Railway Girls

Maisie Thomas was born and brought up in Manchester, which provides the location for her Railway Girls novels. She loves writing stories with strong female characters, set in times when women needed determination and vision to make their mark. The Railway Girls series is inspired by her great aunt Jessie, who worked as a railway clerk during the First World War.

Maisie now lives on the beautiful North Wales coast with her railway enthusiast husband, Kevin, and their two rescue cats. They often enjoy holidays chugging up and down the UK's heritage steam railways.

The Railway Girls

MAISIE THOMAS

arrow books

1 3 5 7 9 10 8 6 4 2

Arrow Books
20 Vauxhall Bridge Road
London SW1V 2SA

Arrow Books is part of the Penguin Random House group
of companies whose addresses can be found at
global.penguinrandomhouse.com.

Penguin
Random House
UK

First published in Great Britain by Arrow Books in 2020

www.penguin.co.uk

A CIP catalogue record for this book is available
from the British Library.

ISBN 9781787463967

Typeset in 10.75/13.5 pt Palatino by Jouve (UK), Milton Keynes
Printed and bound in Great Britain by Clays Ltd, Elcograf S.p.A.

*To the memory of Colette Grant (neé Bourke 1932-2019),
who fought for her independence and worked hard all her life.
She played hard too, travelling the world, throwing the best
parties and moving house more times than you can shake a
stick at. A life lived to the full.*

And to Elizabeth and Ray.

Acknowledgements

I am grateful to my agent, Laura Longrigg, and my editor, Cassandra Di Bello, for the opportunity to write this series. Their editorial input made this a better book. Thanks also to Jennie Rothwell for picking up the baton part-way through.

Special thanks go to Gillian, who kindly responded when I asked a question on social media about the Ritz Ballroom's famous revolving stage. Through Gill I received information from her parents, Fred and Doris Hodson, who generously shared their memories about dancing the nights away in the Manchester of yesteryear. Fred even recalled the name of the music that was played every night at the Ritz when the stage revolved. If you do an online search for 'Tommy Dorsey Lovely Lady', you will be able hear Tommy Dorsey & his Orchestra playing the music.

Thanks also to Melanie Catley, who chose Letitia's name; Jen Gilroy, who guided me through a difficult time before this book was written; Kevin, my tech elf; and Tara Greaves, Catherine Boardman and Aimée Hogston for their support.

In February 1922, at the westernmost entrance to Victoria Station in Manchester, a massive memorial was unveiled. It filled an entire wall, the top half of which was made up of coloured tiles laid out to depict a map of the old Lancashire and Yorkshire Railway. Below this stretched a row of one, two, three, four . . . nine bronze panels in all. The panel at the right-hand end showed St George on his rearing horse, using his spear to slay the dragon. At the left-hand end stood St Michael the Archangel, sword aloft, his foot on the neck of a vanquished Lucifer. These two panels were each flanked by two narrower panels depicting flaming torches, each one bearing a single word: UNITY, STRENGTH, COURAGE and SACRIFICE.

THIS TABLET IS ERECTED TO PERPETUATE THE MEMORY OF THE MEN OF THE LANCASHIRE AND YORKSHIRE RAILWAY WHOSE NAMES ARE RECORDED AND WHO GAVE THEIR LIVES FOR THEIR KING AND COUNTRY IN THE GREAT WAR 1914–1919.

The seven bronze panels in between those of the two saints were engraved with long lists of the names of the fallen, men who had left their jobs on the railway to fight in the Great War. A total of 1,460 men from the Lancashire and Yorkshire Railway gave their lives in the war to end all wars.

In March 1940, a group of women stand in front of the war memorial. They are of varying ages and backgrounds and come from different social classes – a solicitor's wife, a factory owner's daughter, a sewing machinist, a debutante, a working-class housewife, a clerk, a young wife who has been wrapped in cotton wool, and a girl who wasn't tall enough for the switchboard. On the surface, they form a diverse group, but they have one thing in common: their willingness and determination, under threat of invasion, to do their bit in this new world war by rising to the challenge of working as railway girls.

Unity, strength, courage and sacrifice.

Chapter One

'I don't care what war work I do or where I do it – as long as it isn't here.'

Mabel perched on the wooden chair on one side of the acres of scarred wood that formed Miss Eckersley's desk. There was certainly no need for such a huge desk. All it bore was a couple of ledgers held upright between book-ends, and a card index in a box. A hole in the corner of the desk-top held a sunken inkwell, while a long groove housed two sharp pencils and a fountain pen.

Mabel's back prickled with awareness of the townsfolk standing in an orderly queue behind her. Supposedly they were at a sufficient distance to allow her to conduct this conversation in private, but to Mabel, with nerves skittering like mad throughout her body, they felt a jolly sight closer than Miss Eckersley did. She had hoped that by coming here in the afternoon, there would be fewer people present. Maybe there were, but it didn't feel like it. Were they earwigging? Putting two and two together? Drat them to hell and back if they were.

She fixed her chin in what she hoped was a determined line and looked the labour-exchange lady directly in the eye. Miss Eckersley had a reputation locally for keeping more or less the entire population of the town of Annerby, as well as many a moorland village, in regular employment, refusing to permit anyone to skive on the dole.

Miss Eckersley didn't so much as blink at Mabel's outspokenness. 'You have no desire to work for your father, then, Miss Bradshaw?'

'No.' Did that come out too quickly? She smiled – or did she? It had been a long time since she had smiled and her face seemed to have forgotten how. The inside of her cheeks felt creaky. 'I . . . I want to strike out on my own.'

'Indeed?' Miss Eckersley's pencilled-on eyebrows climbed up her forehead. 'You can join the Land Army. There are plenty of hill-farmers in need of an extra pair of hands.'

'I don't want to stay here,' said Mabel.

'Will your parents permit you to move away?'

'I think the war effort trumps parental consent – don't you?' Lord, did that sound upper-crust and spoilt-bratty? Two things she definitely wasn't, even if her parents wouldn't have altogether minded if she had been. Trying for a conciliatory tone, she added, 'Miss Eckersley, I really do want to move away from here. Can't you put me forward for something?'

'Do you imagine I have every job in the kingdom on my books?'

'Of course not.'

Miss Eckersley removed a sheet of paper from a desk drawer. 'Qualifications?'

'School Certificate.'

'Any Distinctions?'

'No.' Or to be more accurate: good God, no. She had scraped through by the skin of her teeth. Even then, it had taken her two goes. She had insisted upon staying on at school an extra year to take it again, not to achieve the qualification, but simply to avoid being sent to finishing school.

'What work have you done since leaving school?' Miss Eckersley laid down her fountain pen – what answer was she expecting?

'None.' Heat flooded Mabel's face. Twenty-two years of age and never done a day's work. It hadn't been for the want of asking. She would have loved nothing better than to be trusted with a role in her father's factory, but all she had ever been called upon to do was shake hands with the clerical staff and give out the small square envelopes containing the Christmas bonuses.

Miss Eckersley handed her the sheet of paper across the desk. They both had to extend their arms.

'Fill in your name, address and date of birth, please.'

Opening the leather handbag that matched her gloves, Mabel took out her gold-nibbed Parker pen. Only the best for Miss Mabel Bradshaw.

Miss Eckersley took back the sheet of details and wrote on a card, which she handed across the desk.

'Take this to Hunts Bank in Manchester on Thursday. You should arrive no later than a quarter to ten for a ten o'clock start.'

'Thank you, Miss Eckersley.'

Working in a bank? You could hardly call that war work. But she had yearned after a clerical position in her father's factory for long enough, so she could hardly turn up her nose, could she? Besides, you didn't say no to Miss Eckersley.

As she departed, she made a fuss of pulling on her gloves and adjusting her brimless fur hat, so as not to make eye contact with anybody in the queue. She opened the heavy wooden door onto a rush of chill, pulling her woollen scarf higher around her throat. Her brown curls bushed up around her cheeks and the back of her neck, like a cat's fur fluffing up to keep warm.

Snow crunched beneath the rubber soles of her galoshes. Oh, the temptation to stuff her hands deep in her pockets, but ladies didn't slouch around like that. Even

School Cert failures who hadn't attended finishing school knew better than that, not least thanks to *The Modern Lady's Guide to Etiquette*, which was Mumsy's adviser for all things. Would you credit it, there were rules about managing your gloves while removing your coat and the correct way to carry a rolled umbrella. There were even instructions on how to glance over your shoulder in a beguiling manner as you left a room, which would have been hilariously funny, if only Mumsy hadn't taken it so seriously.

Something that was less hilarious was Mumsy's insistence on Mabel's use of Mumsy and Pops as the names for her parents. Mabel would have much preferred plain old Mum and Dad, but that would make the family sound lower class, apparently. Mumsy had wanted Mummy and Daddy, but Mabel had drawn the line at that.

'I'd look wet if I called you that at my age.'

So, Mumsy and Pops it was, which made her sound jolly hockey-sticks. But better that than wet.

She picked her way carefully across the road and headed for the old stone bridge, pausing in the centre to look down at the river, which had swollen recently. Would it burst its banks and flood? That would be interesting, as the water derived its colour from whatever the dye-works spewed into it on any given day. At present, the river was covered by a layer of ice, upon which some ducks dolefully slid about. What a shame she hadn't brought food for them, but that probably wasn't allowed under the new regulations.

Darts of cold in her toes reminded her to get going. It wasn't long before she began on what started as a gentle slope before shifting to a more serious gradient. As well as occupying the broad valley floor, Annerby reached upwards along the stretch of hills on this side of the valley. Long streets of terraced houses led off in both directions from the appropriately named Hill Climb. At intervals along both pavements stood fancy-topped iron posts. At this time of year, sturdy ropes were looped from one to the next for folk to grab on to for assistance in getting up and down the road. Mind you, if the war continued, the posts' days were probably numbered. Metal railings and metal gates were already being removed.

Pops had paid for the posts to be fitted, back at the tail-end of the twenties. It was his first act of benevolence towards the town of his birth.

'Aye, benevolence that means no bugger can miss a day's work on account of heavy snow,' Mabel had heard someone mutter on one of her infrequent visits to the factory.

Benevolence was her father's preferred word for it. Not charity. He might be moneyed now, but he came from a background in which being on the receiving end of charity was a matter of shame.

'We have a position to uphold in the community,' he was fond of decreeing, as if they were the poshest of the posh. 'My wife and daughter should be seen to undertake acts of benevolence to the poor.'

Which sounded very grand. But if they had been proper posh, they would have called it charity and taken the gratitude for granted.

Mabel peeled off Hill Climb, steadying herself as she entered Vicarage Lane, where the lines of Victorian cottages had snow almost up to their downstairs window sills. One of Mumsy's acts of benevolence had been to ask for a list of the elderly poor from Sister Beddow, who was in charge of the district nurses, so that she – or rather, their housekeeper – could provide what Mumsy called 'comforts', as if the recipients were soldiers in the trenches.

But Mabel had soon realised that, much as the packets of tea and twists of sugar, the balls of wool and the occasional sack of coal, were appreciated, what these elderly folk craved

7

more than anything was company, so she had taken to doing a series of weekly visits, something she loved. Was there something in her bones that responded to folk from a lower rank of life? A lower rank – what would Grandad have said to that, eh? He had died ten years ago now, but she had never stopped thinking about him and missing him. He had been a wheeltapper on the railways and had never ceased to be amazed by his son's rise to greater things.

What would Grandad say now, if he knew of the terrible thing she had done? She would never have been able to hide the truth from him, she was certain of that. As it was, the accident she had caused had resulted in an outpouring of sympathy from all sides. Sympathy she didn't deserve in the slightest. Sympathy that made her feel raw inside.

Paths had been dug through the snow along Vicarage Lane's cobbled road, and from the roadway to each door. With only a couple of stomach-swooping moments when one of her feet slid from under her, Mabel arrived outside number 8. She didn't want to be here. She didn't want to see any of her old dears any more. She didn't want to see anybody. But she couldn't ignore her duty. It was the only thing she had left of the once-decent person she used to be.

She took a deep breath to prepare herself, then with feigned cheerfulness banged on the door, opening it with a call of, 'Knock, knock. Can I come in?'

Mrs Kennedy, a little mouse of a woman, with swollen knuckles on once busy but now pretty well useless hands, sat in an ancient armchair that, if it had been any closer to the hearth, would have tipped her into the fire. She had a blanket over her knees, a black woollen shawl around her thin shoulders, and covering her fine white hair a widow's cap that was pulled down over her ears and tied beneath her chin.

8

'You're a good girl, coming out in this weather,' she said. 'Bung the kettle on, there's a good lass.'

'You all right for coal, Mrs Kennedy?' Mabel asked as she bustled about.

'Aye, love.'

'Are you telling the truth? I'll be most put out if I come in one day and find you frozen solid because of a bit of pride.'

'Don't be cheeky to your elders.'

Of all her old dears, Mrs Kennedy was her favourite. There was something that made them get along, but today she must be careful about what she said. Not just because of the truth behind the accident she had caused, but also because she mustn't spill the beans about her interview at the bank. She had to tell Mumsy and Pops first. So she breezed through their conversation, hugging her secret to her and trying not to feel disappointed that she was only going to work in a bank when what she wanted to do was proper war work. Had all the bank clerks joined up?

When she left Mrs Kennedy, the afternoon was drawing in. She returned to Hill Climb. With her gas-mask box slung over one shoulder and the handles of her handbag looped over the other, she grasped the rope and proceeded to haul herself up the hill. It only took a moment for her handbag to slide down her arm and dangle from her elbow, which was a nuisance, but she didn't bother restoring it to its original position. Her body warmed pleasantly, then less pleasantly, as she toiled up the hill. The ladies of Annerby had no need of the Women's League of Health and Beauty in this weather.

After she passed the top row of houses, the climb became gentler and what were known down the hill as 'the big houses' came into view higher up, in a position from which the well-to-do could in the most literal sense look down on everybody else – though it wasn't just the townsfolk who were looked down upon. Those families who had lived up here for generations weren't best pleased that Arnie Bradshaw had bought his way into such a privileged position.

By the time she had walked between the eight-foot-tall gateposts topped by stone griffins whose presumably once-sharp features had weathered over time into something more blurred, Mabel's pace had reduced to a trudge and the daylight dazzle of snow had eased into the faded grey of winter's early dusk. She put on a spurt along the drive, between humps of snow beneath which were the shrubberies. Stamping her feet as she marched up the salted steps, she let herself into Kirkland House. The hall, which was full of dark wood everywhere you looked, was gloomy – gloomier than usual, and that was saying something. It was that odd, in-between time of day. Too early for the blackout, but you mustn't put lights on because of the falling darkness.

Shedding her outdoor things, she dashed upstairs in search of woolly socks and her warmest cardy. A few weeks ago, she had shifted her cheval mirror to a different angle so she was less likely to catch sight of herself, but as she rootled around deep in a drawer to find the socks, she caught an unexpected glimpse. The velvet-rayon dress in two shades of green, with its buttoned bodice and matching collar, cuffs and belt, had been a perfect fit not so long ago. Like all her clothes, it had been tailor-made for her. And, like all her clothes, it now hung loosely. She wasn't supposed to know, but Cook was under orders to fatten her up. Some hope. Everything that went in her mouth tasted of sawdust.

The despair that was never far away pounced on her, wrapping her in its jagged-edged gloom. Pain tightened the back of her throat as guilt surged through her. She started to wrap her arms around herself, but dropped them to her sides. She didn't deserve comfort.

Stop it, stop it, stop it.

After pulling on a pair of stripy woollen bed-socks over her faintly damp stockings, she ran downstairs to the drawing room, whose vast old Victorian furniture Pops had purchased along with the house. She paused outside the door at the last moment because she could hear voices within, which made it necessary to adopt the entrance required by Mumsy's dratted etiquette book. Opening the door softly, she entered 'with confidence but without commotion', slipping her hand behind her to close the door while facing forwards. It wasn't a visitor with Mumsy. It was Pops. She could have burst in, after all.

She fingered her necklace as anxiety fluttered through her. She hadn't expected to do this quite yet, but since Pops was here, it must be done now. Oh Lord.

'There you are, Mabel,' said Mumsy. 'Come and sit by the fire.'

She complied. She wanted to hold out her hands to the flames, but it was essential to look her parents in the eye for the next bit.

'Mumsy says you've been out visiting your old dears,' said Pops. 'How about a drop of something to warm you up? It's a bit parky out there.'

Mumsy softly cleared her throat while gazing into the middle distance. Mabel shared an amused glance with Pops. Hitting the decanters wasn't permitted until you were dressed for dinner. Mind you, today might be the exception.

'Actually, I only called on Mrs Kennedy. I had something else to do as well.' Her heart took a few beats in rather a rush, but she straightened her spine. 'I . . . I went to the labour exchange.'

'You did what?' Pops sat bolt upright. His slicked-back, Brilliantined hair gleamed in the firelight.

11

'Mabel, really!' cried Mumsy. 'You know what it's like for us. It isn't easy being new money. If you get a job, it'll give certain people another reason to look down their noses. Besides, you know what we've always hoped.'

Didn't she just? Mabel Bradshaw, heiress to Bradshaw's Ball Bearings and Other Small Components, was widely expected to bag herself a penniless lordling, or at the very least an honourable, and become the mother of an unutterably respectable family.

'I want to do my bit,' she said quietly. 'I want to do war work.'

'I've told you before,' said Pops. 'Young ladies don't go out to work.'

'I think we'll all be going out to work if the war continues – which it will. You're always saying so. Anyway, I have an interview and I have to go. It's all arranged.'

'Where?' Pops demanded.

'Hunts Bank in Manchester.'

'Never heard of it. Mind you, there are so many banks.'

'I suppose being a bank clerk might not be so very bad.' Mumsy's hand fluttered towards the bookcase, then fell away. Had she thought of checking her etiquette book?

'The address is Hunts Bank Buildings, which sounds rather grand, don't you think?' Mabel shamelessly pressed the point and was rewarded with the sight of Mumsy's eyes turning thoughtful.

'But . . . Manchester?' said Mumsy. 'You couldn't do that on a daily basis, especially these days, with ordinary passengers playing second fiddle to soldiers and goods and heaven knows what besides.'

'It would mean finding somewhere to live,' said Mabel.

Pops slapped his hands down on the chair's arm-protectors so suddenly that he almost shoved the cotton covers to the floor as he surged to his feet. 'That's that, then.

You're not leaving home. When is this interview? You simply shan't attend.'

'I have to. I asked to do war work, so I can't not turn up. It would be looked into.'

His fleshy cheeks puffed up and Pops blew out a stream of air. 'Put like that, I suppose you have to go. Bradshaw's Ball Bearings is in line for an important government contract – but you didn't hear me say that. I can't have it said that my daughter tried to dodge doing her duty.'

He stomped across to the sideboard and clattered about among the crystal. When he turned round, he had a whopping three fingers of Scotch. Mumsy opened her mouth, then shut it again.

'Well, my girl,' said Pops, uttering words that were normally an endearment in a completely different tone of voice, 'you've got your own way. I hope you're satisfied.'

Mabel's feet were like blocks of ice when she descended from the train, but she had aimed for elegance rather than warmth when she got dressed, so it was her own fault. Drawing her coat's fur collar more closely round her neck, she headed along the platform, surrounded by the sharp, spicy aroma of smoke and steam mingling together. It was a smell she adored. The railway meant Grandad: simple as that.

Handing over her ticket to the ticket collector, in his peaked cap and polished buttons, she entered Victoria Station's main concourse, where she absorbed an impression of large round clock-faces with Roman numerals, hanging from the metal gantry beneath the station's canopy; a departure board in a handsome wooden frame; large noticeboards in between the sets of platform gates; a long sweep of polished wood-panelling, with ticket-office windows; and a small cluster of interior buildings with tiled walls the colour of buttermilk, above each entrance the words RESTAURANT, GRILL ROOM and BOOKSTALL depicted in elegant capitals against a background of deep blue with white and green swirls, not unlike the Prince of Wales's feathers. And, oh my, that glass dome in the restaurant's roof said *First Class* far more eloquently than any notice ever could.

She made her way out of the station, realising just before she walked outside that this wasn't the main entrance. Before she could turn back, she spotted a blue Austin taxi across the road. Good! But as she approached, she saw no driver.

A middle-aged man in a sturdy hat with ear-flaps that made him look like he was about to trek across Alaska, detached himself from a stall selling coffee and hurried across.

'Could you take me to Hunts Bank, please?' she asked.

'Hunts Bank?'

'Hunts Bank Buildings is the address I've been given.' Honestly, weren't taxi drivers meant to know things like this?

'Are you sure you want taking?'

'Of course.' What a strange question. Only good manners stopped her from looking round for another taxi. The official taxi rank must be elsewhere.

The driver looked at her, making her acutely aware of her felt hat, trimmed with a petersham ribbon fashioned into a cluster of curls to make a rosette, which was definitely not suitable for trekking across Alaska. He glanced down at her high-heeled shoes, their tongues fashioned into tiny pleats forming fan-shapes. Likewise.

'Aye, happen you do want taking, dressed like that.'

Rude fellow. Mabel climbed into the back seat, employing the 'derrière first, ankles together' method advised in a

14

supplement to Mumsy's etiquette book, entitled *Modern Etiquette for the Motor Car*, which Mumsy had sent off for in response to an advertisement in *Woman's Illustrated*, at a cost off five shillings plus thruppence in stamps.

She peered through the window, eager to view her surroundings. As she did so, she secretly scrunched and unscrunched her toes at a furious rate to pump blood into them before they succumbed to frost-bite and dropped off. The taxi drove sedately round the corner and came to a halt.

She leaned forward. 'Why have we stopped?'

'Hunts Bank Buildings?'

'Yes.'

'Here we are.'

'Are you sure? We've only just left the station.'

'I can drop you somewhere else if you'd rather.'

'No, thank you. Why didn't you tell me it was just round the corner?'

'I assumed you wanted to save your pretty shoes. That's two shillings, please.'

'Two shillings?'

'Minimum fare.'

She added thruppence as a tip, not sure that one was deserved, but it would have felt mean not to give something. She scrambled out, too flustered to remember to emerge properly. Far from the high street of smart shops she had pictured, this was a road of imposing, stone-clad buildings. Was it silly to find them unwelcoming? Maybe this was the bank's back entrance. Did interview candidates go in via the back? But the taxi driver hadn't known why she was here.

Well, there was one way to find out. She walked to a door set deep inside a porch and went through it, telling herself not to expect a handsome banking hall, but unable to prevent a dip of disappointment when she didn't find one, a dip that became a positive plunge when she absorbed the plain hall and staircase, and the hatch in the wall.

A man looked up from his desk inside the office as she appeared at the hatch.

'Good morning,' she said. 'I've come for an interview.'

'Do you mean a test?'

'It could be a test, I suppose.' Had Miss Eckersley actually called it an interview?

'Did the labour exchange send you? Have you got a card?'

Mabel slipped her hand inside her bag. 'I hope there won't be a maths test – though I suppose there's bound to be, isn't there? Not my strongest subject, I'm afraid.'

'Maths, English and geography of the British Isles.'

She stared. 'Geography? What for?'

It was the man's turn to stare. 'I'd have thought geography was the most important. A heck of a sight more useful, pardon my language, than the other two.'

'For working in a bank?'

'You what?'

'Hunts Bank.'

'Hunts Bank – as in money?' The man chortled. 'I've heard it all now. Hunts Bank!' He laughed out loud. Catching sight of her confusion, he pulled himself together. 'This isn't a bank. These buildings belong to the railways. The tests are to see if you're cut out for railway work.'

Chapter Two

'Me and my sister have made a pact not to get killed with our rollers in.'

Joan pushed herself out of the collapsible canvas chair to stamp her feet and rub her gloved hands up and down her thick-sleeved arms. It was jolly perishing up here on Ingleby's rooftop, doing fire-watching duty in the pitch-darkness. The charcoal hand-warmers tucked inside her woolly gloves, which had been toasty warm at the start of her shift, had cooled to almost nothing by now.

'Oh aye?' Hunched in her chair, hands thrust deep in her pockets, Margaret waggled her face from side to side, easing out her nose and mouth from behind her scarf. 'So if the bombs start falling—'

'When,' said Joan. 'Not if. When.' It was better to tell yourself 'when'. It kept you on your toes.

'All right, *when*. When the siren goes off and everyone else springs out of bed and legs it downstairs, you and your Letitia are going to jump up and start flinging rollers here, there and everywhere?'

Joan grinned. 'Something like that.'

She turned to look across the rooftops of the centre of Manchester. Not that she could see anything apart from deeper shapes of darkness that denoted where buildings were, and maybe she couldn't really see those. Maybe it was her imagination filling in those dark shapes because she knew they must be there.

It felt as though she lived her whole life in darkness at

the moment. Not even the snow brightened things up. The short winter days meant getting up in the dark and it was still gloomy when she arrived at Ingleby's. Her days were spent in one of the sewing rooms. They had two of them now, the second one having been added last summer when blackout fabric was being sold in huge quantities and many folk wanted their curtains made up quickly. Both the sewing rooms were internal rooms with no windows, and unless Joan bolted her midday meal in order to dash outdoors for a spell, she wouldn't see the outside world again until it was finally time to go home after her now regular overtime, working on WVS uniforms and uniforms for bus conductresses and the like. The sewing rooms were filled with girls and women working overtime, and as well as the extra money being welcome, Joan was glad to feel she was doing something for the war effort. But she would much rather be wearing one of those uniforms than sewing them.

At the end of her long working day, she would walk outside into a darkness that was more complete than any she had ever known.

'I don't care who you're with,' Gran had instructed her and Letitia. 'Make sure they walk on the road-side of the pavement. If anyone's going to stumble into the path of a motor car, I don't want it to be you, Letitia.' She turned to Joan. 'Or you.'

Had she paused and turned to look at Joan to reinforce the importance of her message? Or had she added her as an afterthought?

Tuesday nights were the darkest of the lot, because of fire-watching duty on Ingleby's roof.

Gran was used to it now, but she hadn't been pleased to start with.

'I'm not having you out all night,' she had declared. 'It isn't respectable.'

'I've already registered,' Joan replied. 'It's official.'

Darned right it was. There were some things you didn't tell Gran in advance. It had been Letitia's idea that she should register first and confess later, and she had been proved right.

'Then I want you partnered with another girl,' Gran had insisted – as if Joan would have any say in the matter.

She had been partnered with Margaret from haberdashery – well, Margaret was what Joan called her when they were on the roof, and Margaret called her Joan. In the shop, they were Miss Darrell and Miss Foster. Gran probably thought they maintained that formality up on the roof as well.

It was a long night. During her first stint of fire-watching, Joan's heart had pitter-pattered all night long, but she had soon learned that being on watch was pretty dull. That was the phoney war for you. Not to mention the freezing-cold war, she thought, stamping her feet again. Other fire-watchers had rigged up a canvas wind-shield, and men from the stock-room had shovelled away the snow, but unless you were prepared to spend all night running on the spot, nothing was going to keep you warm. They weren't allowed to have a brazier up here because of the glow, so the only way to combat the low temperatures was to take turns to nip inside and boil a kettle for a hot drink, though the steaming Bovril that warmed you at the time soon sent you racing to the Ladies.

'Cold air plus a hot drink equals a fast sprint,' according to Miss Armitage from ribbons and braids.

'More like a brisk hobble with your legs crossed,' Miss Dent from millinery had said. 'And then you have to fight your way through all your layers before you have an accident.'

Joan wore an extra camisole, two pairs of socks over her stockings, plus two jumpers and slacks beneath her coat. She had run up the slacks in her dinner-hour, using a warm wool fabric provided by Ingleby's, payment for which had been taken from her weekly wages before she received her pay packet.

She kept her slacks in her locker at work. Gran would have kittens if she knew about them.

'They're called "slack" for a reason,' was Gran's opinion. 'Only slack girls wear them.'

Even Letitia, who had been nagging for yonks about shorter skirts, wouldn't dare ask Gran about slacks.

'Will you carry on with your fire-watching if you get this other job?' Margaret asked.

Joan frowned. The tug in her brow made it feel like her forehead would crack open in the cold. 'Don't call it "this other job", as if it isn't important.'

'Golly, you really are keen, aren't you?'

'Yes, I am,' she replied frankly, 'ever since I read about it in *Vera's Voice*. With so many men being called up, there's a great need for girls to take on railway jobs. Women stepped up and did their bit in the last war and we're being called upon again now. The part the railways will play is going to be crucial. There'll be precious little petrol, so everything and everyone that needs to get from A to B will have to be transported by rail. Just look at how the railways coped with evacuating all those children last autumn. It's going to be like that, only more so.'

'Well, I'd rather stay put here, thanks.'

'For as long as they let you, you mean. Girls will be ordered into war work – not straight away, but it will happen.'

'So you thought you'd choose your own job before one was chosen for you?'

'No, I chose it because I want to do something more important than sewing blackout curtains and uniforms.'

'Which brings me back to my original question: will you carry on fire-watching? You'll be working shifts, won't you? Including nights.'

'Working nights doesn't stop folk fire-watching on one of their nights off.'

Indeed, there seemed to be no end to what folk were prepared to do. That was why this new job was so important. Hark at her. This new job – as if she had already got it. Ingleby's were giving her time off this afternoon to sit some tests. Lord, what if she wasn't suitable? Wasn't clever enough?

Oh, she had to be. It mattered so much. She didn't want to spend the war working in Ingleby's. She longed to do proper war work – like Letitia. Well, no, not like Letitia. You had to be really clever to do what she did.

A proper wartime job, that was what she dreamed of, the chance to serve her country in a role that was considerably more meaningful than sewing blackout curtains and WVS uniforms. The country couldn't manage without the railways, not with a war to be won. Was it foolish to imagine the railway lines as lifelines?

Did she have what it took to become a railway girl?

It didn't matter how much you stamped up and down during the night, you were always stiff with cold when the time came to leave the roof. Ingleby's had set aside a small room for male fire-watchers to use for getting changed night and morning, but there wasn't a spare room for the girls, who had to use the ladies' lavatories. Joan and Margaret draped their uniform dresses over the vast radiators, which were starting to warm up, and, oh the luxury, dunked their hands in basins of hot water.

'D'you think it'll give us chilblains?' asked Margaret.

'Like sitting on the radiator is meant to?' said Joan. 'I always wondered if girls said that at school to make you get off so they could get on.'

Modestly turning her back on Margaret, she hastily pulled off her night clobber and drew on her black dress. All the girls' dresses were a perfect fit because they were made to measure in Ingleby's sewing rooms. Joan had made her own, so it was faultless – except for the length. She removed her snood to comb her hair, then tucked it back inside. Wearing snoods was one of Gran's rules. The only time Joan and Letitia didn't have to wear one was when they went dancing.

Checking her appearance in the mirrors over the line of basins, she noted that Margaret was wearing yesterday's collar and cuffs, whereas Gran had provided her with fresh ones, which had spent the night inside a small cardboard box to preserve their starched perfection.

'You're the only girl I know whose C and Cs have their own little gas-mask box,' said Margaret.

Did her ultra-crisp appearance make her look like she hadn't been up all night fire-watching? And what sort of big-head did that make her? Wanting others to know she was doing her bit – honestly! If she passed the tests this afternoon and was given a real war job, she wouldn't have to worry about petty things like that.

After stashing their things away in their lockers, they headed for the staff canteen, where the cook came in early these days to provide breakfast for the fire-watchers and the chaps who manned the local first-aid point up the road. Shortly before quarter to nine, Ingleby's staff rushed up the stairs to the various departments to present themselves for inspection by their superiors at eight forty-five sharp.

Miss Trent, who oversaw both sewing rooms, walked up

and down the rows of sewing machines, beside which the sewing girls stood, hands folded demurely in front. She paused next to Joan.

'Fresh C and Cs after a night on the roof. That's what I like to see.'

The morning seemed to last for ever. At last Joan dashed to the canteen to bolt down a hasty meal. There was an anxious tightness inside her chest, but she was excited, too, as she put on her coat and gloves and slid her scarf around her neck, positioning her beret carefully so as not to disturb her snood. Then she swung her gas-mask box over her shoulder, looped her handbag over her wrist and set off. Which was better? The centre of the pavement, where there was slush, and the danger of getting your clothes splattered, or the edges, where the snow had been stamped on and was possibly more slippery than it looked. Today of all days, she didn't want a broken ankle. She headed along Market Street, passing the huge shop windows crisscrossed with anti-blast tape, before striking off in the direction of Victoria Station. She hadn't been there since the days when Gran used to take her and Letitia on day trips to Southport, and it was further than she had anticipated, but that was probably because of the snow slowing her down.

The sight of the station's handsome and imposing building, with its clock tower atop one elegantly curved corner, brought her to a standstill. Even her breathing slowed. Might she really and truly get a job here? Was there time to pop inside and soak up the atmosphere? No, she mustn't make herself late.

She made her way along Hunts Bank, her pulse quickening as she looked for the right doorway. Here it was, set inside a porch. She blew out a breath. She was early – too early? She wanted to look keen, of course, but she might look daft if she had to sit here waiting for everyone else to arrive.

'Are you here for the test?'

It was a girl about her own age or perhaps a year or two older. Dark brown hair showed in a glossy roll beneath a felt hat with top-stitching and a smart, upturned brim. The girl's wool coat, with its large collar and padded shoulders, ought to have made her look confident and business-like, but there was no disguising the uncertainty in her eyes or that little tug at the side of her mouth that suggested she was biting the inside of her cheek. Good: someone else was nervous.

'Yes,' said Joan. 'I don't want to be too early.'

'I know, but it's a bit chilly to be hanging about out here. Shall we?' The girl glanced at the door. 'My name's Alison Lambert.'

'Joan Foster. Pleased to meet you.'

They went inside, presenting themselves at a hatch in the wall. On the other side, a girl walked across an office, skirting a desk to speak to them, and directed them upstairs. The Stephenson Room was large with frosted windows adorned with the ubiquitous blast-tape. Two big tables butted up against one another to create one long table stretching the length of the room. A number of girls and women already sat around it, all with their hats still on. Having felt too early, Joan suddenly felt late. What a good job she and Alison hadn't waited outside to walk in at what they thought would be precisely the right moment.

'Good afternoon. Names, please?' A middle-aged lady in what looked like a silk blouse, but Joan knew artificial silk when she saw it, smiled at them, her fountain pen poised over a list. 'You may hang up your coats over there. Sit wherever you like.'

There was a rail with hangers. Joan hung up her coat, hoping it wasn't obvious that she was glancing round the table. There were empty seats here and there, but no pairs of empty seats. Goodness, how silly. She didn't need to sit beside Alison. They weren't children. She took the first available place, which happened to be beside a red-headed girl in a hat with a wide satin band that boasted a jaunty bow. Those already at the table smiled and nodded, but apart from a few murmured greetings, no one spoke. There was a distinct air of nervousness.

'It feels like walking into an exam at school,' said Joan.

'I wouldn't know,' said the red-head. 'I never sat any. I don't know why they sent me here. I went to the labour exchange to ask if I could be a telephonist, but they said I wasn't tall enough.'

A couple more girls arrived and sat down. Then another woman walked in. She held herself erect and her chin up, which had the odd effect of obliging her to look down on everyone. Followed by the lady in the artificial-silk blouse, who was giving out pencils, she walked around the table, placing a paper face down on the table in front of each person.

'I'm Mrs Pugh, the invigilator. These are your test papers. You shall sit three tests, in English, maths and geography. Each test will be timed. This is the English paper. Please don't turn it over until I tell you. There are two sets of tests, A and B. A papers and B papers are given out alternately, so no one can copy from the person beside them.'

Alison gave a little toss of her head, as if copying was beneath her. She was beside a woman who Joan thought would be the sort of age her own mother would have been had she lived, except her own mother wouldn't have looked like this. It was impossible to imagine Estelle with a thickened figure and looking, well, motherly. The woman across the table wore a hat that had seen better days, having lost much of its crisp shape, and beneath it showed faded brown hair that was now heading for grey. Although the bags under her hazel eyes suggested she didn't get enough sleep, there was an energy about her.

There was a lady of similar age further down the table, but the two of them couldn't have been more different. This second lady, with her elegant hat and discreet earrings, was slender, with high cheekbones and calm grey eyes. Her hair was ash-blonde, dressed in smooth waves. Was this what Estelle would be like now, had she lived? Beautiful and grave?

'You may start.'

Joan turned over her first test paper and began.

Putting down her pencil for the third and final time, Joan rolled her shoulders. She felt she had done quite well, though it was difficult to be sure. She hadn't done anything of this kind since she had left school and she hadn't been brilliantly clever then.

A flash of memory. Gran saying, 'My two both left school in the summer of '36.'

The polite lady staying in the same seaside boarding-house had looked at her and Letitia. 'They don't look like twins, do they?'

And the triumph in Gran's voice as she delivered her boastful, 'They're not. Letitia is a year older, but she went to grammar school, so naturally she stayed on the extra year until she was fifteen. She was awarded a Distinction in mathematics in her School Certificate, you know. Joan, of course, is good with her hands.'

Good with her hands: Gran's not-so-secret code for 'dim'.

'Thank you, ladies,' said Mrs Pugh. 'Your test papers will be marked and those of you who pass will be required to attend a medical. Thank you for attending this afternoon.'

Joan glanced round, feeling a faint uncertainty, an unwillingness, perhaps, to be the first to stand up and leave. Then the grave-looking lady with the ash-blonde hair rose and tucked her chair under the table. She picked up her handbag and gas-mask box before fetching her coat from the rail.

'Good afternoon,' she said to Mrs Pugh before smiling briefly at the other candidates. 'I hope to see you all again soon.'

As she left, the motherly woman bounced off her chair. 'Well, if nowt else, it's been nice to take the weight off my feet. Now I must dash. Bye, all.'

She came round the room towards the coat-rack. She moved quickly, but without looking as though she was hurrying. It was more as if she lived her life at speed. Was that the only way she could fit in everything?

Joan caught Alison's eye and they left together, walking downstairs at the same time as the red-head and another girl who was quiet-looking and neatly-dressed. They stepped outside into the winter twilight.

'We've been in there all afternoon,' said Joan. 'It's just gone five. My supervisor said I could go straight home after the tests.'

'Where do you work?' asked the red-head.

'Ingleby's.' There was no need to say more than that. Everyone knew Ingleby's, the same way everyone knew Paulden's.

'Cor, lucky you. I wouldn't leave there if I was you.'

'I want to do my bit,' said Joan.

'Of course you do,' said Alison. 'We all do.'

'I'm Lizzie Cooper.' The red-head stuck out her right hand.

Joan shook hands, introducing herself; Alison followed suit. Then the three of them looked at the fourth girl.

She looked back at them. Wasn't she going to join in?

'Mrs Colette Naylor,' she said. Her voice was soft, her smile restrained. Was she shy? 'How do you do?'

They made a quick comparison of destinations. Joan would have liked to share her journey with Alison, but Alison lived to the north of Manchester and it was Lizzie she was paired with. Lizzie lived in Whalley Range, which lay between here and Chorlton.

'We can walk to Deansgate together and catch the bus,' said Lizzie.

'How about you?' Alison asked Colette. 'Where do you live?'

'I'm going to wait here for my husband,' said Colette. 'He's coming to collect me.'

'I wish my boyfriend could come and collect me,' said Alison. 'He would, of course, if he could, but he's at work. I'll have to save everything up to tell him later.'

Joan's feet were starting to feel the cold. She was about to stamp them, then noticed the slushy pavement and decided against it. 'Come on if you're coming,' she said to Lizzie. To the others, she said, 'Goodbye. I hope we'll all see one another again.' She gave Alison a smile, wanting to show her willingness to become friends.

She and Lizzie set off for Deansgate, where the shops were shutting.

Like a homing pigeon Lizzie headed for one of Kendals' windows. 'Come and see these shoes. I've been looking at them for weeks. Aren't they gorgeous? Here – take a look. Quick, before they put up the blackout.'

'Very pretty,' said Joan. They were too. They were evening shoes, with heels high enough to be stylish, yet not too high for dancing – but they were red. Inside her head, she distinctly heard Gran's sniff, and a shiver passed through her. But the shoes were still pretty. Oh, imagine wearing something like that, proper evening shoes, to a dance, instead of the daytime shoes she and Letitia were doomed to wear. 'Red is for tarts,' said Gran's voice.

Lizzie sighed. 'You'd have to buy 'em sharpish if you wanted 'em. They're bound to put clothes on ration, my mum says. You wouldn't want to fritter your coupons on them.'

'We need to cross over,' said Joan. 'We don't want to miss the bus.'

They didn't have to wait long.

'No room downstairs, girls,' said the clippie.

'We'll stand,' said Joan.

'Don't be daft,' said Lizzie. 'Let's go up.'

She swung her way upstairs, leaving Joan no choice but to follow. She hated going upstairs on buses and trams, because of showing her legs – or rather, because of not showing them. There went Lizzie with her coat and skirt dancing around her knees, but Joan's flapped around her calves. She felt like a dowdy old biddy. She might have made her shop dress herself, but she had made it to Gran's instructions.

Lizzie flung herself into a seat. 'I can't wait to tell my mum all about this afternoon. I bet your mum can't wait either.'

A familiar tingle spread through Joan's body. 'Mine died when I was a baby.'

Lizzie turned to look at her. 'Oh, I'm sorry to hear that. Me and my big mouth. I don't know what I'd do without my mum, especially now there's only the two of us. Dad was run over in the blackout in October. Have you still got your dad?'

Joan didn't know whether to be more shocked at Lizzie's way of blurting out private details to a virtual stranger or downright scared. Was she expected to reciprocate? She slapped down the flutter of panic. She had been brought up not to blab. This chatterbox had caught her unawares, that's all.

'My dad died as well.'

'What, both your parents? You poor love.'

'Me and my sister were brought up by our grandmother, Daddy's mother. Are you doing anything this evening?'

'Me and mum have got mending club,' said Lizzie.

'For mending clothes?'

'No, it's things like how to change a plug or unblock a sink. Mum says it's important now we haven't got a man in the house, and we're getting better at doing things. We put up a shelf last week and it's still up. Not like when we fixed the pulley airer and it dropped like a stone the next day and the damp washing landed on the kitchen table in the Yorkshire pudding batter.'

'Oh no.'

'It wasn't that bad. I mean, we jumped out of our skin, obviously, but afterwards we laughed like drains. Mum said it was the best laugh she'd had since Dad popped off, so that sort of made it worth it, if you know what I mean.'

Lizzie looked at her. One bereaved child to another? She couldn't have that. She glanced out of the window.

'Is it your stop in a minute?'

'Lord, yes.'

Lizzie jumped up, slinging her gas-mask box over her shoulder. Joan turned sideways in the seat to let her scramble past.

'Nice to meet you,' said Lizzie. 'Good luck with the test results.'

'You too.'

Lizzie vanished down the stairs, leaving Joan feeling as if she had made friends with a whirlwind. Made friends? Really? No. Lizzie was just a chatterbox who spilled out her personal business to all and sundry. Or maybe, in Lizzie's book, that constituted making friends.

At any rate, one or both of them might not pass the tests, and then they would never see one another again. A frisson of anxiety passed through her. She would pass the tests . . . wouldn't she?

Chapter Three

'Chickenpox? ... Measles? ...' The nurse, neatly attired in a white uniform with a white cap, rattled off the list of childhood illnesses, ticking them off her list. A brief pause saw Mabel breathing a sigh of relief that the questioning was over, only for it to start again, this time with a stream of serious ailments, including a couple she had never heard of. The nurse ran through the list at some speed without looking at Mabel until she had finished, whereupon she glanced up with a cool, professional smile. 'Thank you, Miss Bradshaw.'

'I must be healthier than I thought,' said Mabel. 'I've never even heard of some of those.'

'They're not real. Doctor puts those in to trip people up. If you say you've had one of them, we know you're trying to get out of doing your duty.'

Crikey. Had she wandered into a recruitment room for Wrens and WAAFs by mistake?

'I'll let you know when Doctor is ready for you.' The nurse was already looking at the next girl's paperwork.

Mabel rose and returned to the wooden chairs lined up against the wall, sitting up straight not just because she had been taught to, but also because of nerves. She had passed the written tests, presumably even the maths, in spite of the problems and percentages that had caused her brain to freeze. Now she had to pass the medical. She had no doubt she was healthy enough. She just didn't want to be examined. No one had told her what the examination involved and she didn't like to ask, for fear of making herself look silly. Or were all these other girls also dying to ask but too scared?

The door to the consulting room opened and another nurse appeared.

'Miss Bradshaw.'

Not a 'please' or a 'This way' or 'There's nothing to worry about.' Not even a smile. Oh, well. Mabel stood up and walked through the door to find a small room with framed lists of the local bowling club's chairmen on the walls. Pushed up against one wall was a shabby desk, a pillar of drawers on either side of its knee-hole, at which sat an elderly man who swung round on his chair to face her. Had all the young doctors been called up? He cast her a brief look up and down.

'Henderson,' he introduced himself brusquely. 'Hang your coat over there and sit here, please.'

The moment she removed her coat, there was a loud hissing sound as Dr Henderson sucked in a prolonged breath.

'Way too thin,' he declared. 'Not good for you. Not healthy.'

She froze, her coat halfway to the hook. 'I'm perfectly healthy. I've just gone thin, that's all.'

'Why? You're not one of those silly girls who takes Bile Beans to lose weight, are you?'

'I . . .' Emotion swelled inside her. Cripes, she wasn't going to cry, was she? She breathed in deeply, and not quite as silently as she would have wished, hoping to crystallise the tears behind her eyes. 'I had a . . . There was a death. I, um, I lost weight. I couldn't help it. It wasn't that I stopped eating.'

'Hmm. Well, don't stand there like an idiot. Hang up your coat and sit down.' Dr Henderson plugged the ends of his stethoscope into his ears. 'Top buttons, please.' He pressed the metal against her flesh. 'Hmm. Let's have a look at your blood pressure. Roll up your sleeve, please.' He positioned the cuff around her arm and pumped it up, eyeing the gauge. 'Hmm. Stand here, please, and read the chart on the far wall.' When she had done so, he said, 'Hmm' yet again, followed by, 'Thank you. You can put your coat back on.'

Mabel eyed the scales. 'Aren't you going to weigh me?'

'Don't need to. I can see you're too thin.' Dr Henderson gestured towards the hat-stand. 'Coat.'

Mabel got up and took her coat off the hook, turning back to face him as she fastened the buttons and the belt buckle. He had his back to her, bent over the desk, scribbling away. Dismissal? Apparently so, because the nurse tried to get round her to open the door. Mabel didn't budge. She wasn't going to leave until Dr Henderson had told her his decision.

He glanced round. 'Oh, are you still here?'

'Have I passed?'

'There's nothing wrong with your eyesight or your blood pressure,' said Dr Henderson, 'but your weight is below what it should be.'

'I know I'm too thin, but this isn't the way I normally am.' Nothing about her was the way she normally was and it never would be again. 'Are you going to fail me?'

'That isn't the way to speak to Doctor,' said the nurse.

Mabel stared at Dr Henderson, realising in that moment how very much she wanted to get this job. She had not specifically wanted a railway job. But, since overcoming the surprise of finding herself sitting the railway tests, she had got to like the idea. Grandad had worked on the railways all his life. If she could get a job as a railway girl, she wouldn't just be doing it for the war effort, she would be doing it to honour his memory.

And that was another surprise, because when she had first vowed to do war work, her only thought had been to get away from home.

Something inside her quivered. Was Dr Henderson about to turn her down?

'You're good enough in other respects,' he said, 'but you'll have to stop moping.'

'Moping?'

'There will be many more deaths before this war is over, believe you me. If you mope to this extent over just one, what hope is there for you when things get bad? You need to stiffen your spine, my girl.'

A hot pulse passed through Mabel's body, turning her limbs to lead. No, not lead, though they felt that heavy. It was more a bloated, squashy feeling, as if all her grief and guilt and remorse, together with the terrible, useless desire to undo what she had done, were squeezing out of her muscles and leaking inside her.

'So you'll pass me as fit?' she asked in a brittle voice.

'Yes, you'll do,' said Dr Henderson. 'After all, how fit do you have to be to sit in a ticket office?'

'If all you're likely to do is sit in a ticket office, I don't see why you can't do that here in Annerby,' Mumsy declared. They should have gone in to dinner ten minutes ago, but they were locked in the middle of an argument. 'Or if not here, then one of the stations on the local line. There's no need to leave home. You aren't old enough.'

'I'm twenty-two.'

'You should live at home until you get married. And why Manchester? Why so far away?'

I don't care what war work I do or where I do it – as long as it isn't here.

'It isn't that far.' Mabel aimed for a light tone, though her

35

throat was clogged with guilt. 'You make it sound like the ends of the earth.'

'There's no need for this fuss, Esme,' said Pops. 'I'll place some telephone calls in the morning. I'm sure it can be sorted out.'

'You can't rearrange the war effort to suit Mumsy,' said Mabel. Or could he? 'Pops, it wouldn't be right to pull strings. The factory has that government contract coming up. You have to be above reproach.'

'No one could reproach a man for doing his best for his family. But maybe you have a point.'

'Are you saying there's nothing you can do?' Mumsy demanded.

'We'll see,' said Pops.

For a day or two, nothing was said. Typical Pops. You could chew your nails down to stumps and it wouldn't occur to him to tell you what was going on until he was good and ready.

At last he made his announcement.

'I've arranged somewhere for you to stay in Manchester, Mabs.' He held up a finger to stop her speaking. 'Don't say no, because this isn't open to negotiation. Just because the war is taking you away from us doesn't mean I'm no longer responsible for you. You'll be a guest at a place called Darley Court.'

'A guest?' Mabel repeated. 'Is it a hotel?' She had heard of folk who had decided to sit out the war in deluxe comfort, but such hotels were in places like the West Country, not in cities that were liable to be attacked.

'No, it's a real-life stately home,' said Pops, sitting up straight so he could proudly throw out his chest, though exclamations from Mabel and Mumsy had him backtracking pretty quickly. 'Well, maybe not an actual stately home as such, but certainly a big place that's been in the same family for generations.'

'The Darleys,' said Mabel.

'Exactly. That is to say, the Darleys died out round about the turn of the century and the place was inherited by a distant relation . . . with a different name.'

Mabel pounced on the hesitation. 'A different name?'

'Brown.'

She laughed. She couldn't help it. 'That doesn't sound very posh.'

'Browne with an E?' suggested Mumsy.

'Just plain Brown, as far as I know. And that's where our Mabel will be staying. There'll be bed and board to pay, and she'll have to take her ration book with her, of course, and hand it over.'

'However did you organise it?' asked Mumsy.

'What you might call a family connection.'

'To the Browns? Of Darley Court?'

'There's just Miss Brown, as far as I can tell,' said Pops.

'And we're related to her?' Mumsy persisted.

'No,' said Pops.

'Then what's the connection?'

'If you must know, the housekeeper is my cousin.'

Chapter Four

'A railway girl? You? Well, I suppose it's all you're good for. You're not clever like your sister.'

The clock ticked solemnly on the mantelpiece above the coal-fire. Joan stood, holding the letter that had been waiting for her when she arrived home from Ingleby's. In the darkness created by the blackout, the small fire and the lamps threw out glowing pools that gave the room a cosy feel that it hadn't known before. It was usually a gloomy room, even on the sunniest of days, when the brightest sunshine was turned to amber by the thick net curtains that smothered the windows.

Gran sat in the armchair beside the fire. The arrangement of the furniture showed that in their house, the fireplace was still the centrepiece, even though in some houses, the wireless had become the focal point. Trust Gran to stick to the traditional way.

And trust Gran to pour cold water on her successful application to the railways.

Just this once, couldn't Gran be proud? Joan and Letitia owed everything to Gran. What could be better than repaying her by making her proud? Gran's iron-grey hair was drawn back into a bun. If she hadn't had such a hard life, would her blue eyes be softer, her mouth more smiley and generous?

Gran got to her feet. Might she ask to see the letter? Give her a hug? But she seized the poker from the companion set on the hearth and rattled it among the coals.

'You should have asked,' she said, with her back to Joan. 'Applying to the railways on the sly – I don't know.'

'I didn't. It was the lady at the labour exchange's idea. She said I might be suitable.'

Gran turned to face her. She had a commanding presence that made her seem taller than she was.

'And did you say, "I'll have to ask my gran, who is my guardian and responsible for me until I turn twenty-one"? Did you say, "Actually, I don't need to ask my gran, because she's happy for me to continue doing what I'm doing now"?'

'But Gran—' Joan began.

'Well, I think it's wizard,' Letitia declared and Joan turned gratefully to her beautiful sister. 'Good for you, Joanie. I'm proud of you.' And this time Joan did get a hug. 'You should be proud too, Gran. Joan wants to do her bit and now she's found a way.'

'She's already doing her bit,' said Gran, 'sewing WVS uniforms and blackout curtains.' She resumed her seated position, looking not at the girls but into the fire.

'Oh, Gran, that was never going to be enough for Joan.'

Letitia made it sound as if Joan was famed far and wide for her ambition and initiative. Joan's heart swelled with warmth. Whatever would she do without her sister?

Letitia perched on the arm of Gran's chair, slipping a slender arm around her shoulders. 'Come on, Gran. It's done now and she can't get out of it. Let's make the best of it, eh? It's understandable that she wants to do more than sit behind a sewing machine, what with me doing what I do.'

Joan held her breath. Letitia did this occasionally. She called it playing the clever card. When Joan was in Gran's bad books, Letitia would throw in a comparison with herself that suggested Joan was trying to live up to her, and quite often, Gran would relent. When Joan was younger, she had thought Gran liked the idea of her wanting to be as good as Letitia, but was that the case . . . or did Gran like her being second best?

'Would Daddy be proud?' Letitia asked Gran.

The three of them looked across the room to the studio portrait of Daddy that lived on the sideboard. Gran had put it in the air-raid box last September, it being their most prized possession, but after weeks of no air raids, on Christmas Day she had restored it to its rightful place.

'A special Christmas gift to ourselves,' she had said in the soft voice she reserved for her one and only child, who had been torn from her so tragically when her granddaughters were tiny. Too tiny to remember him.

'You brought us up,' said Letitia, 'telling us that, if in doubt, we should ask ourselves, "Would Daddy be proud of me for doing this?" What d'you think, Gran? How could he not be proud of Joan for this?'

The harsh lines of disappointment in Gran's face shifted and re-settled into a slack sadness. 'Yes, he would – though he wouldn't be proud of the way you went about it,' she added with a sharp glance in Joan's direction.

'I'm sorry, Gran.' She would have said more, but Letitia threw her a frown to shut her up.

'If we're all friends again, and Gran's feeling all soft and gooey,' Letitia said blithely, 'is this a good moment to ask about turning up our hems?'

'Cheek!' Gran swatted at Letitia, who laughed and dodged away, returning to her own seat. 'You know my opinion on that subject.'

But she didn't say it in the uncompromising tone she often used to quell opposition. She said it almost kindly. Not for the first time, Joan boggled at Letitia's talent for coping with Gran. The power of the favourite.

A cheerful rat-a-tat-tat on the front door made Joan's heart leap. What luck she was on her feet.

'I'll go.'

Leaving the parlour, she closed the door behind her, clicking off the light in the hall as she went to the front door. Their front door had a circular window in its top half, so Steven had put up a pole above the door and Joan had made a floor-length blackout curtain. The brass rings rattled as she threw the curtain back. A happy, breathless feeling came over her as she opened the door.

'Steven – come in.'

In her heart, she was flinging the door wide open in welcome. In practice, it was too cold for that. Steven slid inside, his lean, muscular body close to hers. He smelled of chilly air, Imperial Leather soap and, very faintly, tobacco.

'How are you, Joan?'

He shrugged out of his overcoat. If she hadn't had to shut the door and close the blackout curtain, she could have helped him take it off, but she could still hang it up for him. Steven knew where the coat-pegs were though, even in the dark. Their hands brushed as they moved at the same time. Joan's fingers ached with the need to touch him.

Steven dropped his trilby and gloves onto the shelf and opened the parlour door, standing aside to let her enter first. The room's low light crept out, showing his sandy short back and sides and light brown eyes. The scarf Joan had knitted him for Christmas still dangled from his neck and down the front of his tweed jacket, falling longer on one side than the other in an endearing lack of symmetry.

Joan walked into the parlour. 'Look who it is,' she announced, as if they didn't already know.

Letitia stood up and Steven went to her, taking her hands and bending his head to kiss her cheek, and Joan, as happened every time the man she adored walked into her sister's arms, found it impossible to look away.

*

'You're not to tell a soul,' Mabel insisted, trying not to join in with Mrs Kennedy's laughter. Would it be disloyal to her parents if she laughed too? She had no business laughing. It wouldn't just be her parents she was being disloyal to.

'I won't, I promise.' Mrs Kennedy wiped her eyes. 'That's tickled me that has, your dad sending you off to his house-keeper cousin. So much for the Bradshaws' fancy house up the top of the hill. Eh, lass, I don't mean to speak against your dad, but I can picture your grandad chuckling over this.'

Mabel could too. Mrs Kennedy's words created the picture, the certainty, in her mind. Warmth invaded her heart, as it always did when she thought of Grandad. She was going to follow in his footsteps. That was something to be proud of, something to hold on to.

She was setting off tomorrow and she had come to say goodbye to Mrs Kennedy. She had seriously considered not coming. It might have been safer that way. Before every-thing went so horribly wrong, Mrs Kennedy's company had taught her an important lesson; namely, that friendship wasn't necessarily something that occurred only between people of the same age. In spite of the fact that Mrs Kennedy was old enough to be her grandmother, the spark of true friendship had been ignited between them and had seen them talking freely about all kinds of things as they enjoyed one another's company.

That was the trouble. She owed Mrs Kennedy a proper farewell. But she was scared of the old lady now, scared of the friendship that had allowed them to speak freely in the past.

But coming here had been the right thing after all. Dear Mrs Kennedy had laughed at the idea of her going off to a grand address, courtesy of the housekeeper – just as Gran-dad would have done.

They chatted on and Mabel relaxed. When it was time to

go, she kissed the old lady, gently holding her deformed hand.

'I wish you all the best, lass, I really do.' There were tears in Mrs Kennedy's eyes. 'I know you think you can't stay here any more. Oh, don't look at me like that, all shocked. You know what I mean. I haven't said a word before, but now you're going, I want you to know I understand. After what you did—'

'What d'you mean, after what I did?' God in heaven, could the woman read her mind?

'Don't be daft, love. There's not a soul in all Lancashire as doesn't know what you did. So my question for you is this: are you going because you actually want to go or because you're too miserable to stay? It's what your grandad would ask you, you know it is. Are you running away, Mabel Bradshaw?'

Catching her breath, Mabel tried to withdraw her hand, but Mrs Kennedy dropped her other hand over the top, holding Mabel's inside both of hers. The old lady's hands were swollen and weak. Mabel could have pulled free without any trouble, but that might well send pain shooting through Mrs Kennedy's knuckles and she couldn't do that to the old lady.

'Eh, I don't want to hurt you, love. You've had enough upset and I don't want to add to it. I'm trying to make you feel better, though I'm going the wrong way about it.' Mrs Kennedy shook her head, sighing out a huff of sorrow. 'What I'm trying to say is, if it had happened t'other way about, if you had died and your friend had lived, wouldn't you have wanted her to live her life and make the most of it? You wouldn't have wanted her grief over that accident to hold her back, would you? Of course you wouldn't. And she wouldn't want you to be unhappy for ever either.'

Wouldn't she? Mabel wasn't so sure about that.

Chapter Five

'You? A railway girl? Don't make me laugh. A railway old biddy, more like.'

Dot stared at Reg, but he was already peering at the cartoon page of the *Daily Mirror*, which was spread out on the kitchen table. He had lifted his head long enough for a brief smirk and a nod to acknowledge his own repartee, which he probably considered to be of sufficient wit to share later on with his mates down the King's Head. No doubt the family would be treated to a replay of his banter an' all. The rat.

She hovered behind Reg, willing him to shove off and go to work. She needed the kitchen table. She had a hundred things to do this morning. She always had a hundred things to do. But Reg, oblivious or just not caring, reached for his mug without lifting his eyes from the paper and sucked in a sip of tea, swallowing it audibly. He sounded like a snake with a bad throat.

She couldn't hover any longer. She had to press on. 'Get fettling,' said her mam's voice in her head. Eh, Mam would have been that proud of her for passing the tests to be a railway girl. Mam had been one an' all, in the last war. The last war – aye, that was what it had been supposed to be, the last one ever. The war to end all wars. Which smart alec had fed them that particular promise? And what twerps they had been to believe it. Now they were facing the whole thing all over again, except it would be worse this time. It hadn't been so far, but it would be. Give it time.

The expected air raids and resulting devastation hadn't materialised, which had led to the girls, in common with thousands of other mums all over the country, bringing the kids home from evacuation. Pammy had fetched her precious Jenny back, which had more or less obliged Sheila to send for their Jimmy. Dot wasn't sure how to feel about her grandchildren's return. It had nigh on broken her heart last September to wave them off, poor little mites. Even their Jimmy had looked like a poor little mite, with his gas-mask box, cardboard suitcase, packet of sandwiches and the brown luggage label tied to his gabardine lapel – tied with a double-knot so he couldn't swap it for someone else's. He had walked along with all the quietly despairing mothers and children, the only bouncy one in the whole procession, the irrepressible monkey looking forward to the adventure, only for the sight of the coaches lined up along the road outside St Cuthbert's to transform him into a shrunken, whey-faced waif.

Dot's heart had squeezed tight, robbing her of the ability to breathe. Then she had bustled about, searching for the children's teacher, finding out which coach they were on, extracting a promise from Jimmy not to open his sandwiches until he was told to, and firing smiles at her daughters-in-law. Sheila and Pammy had never had anything but moral support and encouragement from her in the matter of sending the kids away, and only she herself knew how she had wept buckets night after night.

Now the children were home and, much as she loved knowing they were close by, she had the never-ending worry of how safe they were going to be when things finally got going.

Dot flung another look at Reg's back. His shoulders were rounded these days, where once they had been broad. Mind you, she was no spring chicken herself. She caught herself: not being a spring chicken didn't make her an old biddy.

She needed the table. She liked doing her meal preparation on it, chopping the veg, mixing the pastry, even kneading her own dough at times. You couldn't beat home-made bread with soup. But Reg didn't look like shifting any time soon, so if she wanted to get fettling, she would have to use the top of the crockery cupboard. Grabbing her chopping board, she made space for the vegetables and took her favourite knife from the drawer, picking up the onion to start with. Her dear old mam had always reckoned she could get a month's worth of flavour out of an onion before she even chopped it. As the mother of eleven surviving children, such culinary dexterity had been essential. Would Dot shortly be following suit? Rationing had already started. Four ounces of bacon per adult per week wouldn't go far.

'Pan's boiling over,' said Reg without moving. He could have stretched out his hand and turned the heat down, but did he? Course not. He was a man and men didn't do owt in the kitchen apart from eat what was put in front of them. Mr Donoghue up the road did the washing-up after dinner on Saturdays and Sundays, but no one was supposed to know that. Dot knew only because she and Mrs Donoghue had got tiddly on the cooking sherry the day after the abdication. Every Saturday and Sunday, Mrs Donoghue closed her kitchen curtains and the one in the scullery so that no one would glimpse Mr Donoghue with his sleeves rolled up. Not that Dot had ever said so to Mrs Donoghue, but there were those in Heathside Lane who said the Donoghues must be at it like rabbits behind those curtains, but at least passionate love-making was a manly thing to do. Washing-up definitely wasn't.

Dot bustled around behind Reg to get to the cooker. She was a great bustler. It was part and parcel of being busy, capable, a fettler. Her thighs rubbed together inside her ribbed-cotton girdle as she bustled.

She reduced the heat that was squeezing the flavour and last lingering goodness out of yesterday's chicken bones and returned to the vegetables. Together, they would make a hearty soup. She was proud of her soups, and rightly so.

'Always put the best you can in your soup,' her mam had taught her, and she always had. When she was a nipper, they had had a really poor family in their road. Everyone was poor round their way, but the Raffertys were the poorest and their soup was made from well-water that they didn't always have the wherewithal to heat up, and carrot and potato peelings that their neighbours donated out of what was destined for the pig bin. Dot and her brothers and sisters used to taunt the Rafferty kids for eating pig-swill soup. Aye, children could be cruel. She had tried to bring up her lads to be kind and considerate, but it hadn't been easy with Reg poking fun at her for it.

'Your mam's soft-hearted,' he used to tell the boys, smiling as he said it as if it was a compliment, though there was an undeniable element of man-to-man joshing that invited them to be like him, not her.

At some point in the years that followed, he had progressed from pretend-compliments to outright jibes.

'You know what your mam's trouble is, don't you, Harry ... Archie?' ... 'You know what you're ma-in-law's trouble is, don't you, Sheila ... Pammy? ...' Even to the children. 'You know what your nan's trouble is, don't you, Jenny ... Jimmy? She sees a pie and she's got to stick her fingers in, that's what.'

He made her sound a right busybody, but she wasn't. She was a coper. She was the one who helped everyone else; the one who'd looked after Jenny when she'd had such a terrible time teething, so that Pammy could snatch some shut-eye; the one who did Mrs Naughton's washing when she had three little 'uns under five all weeping and wailing with the chicken pox; the one who'd chased a so-called window-cleaner up the road when he'd helped himself to old Mrs Porter's life savings, aye, and bashed him over the head with her frying pan an' all; the one who'd cooked and cleaned for Alice Forshaw for a month when she had the baby blues so bad her mam was scared she might top herself; the one who'd helped the Ryans pack up all their worldly goods when they were meant to move house and then helped unpack it all when the rent man gave the new place to someone else.

That wasn't being a busybody. That was being helpful, reliable, kind. It sprang from coping, from caring, from not letting things get on top of her. She was the first person her daughters-in-law turned to, and that was summat to be proud of. She loved helping them. It was a wise woman who loved the girls her sons chose for their wives . . . even if one was posh and t'other a slattern, with the untidiest house you ever saw. But Pammy and Sheila loved her boys and had given her two wonderful grandchildren, so what did anything else matter? Especially now that Harry and Archie were away fighting. Dot had made a private vow that in their absence she would take extra care of their wives and, now that they were home again, double-extra care of Jimmy and Jenny. It was a promise she renewed every night, tacking it onto her nightly prayers for Harry and Archie to stay safe and in one piece.

At what point had she twigged that her prayers and promises didn't include Reg? Did that make her a bad wife? She was certainly a flaming tired one. She was tired of her rotten husband doing her down in front of the family, but that was his way and she couldn't object, because he would delight in telling everybody, 'You know what your mam's . . . ma-in-law's . . . nan's . . . auntie's problem is, don't you? She can't take a joke. She wouldn't recognise a joke if one got up and bit her on the bum.'

Aye, and the biggest joke of the lot was her marriage.

What a thing to happen first thing in the morning – and today of all days! Just when Dot needed everything to run smoothly, to show she could manage her house, care for her family and do a full-time job all at the same time, she had come downstairs to find her saucepans had gone AWOL, thanks to her daft grandson giving them to the rag-and-bone man for melting down.

She hammered at top speed down Heathside Lane. Either she was going at such a lick that the snow couldn't catch her out or else her carpet slippers had a better grip than she would have expected. Carpet slippers! Talk about undignified. Mind you, that was nowt compared to having her rollers on show for the world and his wife to gawp at under the hairnet she wore in bed, which she hadn't had time to exchange for her turban. Even so, it could have been worse. She could easily still have been in her dressing gown.

Her heart swelled and thudded as she made her mad dash to catch up with the horse and cart. Despite the early hour and the grey light, the cart was already piled high with all manner of bits and bobs.

'Any old rags? Rag-bone,' called the bloke in a powerful sing-song.

Dot caught up, clutching the side of the cart to prevent herself from collapsing in a breathless heap. The rag-and-bone man reined in the plodding horse, which wore a blanket covering its back, with an overcoat spread out over the top. The man turned on the bench-seat to look down on her with an expression that was half startled, half amused. He was a tough-looking chap, with gaps where various teeth should be. Not I'll-beat-you-up tough, but out-in-all-weathers tough. White hair stuck out untidily from beneath his cloth cap.

'My, you're keen to hand over your old stuff, love. I don't often get ladies pursuing me down the street.'

Dot pushed herself upright and eyed him with a firmness that would have been a lot more compelling if she hadn't been out of puff with her hairnet on.

'I want my things back.'

'Sorry, love. You gave it freely and I give every one of my customers one of my best donkey-stones.'

'I gave you nowt, freely or otherwise, as you well know.'

The rag-and-bone man shrugged. 'Difficult to say. If you did, you weren't all hot and bothered when you waved me down from your front door.'

'I never waved you down and I never gave you owt, and if I had, I'd have wanted a heck of a lot more than a flaming donkey-stone in exchange for all my pots and pans.' Dot jammed bunched fists on her hips. 'Shame on you, telling a little lad that all spare metal goes towards building planes for the RAF.'

'Come on, missus, it's for the war effort.'

'When I give away my pots and pans, it'll be to an official collection by the Women's Voluntary Service, not to a clever-clogs who's going to make money out of it.'

'Careful what you say, missus. I'm not one of them war profiteers.'

'Prove it,' Dot challenged. 'Give me back my kitchen things.'

'Well, I don't know.' The rag-and-bone man glanced vaguely over his shoulder. 'They could be anywhere in among that lot.'

'Rubbish. You've not had 'em in your possession five minutes. Either you hand everything back – everything, mind – or I'll fetch my sons. I've four lads, all at home, all in reserved occupations. One's a policeman, one's a fireman—'

'All right, you win.'

He jumped down from the bench-seat, causing Dot to take a swift step backwards, one foot plunging straight into a mound of snow. A cold, wet feeling shot through her. *Thank you very much.* Leaning over the side of the cart, the rag-and-bone man rummaged about, probably for show. He brought out her saucepans one by one, a milk-pan with a wonky handle and a bigger pan that did for soup in winter and jam in summer. She performed a juggling act, cramming smaller into larger.

'Thanks.' She turned away, then spun round again. It was ruddy cold out here, but that didn't mean her brain had frozen. 'Frying pan.'

The rag-and-bone man cast his eyes up to the heavens, as if she was the most unreasonable creature ever to walk God's green earth, but he produced the frying pan. Dot wanted to whip it out of his hands, but that would mean putting her other possessions in jeopardy. Bad enough being outdoors in her hairnet without sending her pans flying in all directions and landing splat in the slush.

She managed to free one hand to snatch the frying-pan handle. 'Thank you,' she said in her most clipped voice.

The rag-and-bone man hauled himself back onto the cart. 'Mind how you go, Grandma.'

Grandma? Blooming cheek.

'I'll have you know . . .' she began – but she couldn't say that, could she, because she *was* a grandmother. Honest to God, just because you were closer to fifty than forty, and your hair was more salt-and-pepper than brown, people made all kinds of assumptions. Inspiration struck and she raised her voice. 'I'll have you know, Mr Call-yourself-a-rag-and-bone-man, though really you're a swindler who takes advantage of little boys, I'll have you know that, as of today, I'm a railway girl – aye, a girl. Not a railway grandma, and certainly not a railway old biddy, but an actual railway girl. So put that in your pipe and smoke it.'

Dot dumped her pots and pans on the kitchen table with a crash that made Reg jump. Good. Where had he been while she was fighting to retrieve their worldly goods? Sitting at the kitchen table, that's where, waiting for his breakfast. If the rag-and-bone bloke had spirited her saucepans away so that she could never cook again, Reg would still sit at the ruddy kitchen table in expectation of his next hot meal.

She swung her gaze upon their Jimmy. It was lucky for him he was her grandson and the light of her life, because if he was anybody else's she would string him up by his toes, aye, and give his mam a piece of her mind an' all. She was riled up and cold and all Heathside Lane had seen her larking about in the snow in her hairnet, making a right spectacle of herself. Jimmy looked stricken, as well he might, but it wasn't the way she wanted him to look stricken. It wasn't with awareness that he had done summat wrong, summat downright barmy. It was because she had fetched back her cookware.

Jimmy gazed back at her with irresistible blue eyes. Harry's eyes, his dad's eyes. Blue eyes and freckles on a round face with a happy-go-lucky smile, but Harry had never given her the runaround the way this lad did. He was more trouble than a mattress full of bedbugs.

Look at him now. He hadn't been up half an hour and already his socks were round his ankles. How many times had she sewn pieces of elastic into circles to make garters? And they never lasted. If Jimmy didn't snap them using them as catapults, then Sheila ... well, God alone knew how Sheila the Slattern could have lost so many of them, but she had. Knocked them down the back of the chest of drawers, probably, never to be seen again until Dot arrived on her doorstep one fine day a few weeks from now with the offer of 'Shall I make a start on the spring-cleaning for you, love?'

Anyroad, there would be no more garters for young Jimmy. She hadn't spent all last summer stockpiling elastic just to keep her monkey of a grandson in catapults. It hadn't been possible to get knicker elastic for love nor money by the time the last war ended, and she wasn't going to get caught out this time.

'What did you do that for, our Jimmy?' she demanded. 'Giving away my saucepans, I ask you.'

'The man said it were for the RAF, Nan.'

'Oh aye? And you thought you'd give away your nan's saucepans so your very own Spitfire would appear by magic on the parlour rug?'

Jimmy's eyes widened with surprise and hurt. Yes, obviously he had thought that, the daft ha'porth.

'Don't give away owt of mine ever again without asking,' she said. 'Or anything of your mum's. Or anyone else's,' she added, just in case.

'Get this clutter off the table,' said Reg. 'Where's my breakfast?'

'Hold your horses.' Dot stepped out of her sodden slippers. Her stockings stuck to her feet like dead skin. 'Here, our Jimmy, stuff these slippers with screwed-up newspaper and put them on the hearth to dry. On second thoughts, I'll do it. You aren't capable of setting foot near the hearth without ending up looking like one of them lads chimney sweeps used to send up chimneys in th'olden days.'

Reg made a clucking sound with his tongue. 'Leave it for now, Dot, for pity's sake. Breakfast is more important – isn't it, Jimmy? Your poor old nan gets herself in such a state, she can't get her priorities straight.'

Jimmy grinned, until Dot caught his eye, whereupon he subsided. After a speedy breakfast, she fetched Reg's overcoat and held it for him to put his arms in. He shrugged it onto his shoulders, tucked his scarf inside his lapels and jammed the old bowler that had once been his dad's onto his head. Ten minutes after Reg left, it was time to send Jimmy to school. With Sheila working at the munitions factory, Jimmy was staying overnight with them two or three times a week.

After she had cleared away the breakfast things, she peeled off her stockings and, turning her back to the kitchen fire, lifted up first one foot, then the other, like a horse at the blacksmith's, wiggling her toes in the warmth to try to get some life back into them. Tempting as it was to pull up a chair and toast her tootsies, there wasn't time. There was never time for things like that. She had to put together a cottage pie that she could bung in the oven when she got home from work. It was years since she had worked. That was to say, she had worked all her flaming life, one way or another, but it didn't count when you were a housewife.

It was the women who were the true workhorses. Dot had grown up helping her mam. All the girls did and the oldest ones did the most – cleaning, mending, taking care of the younger ones – while the boys climbed trees and played conkers. They might be sent out to find firewood or pinch a bit of coal from the railway yard, but that was the extent of their responsibilities.

When she was twelve, she had gone half-time at school so she could be a lace-threader in the afternoons, threading the lace-making machines with silk or cotton, a job she had taken on full-time the following year. She hadn't been that fussed about the job to start with, but when she was promoted to apprentice lace-maker and was given her own machine to operate, she took a fresh interest and began to enjoy it. By, that had been a happy time. She hadn't enjoyed it for long, though. She had met Reg and that was that: madly in love at fifteen. Reg had been a handsome devil in those days. He was almost ten years older than she was. Had that been part of the attraction? As one of the oldest in such a big family, with responsibilities from an early age, she had revelled in the novelty of being the young one, of feeling she was being looked after.

Reg had looked after her all right. He had got her up the spout when she was barely sixteen. She had had Archie at sixteen, followed by Harry, practically a year to the day later. Never mind the fancy lace-work. It was the washing and darning and bottom-wiping that she had done as a lass that had stood her in good stead. Much as she loved her boys, and Reg too in those days, it had been grim to realise that she faced the same never-ending grind as her mam.

Except it hadn't worked out that way for her. After Harry, she fell for another baby, who was due to be eighteen months younger, but in the third month, one Saturday morning when Reg was digging the vegetable patch, a dull, dragging pain had started in the pit of her stomach, accompanied by the metallic smell of blood. She had despatched Reg for the midwife, but – he had loved her back then – he had gone for the doctor, who had sent him home with instructions that everything expelled should be collected and he would be along later to examine it.

The doctor had ambled along about teatime. By then, the neighbours who were caring for Dot had gone home to see to their families; Archie and Harry, who had been spirited away, had been brought back; Reg, who had nipped along to his mother's for his dinner, had returned and was in the middle of digging every row in the vegetable patch so as not to intrude on women's matters; and Dot, after a few hours in bed, was up and fettling, with a mound of rags stuffed inside her knickers to absorb any final bleeding.

The doctor peered into the enamel dish that Dot couldn't bring herself to look at.

'Knife and fork, please,' he said without looking round.

Dot opened the kitchen drawer, obscurely embarrassed when it got stuck and squeaked. She offered him her best pair. He was the doctor, after all.

And he used her best knife and fork, the ones with the bone handles, to rootle around in the enamel dish.

'It's all there,' he announced. 'Nothing to worry about. Hot water and a clean towel, if you please. Doctor has to wash his hands. Tell your husband that will be one shilling.'

After that, her womb must have shrivelled in horror, because there was never so much as a late monthly in the years that followed, though that hadn't prevented every nerve-end in her body, every beat of her heart, every shred of her instinct, from crying out for another child.

'Oh well,' said Reg when she told him of her longing, 'having just the two lads makes the money stretch further.'

Was that the best he could come up with? Couldn't he see how much his words had hurt her? Was that when they had started to drift apart? Had she foisted too much attention on her precious sons? Was that why Reg's teasing had taken on first an exasperated, then a sniping, air? It was difficult to say. It hadn't happened overnight. How could summat that had started with passion and high hopes have slumped into an obscure sourness?

Back then, everyone had taken advantage of her family circumstances. In a close-knit, working-class community like theirs, having just the two children meant she was practically childless and therefore available to help all the over-worked mothers of six, eight, ten – the real mothers.

'You've got room for a few more, haven't you, Dot?' asked her sisters and sisters-in-law. 'You can mind mine for me, can't you?' 'I'll send mine round to yours, Dot. Give me a bit of a break . . .' 'You'll like having my lasses for the day, won't you, Dot? It'll be a big help to me.'

As a young mum, she had spent the last war keeping open house for everyone else's nippers. As the war dragged on, and other women went out to work, Reg, home on leave, had made it clear that she wasn't allowed to.

'It's not right for a married woman. Not respectful to her husband. It makes him look like he can't afford to keep her.'

And she was young enough and daft enough to let him lay down the law. Anyroad, Archie was four when war was declared, with Harry only three, and she had wanted to be at home for them.

'Course you do, pet,' Mam had said comfortingly. 'Looking after the bairns is your job when you're young.'

'And when you're not so young. You've still got six at home and two of them are at school.'

'Aye, it never stops. I was going to wait until our Philip and Floss had finished school, but I've decided not to. It's not as though they're tiny bairns.'

'What are you talking about, Mam?'

'I'm off out to work, lass. What does that poster say? "Your Country Needs You." Well, that's me.'

'It means soldiers,' Dot had pointed out.

Mam shrugged. 'I'm going out to work.'

'But, Mam—'

'But what? How will I manage with the kids and the house at the same time? Listen, Dot. Keeping house and looking after the family is what women do, and we do it as well as owt else we're called on to do. Take last week. You helped our Marnie move house, and you helped Agnes with the kids when they was all struck down with that cough, and how many pairs of socks did you knit for the troops? And did that stop you being a good housewife and mother?'

'Course not.'

'Course not, because that's what women do. We're house-wives and mothers, and we take on whatever else wants doing. Well, what I'm taking on is my own level crossing and I'll take good care of it until the level-crossing keeper comes home from the war. Close your mouth, our Dot. You'll catch flies.'

Eh, Mam had been the best sort of woman. Dot hadn't realised it at the time and was sorry now she hadn't seen it sooner. She was the same age now, give or take, that Mam had been when she became a railway girl, and that felt odd. Back then she had thought Mam too old to be doing such things, but she didn't think of herself as old now. She was going to be forty-six this year. Forty-six! If only youngsters could understand how young that felt. Her brown hair might be fading to grey, and her neck might be less firm than it once was, but she still didn't feel old. Not inside.

'I'll do you proud, Mam,' she said out loud as she flew round the house: making beds; doing the day's dusting; sweeping the hall, stairs and landing; and starting on the cottage pie that was going to prove you could take on full-time work and still put nourishing meals on the table. 'You managed with a family *and* a railway job and I will an' all.'

Chapter Six

Joan made her way to Victoria Station, relishing the undeniable tang of spring in the air. The chilly edge to this March morning was nothing after the hard winter they had endured. Her senses were heightened in a way they hadn't been since the day war was declared, but today's awareness was due to excitement, though maybe there was a tremor of apprehension too. She badly wanted to make a good fist of this. No more sewing blackout curtains, no more piecing together uniforms for WVS ladies. This was her chance to do her bit for real.

As she entered Victoria Station, the sound of a train pulling in echoed around the vast building, soaring high above her into the arched canopy and down again. Her heart swelled. This was her new place of work. Would she be behind one of the ticket-office windows that were set in that long line of wooden panelling, each end of which was gracefully curved? She would enjoy handing out tickets and saying, 'Change at Salford Central for the Ribble Valley line to Blackburn.' Or maybe she would be a ticket collector, staffing the gateway between the bustling concourse and one of the platforms. 'Not this platform, madam. You need platform four.' She would have to learn all the routes that left from each platform to do her job properly. Or maybe she would be lucky enough to work on one of the trains. What a thrill that would be.

The letter she had received had instructed her to wait beside the station's war memorial. She could see it, past the line of ticket-office booths. A couple of other girls were already there. She smiled, ready to look friendly and approachable when they acknowledged her – but they didn't so much as glance her way. They stood gazing at the memorial, their attention locked on it. Moments later, she understood why.

The memorial took up the whole wall. The top part was a map showing the routes of the old Lancashire and Yorkshire Railway network. Below this, between end-panels depicting St George at one end and an angel at the other, were bronze panels with the names of the fallen engraved in long lists upon them.

Sorrow spread through Joan. So many men, so many names. All those families. She knew what it was to grow up without a father. But as well as deepest sorrow, there was another emotion. She stood taller as pride flowed through her. Pride. Determination. Willingness. This war memorial and all it represented, this was what mattered. King and country. Duty. Honour. Facing what had to be faced. Doing what was right. And she would. She, along with millions of others, would do all she could to help win this war, so that the glorious dead of the last war would not have died in vain.

'Goodness me!' A voice rang out, clear and confident, in the cut-glass accent of one who didn't just travel first class but had probably been on the Orient Express. 'How magnificent. That enormous map – and all those names. A truly breathtaking piece of design. I simply have to write an article about this.'

Turning, Joan saw that she was now part of a group of girls and women gathered by the memorial, all of them as moved and captivated as she herself had been until their mood of silent respect and reflection had been interrupted. Joan found herself staring at a startlingly lovely creature with violet eyes. She had read stories that featured violet-eyed heroines and had always put the description down to the authors' imaginations running amok, but this girl really did have violet eyes above high cheekbones that were smooth and creamy. Everyone else's cheeks were pink from the day's early chill, but this girl's complexion was the perfect ivory of skilfully applied make-up and her lips were, not the red so many women favoured, but a more subtle rosy-pink. She was even more beautiful than Letitia, and that was saying something.

She was elegantly dressed, too, in a fitted wool coat with an over-sized collar, its buckled belt showing off her slim waist. She wore a matching hat with a curled brim. Even her gloves – leather gauntlets – added a dash of flair.

Could this be another railway girl? Whoever she was, she had cut into the thoughtful mood good and proper. And what did she mean about writing an article?

Another girl caught Joan's notice. She was standing beside the upper-class beauty. Dark hair fluffed out in a cloud of curls from beneath her hat, and her eyes were the rich brown of chocolate – eyes that flicked sideways with a suggestion of vexation as she took a small step away from the upper-crust girl, as if to dissociate herself from her.

'Excuse me butting in.' It was Lizzie, the little red-head. 'Are you new railway girls?'

'I'm not, I'm afraid,' said the upper-class girl. 'I'm merely hanging on to Miss Bradshaw's coat-tails. She's the one you need to be chums with.' She held out her hand to Lizzie, but the chatter of some people walking past prevented Joan from catching her name. 'Miss . . . ?'

'Cooper.' Lizzie shook hands, clearly entranced. 'Lizzie Cooper. It's my first day.'

'Lucky you. You've taken on essential work.' The upper-crust girl turned a fraction, to include her dark-haired companion. 'Mabel, permit me to introduce Miss Cooper. Miss Cooper, this is Miss Bradshaw.'

Miss Bradshaw might have appeared exasperated with the violet-eyed beauty a few moments previously, but she showed perfect manners as she shook hands with Lizzie.

'How do you do? I'm pleased to meet you.'

Nevertheless, Joan couldn't help noticing that she didn't engage Lizzie in conversation. The upper-crust girl seemed willing to be chummy, but Miss Bradshaw was more reserved.

Miss Bradshaw addressed her companion, speaking quietly. 'Why don't you head off to the shops now?'

'I don't mind hanging around,' was the cheerful reply. 'You know, just to see what happens.'

'I'll tell you everything later.' Miss Bradshaw's jawline was so tight, it was a wonder she could get any words out.

'Righty-ho. I'll say toodle-pip.' The violet-eyed girl swept a warm smile over the group. 'Best of British luck in your new jobs, everyone.' To the dark-haired girl, she added, 'I'll see you at home.'

As she walked away, Lizzie bobbed up by Joan's side.

'She looks like one of them mannequins that model clothes. I'm glad you're here, Joan. Imagine me passing all those tests!'

'I bet your mum's proud,' said Joan.

It was the right thing to say. Lizzie beamed, displaying wonky teeth. 'She is – once she got over being amazed.'

'Don't put yourself down.' Alison joined them, giving a nod of greeting. 'We all passed, then.'

'Looks like it.' Joan glanced about, recognising the two older women from the day of the tests: the grave, elegant one and the motherly one.

'Here's Colette.' Lizzie couldn't have sounded more pleased if Colette had been her dearest friend. She had certainly been born with the gift of a sunny disposition. 'Has her husband come with her?'

A good-looking young man in an overcoat had Colette's elbow cupped in his gloved hand. Beneath the brim of his trilby, his eyes were clouded.

'He looks worried,' said Alison.

'Aah,' crooned Lizzie. 'I think it's sweet. Isn't she lucky to have a husband who loves her so much?' She nudged Alison. 'That'll be you one day. Didn't you say you have a boyfriend?'

'You remembered.' Alison smiled confidently. 'Between you, me and the gatepost, it will be me in the not too distant future. I'm just waiting for him to pop the question.'

Lizzie bunched up her shoulders in excitement. 'He shouldn't leave it too long, not these days. I bet he asks you when he's on leave.'

'He isn't away fighting,' said Alison, a trifle stiffly. 'He's in a reserved occupation.'

'Oh aye?' said Lizzie. 'What does he do?'

'He's an engineer at the telephone exchange – and before you say anything, communications are enormously important. Essential, in fact.'

'I know that,' said Lizzie, 'and I wasn't going to say anything – not about your chap, anyroad. I was just going to say that that was the job I wanted. You know, on the switchboard.'

'I remember you saying,' said Joan.

'I'm sorry,' said Alison. 'I get a bit twitchy sometimes. If he was, say, a fireman, no one would think twice, but when they hear he's at the telephone exchange, some people immediately think he's trying to duck out of doing his duty.' She turned to Joan. 'What about you? Are you spoken for?'

'No.'

As the denial shot out of her mouth, heat scalded her

neck, inexorably seeping upwards to her face. Even her eye-lids felt as if they were on fire.

'But maybe there's some lucky fellow you've got your eye on?' Alison suggested.

Hell's bells. 'No. Nobody special.' She tried to sound off-hand. Being in love with her sister's boyfriend was her deepest secret, a challenging mixture of the glorious and the damning. 'Look – is this lady coming for us, do you suppose?'

'Ladies, good morning. If I might have your attention, please.'

Joan could have sunk to the floor and kissed the woman's stout lace-ups in gratitude for the timely interrup-tion. She made a guess at her age. Thirties, maybe? Older than twenties, anyway, but nowhere near the age of the woman with the greying hair who had bustled out of the room when they had sat the test. Her hat and wool suit were smart and business-like.

She waved a hand in the direction of the memorial. 'I especially wanted you all to see this. Up there are the one thousand, four hundred and sixty names of the railway-men who gave their lives for their country. This was the Lancashire and Yorkshire Railway back then. The same year that this memorial was unveiled, it merged with the London and North Western and a year later became part of the London, Midland and Scottish. You're going to be doing important work, ladies. I am Miss Emery and I'm the assist-ant welfare supervisor for women and girls of all grades. Would you follow me, please?'

'Excuse me.' The good-looking man with Colette stepped forward. 'Is there a man I could have a word with about the nature of the work my wife will do?'

'Roles have already been allocated, Mr . . . ?'

'Naylor, Tony Naylor, and this is Mrs Naylor.' His mouth

formed into a half-smile, as if he hoped to win Miss Emery round. 'I know how important war work is, of course. That's why I agreed to let my wife do this now instead of waiting until the government makes all women sign up. But I'm worried about what she might be asked to do. I imagined her in an office, not a . . . railway station.'

'There's no reason to suppose any of these ladies will be required to act beyond their ability,' Miss Emery stated. 'On the other hand,' she added, looking round at her listeners, 'you might be surprised by how far your capability extends.'

A frisson ran through the group. Joan straightened her shoulders. She was going to live up to what was expected of her, and more.

'I'd still like to speak to the man in charge, please,' said Mr Naylor. His manner wasn't obstinate or vexed, just concerned, and Joan felt a tug of sympathy, not to mention a twinge of envy. Imagine if Steven cared for her to that extent. Not that she wanted for one moment to steal him off her sister, but . . . Oh, it was complicated.

It was impossible to tell what Miss Emery was thinking as she looked at Mr Naylor. 'Then you'd better follow us.'

Extending her arm like a lance, she carved a way through the group and headed out of the station. Glancing at one another, the group followed, automatically raising their hands to ensure their hats didn't get blown off as a sharp-edged breeze caught them the moment they left the shelter of the station.

Miss Emery led them at a brisk pace to the building where they had sat their tests. As she went inside, Tony Naylor hastened forward.

'Allow me.'

He held the door open, Colette standing by his side.

'Thanks,' said Joan, walking indoors in time to catch

what Miss Emery was saying through the hatch to somebody in the office.

'There's a husband here who's anxious about what his wife will be asked to do. Please let Mr Mortimer know.'

Followed by her group, Miss Emery headed for the staircase. Halfway up, she stopped and turned round, looking down over everyone's hats into the hall below. Along with the others, Joan looked round. The door was now closed and Mr Naylor was about to follow Colette up the stairs.

'If you would care to wait downstairs, Mr Naylor, I have alerted the office to your presence. Mrs Naylor, will you join the others, please.'

Miss Emery immediately set off again, with the new recruits hurrying after her. There was no time to linger and look back. Was Tony Naylor frustrated at being dismissed, however courteously? Did Colette hesitate before following? Was she one of those helpless creatures who needed a man to do everything for her?

Miss Emery threw open a door to a room no bigger than the parlour at home, and certainly not large enough to accommodate the group comfortably. Miss Emery stood behind a table that took up a disproportionate amount of space. A scattering of chairs faced it.

'I'm sorry, but some of you will have to stand,' said Miss Emery, not sounding at all sorry. 'Don't waste time being polite. If there's a seat, sit on it.'

Joan sank onto a chair, immediately realising that the motherly woman was still on her feet. Feeling rude, she started to rise, but the woman gave her a smile and shook her head. She had a pleasant face.

'First of all,' said Miss Emery, picking up a piece of tired-looking paper that had evidently been written on several times, 'let's make sure everyone is here. Answer "yes" to your names, please. Miss Bradshaw?'

'Yes.' The girl who had been talking to the upper-class beauty sat up straighter as she spoke. She looked like she could do with feeding up a bit. Good luck with that, now that rationing had been introduced.

'Miss Cooper?'

'Yes,' said Lizzie.

'Miss Foster?'

'Yes,' said Joan.

Miss Emery went down the list – well, not so much down it, as round the corner. They were all being encouraged to make use of every scrap of paper as many times as was feasible these days and Miss Emery had evidently scribbled their names around the edge of the sheet.

Joan wished she wasn't sitting at the front. It would look so obvious if she turned round to put faces to the other names. As it was, she only gleaned the names of the two older ladies who had sat the tests the same day she had. The elegant one with the serious face was Mrs Masters and the one who had rushed off at the end was Mrs Green.

'We have a lot to get through,' said Miss Emery when the register was complete, 'so let's make a start. You're here to work on the LMS Railway for the duration of the war and you'll be tackling work you've never done before. That is, I assume none of you has previously worked as a signalman, welder or steam-hammer operator.' She paused. Were they meant to laugh? 'Many jobs involve shift work, including nights, and you'll be expected to fit in your domestic duties around your work. You'll be on three months' probation and for salary purposes, you will all be placed on the starting grades, though naturally you shall not earn the same as the men. Now then, there are a few things we have to discuss before Mr Mortimer arrives. I have a form here for you all to sign, saying you will wear full-length stockings, not the shorter length, at all times.'

'I bought four extra pairs to see me through the war,' said Alison. 'My mother said they were bound to be hard to get.'

'Let's hope that four pairs will be enough,' said Mrs Masters. She wasn't poking fun. There was sorrow in her voice. Was she remembering the last war?

'Next thing,' said Miss Emery. 'The station has no lavatory facilities for women workers, so you shall have to use the ladies' public conveniences. These, of course, operate on a penny-in-the-slot basis.'

'You mean we have to pay every time we . . . ?' asked a voice behind Joan.

'I'm afraid so. Maybe proper facilities will be provided at a later date, but don't hold your breath. Next: I imagine that for some of you, this will be the first time you have worked alongside men. Please raise your hand if this is the case.'

Joan was unsure what to do. Ingleby's employed some men, but not in the sewing rooms, where she had worked.

'It is my hope that your male colleagues will support you in your endeavours, though you may encounter some resistance. All the railway companies have employed women in certain roles for some years, but by and large the jobs you'll be allocated are those which have been left empty because of railwaymen going to serve their country. You'll be provided with uniforms as and when they are available. In the meantime, you'll be provided with a badge to show you are employees of the LMS Railway. Some of the jobs involve hard physical work and you'll be required to wear trousers or possibly overalls. In other positions, where appropriate, you may be given the choice between trousers and a skirt.'

Joan was aware of looks passing round the group. Trousers! Gran would throw forty fits. She couldn't help glancing at Miss Bradshaw. If she was friends with that upper-crust beauty from earlier on, she probably spent half her time striding about in jodhpurs.

'There is a staff canteen in this building for those who work in the offices. Those who work on the station or the trains – porters, ticket collectors and so forth – have a separate canteen over there, called the mess.' Miss Emery consulted her wristwatch and gave her head the tiniest of shakes. 'We haven't nearly enough time, I'm afraid. Mr Mortimer will be here in a minute.'

'Is there time for questions?' asked Alison.

'A couple, if you wish – or I can give you the best piece of advice I can. Your choice.'

More glances.

'Advice, please,' said Mrs Masters. 'We can always come back to you with questions as they arise.'

'I'm afraid that might not be possible,' said Miss Emery. 'This isn't the only place I work. I have a large geographical area to cover. I'll see you as often as I can, but . . .' She let the sentence trail away.

'But, as with waiting for proper WC facilities,' finished Alison, 'don't hold your breath.'

'I'm sure you'll all manage perfectly well,' said Miss Emery.

'We'll have to, by the sound of it,' remarked Mrs Green.

'Quite so,' said Miss Emery. 'Which brings me to the advice. It's very simple. Be friends with one another – regardless of age or background or anything else that would normally come between you. You'll be women in a man's world and some of the men, I regret to say, aren't keen on your being here. Some of you have been assigned to small stations, where you may be the only woman. But several of you will be based at Victoria Station and if you can turn to one another for support, it will help you all.'

There were nods and murmurs of agreement, then the

room stilled as everyone looked at Mrs Masters. Socially speaking, she was the most senior person present. Her response was crucial.

'I think that's an excellent idea,' she said, and the room relaxed. 'Moral support will benefit us all. If things are hard, it'll be heartening to know we can rely on seeing friendly faces. I hope the rest of you agree.'

More murmurs of agreement, louder this time.

'Fair enough,' Mrs Green said. 'If we're going to be mates, let's forget about being Mrs and Miss and go straight to first names.'

'I'm not sure about that,' Mrs Masters murmured. 'It's rather avant-garde, isn't it?'

'I don't know what that means,' said Mrs Green, 'but we're all going to need friends. You young girls probably see me as an old fogey, and Mrs Masters probably sees me the same way she sees her charwoman – no offence – but it's like Miss Emery says: regardless of age or background. We're all in the same boat, girls. We can be formal in front of other people, because that's only polite, but when it's just us, I vote for first names. I'll start, shall I? I don't mind putting my money where my mouth is. I'm Dot, short for Dorothy.'

She looked at Mrs Masters. So did Joan – and everyone else. This couldn't be done without the cooperation of this middle-class lady.

After a moment, Mrs Masters nodded. 'I'm pleased to meet you, Dot. My name is Cordelia.'

Cordelia, yes. Such an elegant, self-possessed lady was bound to have a lovely name.

'Your turn, girls,' said Mrs Green – Dot.

The others gave their first names. Joan missed a couple because she was wondering how she would ever dare be so familiar with the group's older women. It was probably best not to mention it to Gran. Everyone glanced round at one another, exchanging hesitant smiles. Was it possible to become friends just like that, because you had been told to? But Miss Emery must know what she was talking about.

Miss Bradshaw hesitated before saying, 'My name is Mabel.' Reluctant to dive into instant intimacy? Well, yes, it was a bit disconcerting. 'I don't wish to presume,' Mabel added, 'but might I ask for help?'

'Already?' grinned Lizzie.

'I'd like to find a new billet, if anyone knows of a likely place. I can afford the rent.'

'Don't you live with that girl who arrived with you?' asked Alison.

A faint flush invaded Mabel's cheeks. 'Not exactly.'

'What was her name?' Joan asked. 'I didn't quite hear.'

'Persephone Trehearn-Hobbs.'

'Per- . . . whatsit?' asked Dot.

'Per-sef-onny.' Mabel sounded it out.

Lizzie made a trilling 'Oooh' sound. 'Very posh.'

'It's from Greek mythology,' said Cordelia. 'Wasn't she the one who was kidnapped and married by the king of the underworld? But once a year, she's allowed to come back up, as it were, and that's when we have springtime.'

'Blimey,' Lizzie murmured.

'What d'you mean, you don't exactly live with her?' asked Alison.

'We're staying at the same place for now,' said Mabel, 'but I'd like to look for somewhere else.'

'I may be able to help you,' said Cordelia.

'I'll ask my mum,' offered Lizzie.

'Thank you.' Mabel smiled politely, but there was a tightness about her lips.

'Good,' said Miss Emery. 'This is what I mean about supporting one another. Before Mr Mortimer arrives, can I ask if any of you know Pitman's shorthand?'

'I do,' said Cordelia. 'That is, I learned it when I was young, and, although I never actually went out to work in the end, I've practised it from time to time, just to keep my hand in, you know.' She gave a light shrug. 'It gave me something to do.'

Dot laughed out loud. 'If you ever need summat to do, love, come round my house. I'll keep you busy. Guaranteed!'

'I'm nowhere near dictation speed,' Cordelia told Miss Emery.

'You don't need to be. The clerks write in Pitman's shorthand and the typists read it and do the typing.'

'So I'll be a typist?' Did Cordelia sound disappointed?

'Not at the moment, I don't think, but I'll make a note that you know Pitman's, so you can be called on in the future, if necessary. Ah, here's Mr Mortimer.'

Everyone looked round as the door opened. There was a bit of faffing about, as chairs had to be moved aside to let in the newcomer, and then those who had been sitting offered their chairs to those who so far had been standing. While everyone settled themselves, the gentleman positioned himself behind the table, taking the place in the centre, where Miss Emery had previously stood. He was immaculately turned out in pinstripes and a bow-tie, with a watch-chain hanging in a loop from the little pocket in his waistcoat, which was a perfect fit across the ample girth that matched rounded cheeks, run through with fine red lines. His hair was slicked back, his moustache neatly trimmed. At first glance, he looked like a jolly old uncle. His cheeks bunched up beneath his eyes as he smiled round the room.

'So these are the good fairies who are going to assist us in all things, eh, Miss Emery? Splendid, splendid. I am Mr Mortimer and I'm here to welcome you to the London, Midland and Scottish Railway.' With the air of a conjuror, Mr Mortimer produced a small piece of card from his pocket. 'The following ladies will be working on small stations in the locality. If you would kindly leave the room, Mr Kiernan is waiting in the corridor to spirit you away.'

Joan looked round, catching a few glances. Which of them would stay here to work at Victoria Station? She was relieved when her name wasn't read out. She, Lizzie and Alison smiled at one another as others eased their way out of the crowded room.

When the door closed, Mr Mortimer smiled round the room. 'You will be based at Victoria.' He waggled his piece of card. 'These are the jobs you'll be doing.'

'Won't we all be together?' asked Lizzie.

Mr Mortimer looked round for the source of the voice. Lizzie wiggled her fingers at him.

'No, my dear. As much as you might like to huddle together, safety in numbers and all that, it isn't possible. Will you kindly make your good selves known to me when I say your name? Cooper, Miss Elizabeth, are you here? Ah, young lady, it's you. You're going to be a station porter, but because you're under eighteen, you have to be a lad porter.'

'Not a girl porter?' asked Dot.

'No such thing, my good woman. Miss Cooper will be a lad porter. Foster, Miss Joan?'

Joan half raised her hand. Pulses jumped in her neck and wrists. This was it – the moment she had been waiting for.

'You'll be a clerk.'

Disappointment swamped her. A clerk? That wasn't why she had applied to the railways. 'But I don't know Pitman's shorthand. Miss Emery said the clerks use Pitman's.'

Mr Mortimer addressed the room. 'Ladies, you'll receive full training in whatever job you are asked to do. This might, if necessary, include teaching you Pitman's. In your case, Miss . . .' he glanced at his piece of card, '. . . Foster, shorthand isn't necessary.' Another glance at the card: he was looking at the next name.

Joan couldn't stop herself. She had to know. 'Please, sir, the jobs we're given today, are they the ones we'll stay in for the duration?'

Mr Mortimer looked at her. 'My dear young lady, one cannot chop and change at will. There is a war to be won.'

Feeling her chest curving inwards, she forced herself to sit up straight, even though a heavy flush seeped across her cheeks. She had made herself look a real fathead. What a rotten start.

'Bradshaw, Miss Mabel?'

'Here.' Mabel lifted her hand a short way.

'You shall be a driver,' said Mr Mortimer.

A collective intake of breath sounded softly round the room.

'A train driver?' asked Lizzie, turning in open admiration to Mabel.

'Good Lord, no, what a ridiculous idea,' said Mr Mortimer. 'Women can't drive trains. How absurd. Miss Bradshaw will drive a delivery van. The railways carry all manner of items from one place to another and they all have to be delivered safely to their final destination.'

Joan couldn't believe her ears. Envy sucked the marrow out of her bones. But Mabel had gone rather white about the gills.

'I can't drive.' Mabel's voice was quieter than normal.

'I don't suppose you can,' said Mr Mortimer. 'We'll teach you.'

'No,' said Mabel, and this time her voice was louder – and harder. 'When I say I can't drive, what I mean is – I won't.'

Chapter Seven

What the heck had made her do that? Dot could have kicked herself. This girl – Mabel – wasn't family. And never mind all that stuff about being friends. That didn't make Mabel her responsibility. She had quite enough responsibilities on her plate already, thank you very much. Yet she had done what she always did when a problem presented itself. She had stepped up – pushing herself forward, Reg called it – ready to sort it out. Good old Dot, the one everybody relied on.

In the consternation that had followed Mabel's announcement, Dot had, without a second thought, made her offer.

'I'll do it. I'll be the delivery driver and Mabel – I mean, Miss Bradshaw – can do whatever you've put me down for. I don't mind learning to drive.'

Don't mind? Imagine the family's faces when she told them that. Wouldn't that be grand? Or would Reg's howls of derision set everyone else against her doing any such thing? He was the head of the family and his influence counted. There must be some men out there who deserved such influence and used it wisely, but Ratty Reg wasn't one of them.

Mr Mortimer puffed up his cheeks and blew out a breath. 'Extraordinary! A woman, and a mere slip of a girl at that, actually refusing the job she's been put down for. This is unprecedented. Miss Bradshaw, I am shocked. And you, my good woman, Mrs . . . ?'

'Green,' said Dot. 'Mrs Dorothy Green.'

'Mrs Green, it isn't your place to make an offer like that, though it should be said that your attitude does you far more credit than Miss Bradshaw's does her. You've let yourself down badly, Miss Bradshaw. This will put a black mark against your name – and not just your name, but the names of all the women. It will reflect badly on all the women who work here. You've made everyone appear scatterbrained and unreliable.'

Dot glanced about, taking in the hardening looks on the faces around her. Even Lizzie, who had seemed such a bubbly little thing, had a flat, narrow-eyed expression. Alison had folded her arms.

'I never intended—' Mabel began.

'Your intentions are beside the point,' said Mr Mortimer. 'I've a good mind to ask you to leave immediately and apply for work elsewhere.'

'Mr Mortimer.' Miss Emery stepped in. Her voice was quiet and respectful, but with an underlying firmness. 'Perhaps we could discuss this at the end. We do need to send Mrs Green and Miss Foster on their way.'

'Yes, we do. Mrs Green, you'll be working on the trains as a parcels porter. Today there's a special job for you and Miss Foster. Miss Emery, will you do the honours?'

'If the rest of you wouldn't mind clearing a path to the door,' said Miss Emery, 'I'll show you where to go.'

'I'm a clerk, not a porter,' said Joan.

Mr Mortimer raised his eyebrows at her. 'Are you declining to do as you're told?'

'Of course not. I just—'

'Then kindly follow Miss Emery.'

Miss Emery marched from the room, Joan standing back politely to let Dot go next. Without a word, Miss Emery ran downstairs. It looked as if she might be about to rush straight out of the building, but instead she ducked through a door opposite the hatch, turning to face them. She waited for Joan to close the door.

'You're going to do an important job today. This is your chance to show what you're made of.'

'What is this job?' asked Dot.

'You'll have to wait and see.' Miss Emery opened the door, then pushed it to and added in a low voice, 'Afterwards, you're to keep quiet about it. Understood?'

They left the building.

'Aren't we going on a train?' asked Dot as Miss Emery passed the station entrance. 'Didn't you say I'd be on the trains?'

'You will, but not today.'

Dot and Joan scurried behind Miss Emery as she hastened down the road, along the length of the station's soot-encrusted, four-storey building, beneath the ornate ironwork canopy on which some of the railway's destinations – Scarborough, London, Blackpool – were displayed. At the point where the building curved round the corner, and the words *Lancashire and Yorkshire Railway* were carved high up beneath the clock, Miss Emery stopped beside an unusual vehicle painted in the LMS's distinctive maroon. It had a snub-nosed cab with a single wheel at the front. Attached to its two back wheels was a large trailer, again painted in the company colour, in which lay a pair of sack trolleys. Beside the vehicle stood a man whose uniform boasted the company buttons and a badge on his lapel.

'Mr Hope, thank you for waiting for us,' said Miss Emery. 'May I introduce Mrs Green and Miss Foster?'

'How do?' Mr Hope had the same sort of moustache as Clark Cable in *Gone With the Wind*, though that was where the similarity ended.

'Pleased to meet you,' said Dot. 'I've never seen a van like this before.'

Mr Hope gave it a pat. Was he the one who had polished it to such a high shine? 'It's not a van. It's a Scammell Mechanical Horse with a trailer.'

'Is it used for deliveries?' asked Dot. Was this the sort of vehicle Mabel would have driven?

'That's right. In you get, girls. It'll be a bit of a squeeze with three of us.'

They set off, Dot in the middle.

'Can you tell us what we're doing?' Joan asked.

'I don't know the answer to that myself,' Mr Hope replied cheerfully. 'I just know where we're doing it, that's all.'

Dot smothered a sigh. Ought this to be mysterious and exciting? Actually, it was more sobering than anything else. Scary, too, to think that in wartime, secrets and silence were so important. What was this job they were going to do? And what would she say later at home when she was asked about her first day? Was her first day on the railways to end with her telling lies to her family and her neighbours?

Mr Hope drove them out of town in the Longsight direction, checking road names as he went, and drew to a halt outside a church hall set back from the road in what might once have been a garden but was now cleared ready for vegetables.

They walked up the path. The door handle was a big ring that squeaked as it turned. The door didn't budge. Mr Hope had another go.

'Locked,' he said.

He was about to knock when there was the sound of a key on the inside and the door opened to reveal a bespectacled young man with his sleeves rolled up. His general appearance was smart, but in a not-quite-enough-money kind of way. Though his shirt was neatly pressed, there was a suggestion of wear on the collar. His shoes were well polished but his trouser-legs weren't quite wide enough, his turn-ups not quite deep enough.

'We're from the LMS,' said Mr Hope. 'We're to report to Mrs Bateman.'

'Names, please.' The young man consulted a list.

'My name's Hope and these ladies are Mrs Green and Miss Foster.'

'Peter Lofts. We're expecting you. Come in. Just a mo while I lock the door behind you.'

Their heels tapped on bare floorboards as Mr Lofts led them along a corridor into the church hall, a huge room with high windows. Trestle tables stood in rows down the middle of the room and large cardboard boxes were stacked along the walls. As well as a group of men, there were some WVS women, easily recognisable by the badges on their lapels.

A middle-aged woman walked down the room towards them. She was dressed in the full WVS uniform of a greenish-grey jacket and skirt, a red blouse, and a hat with a badge on the front of the ribbon around the crown. The matching coat and scarf were draped over her arm, as if she wanted to make the point that she owned them. Blimey. That lot would have set her husband back the best part of a tenner. More money than sense, some folk.

'The people from the LMS,' said Mr Lofts.

'I'm Mrs Bateman.' As well as ten quid's worth of smart new uniform, she had the voice to go with it. 'Have you been told what we're doing today?'

'Corned beef!' Mr Hope exclaimed.

Dot followed his gaze. There was indeed corned beef, a mountain of it in tins on a table by the wall.

'As you can see,' said Mrs Bateman, 'corned beef . . . Tins of biscuits over there . . . Tinned soup . . . Tea and sugar at that end . . . Condensed milk behind you . . . And so on. We're organising provisions for food dumps. Mr Lofts, the paperwork, if you'd be so good.' Without sparing him a glance, she held out her hand and he put a clipboard with a wodge of paper attached into it. 'We need to count all the tins and packets and check that the quantities tally with these lists here.' Mrs Bateman riffled through the sheets on her clipboard. 'Then we can make up the food crates, double-checking the contents going into each one.' More riffling. 'Lastly, the crates are to be labelled, as per these instructions.' Riffle, riffle. 'Got that? Good.'

'What are the food crates for?' asked Dot. 'Is this in case of shortages?' Goodness knows, they had repeatedly been told to expect those.

'You don't need to know, Mrs Brown.'

'Green,' said Dot. She would bet any money that Mrs Bateman wouldn't have got Cordelia's name wrong.

As Mrs Bateman bustled off, Peter Lofts sidled up to them.

'It's not for shortages . . . as such. Not the way you mean, anyway.'

Dot looked at Joan. 'Are you as much in the dark as before, or is it just me?'

Joan smiled. She wasn't a raving beauty, not like that Persepher-whatsit girl from first thing this morning, but she had pleasant features and clear skin. Her blue eyes looked serious, but that could just be because this escapade felt weighty. Being kept in the dark didn't help.

The first job was to count up how many there were of each type of tin or packet.

'This is because we have to put together collections of different sizes,' Peter Lofts explained, 'and every collection has to have each type of food in the same proportions.'

Dot was allocated the task of counting the tins of corned

beef and sardines. Once the counting was under way, Mrs Bateman started stalking around the hall, placing a card on the corner of each table. The cards looked like – yes, old library catalogue cards. Dot picked one up. An address had been written on the reverse of a card for HARDY, Thomas: *A Pair of Blue Eyes*.

'Hands to yourself, please.' Mrs Bateman twitched the card from her fingers as deftly as any pickpocket and replaced it precisely so on the corner of the table.

When the counting was finished, the totals were collected from the helpers and various lists had to be certified by Mrs Bateman and a gaunt, silent gentleman in tweeds, who wore a monocle on a cord. Each time a page was presented to him, he elongated his face, thrust the monocle into position and locked it there by snapping his face back. Then, having initialled or signed using a gold-nib fountain pen, he stretched his eyes and contorted his mouth, whereupon the monocle pinged free.

'Each table has an address card on it,' said Mrs Bateman. 'We've worked out the numbers of each item for each address. Mr Lofts will give out the lists. Remember, each address will receive a different quantity, so don't get mixed up.'

Mr Hope, standing beside one of the tables, looked round for Dot and Joan. 'This is the address we'll be delivering to. Let's get our crates packed and sealed, then we can help the others. If you two gather the tins, I'll do the packing.'

It was a bit like that children's game when you had to rush about without bumping into anyone. People milled around, consulting lists, counting tins and carrying armfuls.

'I'll count the tins,' Dot said to Joan, 'and you carry them to our table.'

She seemed to be surrounded by folk who were all counting not quite under their breath and it interfered with her own counting. She took a moment to dig a pencil out of her handbag and used it to mark every tenth tin with a cross, then all she had to do was count the tens. Easy!

As each collection was completed, there was a round of initialling by Mrs Bateman and the man with the monocle.

'Where's your collection going to?' asked another WVS woman. She didn't have the full clobber like Mrs Bateman, just the hat and the jacket.

'I don't think we're supposed to say,' said Dot.

'Several are going to farms,' said Joan. 'I noticed as I went round.'

'Lots of space, I suppose,' said Mrs WVS. 'All those barns.'

'I'll fetch the sack trolleys,' said Mr Hope. 'Once we've loaded the trailer, there's a tarpaulin to put over the crates.'

'In case any members of the public have X-ray vision,' Joan murmured.

'It isn't a joking matter,' said Peter Lofts, though he didn't say it in a telling-off voice.

'Since it's to do with the war, I'm sure it isn't,' said Joan, 'but I still don't understand what all these crates are for.'

Peter Lofts replied by tilting his chin towards Mr Monocle, who was going through the many pieces of paper and seemed to find them fascinating.

Dot shifted. 'Who is he, anyroad?'

'He's from the Invasion Committee. Food is being stored in locations all over the country to be used if we're invaded.'

Chapter Eight

'Blow that for a game of dominoes,' said Mabel. 'I absolutely refuse to wear stockings to do this. They'll get ripped to shreds.'

The other girls laughed. They could afford to: they were wearing trousers. And – not to be rude or anything – their overcoats hadn't exactly been tailor-made by exclusive dressmakers, and they wore their hair tucked away in turbans. Mabel's hat wouldn't stay on, not with bending over to hoe up the weeds on the tracks.

'I can't wear this either.' She snatched it off, almost glaring at it in frustration. The petersham rosette on the hat-band, which she had always thought of as debonair, looked positively flashy out here in this setting.

Bette grinned. 'And there was me, thinking you were aiming for the film-star look.'

Mabel forced a smile. It was no good getting hot under the collar. These were her new work-mates and she wanted to get on with them. Closest to her in age was Louise, and it wasn't just being in their twenties they had in common. Her first glimpse of Louise's sharpened cheekbones had occasioned an uncomfortable twinge in Mabel. Louise's thinness was the real thing, thinness that came from a hard life. Bette, who had been introduced by Louise as 'Bette with a double T, E, like Bette Davis,' was older – in her thirties, maybe? Copper-coloured hair peeped out from the front of her turban, while the fall of her coat suggested an hour-glass figure. The eldest was Bernice, who was the same sort of age as Dot Green, and with the same thickened waist.

Aware of the others' smiles, Mabel opened her gas-mask box.

'You're never going to do that to your nice hat.' Louise's amusement turned to horror.

'It's felt,' said Mabel. 'It folds up.'

'Aye, thin felt does,' said Bernice, 'but yon hat doesn't look cheap. Are you sure it's the squashy sort?'

Mabel folded it several times and forced it inside the box. 'It is now. Mind you, that rosette will never be the same again.'

She expected laughter, but instead intercepted the glances exchanged by the other three. Crumbs. She thought swiftly. Two choices. Say nothing and let the others base their opinion of her on it; or bring it out into the open and hope for the best.

'I apologise. You must think me a spoilt rich girl, to treat a hat like that. And I'm not, truly. My father's an ordinary working man, who's done well for himself and his family.'

'He can't be as ordinary as all that.' Bette dealt Mabel's appearance a significant glance.

Mabel looked down at her loose-fitting woollen coat, its stand-up collar brushing against her chin. The sleeves boasted a slight puff at the shoulder and were deeply cuffed. Compared to the others, she looked like something out of a magazine. Did her sensible shoes add a touch of the ordinary? Striding about on the moors and up and down the steep hill to and from Annerby had made flats her normal footwear. But her leather shoes were obviously far newer and more costly than the worn-looking shoes on her companions' feet.

'What can I say?' she replied. 'He worked hard, pulled

himself up by his bootstraps, and now he's got his own factory. But my grandad was a wheeltapper and I'm proud to follow in his footsteps.'

'Good for you, lass,' said Bernice.

'I shouldn't have screwed up my hat like that. It was a silly thing to do and – and it was disrespectful to you. I'm sure you would never treat your belongings like that. Neither would I, normally.'

'Aye, well, I don't suppose you came in on your first day expecting to be shovelling ballast,' said Bette.

'No one comes in on their first day expecting that,' said Louise.

Was it meant to be a punishment for refusing to get behind the wheel of a delivery van? That wasn't the way Mabel saw it. With Grandad having been a wheeltapper, she was well aware of the number of outdoor jobs on the railway. There was a lot more to railway work than punching tickets.

'We'd best get on,' said Bernice. 'We've plenty to do before we can stop for us dinner. What are you going to do about them stockings?'

'Take them off,' said Mabel. She didn't want to sound loose or ill-bred, but honestly, no one could justify wearing stockings to do this job.

'What about that form you signed?' Louise kept a straight face, but Mabel decided to take it as teasing.

'I'll put them on again before we go back to the station.'

As the others hooted with laughter, Mabel discreetly turned her back, opened her coat and flipped up her skirt. Even before her fingers could locate her suspenders, a blast of whistles and cat-calls had her dropping her hem, cheeks flaming. A group of workmen were grinning broadly from further along another track. She had just treated them to a flash of thigh. And she had turned away from the other women to do it – as if she was intent on giving the blokes an eyeful. What must they be thinking?

'Here, lass, we'll do the honours,' said Bernice.

She, Bette and Louise unbuckled their belts and unfastened their coats, then held out the front panels sideways like wings. Standing around Mabel, chuckling their heads off, they formed a screen to protect her modesty.

'Eeh, we must look like a load of flashers,' said Bernice, and the other two laughed even harder.

Mabel had no idea what a flasher was. She didn't care, either. All she cared about, as she peeled off her stockings at top speed, balled them up and stuffed them deep into her pockets before shoving her feet back into her shoes, was coming to work appropriately attired tomorrow.

'Now let's get back to work,' said Bette, fastening her coat.

Mabel set to with a will. After the fiasco of her hat, she had something to prove. She, Bernice, Louise and Bette, working as a group of four, were lengthmen – or should that be lengthwomen? The previous fourth member of the group had left yesterday with no notice 'on account of women's troubles,' according to Bernice, 'which means you've popped up at exactly the right moment.'

Mabel was grateful to Bernice, not least because she had advised buying a barm cake in the station first thing. Bernice had then explained a few things as the four of them had walked out of the station beside the tracks.

'A length is the space from one set of joints in the track to the next and we have to do a certain number of lengths every day. Usually, we go by train to wherever we're working, but today we're near enough to get there by shanks's pony.'

'Get yourself a knapsack like the rest of us,' Bette had told her, 'and put your dinner in it. We don't go back to Victoria until the end of the day.'

The others now set aside their hoes.

'That's the easy bit finished.' Louise gave Mabel a wicked smile. 'Let's see how you manage the important stuff.'

'Our main job is to re-settle the ballast,' said Bernice. 'These stones are the ballast. As the trains go along the tracks, the ballast eases out from under the sleepers – railway sleepers?' She lifted an eyebrow at Mabel.

Mabel nodded. She knew what sleepers were – the broad pieces of wood on which the track was laid.

'The trains vibrate the tracks and the ballast jiggles out from under the sleepers,' said Bette, 'so we have to pack it back again.'

'We do it in pairs,' said Bernice. 'One lifts the edge of the sleeper with a pickaxe or a crowbar and t'other shovels the stones back under. Feeling up to it?'

'Definitely.'

'You can do the shovelling, to start with, as that's easier, but we take turns, mind.'

Mabel nodded. She drew in a breath, not so much of air as of pure resolution. She might have made a twit of herself over her hat, and she might be hideously over-dressed, but she was jolly well going to show what she was made of. She smiled to herself. Mumsy would faint clean away if she could see her now, bare-headed, bare-legged and working on the tracks – or the permanent way, as she had been told to call them. She remembered Grandad calling them that.

It was hard work, to put it mildly, but, goodness, when they stopped to watch as a train passed on the opposite line, that great locomotive puffing clouds of steam into the air, the long line of carriages trundling rhythmically along the tracks, with every single passenger on board relying on the railways to get them where they needed to go, the thought that she, Mabel Bradshaw, granddaughter of Ernie Bradshaw, wheeltapper, was helping to keep the railways running smoothly – well, she was so proud that her bones all but melted.

By the time Bernice said they could stop for dinner, Mabel was ready to drop and she was sure she had pulled a dozen muscles.

'You'll get used to it,' said Louise.

'I hope so,' said Mabel. 'Right now, I feel I may never stand up straight again.'

'Usually we sit in one of the gangers' huts to have us dinner,' said Bernice, 'but we're a bit of a distance from one here. We'll get more of a sit-down if we stop outdoors.'

'It's a bit nippy,' said Louise.

'Please, I just want to sit down,' begged Mabel, 'though you'll have to find a crane to lift me up again.'

Bette laughed. 'We'll park our bums over there, next to that shed, and we can lean against it.'

'You make it sound like a garden shed,' said Mabel. 'It's huge.'

It was brick-built and plenty big enough to house a locomotive, though no track led into it, so it wasn't an engine shed. At one end was a wide, arched doorway, with a pair of wooden doors.

'If we sit at the other end, we'll be sheltered from the breeze,' said Louise.

They settled themselves. As Mabel lowered herself, a groan was wrenched from her, which prompted chuckles from the others.

'No offence, love,' said Bernice. 'We all started out like that, wailing and moaning like ghosts. But you'll be used to it before you know it.'

Mabel unwrapped her barm cake. 'Bernice is an unusual name.'

'Our Bernie were named after a music-hall act, weren't you, B?' said Bette.

'My old mam adored the music hall,' said Bernice. 'Her favourite act was Maximilian Martino, Master of Magic and Illusion, and his beautiful assistant Bernice.'

'Poor old Bernice.' Mabel shifted position, hoping to ease the pressure on her bladder. 'She sounds like an afterthought.'

'It's a good job his act didn't include a troop of dogs,' said Bernice, 'or she'd have been even further down the pecking order – "his Performing Poodles, and his beautiful assistant Bernice".'

'It's a nice name, anyway,' said Mabel.

'One of my sisters is Marie, after Marie Lloyd. Mam wanted to call t'other one Vesta, for Vesta Tilley, but Dad said no daughter of his were going to be saddled with something that sounded like she'd been named after a box of matches, so Mam settled for Florrie instead, after Florrie Forde.'

Bette burst into an unexpectedly good rendition of 'It's a Long Way to Tipperary', before being howled down by Louise and Bernice.

'Were you a singer before the war?' Mabel shifted position again.

'Eeh, what an idea. No, love, I was a barmaid, though I'm a bit long in the tooth for that lark now. Barmaids need to be either young and beautiful or else young and saucy. When you get past thirty, if you're not married to the landlord, you start to look pathetic.'

'Surely not—' Mabel began.

'Oh aye, you do. I remember myself fifteen years since, looking at a barmaid who was closer to forty than thirty, and feeling sorry for her. I always swore I'd not let that happen to me. Not that I want us to be at war, but it came along at the right time, as far as I'm concerned. And I'm enjoying working just during the day an' all, instead of 'till gone closing time.'

'That's one good thing about being a lengthman,' Louise added. 'We don't do shifts or nights.'

'But the days will get longer now we're leaving winter behind,' Bernice pointed out, 'and the first few hours of overtime are compulsory, not voluntary.'

Mabel couldn't wait any longer. 'What happens about spending a penny out here?'

'If we're near a gangers' hut,' said Bette, 'there's usually a little add-on with a bucket.'

'A bucket?'

'As for out here,' said Bette, looking over her shoulder, 'there's bushes over yon.'

'Bushes!'

'Don't tell me you've never been caught short outdoors and had to nip behind a bush.'

Well, needs must. Mabel stood up. She must have looked pretty fierce, because the others laughed. If nothing else, she had provided plenty of hilarity today.

'We'll all go,' said Bernice, 'and we'll stand look-out for one another.'

Leaving the shelter of the building, they headed towards a few bushes that didn't look anything like plentiful enough for the proposed purpose.

'Hey, look at this.' Louise veered off round the far side of the building. 'Is this what I think it is?'

Attached to the side was a small, brick-built add-on, of a size and shape that suggested . . .

'Oh, please,' breathed Mabel.

Virtually all the paint on the door had long since flaked off. The upper hinge had dropped and the diagonally opposite bottom corner had rotted away on the ground. It took Bette and Louise, working together, to heave the door ajar, with Mabel grateful not to be needed, as she might well have wet herself if she had had to take the strain.

'Don't push it too far,' said Bernice. 'Just enough for us to squeeze in and out.'

Bette stuck her head round the door. 'Lord, what a pong. Looks like an ancient earth-closet.'

'You first, Mabel.' Bernice's eyes, dark as raisins, twinkled. 'Your need is greatest.'

Mabel held her breath against the rank smell and also against the possibility of slathering her lungs with a thick coating of dirt. And no matter how desperate she was, she wasn't going to use the closet until after she had tested the door on the inner wall. If there was anybody inside the building, she wasn't having them bursting in on her when she was mid-performance. But the door was either locked or stuck fast. An increased urgency in her lower belly saw her fumbling with her clothes.

'Here y'are, love.'

A hand appeared round the wonky door, waving – was that toilet paper? Mabel grabbed it.

When she emerged, Louise twisted her way round the door and went in.

'That's a weight off your mind,' grinned Bette. 'I expect you've got proper indoor plumbing at home, haven't you?'

It was said in a jokey way, but it was a challenge of sorts. Mabel took it on the chin.

'I'll have you know, there are nosegays of flowers painted round our lavatory pan.'

'Nosegays?' Louise appeared. 'You need a nose-peg to go in there.'

A few minutes later, they were about to return to work when the sound of a motor engine chugging closer made them look round.

'This way,' said Bernice.

They walked to the far end of the building, weaving their way through a small graveyard of rusty old tenders and piles of weathered sleepers. At the front end of the building, where the arched doorway was, there was a road-way of what must have started out as cinders, but which had been flattened and hardened over the years.

Coming to a halt was a curious-looking vehicle, the like of which Mabel hadn't seen before, though the others made no comment, so she stilled her tongue.

Joan emerged from the vehicle, followed by Mrs Green – Dot. Good manners propelled Mabel forwards. 'Miss Foster, what are you doing here?'

'You're supposed to call me Joan,' said Joan, sounding a tad awkward.

Mabel nodded a greeting to Dot. That was as far as she was prepared to go. Call a middle-aged woman by her first name? Plain impossible – though presumably if all the others in their group did it, she would have to follow suit.

Her muscles tensed as reluctance coursed through her. She didn't want to get close to them. She wanted to keep herself to herself. It was one thing to be chatty with Bette, Louise and Bernice. That wasn't friendship. It was simple comradeship, the pally feeling between work-mates of getting along. But Miss Emery had proposed actual friendship for her new recruits and Mabel wasn't keen. She couldn't face the complications that were part and parcel of caring about others, and she didn't deserve to have them caring for her.

Had she been foolish to ask for help in finding another billet? Possibly. But her need to escape from Persephone had in that moment been greater than the necessity of hold-ing herself aloof.

She performed a flurry of introductions, knowing the precise order in which to do it. Mumsy would have been proud. When she came to the uniformed man, she glanced at Dot, who introduced him as Mr Hope.

'What brings you ladies here?' Mr Hope looked

uncomfortable. Too many working women in one go? Get used to it, pal.

'We're lengthmen,' said Bernice, which had to be followed by a quick explanation for Joan and Dot's benefit. Mabel saw the way they looked at one another. She didn't have to be a mind-reader. They were wondering whether she had been put into this job as a punishment.

Bette nodded at the long trailer, the heaped contents of which were covered with a tarpaulin. 'What have you got there?'

Joan and Dot both opened their mouths to answer, but Mr Hope beat them to it. 'Nothing you need to know about.' Did he imagine Joan and Dot would have blabbed?

'Fair enough,' said Bernice. 'We need to get back to work, anyroad. Come on, girls. Nice to meet you.' She nodded farewell to the newcomers.

Joan darted to Mabel's side. 'What time do you finish? Come to the station buffet for a cup of tea before you go home.'

It would be rude to refuse. Besides, an apology was in order. 'Will do.'

'As long as you don't gossip about what we've been at today,' Mr Hope said to Joan. He said it with a smile on his face, but he wasn't entirely joking. 'We all know what you girls are like when you get together. Natter, natter, natter.'

Chapter Nine

It wasn't that she minded helping to load the Mechanical Horse and bringing the food supplies to the disused building beside the railway, but by the time they had made two journeys to the church hall and then to the railway shed, Joan was itching to get to her proper job. All she knew was that she was to be a clerk of some sort. That hadn't sounded altogether appealing back in that cramped room with Miss Emery, but now, having assisted with the necessary paperwork and taken to their hiding place two deliveries of tinned goods, to be used only in the event – God forbid – of invasion, she could see that clerking was more relevant than she had imagined. When you thought about it, there must be masses of admin involved in keeping the railways running, and anything that kept the trains moving was essential work.

They had stopped for a bite to eat during their second stint at the church hall. Now they were back at the railway shed, ready to unload and store the second delivery. Mr Hope let down the back of the trailer and lifted out the sack-barrows with a practised ease that made them look lightweight. Feeling like an expert by this time, Joan climbed onto the trailer to push the crates towards the edge, from where Mr Hope manhandled them onto the sack-barrows. He had shown them how to put one foot on the bar near the bottom of the back of the trolley and swing their weight onto it to tip it backwards, ready to be pushed along.

Mr Hope had been reluctant initially to let Dot push a trolley.

'No offence, but it isn't right for a lady of your years.'

'Fiddlesticks!' Dot had been good-humoured but determined. 'If I'm to be a porter, I have to do everything the men do or else why am I here?'

As they were tackling the last of the stacking inside the shed, two gentlemen in smart overcoats and bowler hats walked in.

'Good afternoon,' said one of them. 'Just about finished, are we?'

'Yes, sir.' Mr Hope went over to speak to the men.

'Just like the bigwigs to waltz in when all the heavy stuff's been done,' Dot murmured, mopping her brow with her hanky.

Joan, too, felt hot, even though she had shed her coat. She was achy as well and rolled her shoulders, aware of the men's eyes following her and Dot as they headed for the nails where they had hung their coats.

'No, sir, it hasn't been a trial at all to have them along,' said Mr Hope. 'They've pulled their weight all right.'

That might have been flattering, but for the surprised sounds the bigwigs made.

Joan, Dot and Mr Hope left the shed. Outside, parked behind the Scammell was a posh motor. Leaning against the bonnet, with one ankle crossed over the other, was a uniformed chauffeur, puffing away on a cigarette. He nodded a greeting at them. They climbed into the Scammell, but Mr Hope couldn't turn the vehicle round until the important men had finished the job of locking and padlocking the building, and the chauffeur had driven them away.

'If you're a parcels porter,' Mr Hope said to Dot once the Scammell was back on the road, 'I can show you where to go, but I don't know owt about clerks, miss. What kind are you?'

'I don't know,' said Joan, adding 'yet', because it made her sound less helpless. 'I'll sort myself out.'

She concentrated on feeling determined rather than anxious as she went to Hunts Bank and presented herself at the reception office hatch.

'Can I help you, Miss . . . Foster, isn't it?' came Miss Emery's voice from behind her. 'You need to be shown to your place of work, don't you? This way.' She set off at a rapid pace through the front door and down the road. 'You'll be in charging, which is part of deliveries. Here we are.' Stopping outside a door, she consulted her wristwatch. 'Upstairs, second or third on the right, not sure which. Ask for Mr Clark. Excuse me. I have to . . .' And off she went.

At the foot of the stairs, Joan hesitated. It would have been much easier to be shown in, but this was no time to be feeble. She went upstairs, where an old gent, who must have been brought out of retirement for the duration, took her to the correct door and gallantly opened it onto a fug of tobacco smoke. The room was filled with desks all facing the same way, like at school, and at every one there was a girl or woman sitting up straight in front of a typewriter. Was this to be her war work?

'Excuse me.'

She hovered beside a typist with masses of blonde curls on top and the rest of her hair swept behind her ears to fall down the sweep of her neck, like Greta Garbo in *Anna Karenina*. The girl finished the bit she was typing before glancing up, seizing the opportunity to take her half-smoked cigarette, the end of which was lipstick-red, from a saucer that was crusty with ash. She inhaled sharply, exhaling a stream of pungent smoke in Joan's direction. Joan parted her lips slightly, trying to blow the smoke away without being obvious. She had tried smoking, but had never got the hang of it.

'Can I help you?' asked the typist.

'I'm new. My name is Joan Foster. I've been told to ask for Mr Clark.' She glanced round. There wasn't a man to be seen.

'Lucky you. Through that door over there.'

Lucky? Why? Was Mr Clark impossibly handsome? It didn't matter if he was. Joan's heart was spoken for.

When she knocked on the inner door and went in, she almost stopped in her tracks. The room was full of men. Well, of course it was. This was the railways and even though many railwaymen had been called up, the remaining ones still far outnumbered the women.

The walls were lined with shelves of ledgers and the smoky atmosphere was quiet enough for everyone to look up at her arrival. They all seemed to be old enough to be her father, if not her grandfather, except for a weedy-looking younger man at his desk near the door.

'May I help you?' he asked.

'I'm looking for Mr Clark.'

'I am he,' boomed a voice from the other end of the room. 'Send her this way, Hargreaves.'

She turned to shut the door behind her.

'Leave it open,' Mr Hargreaves said quietly. 'You're not supposed to be on your own in a room of men.' His blush was as vivid a red as the blonde typist's lipstick.

As she walked between the desks, Joan glimpsed paperwork with – yes, lots of sums, long multiplication, and columns that suggested pounds, shillings and pence. She came to a halt in front of the desk where Mr Clark had risen to greet her. He was a ruddy-cheeked, mustachioed man with a pot belly.

'You must be the handmaiden promised to me by Miss Emery. Miss Forster, if I'm not mistaken.'

'Foster.'

'You'll join our typists through there, Miss Forster, but first – I say, Hargreaves, close that door, will you? There's a good fellow. I can't hear myself think with all that clattering going on.'

The young man left his desk and shut the door. Joan's heart bumped, but that was plain daft. She wouldn't have felt at all self-conscious if Mr Hargreaves hadn't told her about not being in a room full of men.

'But first,' Mr Clark repeated, 'let me explain what we do here. The simplest way is to show you the paperwork. No spare chairs, I'm afraid. You'll have to share mine.' So saying, he sat back down, this time on one side of the chair . He looked up at her, his expression bland as he patted the other side. 'No need to be shy.'

Joan froze. Tension tightened her stomach. She glanced round at the other men, half expecting, half hoping one of them would say something to prevent this, but no one said a word. Did that mean it was an accepted thing? After all, if there were no spare chairs . . .

Her feet took her round the desk and she perched on the edge of the seat. Her heart thudded – or was she being stupid? Nobody so much as raised an eyebrow. Was this the chair-equivalent of re-using paper until there was no space left to write on?

'This is the kind of thing you'll be typing up. It's important you understand it. Here is the destination of the goods, including delivery by road at the end of the rail journey. These sheets come in from the checkers. Their job is to check what arrives for delivery, see? And they record the weights here in these columns, starting with tons and – do you know what CWT stands for?'

'Hundredweight.'

'Good girl. Clever girl. This is the charging office. A rate of payment is allocated to the delivery, depending on what the goods are, and the chargers calculate the cost. Then the ladies next door type the invoices.'

'I see.' This wasn't the moment to mention she had never used a typewriter in her life.

'It's very straightforward. Not too much to tax your sweet little brain, eh? What you need to be careful of is not getting the weight mixed up with the wagon number. We don't want anybody being charged by the wagon number instead of the weight, do we?'

Was that a joke? 'No, Mr Clark.'

Mr Clark shifted a fraction. It would be rude to slide away, and besides, she was on the edge of the chair already and might fall off.

Mr Clark dropped his voice and spoke softly. 'I hope you won't let me down, Miss Forster. It's all over the shop that one of the new girlies all but turned tail at the thought of learning to drive. Panicky creatures, females. Like horses, only not so sensible. If this new lot of wenches is a dud batch, I don't want you anywhere near my charging office, do you understand? What do you say? Can I depend on you?'

'Yes, Mr Clark.' Ruddy Mabel!

'I hope so, Miss Forster. Any questions concerning the job?'

Even if she'd had a dozen urgent queries, she wouldn't have admitted it. Leaping up, she uttered a thank you through gritted teeth and headed for the closed door, forcing herself to walk at a normal pace with her head up instead of flying as though the hounds of hell were at her heels.

The station concourse was packed. It was a busy time of day, but the large volume of passengers told Joan that some trains must have been delayed because of priority being given to those carrying troops or freight. Some lucky folk had seats on the station's wooden benches, though maybe they weren't as lucky as all that, come to think of it, considering what a squash it looked, elbows tucked in, handbags and brief-cases on knees, shopping bags and suitcases so closely clustered around feet that there was a serious danger of tripping over one when you attempted to get up. Making slow but steady progress through the crowd, Joan dodged round a suited man in a trilby, who was determinedly reading his newspaper regardless of the crush all around him, and stopped to give way to a porter steadily pushing a flatbed trolley loaded with suitcases.

Walking in the wake of a well-dressed couple, she almost followed them into the first-class waiting room with its glassed dome, but veered off into the cosy atmosphere of the station buffet. Shelves of crockery lined the wall behind the curved counter with its wood-panelled front, on which stood a three-tier glass display case. On the opposite side of the room from the fireplace with the clock above, Lizzie waved to her from a corner table, where she sat with Cordelia and Alison. Joan asked for a cup of tea and took it across, warmth radiating through her. Her first meeting with her fellow railway girls!

'Have you had a good day?' Alison shunted her chair round a bit to make room. 'Lizzie was just telling us about being a porter.'

'I'm going to have a uniform,' said Lizzie, 'and I've got to make sure passengers get onto the right trains, as well as shifting parcels and boxes about.'

'It sounds as if you're going to enjoy it,' said Joan. It was difficult to imagine cheerful Lizzie not making the most of anything that came her way.

'I think so,' Lizzie agreed. 'What job have you been given?' She looked at Cordelia – to avoid using the older lady's first name? It was going to take a bit of getting used to.

'Lampwoman,' said Cordelia.

'You mean lampman,' said Alison.

'They can call me what they like, but I'm going to call myself a lampwoman.'

'What does it involve?' Joan asked.

'I have to remove, clean and replace all the signal lights on a stretch of the railway and do the same for the side-lights and tail lights on the wagons in the marshalling yard.' Cordelia smiled. It wasn't an infectious, sunny smile like Lizzie's, more a restrained pleasantry. 'I said that as if I know what a marshalling yard is.'

Joan's ribcage delivered a squeeze of envy. That was a proper railway job. Typing invoices for deliveries was important too. Indeed, it was an essential part of the process. But all professions had clerks and typists. Only the railways had lampmen – lampwomen.

'What about you?' Cordelia asked her.

Joan explained about the work of the charging office.

Lizzie gasped dramatically. 'I'd be terrified of getting the sums wrong.'

'I'm not doing the maths, just typing the invoices. Look, here comes Dot.'

She might feel reluctant to use Cordelia's name as yet, but after spending much of today in Dot's affable company, she had no qualms about saying that lady's name out loud. Dot was good-natured without being a push-over, kind without being mushy, and capable without being severe. Having grown up with Gran, it always came as something of a revelation to meet someone who was capable but not severe. Dot's family was lucky to have her. She must be a great mum. How lucky some folk were with their mothers. Not like her and Letitia. Estelle had ruined all their lives.

Dot came straight to the table without fetching a cup of tea.

'I can't stop. I've a family to feed and I've got both the grandchildren this evening.'

'What are their names?' Lizzie asked.

'Jenny and Jimmy.'

'They sound like twins.'

Dot's face softened. 'They're cousins, but we call them birthday twins, because they were born on the same day.' She turned to Cordelia. 'Do you have family?'

'A daughter. She was fourteen in November.'

'So this is her last year at school,' said Lizzie.

'No, she'll be there another year to sit her School Cert.'

'Clever girl,' said Dot.

'Cleverer than I am, I hope,' said Mabel. 'It took me two goes and even then, I only got through by the skin of my teeth.'

'I don't think my husband will mind if Emily sits it half a dozen times,' said Cordelia, 'as long as she stays in a safe place.'

'Was her school evacuated?' Joan asked.

'Yes, but unfortunately not to a sufficient distance to give my husband peace of mind. He decided to send her to a different school, further away.'

'That must have been an upheaval for her,' said Dot, 'but you have to do the best you can for your children. Listen, how are we going to see one another now we're doing different jobs? There'll be shifts and compulsory overtime and what have you. We ought to meet up regular. I know I'm saying it as shouldn't, being as I'm about to dash off, but I do think it's important.'

'It would be nice if we could sit down and have a cuppa together,' said Lizzie, 'but some of us are meant to use the Hunts Bank canteen and others are supposed to use the mess over here.'

'Perhaps we could use this buffet,' said Cordelia. 'We could ask if we might leave a little notebook under the counter. We could write in it the times we can manage and take it from there. It doesn't have to be all of us every time. But I agree with Mrs . . . with Dot.' Was that a faint blush at breaching the class divide? 'We should at least try. Should I speak to the women behind the counter?'

'You do that,' said Dot. 'I must go. See you soon, girls.'

Joan watched her leave. Fancy doing a day's work, then going home to care for the family, not to mention doing the housework. As Dot approached the door, it opened and Mabel appeared. She bit her lip as she walked across. There was a spare chair, but she didn't sit down.

'This is awkward, so I'll come straight out with it. I know word has gone round about my refusal to drive. The women I'm working with heard it from a couple of lengthmen and they weren't best pleased, I can tell you. So if any of you have had an ear-bashing because of me, I apologise. If you want me to clear off, I'll understand.'

Joan exchanged glances with Alison. Had Alison, too, been likened to a skittish horse? Joan's hands formed briefly into fists as annoyance surged through her. How rude of Mr Clark! How patronising.

'I'll say it,' said Cordelia, 'since we're all thinking it. Yes, I was on the receiving end of a few words from the head lampman, not to mention a couple of the lampwomen.'

'I'm sorry,' said Mabel.

'Your conduct has no bearing on my ability to do my job, and that's what I told them.'

Yes, Joan could imagine Cordelia quietly putting them in their place. That was the confidence of the educated middle classes for you.

'It was mentioned to me as well,' said Joan, though she hadn't put anyone in their place, not Mr Clark and not Miss Bligh of the Greta Garbo hair and the lipstick-tipped cigarette, who had introduced her to the complexities of the typewriter.

'Likewise,' said Alison.

'No one said a word to me,' Lizzie chipped in. True? Or saving Mabel's feelings?

'I apologise – to all of you,' said Mabel. She looked at Cordelia. 'Thank you for what you said to your new colleagues.'

'I didn't do it for your benefit,' Cordelia replied coolly. 'I did it for my own, and for that of the other girls. Mr Mortimer was correct to say you've scored a black mark against all of us. Well, I've made my position clear, namely that I expect to be judged according to my own performance, not yours.'

'That's a bit stiff, isn't it?' Lizzie ventured.

'I don't believe so. I consider it perfectly reasonable.'

'Well.' Mabel blew out a breath and blinked once or twice. 'I'd best sling my hook, hadn't I?'

'No,' said Alison. 'You're one of us.'

'You've made us all look bad,' said Cordelia, 'but it's something we all have to rise above – including you. Alison is right. We aren't going to throw you out of our group. On the contrary, it's up to us to help you settle in. That's what Miss Emery meant about supporting each other and it's certainly what I intend to do. You're one of us, for better or worse, so sit down. After all, if the worst that happens to us is a few sharp words because you won't drive, then we shan't have done too badly, shall we?'

Joan cringed on Mabel's behalf, but Mabel took it in her stride. 'Did you use to be a teacher? I can imagine the Third Form shaking in their shoes in anticipation of a wigging from you.'

'As a matter of fact, I've never worked before, except for charity, of course. I went straight from my parents' home to my husband's.' Cordelia glanced round their table. 'A word of advice, girls. It's horrible to be at war, but seize every opportunity that comes your way.'

Joan didn't know what to make of Cordelia. She was

measured and grave, and she spoke her mind, but her words to Mabel hadn't been said with the intention of crushing her. Not like Gran would have done. Cordelia had simply been stating her case. She was cool and – was remote too strong a word? Would she warm up on closer acquaintance?

'Get a cup of tea,' Joan said to Mabel, 'and then you can have Dot's seat.'

'We'll need another for Colette,' said Lizzie.

'I saw her on my way here,' said Mabel. 'Her husband's collecting her, so she can't join us.'

'She could have waited for him in here,' said Alison. 'That's what I'll do if my boyfriend comes to collect me.'

Mabel fetched herself a drink and sank into the chair vacated by Dot.

'We want to hear all about your job,' said Lizzie. 'Were the others beastly to you about not driving?'

'Well, they weren't impressed. Neither were they chuffed to think I'd been foisted on them as a result. I'm going to have to prove my worth with a vengeance.'

'What does a lengthman do?' Lizzie asked.

'I'll tell you in a minute.' Mabel leaned forwards, looking round at them. 'First, can you tell me something? What exactly is a flasher?'

Joan opened the gate and walked up the side of the house to the back door, where Letitia's bicycle leaned against the coal-bunker. She stepped into the kitchen. A pan of potatoes was coming to the boil and a chunk of corned beef sat on a plate under a fly net, but her call of greeting died unuttered as she heard raised voices. Anything above an ordinary tone counted as raised in the well-ordered Foster household, so Letitia's voice, clearer and firmer than usual, rooted Joan to the spot, one hand clutching the edge of the door.

'I'm twenty-one next year, so I should be able to wear what I choose.'

'You know my opinion on these tarty short skirts,' said Gran.

'They're not tarty. They're fashionable. I'm sick of wearing calf-length skirts. Wearing knee-length wouldn't turn Joan and me into tarts.'

'If you look like one, men will treat you like one.'

'Let them try,' Letitia retorted. 'You ought to know we're trustworthy. You brought us up.'

Joan threw the back door shut, calling 'I'm home' into a sudden silence. She went into the hallway to hang up her things.

Gran appeared from the parlour. 'You're home.' Her voice was bright, but her lips were pursed and she touched her hair as if it needed tidying, which it never did. Appearances were everything to Gran – the way she looked, the way her house looked, the way her girls looked. Everything was just so.

Joan kissed her hello. Gran smelled of Erasmic Violet soap.

'Get changed,' said Gran. 'Tea will be on the table in ten minutes.' Not 'How was your first day?' Not 'I want to hear everything.' She vanished into the kitchen, snatching her wrap-around pinny from the hook just inside before snapping the door shut behind her.

Letitia came out of the parlour.

'I heard what you were saying,' Joan whispered.

Letitia answered with an eloquent glance up the stairs. She ran up, Joan following. They shared the bedroom at the back of the house – shared the bed too. Dumping her handbag and gas-mask box, Joan plonked herself on the yellow candlewick bedspread to remove her shoes.

'You weren't supposed to hear,' said Letitia. 'I wanted to say my piece before you came home.'

'It sounded as if you were having a real go at her.'

'I didn't mean to. It just came out that way. She's so stubborn and I'm tired of asking. She makes us dress like old women. It's ridiculous.'

'You could wear a postal sack and you'd still look like a glamour girl.'

'Don't be daft,' said Letitia, but Joan could see she was pleased. And so she should be, with looks like that. She had eyes of soft blue-grey and her light blonde hair did as it was told, falling in beautiful waves. No wonder Steven had fallen for her. Who would look twice at any other girl in the room when Letitia was there to be admired?

Joan hitched her skirt up experimentally to her knee. 'The world must be full of tarts, because everyone else wears dresses this length.'

Letitia put on a clipped, formal voice, like those on the wireless. ' "And what's your ambition in life, Miss Foster?" "Why, to look like a tart, of course." '

'Very funny, but you've probably scuppered our chances after what you said.'

Should she add that Letitia had also scuppered her own chances of holding centre stage with tales of her new job? But Letitia hadn't done it on purpose. Besides, given the secrets she had brought home with her, it was probably just as well. She was going to have to make typing invoices sound utterly riveting when they sat down to their corned-beef hash.

Chapter Ten

On the doorstep, Dot took a moment to push back her shoulders and plant a smile on her face. She couldn't have Reg crowing over how she had taken on too much and her rightful place was chained to the sink, fettling for the family. She could do both. She, along with thousands of other women, could do both.

She opened the front door to a cry of 'There you are . . .' and her heart leaped in delight. Sheila was here, eager for all the details of her first day. How kind. Except that what Sheila actually said was, 'There you are at last, Ma.' Complaint or panic?

'Aye, here I am.' She used her most down-to-earth voice. 'Everything all right, love?'

'Sheila, you might at least have let Mother through the front door.'

Pammy appeared, looking picture-perfect, as always. Dot reckoned their Pammy didn't open her front door to fetch in the milk unless she had a full face of make-up. Goodness knows what she would do when shortages struck. She would probably lock herself away for the duration if she couldn't get her hands on her favourite Snowfire face cream.

Dot could spot a problem a mile off, but first things first. 'Is the cottage pie in the oven?'

Pammy and Sheila looked at one another.

'Never mind,' Dot said before they could play the blame game. Honest to God – two young women indoors at teatime and neither one of them with the wit to put the oven on. 'I'm gasping for a cuppa.'

'That you, Dot?' called Reg. 'About time. What's for tea?'

'Nan!'

Scuffling preceded the children's appearance in the hall. Everyone had come to greet her, except her husband.

'Get the oven warmed up, girls,' said Dot, 'while I say hello to my grandchildren.'

She opened her arms as they scampered towards her, though Jimmy stopped just out of reach.

'You should help Nan off with her coat,' Jenny told him. 'That's what gentlemen do.'

'I'm a schoolboy, not a gent.'

'You're never too young to learn.' Jenny parroted Pammy. 'I'll show you. You stand behind the lady and hold your hands just so, ready to take her coat as it slips elegantly from her shoulders. She shouldn't even need to turn round to make sure you've done it.'

'So you can let it fall on the floor and she'd never know,' Jimmy said before he nipped away.

'Thanks, pet,' said Dot as Jenny took her coat. Jenny was a love and Dot adored her, but did Posh Pammy have to be so dead set on making a little lady out of her?

In the kitchen, Reg was at the table, with the newspaper. Of course. Where else would he be? Pammy and Sheila were sitting at the table an' all.

'Don't get up,' Dot said automatically.

She crossed the small room, weaving behind Reg's chair to turn on the oven and get to the kettle. Some men kissed their wives hello when they got home. Some men probably even got up off their arses to do it, but not Ratty Reg. He stayed put, attached to his chair by bum-glue.

When the kettle started to sing, Dot warmed the pot and opened the oven to check the temperature. Bugger whether it was hot enough: in went the cottage pie. Her tummy growled. She had worked hard today. She put the pans of carrots and winter cabbage on the stove before reaching for the battered old tea caddy, with its fading picture of an old biddy, shawled and widow's-capped, using the bellows on the fire, above which, from the roof of the fireplace, hung a kettle on a chain.

'You're so efficient, Mother,' said Pammy, 'a real example to us all.'

'You put me to shame,' said Sheila, which might have been true if Sheila had been capable of feeling shame about her slapdash ways.

Reg glanced up from his paper. 'It's time to tell all.'

Dot turned to him in surprise. A show of interest? Support? That would mean a lot.

Reg cast his eyes heavenwards. 'You'll never guess what our Sheila's done.'

Dot refused to be disappointed. It was her own fault for thinking Reg could be interested. She fixed her attention on Sheila, but it was Pammy who spoke.

'A man claiming to be from the Food Control Office knocked on her door and asked for her ration books.'

'He said they were from a faulty batch,' said Sheila.

'I've never heard of the Food Control Office,' said Dot.

'That's because it doesn't exist,' said Reg. 'She's only gone and given away her and Jimmy's ration books to a con artist.'

'I thought you'd know what to do,' said Sheila. 'Pa just called me a daft bat.'

'Well, you are one,' said Reg. 'Is that tea brewed, Dot, or are you waiting for it to climb out of the pot on its own?'

Dot prepared the tea, her mind on Sheila's problem. 'What a rotten trick. Some folk want stringing up, they really do.' A frown pulled at her brow. 'I expect there's a rationing office in the Town Hall. I could dash over there in my dinner-hour – well, I can if—'

'Oh, Ma, could you?' Sheila cried. 'It'd save me a heck of a lot of bother. I don't know when I'd get the chance to report it, me being full-time.'

There was nowt to be gained by pointing out that she was full-time now an' all. She worked in the middle of town, so it would be easy for her, compared to Sheila. A small fire ignited inside her belly. She wasn't having her Jimmy, her Harry's lad, in danger of going without. She would deal with it tomorrow.

Unless . . . The words that had died unspoken beneath Sheila's interruption flooded back. Unless she was put on a train tomorrow. Some parcels porters worked on the station, others on the trains, and she was one of the latter, but surely she wouldn't be let loose on the railway network on only her second day.

'Are you all right, Mother?' asked Pammy. 'You're miles away.'

'Just planning tomorrow.' No need to mention the possibility of not being able to sort out Sheila's ration books. She laid her hand on top of Sheila's. 'Don't you fret, love.' Placing the teapot on the table, she added milk to the cups – sugar an' all. They must get used to less sugar now and Reg hadn't taken kindly to being denied his normal three heaped teaspoons. 'Did your friend collect your name-tapes from Ingleby's, Pammy? Are you pleased with them?'

'I don't know why you have to have name-tapes anyroad,' said Sheila. 'A laundry marker is good enough for the rest of us.'

Pammy sniffed and tossed her head, making her blonde hair shimmer in the gas-light. She styled her hair with a centre parting, finger waves at the sides drawn back and above her ears, and deep, full waves at the back.

'Pardon me for wanting the best for my family,' said Pammy. 'And no, Mother, I'm not pleased, as it happens. The foolish girl who wrote down the order made a mistake and the name-tapes have come back saying "J. Green" instead of "G. Green".'

There was a moment's silence. There usually was when their Jenny's true name was flaunted in front of them.

'It's an understandable mistake,' said Dot, 'but it's vexing for you.'

'I won't stand for it,' Pammy declared. 'I'm not sewing the wrong name on my daughter's clothes.'

'It's only one letter,' said Sheila, 'and everyone knows her as Jenny, so where's the harm?'

'The harm is that it's wrong. Her name is Genevieve. If she's evacuated again, I'm not sending her away without every item of clothing correctly labelled. She's already come home once with some other child's inferior clothing in her suitcase.'

'I'm sure that was just a mistake,' said Dot.

Pammy pursed her lips. 'You're too trusting, Mother. Anyway, the point is that the name-tapes have to be returned.'

'I'll have 'em,' said Sheila. 'They'll do for our Jimmy.'

'You?' Pammy lifted a single eyebrow in a perfect arch. 'You'd never get round to sewing them in.'

'Ma would help out, wouldn't you, Ma?'

'The name-tapes have to go back,' said Pammy, 'so that they can be replaced. The trouble is,' and she did that doe-eyed thing at Dot that Archie fell for every time, 'they need to be returned quickly and when am I to get into town? You know I wouldn't ask, but since you're working there now . . .'

'Leave it to me.'

Ration-books tomorrow, name-tapes the day after; and

just how was she to fit in her own shopping, especially if she was to be on the trains?

But she would manage. She, along with thousands of other women, would manage.

After her day working on the permanent way, Mabel would have sold her soul for a luxurious soak in hot water scented with rose crystals, but the best she could hope for was the regulation four inches, as designated by the black mark around the inside of the bath. Four inches! What use was that to a body that had been reduced to an all-consuming ache? Blisters had sprouted on her palms as well. Might the gardener lend her a pair of thick gloves?

She tramped up the long drive to Darley Court. It was easier for Mumsy and Pops to picture her in grand surroundings to be proud of, rather than some anonymous billet, but already Mabel knew she had to move out. She simply couldn't sit out the war alongside the Honourable Persephone Trehearn-Hobbs. Oh, Persephone was a likeable enough soul. It wasn't that. It wasn't even that Persephone was the real thing, with a family line that probably stretched all the way back to the Norman Conquest, whereas the Bradshaws were new money through and through. It was because—Mabel's heart sank, just as it had when she had arrived at Darley Court and allowed herself to be introduced as if the Honourable Miss Trehearn-Hobbs was a perfect stranger to her. Not that they had actually met before as such. They hadn't. But she knew Persephone by sight from the London Season for which Pops had paid through the nose. It seemed Persephone hadn't recognised her, and that was the way Mabel devoutly hoped it would stay; and the safest way of ensuring it did was by upping sticks and leaving Darley Court, regardless of how Mumsy and Pops would react. Persephone would soon forget her. Out of sight, out of mind.

That was one reason for wanting to quit this place, and today had shown her another. Bernice, Bette and Louise had accepted her down-to-earth explanation of Pops as a factory man made good, and they had taken the description of the lavatory pan painted with nosegays in good part, but they had been deeply unimpressed upon hearing that she had refused to become a driver. If on top of that they found out she was residing in an old manor house, they would dismiss her as a spoilt rich kid, and she couldn't bear the thought of that.

Being new money, for all its undoubted advantages, had always had its uncomfortable side, and today's experiences, including meeting the variety of women who were to be her colleagues, had filled Mabel with the determination to fit in. Were her family's working-class roots coming to the fore in her? Mumsy would have kittens, that was for sure. But dear old Grandad would have approved. He would have understood that for a girl from new money, Darley Court was a big step up, and it was a step she didn't want to take.

Darley Court had been in the same family for umpteen generations, even if the title and the Darley name had died out at the turn of the century. Darley Court represented wealth, privilege and entitlement. That wasn't what the war effort was about. The war effort was about everybody pulling together, regardless of class. It was about every single person doing their bit. And for her, it was about being the same as her fellow workers. Grandad would have understood.

As she strode up the drive, she ignored her tiredness, fixing her attention on the massive covered porch that stuck out at the front of the building. In the olden days, carriages would have halted beneath it to protect the grand ladies and gentlemen from the weather as they alighted. The heavy front door swung open as she approached.

'Welcome home,' Persephone called. Over her red knitted cotton jumper and herringbone wool skirt, she wore a disgraceful old cardy that had probably belonged to her father years ago before he gave it to the dogs to sleep on. That was the upper class for you – the real upper class, the old, established one, not the brand-new pretend one with money and no pedigree. 'I've been watching for you. I'm running round doing the blackout and after that I want to hear all about your first day.'

'Should I give you a hand?'

'No need. Go and get warm.'

In a place this size, the blackout was a sizeable job. It would keep Persephone occupied for a while. Mabel didn't especially want to discuss her day. Was that mean of her? But Persephone used to write juicy little snippets for a society column before the war and now she had ambitions to become a real reporter. Mabel had no intention of seeing her own experiences reproduced in print. She would have to hand over some information, of course, but it would be strictly limited.

Like her, Persephone had been sent here by her parents, though in her case, it had been to remove her from the south-east.

'Daddy was expecting Jerry planes to come swooping across the Channel on their way to London,' Persephone had explained. 'Our country seat is in Sussex and therefore in danger of having left-over bombs dropped on it when the Luftwaffe heads for home. I wanted to be in London, natch, to be in the middle of things, like any good reporter, but Mummy and Daddy wouldn't hear of it. They bundled me up here instead.'

'Did you mind?' Mabel had asked.

Persephone shrugged, an elegant gesture that might well have been drummed into her at finishing school. 'The whole family ganged up on me, all the aged rellies, plus my brothers. And of course, I've been doing war work here, so that gave me a real reason to come.'

Darley Court had been put to bed for the duration. That was practically the first thing Mabel had learned when she arrived. The sight of the wood panelling covered in plain old hardboard had come as a surprise, to say the least. Was it only the nouveau riche who treasured their oak panelling, then, and left it on show in wartime? It must have shown in her face, because Miss Brown, the elderly owner, had looked at her over the rims of her spectacles. Quite why she wore them, other than to appear intimidating, Mabel still couldn't tell. She certainly didn't seem to use them for focusing. She was more likely to take them off and use them for pointing.

'Protection,' Miss Brown declared. 'You can't imagine the trouble we've had trying to work out the least damaging places for the nails to go. The paintings have been covered in hardboard too.'

'Couldn't they be stored in the cellar?' Mabel asked.

'I fell for that last time.' Miss Brown sighed. 'Damp, my dear. Fortunately, we found out before the damage was too bad, but even so it cost a fortune having them restored. In any case, there isn't room for all these paintings in the cellars this time. We're providing storage for various collections from the museum and some private collections.'

'But if the cellars are damp . . .'

'That happened because the air-bricks were bunged up with lichen, but they've been kept clear ever since, so that shouldn't be a problem this time round. And, of course, we've had to make all kinds of promises about temperature and what have you. But anything – anything, mark you – is worth it to keep the old place free of bored soldiers and marauding schoolchildren. Worse than being bombed.'

Persephone had been involved in putting the house to bed. She had shown Mabel around the acres of cellars, where crates were stored, each one carefully labelled.

'I helped draw up the lists of contents,' she explained.

Well, if that wasn't the poshest war work ever! Mabel was glad to be doing something in the open air, something physical, something that made a day-to-day difference. She was helping keep the railways running. She was going to work her hardest and show everyone what she was made of.

That evening, at the end of her first day as a railway girl, she dined with Miss Brown and Persephone in Miss Brown's sitting room, where a bookcase and a sideboard had been shunted aside to make room for a drop-leaf dining table. As an arrangement to save on heating, it was ideal, but the sense of cosiness it engendered made Mabel feel rather a heel for wanting to find somewhere else to live.

Aware of how horrified Mumsy and Pops were going to be, she was curious to see how elderly Miss Brown and upper-crust Persephone would react to her description of working as a lengthman.

'You could probably do with some liniment to rub into your muscles,' said Miss Brown.

Persephone laughed. 'You make Mabel sound like a horse.'

'She'll jolly well have to work like a farm horse, by the sound of it. Good for you, child.'

'You don't mind?' asked Mabel. 'You don't find it inappropriate?'

'Lord, no. The men are away, so who else is there to do it? Besides, I'm in favour of women doing jobs they aren't supposed to. When I inherited this old heap, I was expected to hire a land-agent to run it for me, but I never did, which was rather outrageous in those days. Apparently, I was too old to learn, not to mention the fact that being female meant

I wasn't clever enough in the first place. I was thirty-five then, which I know sounds like one foot in the grave to young things like you. I've kept this place ticking over nicely, though I do say so myself.'

A dull, heavy feeling invaded Mabel's chest. Miss Brown's words made her feel even worse about leaving, but she really couldn't stay. What if Persephone mentioned her by name in a letter home and her mother replied with a scathing sentence about that frightful new money who had been obliged to pay a cash-strapped dowager to present their daughter at court?

Mabel had been careful not to spend all her time hobnobbing with Miss Brown and Persephone. It was through the kindness of her father's cousin that she was here and the least she could do was express her appreciation by nipping below stairs regularly.

She went downstairs that evening, ostensibly to say thank you for the meal, but ready to stay for a natter if an invitation was issued, which it was. She had taken to the housekeeper, liking her kindly, forthright nature.

'I'm your dad's cousin Harriet,' she had said when they met, 'but I'm Mrs Mitchell to you. Miss Brown knows your background, but there's no call for anybody else to know.'

Had she been thinking of saving Mabel's face in front of the extremely well-connected Persephone? Mabel didn't know, but God bless her if she had.

Cousin Harriet – Mrs Mitchell – had a small sitting room of her own a hop and a skip from the kitchen. Mabel settled in one of the armchairs, with her feet tucked up beneath her in a way that would never have been permitted at home. Mrs Mitchell sat opposite, the kitchen cat on her lap.

Mabel explained about being a lengthman. 'So could you please provide some suitable tuck for me each morning?'

'Pleasure – for as long as you're here.'

'You say that as if I'm leaving.'

'Aren't you? Don't get me wrong. I'm happy for you to be here, but it was your dad's idea, not yours.' Mrs Mitchell shrugged. 'I'm just saying.'

Should she confide? Yes, it would be a relief. 'I wouldn't mind finding somewhere else, but it's not as though I know anyone who can help me. I asked a couple of people I met today at work, but I'm not expecting anything to come of it.' The flutter in her lungs made it difficult to breathe. Whatever she had expected when she started on the railways, it wasn't being told to drive.

'I can see it might be tricky for you,' said Mrs Mitchell. 'I can tell you now that I won't have you moving just anywhere. That wouldn't be fair on your parents.'

'With the greatest respect, Mrs Mitchell—' Mabel began.

'Oh aye? That's what folk say just before they say summat extremely disrespectful. Are you about to say that if you choose to leave, I can't stop you? Save your breath, chick. What I was going to suggest was, suppose I find you a suitable place to go?'

Chapter Eleven

The flatbed trolley was loaded not just with luggage but also with parcels. Dot eyed it, hoping she was hiding the uncertainty tweaking at her insides. The trolley looked jolly heavy and would take some manoeuvring. Please don't let her crash into anything. Her eyes narrowed. This wasn't just any old railway trolley – it was *her* railway trolley, and she was going to show it who was boss. She was going to show all the men that she could cope an' all. Most of her male colleagues were real gents, but she had heard a few remarks – aye, and had had more than one remark made to her face – about how, when a flatbed trolley needed to turn one way, you had to push the handle the other way, and how could you rely on a woman to remember to do that?

Grasping the long handle, Dot got the trolley moving. Slow and steady, she told herself, as she pushed.

'Off you go, Mrs G,' called a cheeky young porter whose acne looked like raspberry blancmange that had suffered a bad accident. 'Mind you don't run down any passengers.'

Guiding her trolley, Dot set off towards the line of platform entrances, her nose twitching at the combined aroma of smoke and steam. It was the smell of the railways, the smell of travel. It was the smell of her very first day as a parcels porter on the railways.

As she approached the platform, the gates opened. 'Thanks,' Dot called, but she was too busy watching her trolley, still not trusting it not to take off like a runaway horse, to look at the person who had helped her – her train guard, perhaps. Mr Bonner. She hadn't met him yet, but if he was the kind to open the gates for the trolley, then he must be a good sort.

But no, here came a man in a guard's uniform walking down the platform towards her, passing the line of maroon carriages, their doors open ready to welcome passengers aboard. Dot stepped around the trolley to meet Mr Bonner, ready to shake hands if need be. She gave him her usual friendly smile, only to be greeted by knowing, intolerant eyes and a mouth with an upside-down curve. Some folk had those odd upside-down smiles, but this wasn't one of them. This was an upside-down horseshoe of disapproval, an expression of such length that its ends practically dangled from his chin.

Her smile faltered at the sight, but she wasn't going to let it get to her. Civility was all that really mattered.

Except that even that seemed to be beyond Mr Bonner's abilities.

'Here,' he said. 'This is for you.'

And he gave her – or, more accurately, he tossed on top of the parcels and boxes on the trolley beside her – a small metal badge. She picked it up. Pride flashed through her. Her own LMS badge? Would they let her keep it when she left?

It had a number on the back.

'What's that for?' she asked, interested.

'That's in case you're blown up,' Mr Bonner stated in a flat voice, 'and there's no other way of identifying you.'

And that set the tone for everything else.

She wasn't going to be welcome on Mr Bonner's train. It was as simple as that. He was the guard, in his black serge jacket with LMS embroidered on the collar. You'd have thought he would be glad of a regular parcels porter, and he might have been if he had been assigned a man. He was one of those men who didn't think a woman could do a man's job. Would he look for reasons to criticise her behind her back? Well then, it was up to her to make sure he had nowt to complain about.

'It'll be your job to get all the parcels into the guard's van, though how they expect a woman to do that, I don't know. The parcels have to be stacked according to destination.'

'So I've been told,' said Dot. 'So they can be dropped off at the right station.'

'At the right station from the right door. Not all stations can receive from the guard's van. Most receive from else-where on the train. That'll be your job – to get the parcels to the right door in the right carriage. You'll be in charge of the train's blackout as well and, um, I'll expect you to deal with any . . . ladies' matters that arise.'

'You mean I have to deliver the babies?' asked Dot, but her light-hearted remark was misplaced, to say the least.

Mr Bonner flushed deep red, muttered something unin-telligible, then stood up straight.

'Women aren't up to the job,' he informed her. 'It takes training and experience for work like this. It's born into a man, see, that a job is for life. Women aren't meant to work outside the home, in my view, but if they do, if they must, it's just a temporary thing until they get married. That's the female brain for you. It's not equipped for a lifetime job.'

Not equipped for a lifetime job! What did he think it was to be a housewife and mother? Dot felt like grabbing his whistle and sticking it where the sun didn't shine. But she wouldn't rise to the bait. Indeed, he wasn't baiting her. Mr Bonner was simply expressing his opinion, laying down the law in that know-it-all way men had. She got quite enough of that at home with Ratty Reg. She wasn't going to have to put up with it at work an' all, was she?

She kept her voice polite.

'Well, I'm here for the duration. I'd give ten years of my life for the war to be over this time next week, so my lads could come home safe and sound. I'd be happy to be temporary in those circumstances. But the war is here for goodness knows how long, just like the last one, so best think of me as a permanent fixture.'

Whereupon Mr Bonner turned his back and stalked along the platform to talk to another uniformed man, an inspector to judge by the braid on his peaked cap. From the way they glanced in her direction, Dot was in no doubt as to what their topic of conversation was.

She was taken aback. Mr Bonner was her boss. Shouldn't he be showing her what to do? She already knew in general terms what her job involved – and that was just as well, if Mr Bonner wasn't going to bother with her. Mind you, no doubt he would be quick enough to drop her in the soup if she made any mistakes.

Best get on with it, then. She eyed the flatbed trolley. She had to push it to the guard's van. Better find that first.

'The guard's van is down t'other end. It's the one where the doors open inwards.'

She turned to find a chap in a ticket collector's uniform. He was well into his fifties. His cheeks were rather sunken, which might have been due to age or childhood deprivation or to the effects of the last war. Some men had never really recovered from that. He had a beaky nose and not much chin to speak of. It made a man look weak, not having a strong chin. His eyes were brown and gentle. She liked brown eyes. Reg had brown eyes and she had watched Archie's and Harry's eyes like a hawk when they were babies, waiting, hoping, for their eyes to turn brown, but they never had.

'I'll bring the trolley for you, if you open the door,' offered the ticket collector.

Oh aye, and how would that look to Mr Bonner? Like she couldn't cope on her own and had turned to the first available man for help. She wasn't having that.

'Thanks, but I can manage.'

Resuming her place behind the trolley and grasping the handle, Dot set off along the platform. Mr Bonner might not have taken a shine to her, but that didn't stop her experiencing a rush of pleasure as she passed the dark-red carriages. Some passengers were already aboard; she glimpsed a pale face beneath a hat-brim at one window, a newspaper being read at another, but mainly she concentrated on where she was going.

Stopping beside the guard's van, she opened the door and hoisted herself aboard. Most of the carriage was sectioned off behind a wire wall with a door in it. This was where the parcels would be stored for safe keeping. Beside the length of the wire cage was a narrow walkway so you could get from one end of the guard's van to the other and through into the adjoining carriages.

She tried the door in the wire wall. It was locked. She should have expected that. And Mr Bonner had the key.

She climbed down from the train and looked pointedly in Mr Bonner's direction. He and the ticket inspector shared a glance, then he stalked along the platform to the guard's van. Did he realise she was determined to do her job properly, with or without his encouragement? She allowed herself a moment of satisfaction. Mr Bonner climbed aboard, unlocked the wire cage and left her to it.

'Excuse me, miss.'

She turned round and came face to face with a gentleman in a cavalry-twill overcoat and bowler hat, a leather briefcase in his hand. His eyes widened and he raised his hat to her.

'I beg your pardon. I mean, madam. I knew that ladies

124

were being taken on as porters, but I imagined . . . That is to say, a lady of your, um, years . . .'

'Don't be fooled by my looks,' said Dot. 'It's this job. It puts years on you. I'm only twenty-two.' Could he take a joke?

Yes, he could. He smiled ruefully. 'I beg your pardon for referring to a lady's age. But I am concerned to think of you . . .' He looked at the laden trolley, then at the guard's van. 'You must allow me to assist.'

'I'm fine, really—'

'I insist, and I'm sure I'm not alone.' Appealing to a group of three businessmen coming along the platform, he said, 'Gentlemen, this lady porter could do with our help.'

They immediately put down their briefcases and set to. Dot tried to stop them, then realised that fluttering about wasn't helping and probably made her look even more like a damsel in distress. So she took charge, telling them which parcels and boxes she needed in which order and where to place them inside the cage.

When they had finished, the men descended to the platform, laughing and puffing. Dot tried to thank them, but they waved her words aside amid jokes about a spot of exercise first thing in the morning. Dot's heart expanded with gratitude. Weren't folk kind? The gentlemen raised their bowlers to her, wished her well and seized their briefcases before heading along the platform towards what Dot assumed was their regular carriage.

Regular. She liked the sound of that. Would she have regular passengers whom she would get to know by sight?

'Excuse me. Is this the Southport train?'

Dot gave the anxious-looking young woman her best smile. 'Yes, it is. May I help you with your bags?'

'That would be kind. If you wouldn't mind taking this one, I can manage the other.'

Dot felt a sense of calm and ease. She could do this job. Confidence warmed her. She would enjoy it an' all.

Usually, going home was a mad dash, but this evening there were no kids to look after, no ironing pile to wade through and no knitting circle to attend. Dot had even finished her spring-cleaning – aye, and not because she had skimped on it either. She'd had a go at talking herself out of helping Sheila the Slattern with hers, though she knew herself well enough to accept that she was bound to end up doing it. She only had to walk through Sheila's front door and her fingers itched to grab a duster. Proper homes were meant to smell of lavender polish and soda crystals and, on the days you cleaned the inside of the windows, diluted vinegar. Proper homes smelled of clean linen, fresh flowers if you were lucky (Dot wasn't) and something savoury bubbling away on the stove. Sheila's house smelled of old cooking and closed windows.

This evening there was nowt to do at home except feed Reg, and he would moan whether she was home on time or not. Ratty old sod.

So her visit to the buffet this evening would be a leisurely one, which would make a pleasant change. On her way there, she bumped into someone coming round a corner – Colette. They collided and exclaimed as a package Colette was carrying fell to the ground. They both stooped, almost bumping heads. Dot picked it up. It was squashy. She handed it over.

'Thank you, Mrs Green.'

'You're welcome, love – and it's Dot. You know what we agreed about names.'

'Dot.' It wasn't much more than a whisper. Colette's quiet nature was appealing.

'Where's the fire?' asked Dot.

'Pardon?'

'What's the rush? Hurrying to the buffet to see the rest of us before you go home?'

Colette flushed, her fair colouring making it all the more noticeable. 'My husband is collecting me. I had to stay on to get something finished. He'll be worried about me.'

'Make sure you come to the buffet another time. I'd like to know you better.'

'You would?'

'Course I would. Are you sure you can't spare a minute to pop your head round the door?'

'I really mustn't.'

'Well, I know what it's like to have to go home and get the tea on the table.'

'Excuse me, Mrs – Dot. I have to go.'

'And I've kept you talking.' What a silly the girl was, getting into a tizzy in case she kept that nice husband of hers waiting. 'Tell you what, let's walk together and I'll tell your hubby it's my fault.' So saying, Dot slid her arm through Colette's and bore her away. 'What's in your parcel? It felt like fabric. What are you making?'

'A dress. It's got padded shoulders. I've never done those before. I hope I don't make a mess of them. The lady in Ingleby's said everything has padded shoulders now.'

'I'm sure you'll manage just fine, and if you don't, bring it to the buffet and let the rest of us take a look. What colour is it?'

'Blue. Here, have a peep.'

Without breaking her step, Colette freed her arm from Dot's and opened one end of her parcel to reveal material the colour of bluebells.

'That's pretty,' said Dot. 'It'll suit you.'

'Do you think so?'

'Aye, with your colouring.'

Colette smiled. It was a small smile, but not a reserved one like Cordelia's. It was small because she was shy. Dot warmed to her.

'Promise you'll drop into the buffet when you can.' Dot tucked her arm back in Colette's. 'You know about the notebook under the counter, don't you? It would be lovely to see you.'

But Colette wasn't listening. Dot had barely linked with her again before the girl drew her arm away and put on a spurt. That good-looking husband of hers was waiting, his gaze darting about, posture rigid. Poor fellow, what a worrier. He glanced at his watch.

'Tony!' Colette called, hurrying his way. Catching his arm, she smiled up at him before looking at Dot. 'This is Mrs Green. We started on the same day.'

'Of course.' Mr Naylor raised his hat to her. 'I recognise you. Where have you been, darling?' he asked Colette, looking down at her.

'That's my fault, I'm afraid,' said Dot. 'I kept her talking.'

'I was worried,' Mr Naylor told Colette.

Blimey, what a fusspot. 'Well, she's here now,' said Dot. To Colette, she said, 'Remember what I said, love. We all want to be friends with you, so make sure you come and have a cuppa with us. Speaking of which, I must make tracks. G'night.'

'Yes, I must get my special girl home,' said Tony Naylor.

Dot watched as he bore Colette away. She felt mushy inside. There was nowt like a young couple in love to warm the cockles of your heart. She had been Reg's special girl once.

Turning on her heel, she hurried to the buffet, eager to make the most of her time there. The others would be pleased that she had seen Colette. She walked in, her gaze swiftly searching for the group, but only Alison was there so far.

Crossing the floor with her tea, Dot saw Alison's expression before Alison realised she was there. The girl's pretty face was downcast. Then Alison saw her and perked up.

'Summat wrong, love?' asked Dot. 'Tell me to mind my own business, but you looked glum.'

'It's nothing, Mrs Green – Dot. It's not easy getting used to calling you that.'

Now she knew summat was wrong. 'I think that's what is known as changing the subject.'

Alison laughed, more of a forced laugh, really. She shook her head. 'It's nothing, honestly. Just me being daft.'

'You don't strike me as daft. Listen, love. If you want to talk, I'm a good listener and it won't go any further.'

Alison caught her breath. She glanced towards the door and Dot looked too. No sign of the others.

'It is daft, actually,' said Alison. 'My boyfriend is going to propose.'

'What's daft about that?'

'It's not that simple. I mean, it ought to be, but it just . . . isn't.' Alison leaned forward confidingly. She had such pretty brown eyes. 'Everyone knows we're going to get married and they're waiting with bated breath for the announcement. Obviously, he wants to surprise me with a romantic proposal, but how can he? I thought he might propose at Christmas, but he didn't; so then I thought maybe Valentine's Day . . .'

'But he didn't,' Dot finished for her.

'I even . . . I even thought of doing the proposing, this being a leap year, but I just couldn't.'

'Why not, if it's what you both want? Some folk would call it romantic.'

'And others would call it desperate.'

'I can see you're upset. Can't you talk to your mum?'

Alison rolled her eyes. 'She's one of the people dying for

him to go down on one knee.' She chewed her lip. 'It's important that everybody thinks I'm happy with things as they are – and I am. Of course I am. I can see it from Paul's point of view.'

'No one wants to announce their engagement to a rousing chorus of "About time too", eh?'

'Precisely. Oh, Dot, thank you for understanding.'

She patted Alison's hand. 'He'll do it in his own good time, love. He wants to make it special for you.' She was glad to have brought brightness to Alison's eyes.

'Thank you. You must be a wonderful mother.'

Ah. Yes. A wonderful mother. That was the trouble, wasn't it? She was everybody's mum. Not just Harry and Archie's; not just Sheila and Pammy's. She was mum to anyone and everyone who needed help, advice or a slice of toast.

But she didn't want to be mum at work. She wanted to be . . . herself. Dot. Dorothy Green. Dorothy Simpson-as-was. Capable, reliable, hard-working. Not a mother hen. Just a railway girl.

Dot's day started and ended in the parcels office, helping to sort the many boxes and parcels into the various areas of floor space and shelving, according to whichever railway line they would travel by. It was important to be familiar with all the lines, not just your own, because you never knew if you might be assigned to a different train. Dot wouldn't have altogether minded being transferred to a different line, so as to leave Mr Bonner behind, but chugging up and down to Southport was handy, because her current hours were pretty good for her home life.

A clothes brush for everyone's use hung on a hook beside the door. She gave her uniform jacket and skirt a brisk going-over before stepping outside. Golly, but her feet were aching. Her shoes felt tight. Either her feet had expanded from the heat or else she was sprouting bunions. Dear old Mam's bunions had grown so big that she had had to get the cobbler to put slits in the sides of her clogs.

'How do?'

It was that ticket collector, the one who had wanted to help her on her first day on the trains. Dot's heart gave a little leap. She had wanted to see him again, but their shifts hadn't coincided.

She smiled. 'I've been hoping to bump into you.' Goodness, how did that sound? 'To apologise,' she added quickly. 'I think you must have been the person who kindly opened the platform gates for my luggage trolley on my first day and I was so busy concentrating that I never said thank you. You offered to lend a hand an' all and I refused.'

'I'm sorry if I caused offence, but it's difficult for fellows like me to see a lady tackling a heavy job.'

'You didn't cause offence. I wanted to do it myself, that's all.'

'Fair enough.'

'But then those businessmen helped me whether I wanted them to or not, which was very kind of them. Most folk are kind.' That was something she didn't doubt. 'But I don't know what you must have thought. You offered help and I said no, then the other men . . .' She shrugged. 'Anyroad, I've been keeping an eye out for you since, so I can apologise.'

'No apology necessary. I was pleased to see you getting help, truth be told.'

'I just wanted to make sure you knew I didn't intend to rebuff you.'

'That's good of you to say.' His smile pushed flesh into his hollow cheeks, giving them more substance. 'You've made my day by bothering to explain. Small kindnesses: they're what keep us going.'

She liked the sound of that. 'I must get on.'

He touched the peak of his ticket-collector's cap to her as they parted. What a pleasant man. She was glad to have spoken to him. Small kindnesses.

The next morning, he was the ticket collector assigned to her platform. He opened the gates for her to push her loaded trolley through. Aye, and he opened them in good time so she didn't have to stop the trolley and wait. The ticket collector who had manned the barrier the past few days had waited for her to arrive at the barrier before opening it. She was accustomed now to controlling the trolley, no matter how heavy it was, so stopping wasn't a problem, but it made life easier to keep it moving.

'Thank you,' she called as she went through onto the platform.

Coming to a halt beside the guard's van, she realised the ticket collector had followed her.

'I noticed these here long parcels,' he said. 'Have you been shown the best way to shift them? Let me show you.' He cocked an eyebrow at her. 'If that's all right?'

She laughed. 'Please do.'

He demonstrated how to tilt the long parcel so one end touched the platform. Then he stood it upright, taking hold of either side.

'See? Then you "walk" it along, like this.'

Dot tried with the other one. 'Thanks. I'll remember that.'

'I must get back to the barrier.' Touching his cap to her – how polite he was – he made his way back down the platform.

As Dot turned back to her trolley, a couple of porters, a man and a woman, stopped to lend a hand. Women always helped one another. Dot could understand that. As for the men here, they fell into two camps: the ones that accepted their new female colleagues and looked out for them, and the ones that didn't want them here at all, like Mr Bonner. She sighed. It was a sigh that came all the way up from the soles of her shoes. How different her job would be if, instead of Mr Bonner, she worked for a guard who was more like – she didn't know his name. That nice ticket collector.

Chapter Twelve

Once again the station was packed solid. The trains were running late because they were giving way to troop trains, which meant the concourse was heaving with passengers and their luggage. With many an 'Excuse me', Joan eased her way through the crowds, catching a whiff of Evening in Paris here and a snatch of Yardley's English Lavender talcum powder there, little moments of sweetness within the ubiquitous aroma of tobacco. There was something pleasurable about being an official employee, a veteran of four whole weeks, in the middle of all these travellers. It was a shame in a way not to have a uniform, though she had been given an LMS badge, with its linked emblems of an English rose and a Scottish thistle beneath a wing with the cross of St George. She wore it with pride.

'Excuse me . . . excuse me . . .'

She headed for the buffet. Was there any hope of a free table on a day like today? Cordelia's idea of writing messages in a notebook worked well – up to a point. It wasn't easy to pinpoint suitable times and it was downright impossible to make an arrangement that suited all of them, but in a funny way that made it better when any of them did meet.

She pushed open the door, standing on tiptoe to see across the crowded room. Cordelia, Dot and Mabel sat at a tiny table, with Lizzie standing crushed in the corner beside them. She was dressed in her porter's uniform of jacket and skirt with a peaked cap. It was smart but it made her look very young. There was no sign of Colette – that didn't come as a surprise. If she had been here, *that* would have been the surprise. No Alison, either, which was a shame. She liked Alison.

'Even if there was room for another chair at this table,' said Mabel when Joan arrived beside her, 'there isn't a single one to be had. You'll have to share with me.'

Joan was instantly thrown back to when she'd had to share with Mr Clark. A small shudder passed through her. Putting down her cup of tea, she sank onto the edge of Mabel's seat.

'Don't you want to sit down?' she asked Lizzie.

'Not allowed,' said Lizzie. 'Not in front of the passengers while I'm in uniform.'

'I hadn't thought of that,' said Joan. 'Who else will get a uniform?'

'I don't have one at present,' said Cordelia, 'but if they provide one, I shan't travel to and from work in it. There's a big walk-in cupboard in the lamp shed which the women use as a cloakroom of sorts. I'll get changed in there.'

'I've got my uniform on under my coat,' said Dot. 'Standing up is all well and good for a young thing like our Lizzie here, but by the end of the day, I want to take the weight off my feet.'

'What about in the summer when it's hot?' asked Mabel.

'I always wear my coat,' said Dot. 'My dear old mam was a shawlie all her life and she never set foot outside her front door without her shawl. It's the same with me and my coat.'

'Busy today, isn't it?' said Joan. 'How is everyone?'

There was a chorus of 'Fine.' She leaned forwards. The background babble was more babble than background.

'How are you getting on in your office?' Mabel asked.

Joan smiled. 'I've realised why we had to sit that geography test. I feel as if I'm learning the names of every town and village in the kingdom.'

'I'm the same,' Lizzie agreed. 'All those luggage labels. Still, never a dull moment.'

'Do you find it interesting?' Cordelia asked Joan.

Joan was determined not to sound disappointed in her job. 'It's important to concentrate, obviously. We have to produce a score every day.'

'Twenty invoices a day?' Mabel and Lizzie spoke as one, clearly meaning *Is that all?*

'Your score is the minimum you're required to complete,' said Joan. Her own score was gradually creeping up. 'I'm getting to know the other girls. One of them is getting married and we're saving the little circles of paper from the hole punchers for her confetti.'

'I wouldn't fancy slaving over a typewriter every day,' said Lizzie, 'doing the same thing over and over.'

'It is rather samey,' Joan admitted. She tried to make light of it. 'But that's a good thing. It's better than the inspectors descending on us without warning. Everybody dreads that, though it hasn't happened while I've been there. And once a month, we have to wear our gas masks all day.'

The others stared, then Dot and Lizzie snorted with laughter.

'I'd love to see that,' said Dot.

'But I bet you've got proper ladies' conveniences over there in the admin buildings,' said Lizzie. 'There's no such thing on the station. We have to use the public conveniences. One of the lady porters has hung an "Out of Order" sign on one of the doors, so there's always one available for us. We all go together and hold the door for one another, so we use just the one penny.'

'At Southport Station,' said Dot, 'the girls use a bent nail to turn the penny-lock.'

'That's what we need, then,' Lizzie declared jubilantly. 'Some bent nails.'

Lucky Dot! She was the most fortunate of them all. Goodness knows, Joan was envious enough of Lizzie for working on the station, and of Mabel and Cordelia for their jobs on the permanent way, but Dot was actually on the trains. What could be more interesting or satisfying than that?

'Mabel,' said Lizzie, 'my mum thinks she's found you a new billet, near us in Whalley Range.'

Mabel looked startled. 'Really? Only I've already found one. Or rather, someone I know found it for me. Golly, I'm sorry. I didn't realise you were searching.'

'I told you I'd ask my mum,' Lizzie reminded her.

'I know, but – well, I didn't know whether you would after . . .' Mabel's voice trailed away. After she had refused to be a driver.

Joan would have sold her soul for driving lessons. Not for the first time, she wanted to ask Mabel to explain herself, but what if Mabel was scared of learning and felt hounded by the question? So she held her tongue.

'I apologise if I put your mother out,' said Mabel. 'You, too,' she added to Cordelia, 'if you've been looking on my behalf. It was wrong of me to think you wouldn't bother. I should have known you'd be more generous than that.'

Cordelia acknowledged the compliment with a slight nod, but Lizzie beamed. It was impossible not to feel warm towards Lizzie. She was all heart.

Cordelia looked at her watch and stood up. 'Excuse me. I must go for my bus.'

'Aye, I must dash an' all.' Dot got up too.

As they left, Joan moved across into one of the spare chairs. 'Tell us about your new billet. Where is it?'

'Chorlton-cum-Hardy,' said Mabel.

Joan sat up straight. 'I live in Chorlton too. Torbay Road.'

'I'm on Nell Lane, near Southern Cemetery. Do you know it?'

'That's the other end of Chorlton to us. Still, it's near enough for us to go out together, if you felt like it.'

'Perfect!' cried Lizzie. 'We could go to the pictures. I live in Whalley Range, which isn't far from you two. I'd love to see *Goodbye, Mr Chips* and it'd be fun to have chums to go with. I normally go with my mum, but she's always on at me to go out with girls my own age.'

'Robert Donat's in *Goodbye, Mr Chips*,' said Joan. 'He's so handsome. I loved him in *The Thirty-Nine Steps*. Count me in – and my sister, if you don't mind.'

'Do you and your sister do a lot together?' asked Mabel.

'Gran likes us to and that's always suited us. We both like dancing.'

'So do I,' said Lizzie. 'Would you mind if I tagged along sometimes? Mum says I'm not old enough to go on my own. I say, do you remember those red shoes we saw the day we sat the railway tests?'

'They were rather lovely,' said Joan. 'And yes, of course you can come. We usually go with my sister's boyfriend.'

'Don't they mind you playing gooseberry?' asked Mabel.

'It's not like that.' Joan fanned her face with her hand. 'It's warm in here, isn't it?' she remarked, to account for the colour seeping into her cheeks. Wanting to divert attention from herself, she said to Mabel, 'You haven't said whether you want to come to the flicks.'

'I'm not sure,' said Mabel. 'I want to do voluntary work for the war effort.'

'I was a fire-watcher where I used to work,' said Joan. 'I ought to find another fire-watching station.'

It was on the tip of her tongue to suggest they might all find a fire-watching place together, but that wouldn't work. Two of them might get assigned together, but not three, and she did want them to do something together. A little flurry of excitement and comradeship wrapped around her. Was she already forming a bond with her fellow railway girls? Did the others feel it too?

After that, it felt rather flat and ordinary to go home to the grey restraint of Gran's house. She arrived home to find Gran and Letitia examining the contents of the air-raid box, which was open on the table in the parlour. A chill ran through her. Letitia had insisted they put together their air-raid box as soon as their Anderson shelter was ready. All the men in their road had got together and done all the digging in the narrow back gardens. Steven and his dad had mucked in too. Steven had agreed with Letitia that they must prepare their air-raid box, using it as a safe place to store paperwork and precious things – such as Daddy's photograph.

'There you are, Joanie.' Letitia glanced round as she walked in. 'We're discussing whether to put Daddy's picture back in the box. Everyone at work says that now Germany has invaded Norway and Denmark, it's only a matter of time before the phoney war comes to an end.'

The hair on Joan's arms stood up. Hitler was getting closer.

'Do you think Daddy's picture should go back in the box? Just in case?'

There was a silence. The Daddy silence. The shared awareness of their family tragedy. The bond that held the three of them together.

'I like having it where we can see it,' said Joan, 'but we do want it to be safe.'

'We could have it on display during the day,' said Gran, 'and put it in the box at bedtime.'

'That presupposes that air-raids will happen only at night,' said Letitia.

'Let's leave it out for the time being,' said Gran, 'and we'll see what happens.' She sighed, then bucked up. 'The tea's nearly ready. I'll dish up.'

'Do you want a hand?' Letitia offered.

'No, thank you, dear. You work hard enough. Joan will help, won't you?'

Joan exchanged smothered smiles with Letitia. It had always been like this. Letitia, the grammar-school girl, now using her Distinction in School Cert maths at the munitions, had never been required to lift a finger. Joan, on the other hand . . .

After tea, they settled down for the evening, waiting for *Monday Night at Eight* to start on the Home Service. Gran took up her knitting and Joan and Letitia sat at the table with a half-finished jigsaw of Loch Lomond.

'Have you heard of these new first-aid parties?' Letitia asked.

'Parties?' asked Gran.

'Not fun-and-games parties. Parties, as in groups. They want to train people to administer first aid in the event of air raids. There will be groups, working together and receiving instructions by telephone from headquarters as to where they should go. I wondered about us joining, Joanie. We'd have to do a first-aid course, then attend a big first-aid event where everyone's skills will be assessed.'

'Yes, let's,' Joan agreed at once. 'Maybe a couple of girls from work would be interested as well. We were talking earlier about volunteering for something.'

'Girls from your office?' asked Gran.

'No, girls who started on the same day as I did. We promised to be friends. Actually,' she added to Letitia, 'one of them, Lizzie, asked if she might come dancing with us. Would that be all right?' She trembled inside as she added casually, 'Steven wouldn't mind, would he?'

The three of them were going to the Ritz in Whitworth Street on Friday. For a wonder, despite Steven's shifts and

Letitia's compulsory overtime the pair of them would have a free Friday evening together.

Letitia slotted in a piece of sky. 'Well, maybe not this Friday.'

'Why not?'

'No reason. Just save it for another time, eh?' Looking up from the puzzle, she turned to Gran. 'I think the family papers ought to be put in the air-raid box. You know, birth certificates and so on.'

'We've discussed this before,' Gran said as if that was the end of the matter.

But Letitia persisted. 'I know you like keeping them in your handbag, but I'm not sure that's the right place.'

'They're safe in my bag,' said Gran. 'I always have that with me.'

'Then what if you carry the insurance papers and things while Joan and I have our own birth certificates?'

'There's no need. You've got your identity papers. That's what matters in an emergency.' Gran's mouth tightened. Her lips turned into a series of tiny vertical lines like spikes. 'It makes sense to keep all the family papers together.'

'I'm twenty-one next year,' said Letitia. 'You do remember what my war work is, don't you? I double-check the maths of the engineers responsible for the shells. So I'm clever enough and grown-up enough to do that, but I'm not grown-up enough to be responsible for my own birth certificate.' She bounced to her feet so suddenly the table jiggled. 'I'm sick of not being trusted.'

'Not trusted?' Gran dropped her knitting onto her lap. 'Have I ever stopped you seeing Steven? *That's* trust, if you please.'

The parlour jangled with shock at the oblique reference to Estelle.

Letitia lifted her chin. 'It isn't enough. We're adults with responsible wartime jobs. I've had enough of being treated like a child. I want you to give me my birth certificate so I can decide where to put it for safe keeping.'

'That's no way to address me,' said Gran. 'I'm your guardian as well as your grandmother. I brought you up and you owe everything to me. Haven't I protected you from what your mother did? Haven't I given you a decent upbringing in spite of it? I am entitled to your respect. Now kindly sit down.'

She and Letitia glared at one another. To Joan's relief, Letitia resumed her seat. Gran made a show of picking up her knitting and studying the pattern, but she wasn't really seeing it. She was wearing her thinking face, a look of intense concentration mingled with displeasure. Joan felt that familiar wriggle deep inside. She couldn't help squirming. No matter how grown-up she was, Gran could still make her feel like a naughty child who deserved punishment.

Gran huffed out a sharp breath. 'I'm not happy about this, but – well, I am prepared to trust you.'

'To take care of our birth certificates?' Letitia asked.

'I will permit you to wear your hems shorter. You've been going on about that for a long time. It's up to you, mind, to show me you can dress in this modern way without behaving like your mother. If I think for one moment that you've inherited her ways . . .'

'We haven't.' Letitia was all warmth, now she had got her own way. 'We know what she did and we're not like that at all. We're Daddy's girls, aren't we, Joanie?'

Yes, indeed. They were perfect little daddy's girls. Not like Estelle, the tart who had ruined all their lives.

Joan had to duck her head to hide the flame in her cheeks. If she was Daddy's girl, how come she had fallen in love with her sister's boyfriend?

*

Leaving Gran listening to the wireless, Joan and Letitia demurely went out of the room before heading upstairs in a mad dash, arriving at the top in a laughing scramble. In their bedroom, they hugged one another.

'Thank you, thank you, thank you.' Arms flung wide, Joan threw herself backwards onto the bed they shared, then pushed herself up on her elbows. 'You talked her round. I could never have done that.'

'You mean I nagged her into submission. I never thought she'd give in, but she did and that's all that matters. We'll turn up your work skirt first. No arguments. Change back into it.' Letitia positioned the wooden chair in front of the dressing-table that stood crammed into the corner. 'Hop up and we'll see how much needs to come off. Stand up straight, soppy. It's no use bending down to see. Look in the mirror.'

Letitia sank onto one knee as if she was about to propose. She folded back the hem and, bewitched, Joan gazed at her reflection.

'You've got legs!' Letitia exclaimed, making Joan tingle all over with self-consciousness. 'Nice legs, too. Slender but shapely. It's probably not a good idea to look so thrilled. We mustn't rub Gran's nose in it. She might take back permission if she thinks we're crowing.'

'We need to get cutting so she can't change her mind.'

Letitia laughed. 'We'll get this skirt finished tonight and you can wear it for work tomorrow.'

Joan jumped down from the chair and hugged her. 'You're the best sister ever.'

'No, I'm not, but I'm the most impatient. I demand that we do one of mine next.'

'And we'll turn up our dresses for Friday,' said Joan.

Would there be time? It wasn't as though Gran was going to lend a hand and get the hems finished while they were out at work.

Nevertheless, both dresses were done early, Letitia's lilac with elbow-length sleeves, round collarless neck and matching belt, and Joan's V-necked, white-spotted navy. There was much giggling and parading as they tried them on, though this was done only upstairs. There was no point in going downstairs to show Gran. She might have conceded the point, but that didn't mean she had an ounce of grace in her on the subject.

Joan was dying for Friday night, but guilt tugged deep inside her tummy when she thought of Lizzie. Why had Letitia said not to invite her? Joan hadn't felt able to tell anyone in the buffet about her Friday-night plans. Alison had said once that she and her boyfriend occasionally went to the Ritz. What if they happened to be there that Friday and saw Joan, and then Alison mentioned it in front of Lizzie next week? Oh, she was getting herself into a tizzy, and probably all over nothing.

On Friday evening, Joan and Letitia helped one another with their hair and dabbed on the teeniest drop of lily-of-the-valley scent. Gran said they had to make it last till the end of the war. Then they put on their dresses. What a difference the loss of four inches could make. They clambered onto the bed to stand beside one another and look in the mirror, giggling and clutching each other as the mattress dipped, sending them swaying.

'From dowdy to delightful,' said Letitia.

'Frumpy to fascinating.'

'Grim to gorgeous, glamorous and – I can't think of another one.'

'Idiot.' Joan laughed. Her reservations about not inviting Lizzie had evaporated, leaving pure anticipation.

When they presented themselves downstairs, Gran's eyes widened. What flashed into her mind in that moment? Then she made a humphing sound and turned away, but

Joan felt too giddy to care. Gran was a stern old bag. She and Letitia were young and they were going to enjoy themselves.

Steven arrived, setting Joan's heart clattering until he took Letitia's hand and raised it gallantly to his lips, all the while keeping his eyes fixed on her face. Letitia laughed. Joan could have crowned her. She wouldn't have laughed if Steven had done that to her. She would have had a hard job to stop herself from swooning.

They caught the tram into town, Joan and Letitia sitting beside one another, Steven on the seat in front. He turned sideways so he could face them.

'You two look pleased with yourselves.' He frowned, but it was a frown of amusement. 'Have you told her?' he asked Letitia.

'Told me what?' asked Joan.

'You'll see,' Letitia answered, and that was all she would say.

They arrived at the Ritz, queueing for a minute or two to hand in their coats and hats. Excitement radiated through Joan's body as she removed her coat and revealed her fashionable dress-length to the world. With a sister on each arm, Steven escorted them into the ballroom and Joan felt the surge of pleasure she always experienced at being here in the ballroom, with its sprung floor, its pillars and art deco features, and the balcony above, where you could sit at the tables and look down onto the dancers and the famous revolving stage. The band was playing a quickstep and couples slow-slow-quick-quick-slowed past, some gliding with perfect grace, others not so skilled.

With the swing of the music invading her senses, Joan looked about for an empty table, vaguely aware of a young man heading their way.

'There's a free table over there,' she started to say before realising that Steven and Letitia were smiling at her in a way she hadn't seen before.

Letitia, on Steven's other side, dropped his arm and came round to position herself beside Joan. Not just beside, but close to. Protective. Encouraging . . .

'Evening.' The young man whom she had barely noticed had stopped in front of them. He was dark-haired with a narrow face and humorous eyes.

'Joan.' Steven gave her arm a squeeze with his own. 'This is Toby Collins, a fellow copper.'

'And this is my sister, Joan,' Letitia added.

Toby nodded. 'Pleased to meet you.'

'Why don't you two have a dance?' Steven suggested and before Joan knew what was going on, the man she adored had handed her into the waiting arms of another.

Chapter Thirteen

It was turning out to be a heck of a day. Dot might have called it a hell of a day, except that her dear mam had forbidden her children to use the H word under any circumstances, and by crikey, was Dot seeing some circumstances today. First off, she arrived at Victoria to find it extra busy because the early trains had given way to whatever trains had to give way to these days – troop trains, munitions wagons. Anyroad, it meant she had to push her parcels trolley at a snail's pace so as not to bash anyone as she made her way through the crowd.

'You took your time,' sneered Mr Bonner when she drew to a halt beside the guard's van. 'I never have this trouble with real porters.'

'Good morning to you an' all.' Dot kept her voice cheerful even though she felt more like spitting in his eye. She had to be polite or he might report her.

When she had loaded her parcels, Mr Bonner quickly checked the various piles of packages and boxes, as was only right and proper, but it still galled her because of the long-suffering way he did it, which suggested that if she hadn't made any mistakes, it was more through luck than competence.

Mr Bonner's despairing air changed to one of triumph and Dot felt herself shrink inside. What had she done wrong?

'This box,' Mr Bonner declared, 'should be with those over there. No.' He held up a hand, as through stopping traffic, as she stepped forward to rectify her mistake. 'I'll move it. It is essential it ends up in the correct place.'

He couldn't have handled the crown jewels with greater attention. Mr Bonner set down the box with extravagant care and turned to her. She braced herself. This was the moment for him to indulge in some serious gloating.

'I'm sorry, Mr Bonner,' she said.

But instead of gloating, his attitude was dismissive, which was somehow worse. She felt two inches tall.

'It's only what I expect from a porterette. Kindly return to the parcels office. I believe you've left something behind.'

'Pardon me, but I haven't.'

He was already turning away. 'If you say so.'

Dot dithered, but only for a moment. If she really had left something behind – which she knew she hadn't – but if she had, and she didn't go back for it, she would be hauled over the coals good and proper. She might even be sacked. So she had no choice but to ease her way back through the crowd to find out.

There were grins all round as she walked into the office. Was she the victim of a silly joke? Then one of the senior porters appeared, leading a pair of goats. Goats! Round its neck, each goat wore a loose rope collar, from which a stout piece of string acted as a lead. Dot's mouth dropped open, but her hand automatically extended to receive the leads even as her thoughts struggled to catch up.

'They're goats,' was all she could say.

'They're parcels, Mrs Green. Pets and livestock are parcels.'

'Get them two settled,' called a cheery voice, 'then come back for the rest.'

'Take no notice,' said the senior porter. 'It's just these two. Here are their luggage labels. Make sure they don't eat 'em.'

'Eat anything and everything, goats do,' someone added helpfully. 'They'll go through yon guard's van like a flame-thrower, if you don't watch out.'

Dot stared at the animals. They had short-haired white coats, with tufty little tails. At least they didn't have horns, but those horizontal pupils weren't exactly endearing. With laughter echoing in her ears, Dot led her charges to the platform, passengers making way with grins on their faces. As she passed through the barrier with them, the ticket collector couldn't have laughed any more heartily if Harry Champion had popped out from behind a pillar to sing a rousing chorus of 'I'm Henery the Eighth, I Am'. What a pity it wasn't that nice ticket collector. Yes, he would have had a chuckle, but he would have said summat encouraging an' all. She could do with a spot of encouragement.

The goats weren't keen to get on the train, but finally allowed themselves to be tugged aboard. Maybe they were fed up of being laughed at. Lord knows, Dot was. Hey, what was the matter with her? It wasn't like her to be grumpy. This was funny, really . . . or would be when she looked back on it one day in the dim and distant future. She let her head fall back in relief when the goats allowed themselves – and she had no doubt that their consent was involved – to be led inside the parcels' cage. She couldn't have them running riot, could she, so she used the Southport boxes and parcels to build a wall in a corner and penned them in. Crikey, it felt like she had done a day's work already.

Mr Bonner appeared just as she was mentally patting herself on the back. Talk about impeccable timing.

'Here are our special passengers.' She gave Mr Bonner her most dazzling smile. Not for anything would she let on how fraught things had been.

'They're parcels, not passengers, and if they make a mess, it's your job to clear it up.'

She locked her smile in position. 'Lucky for you, you've got a porterette on board. A man would be squeamish about such things. Me, I've changed more mucky nappies than you've had hot dinners, and a bit of goat mess is nowt.'

If she'd imagined that that was the hardest part of the journey over and done with, she was wrong. The train was full, with plenty of passengers standing in the corridors or sitting on upturned suitcases, which made it tricky for her to get her parcels to the correct door before arriving at each station, especially as folk kept asking her questions about arrival times and connections. After Salford Central, where she got the last of her parcels to the door by the skin of her teeth, she reckoned the only way to cope was to start shifting parcels as soon as they pulled out of each station. What with that, and keeping an eye on the goats, she didn't have a moment to sit down.

At last the train pulled into Southport. Dot swore the sky was bluer here. The train doors started banging open before the train came to a halt at the buffers. Passengers streamed out, some in a purposeful hurry, others getting in their way by pausing to look around for whoever was meeting them. The air was filled with the sharp-sweet smell of steam.

Miss Lofthouse, one of the parcels porters, had positioned her empty trolley in precisely the right place to receive the Southport deliveries from the guard's van. She was a sturdy woman of a certain age, whose previous working life had been spent in a laundry, heaving sopping sheets out of giant coppers and turning the handles on industrial-sized mangles, all of which meant she had developed a strength that a man wouldn't be ashamed of. Parcels were nothing to Miss Lofthouse. No matter the size or weight, she heaved them about with an ease that filled Dot with a mixture of admiration and sorrow. By, but this woman had had a hard life. You could say what you liked about Reg, but he had always provided for her and her boys.

Miss Lofthouse peered inside. 'What's them?'

'Goats.'

'I can see that.'

'Though why somebody is sending goats from Manchester to Southport, I don't know,' said Dot.

With no discernible difficulty, Miss Lofthouse picked up a box that had brought Dot out in a sweat when she'd loaded it onto the train. 'Perhaps they're on a day trip and you'll be taking them home again later.'

'Don't even joke about it,' said Dot.

She had to admit, though, that her unusual parcels had been good as gold all the way from Victoria. Transporting animals wasn't so bad after all. As the wall around them vanished, Dot grasped their leads, letting Miss Lofthouse finish the unloading. Finally, she led the goats from the train. Having baulked at getting on, now they weren't keen to get off, but a good tug got them moving. Miss Lofthouse set off with the trolley, Dot following with the goats. This time, she enjoyed the curious looks and the smiles. She returned the smiles, feeling proud. Jimmy and Jenny would love hearing about this.

Maybe it was her own fault, maybe she was too busy revelling in the moment, but next news one of the goats put on a spurt and its lead slipped through her fingers. She stared in horror as the goat headed off at a smart clip, like a POW making a bid for freedom.

'Don't just stand there,' Miss Lofthouse roared.

Dot thrust the other lead at her.

'Stop that goat!' she yelled down the platform. 'It's a parcel!'

She gave chase. By, but there were some things a lady her age shouldn't be called upon to do, and zigzagging around startled passengers in pursuit of an independent-minded goat was one of them. Most of the passengers stood there like a load of lemons, aye, and the staff an' all, but fortunately one fellow in a tweed jacket and trilby had the presence of mind to stamp his foot hard on the trailing lead and brought the goat to a standstill.

'Yours, I believe.' He handed her the lead as she puffed up to him.

After a brief tug-of-war, which Dot was in no mood to lose, she persuaded the goat to return to where Miss Lofthouse was waiting. Dot took the other lead and, winding the pieces of string several times round her wrists to prevent further mishaps, led the animals down the platform and straight to the parcels office. She couldn't hand over the dratted beasts fast enough.

A straightforward journey home was what she needed now, but the swell of the crowd in the station suggested it was a forlorn hope. After her break, she took a minute to fuss the station cat, who was spark out on top of a pile of wicker hampers, before she set about loading the guard's van for the return journey. The train was even fuller going back, making it harder to get the parcels to the various dropping-off points in the carriages.

After unloading Appley Bridge's parcels, she made her way back to the guard's van, squeezing through the jumble of passengers inhabiting the corridors. As she smiled and excused herself through one corridor, a pretty girl in her twenties, dressed in a lightweight wool suit and a lacquered straw hat, murmured, 'Excuse me,' in such a soft voice that Dot barely caught her words.

'Can I help you?' She had already answered umpteen questions about the timetable and where to change for Bolton and she was all set to reel off a quick reply when she twigged that the flush in the girl's cheeks wasn't due to the warmth of so many passengers crammed in together. Instinctively she leaned closer. 'What is it?'

The girl's gaze shifted from side to side. She put her mouth close to Dot's ear and whispered, 'Someone, one of these men, touched me.'

'It is rather packed in here.' Dot was about to apologise for the crush.

'No, I mean he *touched* me . . . on the derrière.'

'On the what?'

'On my . . . on my BTM.'

The dirty bugger! She managed not to exclaim it aloud. Her gaze flashed round. The rotund gentleman with the bowler? The young fellow with the acne-pitted cheeks? The spivvy-looking bloke with the fag dangling from his lips? To her astonishment, she felt – so softly that she could almost believe it wasn't happening – a whisper of a touch on her derry-whatsit. She sucked in a breath, but it wasn't air that poured down her throat. It was sheer disbelief.

For a moment, she didn't move. Then – she would get one chance at this, and one only – she whipped her hand behind her back and seized a wrist, clamping her fingers round the cuff.

Yanking the wrist up into the air, she demanded loudly, 'Whose hand is this?'

Everyone stirred; everyone looked. Conversations stopped. The rotund gentleman in the bowler hat turned puce and tried to pull free of her. He didn't manage it on the first attempt, but he did on the second.

'How dare you?' he spluttered.

'How dare I? How dare you, you mean. Touching ladies in a public carriage.'

'I did no such thing. It's jam-packed in here. I admit I may have brushed against you accidentally.'

'Oh aye, accidental, was it, that your hand ended up in a

153

place I won't mention, which is where I pulled it from? And not just me, neither, but—' She reined in her tongue to spare the girl's blushes. 'Another lady has complained an' all.'

'This is outrageous. I shall lodge a formal complaint—'

'You do that, matey, and see where it gets you. Up before the beak for indecent behaviour, that's where.' Crikey, where were these words coming from? Her pulse was hopping all over the place. She addressed those closest. 'I suggest you move your wives out of the way, because this one's got hands like a flamin' octopus. You come with me, love,' she added quietly to the girl. 'You can sit in the guard's van. Mind out, all, please. Coming through!'

Mr Bonner wasn't best pleased at having a member of the public invade his private kingdom.

'This lady is feeling faint,' said Dot. 'She couldn't stop in that corridor, on her feet all the way to Victoria. Sit on this trunk, love.'

'Don't call the passengers "love",' hissed Mr Bonner.

'Everyone's "love" when they need a spot of looking after.' It was tempting to add 'Even you,' but she mustn't push her luck.

When they pulled into Victoria and the doors burst open, the girl got up, giving Dot a self-conscious smile.

'Thank you for . . . you know.'

'You're welcome, lass – I mean, miss. If us women can't look out for one another . . .'

The girl hesitated. For a moment, Dot wondered if she was about to receive a peck on the cheek, but the girl just nodded and stepped down onto the platform.

By the time Dot had ferried her parcels to the office to be sent on the next stage of their journeys, she felt like she had been flattened in a stampede. Aye, it had been one heck of a day and no mistake, what with goats and the packed train and that dirty old man, but you know what? It had been a bloomin' good day an' all. She had coped, maybe not always with dignity, but she had coped, and she couldn't wait to tell her friends in the buffet.

Dot Green, railway girl.

Normally Dot went up and down to Southport three times in a day, but today, for reasons that weren't explained to her, she spent the rest of the day ferrying sack trolleys of parcels outside for loading onto delivery vans and Scammell Mechanical Horses, the sight of which put her in mind of her first day. Although she was proud to have done something so important as help deliver foodstuffs in case of invasion, she couldn't prevent a loose, wobbly feeling in her tummy when she thought of the implications. The struggle for Trondheim was under way. She had never thought of Norway as being a near neighbour. Well, you didn't, did you? You thought of France and possibly Belgium. But right now, Norway felt like it might be at the other end of the East Lancs Road.

Wheeling her empty sack-barrow back inside, she glanced at the clock. You were never short of clocks to consult when you worked in a station. They were an essential piece of equipment for staff and passengers alike. She was due a break, but couldn't take it until all the parcels for Withington and West Didsbury had been loaded. She lived in Withington. Had she perhaps loaded a parcel that was destined for one of her neighbours? The idea tickled her, gave her a sense of being more than just a housewife from Heathside Lane.

Just a housewife? Blimey, housewives and mothers were the backbone of the country. Look at how women had answered the call when their menfolk went away; women who worked jolly hard all day long and then clocked off and started all over again in the house.

When she took her break, Dot didn't go into the mess.

She didn't feel like sitting down. If her aching muscles were anything to go by, she might not be able to get up again without a lot of heaving and groaning. Being a railway girl – 'railway old biddy', said Reg's voice in her head – wasn't altogether easy, especially after a physically taxing day like today, and she didn't want anybody feeling they had to make allowances for her. It could be difficult enough being female, and therefore considered to be of dubious competency, without being a poor old duck an' all.

Perhaps she would find a quiet spot on the platform near the ticket barrier, out of the way, and watch the world go by while gently rolling her shoulders so they didn't seize up. As she settled down, a porter pushed an empty trolley with a squeaky wheel down the platform, stopping at what looked like a random place, though Dot knew it would be exactly the right spot for the unloading of all the parcels. Two minutes later, she saw the puffing of approaching white clouds and heard the familiar rhythmic chuffing sound as a train approached. Both stopped as the train coasted alongside the platform. A sharp hissing sound emerged from the top of the engine as the train headed towards the buffers. The brakes screeched, followed by a clunk as the vast machine was brought to a halt. Already doors were banging open and passengers were spilling onto the platform, hurrying on their way, clutching bags, newspapers and rolled umbrellas.

Sitting in her private spot, Dot observed the bustle and hurry, grateful to have a few minutes to herself. Presently, the platform quietened again.

'Afternoon.'

'Oh – good afternoon,' said Dot.

It was that nice ticket collector.

'I think this is the first time I've seen you without a goods trolley or a sack-barrow,' he said.

She laughed. 'Make the most of it. I'll be shifting parcels again at the end of my break.'

'Not having a cuppa?'

'Not today. I thought I'd hang about here and watch the world go by.'

'Ah, a bit of thinking time. I can understand that. I won't disturb you.'

'I've just been sitting here looking at yon train. My young grandson is very interested in planes and has his aeroplane-spotter's book, but it'd be nice to be able to talk to him about trains.'

'Allow me to help out. That's the engine at the front. It's a handsome brute, isn't it? And behind it, that's the tender, where the coal and water are stored. The driver and the fireman work on the foot-plate – there, see? The fireman shovels coal into the fire-box.'

'There's still a bit of smoke and steam coming out of the funnel.' She wanted to show she knew something, however small.

The ticket collector smiled. She knew, just knew, he was about to correct her, but she also knew that he would do it in a kindly way. He wouldn't jeer at her like Reg would.

'You only get steam when the train is on the move. Anything that escapes when the train is stationary is smoke and hot gases.' His eyes twinkled. 'We have to make sure you know what you're talking about so you can impress your little lad.'

He looked at her, as if hoping for a signal to continue, but ready to withdraw if he didn't get one. He was pleasant company. Besides, Jimmy would be interested. Dot nodded.

'This long cylinder here, that's the boiler. There's water inside, and lots of tubes from one end to the other. When the fireman stokes the fire-box, hot gases get sucked through the tubes.'

'Like when the air draws on the fire at home.'

'Something like that. That's how the water is heated, and it's why you get both smoke and steam pouring out of the funnel. This round part at the front of the boiler, like a clock face without the numerals, is where the smoke-box is. Ashes build up inside there. At the end of the working day, or more often if the engine has had to work especially hard, the clock-face is opened up for the ashes to be removed.'

'Like emptying the ash-pan at home.' Dot smiled. 'Only with a lot more ashes.' She would enjoy telling Jimmy everything.

The ticket collector took a step backwards. 'I do apologise. Here's me saying I won't disturb you and what do I do but blather on about tubes and smoke-boxes.'

'You aren't disturbing me,' said Dot. 'After the day I've had, I'm glad of a friendly face.'

He smiled and his eyes crinkled. 'Been difficult, has it?'

'Interesting.'

He nodded. 'Good for you.'

'I'm sorry?'

'Making the best of it. Not complaining. Believe me, I know how much there can be to complain about at the end of an interesting day.'

The stiffness dribbled away from Dot's shoulders. A pleasant warmth, incorporating a suggestion of rejuvenation, infused her body. Rejuvenation? How daft. As if a few kind words could buck you up like that. But it was heartening to be complimented. And that was daft an' all. He didn't mean it as a compliment. He was just commenting.

'I shan't be offended if you say no,' he said, 'but I'm due a break now and I'd like to hear about your day, as long as you don't complain about it, of course,' he added with a twinkle. 'Here comes Miss Johnson to take over from me. Charming girl. I trained her.'

'How do, Mr Thirkle.' Miss Johnson was all rosy cheeks and confidence. Very jolly hockey sticks.

Thirkle. That was an unusual name. Mr Thirkle smiled and nodded to Miss Johnson as he and Dot walked away.

'Let's walk up and down the concourse,' she said. 'We might actually be able to do it without tripping over anyone's luggage.'

'That'll make a change, after the crowds earlier.' He fell in step beside her, clasping his hands behind his back. 'You possibly heard Miss Johnson call me Mr Thirkle.'

'And I'm Mrs Green.'

'Pleased to meet you properly.'

'Likewise,' said Dot.

They ambled past the long wood-panelled ticket office, with its elegant curve at either end and the line of windows where passengers queued to purchase their tickets from the booths. Above the centre of the office was a panelled wooden arch with a clock in the middle. Dot described her crowded train and the problems of shunting her parcels about, then went on to her adventure with the goats, chuckling along with Mr Thirkle.

'Thanks for being understanding,' she said. 'I'm afraid Mr Bonner will tell everybody what a hash I made of it.'

'It doesn't matter if he does. All the best railway stories involve animals. "Stop that goat – it's a parcel!" That's a classic, that is.'

'Is it?'

'Good enough to be a catchphrase on *It's That Man Again*.'

'I love listening to *ITMA* on the wireless. Who's your favourite character?'

'Excuse me.' It was a harassed-looking young man. 'Can you direct me to Lost Property, please?'

After that they were asked about platform tickets, taxis and Left Luggage.

Mr Thirkle smiled ruefully. 'So much for having a chat.'

Dot looked at the clock. 'Time for me to start again.'

'I'll walk back to the parcels office with you, if I may. How are you getting along with Mr Bonner?'

'I take it you're aware of his opinion of women working on the railways?'

'He isn't the only one, Mrs Green. There's a lot of ill-feeling about it, which, given the circumstances, is unfortunate, to say the least. What you have to remember is that Mr Bonner – well, no, it isn't my place to talk about him. But to become a train guard takes, I don't know, twenty-five or thirty years maybe, starting out as a lad-porter and working your way up. It's the same to be a ticket inspector, though you'd do that through ticket work, not portering. And now, all these ladies have come along . . .'

'And we've been put straight into jobs that men had to work up to,' said Dot. 'But that's not our fault. There's a war on.'

'I know, Mrs Green. I remember the sterling work that was done by ladies in the last war. But I can also see why it's hard for some railwaymen to swallow what's happening now.'

'They should think a bit less about their pride and a bit more about what their country needs – oh, I'm sorry, Mr Thirkle, I don't mean to snap at you. In fact, I ought to thank you for bothering to explain to me.'

'My pleasure. Is Mr Bonner making things difficult for you?'

'Not really. I know my job and I do it. But . . .' Yes, she would say it. 'I don't feel I could turn to him for support.'

Mr Thirkle nodded, but didn't encourage her to expand. She liked him for it. He wasn't nosy.

'Has he explained to you Rule 55?' he asked.

'Rule 55? What's that?'

'That means he hasn't. Don't get me wrong. It isn't in the rules that the parcels porters should be able to follow it, but I think, in our present circumstances, that they should be trained. But that's just me.'

'What's Rule 55?'

'It's to do with keeping the train safe if it has to stop unexpectedly.'

'I'll ask Mr Bonner to show me,' said Dot, immediately following it with, 'No, maybe not. It'd only get his back up.'

'I could maybe find a guard who'd show you.'

'Really? You'd do that?'

'Like I say, I think it should be automatic that you're trained. Just in case, you know.'

Someone walked over Dot's grave. *Just in case.*

'Thanks for the offer,' she said. 'I appreciate it, but I'd rather sort it out for myself. No offence.'

'None taken. You're an independent lady, I can see that. But if you can't find someone to show you, come back to me, won't you? Don't be proud.' Mr Thirkle stopped. 'Here we are.' They were a few yards from the door to the parcels office. 'Thank you for your company, though I'm afraid most of the company was courtesy of members of the public.'

'That doesn't matter. Helping folk is part of the job. They weren't to know we were meant to be having a break.'

'Well, it was nice to see you, anyroad.'

Dot gave him a nod and went back to work. Mr Thirkle's insight had given her something to think about and, later on, she talked it over with her friends in the buffet.

'. . . so, you see, that's why some of the blokes aren't pleased to have us here,' she finished.

'You're not telling us you've softened towards Mr Bonner,' said Joan, 'after the way he's behaved?'

'No, I've not softened, but I'm glad to have an

understanding of his point of view. I'm not saying the way he treats me is right. I'm just saying I can understand it better.'

'Well, I think that's very magnanimous of you,' said Alison, 'and far more than he deserves. So what if he worked for donkey's years to achieve his position? The country is at war, for heaven's sake.'

'He should be glad of the help,' said Mabel, 'and so should all the other men.'

'Especially those that are working alongside someone like you,' Lizzie added.

Dot was warmed by their support and made a point of giving each of them a special smile as, one by one, they left to go home. Then it was just her and Cordelia at the table.

Cordelia smiled. 'They were certainly fierce on your behalf, weren't they?'

'I hope I haven't turned them against their male colleagues.'

'They're sensible girls,' said Cordelia. 'They know that most of the men are perfectly decent.'

Aye, Mr Thirkle was, for one. What a shame they hadn't had the chance for a proper chat. Dot sensed they would get along.

The next day, as she was hurrying out of the station to head for home, she passed him standing beside the war memorial. She stopped. He seemed to be reading the names. She bit her lip, undecided. Then she went to stand beside him.

'Evening,' she said softly. 'Tell me if I'm intruding.'

'Good evening, Mrs Green. No, you're not intruding. I'm just . . . well, I like to spend a bit of time here now and then.'

Dot looked at the lists of names. A wave of emotion coursed through her. Her own boys were far away. Would she ever see them again? Oh, please, let them come home safe. *This tablet is erected to perpetuate the memory of the men . . .* Her knees felt no more solid than trifle with too much sherry in it. Would Archie's and Harry's names one day be commemorated like this? She couldn't bear it.

'Mrs Green?'

And here she was, with emotion rolling around inside her, when this was Mr Thirkle's special time at the memorial. She should be supporting him.

'Did you know any of them?' she asked. *Pte Colman, W A . . . Pte Commons, J . . . Pte Conlan, T . . . Sgt Connolly, B J . . .* 'Eh, I'm sorry.' She threw her hand across her mouth. 'Hark at me, asking you that like it's a piece of gossip.'

Mr Thirkle let his fingertips rest briefly on the bronze. 'I did know some of them. I think of our boys going off now to fight in a war that was never meant to happen. The war to end all wars: that's what we were told about the last one. And here we are, with another generation of men heading off to war, already there, most of them.'

'Oh, Mr Thirkle.' Dot felt a need to put her hand on his arm, wanted to show him that she understood, but of course she didn't touch him. 'Folk of our generation carry such sorrow, don't we?'

'I look at all these names listed here and feel as if I knew every single one of them.'

Chapter Fourteen

Joan sat at her desk, transferring numbers and costs from charging sheets to invoices, pleasantly aware of her new, fashionable skirt length. She didn't feel the need to tuck her legs away any more. Now she was happy to place her feet forward of her chair, one ankle demurely hooked behind the other. She felt trim and modern. It even made her feel better about typing invoices all day long.

The door to the charging office opened and Mr Clark came through, as he did every day, to walk between the desks, nodding a greeting here, pausing there to pick up an invoice and scrutinise it.

'Just so we know we're all working for him,' according to Miss Bligh of the Greta Garbo hair. 'As if we could forget!'

Mr Clark proceeded slowly up the office, making one or two stops along the way. Then he halted beside Joan's desk. A dull, sinking feeling crept into her tummy. She ignored it, or tried to. She finished typing the invoice and checked it against the paperwork beside her typewriter. But she wasn't really checking. Although her eyes moved between the two sheets of paper, her mind didn't join in. She wound the invoice out of the machine. Mr Clark would be gone in a moment.

'May I?' He held out his hand.

She gave him the charging sheet and her invoice. It would be polite to look up at him while he examined them, but she didn't feel polite. She felt wary and self-conscious.

Trapped. That was how he made her feel. Trapped. Ever since the horrid occasion when he had made her share his seat. And she had gone along with it. What would Gran say to that? She would be outraged at Mr Clark's behaviour, of course – but she would also read something into Joan's behaviour. Sharing a seat with a man was the sort of thing her mother might have done.

'Good work. Thank you, Miss Foster.'

Mr Clark didn't hand her the sheets of paper, didn't oblige her to receive them from him. He laid them on her desk, which made her feel daft. Honestly, the sharing-a-chair thing had been a one-off, and there really hadn't been any spare chairs in the charging office. Was she making something out of nothing? Her tingling skin didn't think so. It hadn't thought so then and it didn't think so now.

Mr Clark moved on. Joan picked up the next charging sheet and was halfway through typing it when Mr Clark reappeared beside her. He didn't ask for anything. He bent over, placing one hand on the edge of her desk and the other on the back of her chair. She fixed her gaze on the invoice poking out of the top of her typewriter.

'Nice legs.'

Shocked, she couldn't help glancing up at him, couldn't help but see the cocksure way he raised his eyebrows at her. She looked away at once, but couldn't un-see it. Heat erupted in the back of her neck, sweeping round to fill her face. She ducked her head over her work. If only she had lots of hair, like Jeanette MacDonald in *The Girl of the Golden West*, so she could whip out her hair grips, let it swing across her face and hide behind it.

She wanted to hide her legs too, tuck them away out of sight under her chair, but that would be tantamount to admitting she had done something wrong. And she hadn't.

She was a nice girl. Not like Estelle, not like her mother. She was a decent girl.

Wasn't she?

'What's the matter with him?' Letitia demanded from her place in front of the dressing table, where she was titivating her hair. Rollers lay scattered across the dressing table's polished wooden surface. One had landed in Joan's trinket dish, where she kept her emery board, tweezers and nail scissors.

'Nothing's wrong with him.' Did there have to be something wrong with Toby Collins for her not to want to go out with him? Joan felt a flutter of frustration. Standing behind Letitia, she unwound her rollers, reaching around her sister to drop them into the ceramic dish painted with daisies, on her side of the dressing-table. 'He's perfectly agreeable.'

'And he can dance. You have to admit he can dance.'

'So can lots of chaps. It doesn't mean I want to have them as boyfriends.'

'It would be lovely to go out as a foursome.'

Joan froze, arms raised, elbows sticking out, fingers on a roller. She flexed her fingers to get the blood moving again and unwound the roller, dropping it in her dish.

'Are you tired of me tagging along when you and Steven go out?'

She would die if the answer was yes. She would die if Steven was fed up of her.

Letitia gave her fair hair a final twiddle, then carefully tucked it inside her snood. She turned round. 'Oh, sweetie, don't say that. Don't ever say that. We love having you along. Steven's ever so fond of you, you know that.'

Ever so fond. Oh aye, ever so fond, in a big brother, little sister kind of way. Joan's muscles suddenly felt rigid and sharply defined. It was wrong, wrong, wrong to have feelings for her sister's boyfriend. What if anyone should find out? The thought brought a thick sensation to her throat. But no amount of shame would make her feelings for Steven go away.

'Here, let me help.'

Letitia expertly twisted the remaining rollers from her sister's hair, Joan intercepting them before she could fling them willy-nilly onto the dressing-table to get mixed up with her own. She stood with her hands cupped in front of her for Letitia to drop the rest into, then opened her hands above the daisy-painted dish.

'I'll do your hair.' Letitia picked up the comb. 'Sit down. Are you positive you don't want to go out with Toby Collins?'

'I've already said.' Umpteen times.

'He's a good egg. Steven and I would never have got you together if we hadn't thought he was suitable. Why not give him a chance?'

'There's no point. I'm sure he's very nice and all the rest of it, but I just didn't like him in that way.'

'That doesn't mean anything.'

Letitia drew on Joan's snood, gently lifting her hair into it so as not to spoil the curls. Times were when wearing a snood had made Joan feel grown-up, but now she would much rather wear her hair loose. Not that Gran would ever permit it.

'I'd known Steven a while before we clicked,' said Letitia.

Joan stared at her in the mirror. Letitia hadn't fallen instantly in love with Steven? Unbelievable. Personally, she had fallen for him the moment she'd set eyes on him.

'There was an article, apparently, in one of the Sunday papers,' Letitia went on, 'written by some lord or other. The girls at work were talking about it. He said that any girl in this war who ends up not married simply isn't trying. Well, that's you, my girl.' She bent over, putting her face beside Joan's so the two of them could look at their reflections. 'You're not trying.'

Are *you* trying? Cold poured through Joan. She didn't dare ask out loud. A good and loving sister would want to bask in the details of her sister's romance, but Joan couldn't ask those questions. She couldn't bear Steven to get married, but at the same time she did want, she truly did want, her beloved Letitia to be happy, and if that meant her marrying Steven . . .

Joan rose and scooped up Letitia's scattered rollers, dumping them in the small wicker box on Letitia's side of the dressing table.

'I mean it,' she said, hands busy, face averted. 'I don't want to go out with Toby. Can you tell Steven to make sure he knows?'

'If I must.'

'You must.'

Letitia picked up her leather handbag with the padded handle and her gas-mask box. 'But I'm not seeing him for a day or two, so you've still got time to change your mind.'

First to arrive in the buffet, Joan bagged a table and settled down to wait for the others. Cordelia was next through the door, and a minute later Dot joined the queue. Joan chewed her lip. She would much prefer the company of one or two of the girls her own age. But why? If the whole group was meant to be friends, then the chance of a few minutes with Cordelia and Dot before the others arrived was a good thing, surely?

Dot and Cordelia took their seats and the three of them exchanged pleasantries.

'Have you started your first-aid classes?' Cordelia asked Joan.

'Yes. I'm in a class in Seymour Grove with Mabel and Lizzie. I'd have liked Alison to be in the same class, but you have to train near where you're going to be stationed, supposing you pass the test, of course.'

'There's no need to ask how you're getting along with Lizzie,' Cordelia remarked. 'I can't imagine her failing to get on with anyone. But I wonder how you're getting on with Mabel?'

Had she hidden how startled she felt? 'Fine.'

'Really?' Cordelia raised an eyebrow. 'I'm asking because of all you young girls, Mabel seems – reserved is the only way I can describe it. A girl with the confidence to move away from home isn't a shy little scaredy-cat, yet she doesn't seem to join in with the rest of us.'

Joan nodded. 'We had to twist her arm to get her to come to the pictures.'

'She's a bit of an oddity,' said Cordelia.

'But likeable with it,' said Dot. 'It'll all come out in the wash.'

Joan thought about it afterwards. What if she sought Gran's permission to invite Mabel and Lizzie to come home with her after work on first-aid nights, so they could go to class together? Lizzie would love it, she felt sure, and maybe it would encourage Mabel to let down her defences. It was worth a try.

When she suggested it in the buffet, Lizzie pounced on the idea and, the following day, reported that her mum was all in favour.

'She doesn't like me going to Seymour Grove and back on my own of an evening, but thanks to your kind invitation, I'll go to first aid with you and we have a neighbour who works evenings in a hotel near where we do first aid and she says we can travel home together.'

'A sensible arrangement,' said Gran when Joan told her. 'Naturally Lizzie's mother wants to protect her.'

Gran was all in favour of protective parents. She was a bit iffy when she heard about Mabel – a girl of twenty-two, living away from home.

'That's not right,' she declared. 'What sort of family lets a girl that age go off on her own?'

'Plenty of girls are joining up,' said Joan.

'That's different,' said Gran, 'and don't answer back. Where is her family, anyway?'

'I'm not sure. Lancashire somewhere.'

'And they let her leave home and come here to live on her own? They should know better.'

'She had to come here,' said Joan. 'This is where she was given her railway job.'

'Then the authorities should know better,' Gran retorted.

'It's wartime, Gran.' Letitia joined in on Joan's side. 'All sorts of old-fashioned rules are being set aside.'

Gran sniffed. 'In wartime, it's all the more important for old-fashioned rules, as you call them, to be respected. I'm not convinced that this Mabel girl sounds the right sort.'

'Oh, Gran, I promise you she is.' A twinge of anxiety flicked its way through Joan. Gran wasn't going to decline having Mabel in the house, was she? 'She's obviously from, if not the top drawer, then a drawer not far from the top. Wait until you see her clothes. They weren't run up in her spare time on her mum's sewing-machine.'

'Hmm.' Gran pursed her lips thoughtfully. She was a great believer in the upper classes knowing best. Her frown lifted and smoothed out. 'We'll see.'

Lizzie and Mabel's first visit to their house was a success. With her perfect manners, Mabel was just what Gran liked.

She had brought a jar of honey and a box of Cadbury's Roses with her.

'Please accept them with my good wishes,' she said to Gran. 'You'd be doing me a favour, really. My mother sends me tuck boxes, would you believe? Honestly, you'd think I was at boarding school.'

'Cadbury's Roses,' said Gran. 'I've heard of those.'

'They've been around a year or so,' said Mabel. 'They're all wrapped up one by one in crinkly paper. Our cat loves it. We screw up the paper and flick it across the room for her to chase – well, Pops and I do. My mother despairs of us. I can see you would too, Mrs Foster.' Mabel waved a hand to indicate the parlour. 'You keep your home spotless.'

Joan held her breath. Would Gran take offence? But Gran said, 'Aye, I do. And thank you for the gifts, though they weren't necessary. My girls' friends are welcome here.'

'Thank you,' said Mabel.

And Gran was just as pleased with Lizzie, if not more so. Well, that was hardly surprising. Everyone warmed to Lizzie. She was such a love, with her happy smile and a good word for everyone. All heart, was Lizzie. Gran didn't exactly warm to her. It was hard to imagine Gran warming to anyone. But Joan could see she approved of Lizzie and she certainly approved of Lizzie's loving, watchful mother.

'What a handsome man,' said Lizzie when Gran had left the room to put the kettle on. She was gazing at the studio portrait of Daddy, with rather the same expression that came over her face when she talked about Clark Gable. 'Is that your father?' She sounded wistful. Remembering her own dad? 'I remember you said he died a long time ago.'

'That's right,' said Joan.

'I like the way he's not looking at the camera, but into the distance,' said Lizzie. 'It makes you wonder what he's thinking about.'

'His beautiful wife and daughters, I expect,' said Mabel.

Joan froze. She and Letitia had grown up fielding remarks about Estelle and diverting the conversation, but that didn't mean it was easy or painless. The never-ending shame was always there, hidden mostly by a false smile or in an unseen tremble.

'That picture was taken long before he got married,' she said. There was something startling about hearing Estelle referred to as beautiful. Of course, Mabel was only being polite, but even so. Gran had never said Estelle was beautiful, but then she wouldn't, would she? Was it unusual not to have any idea what your mother looked like? Or was that something that was confined to families like theirs – families with secrets?

'I can see where your Letitia gets her looks from,' said Lizzie.

Nature had given Daddy and Letitia the same features, carving them into perfect versions of masculine and feminine. They shared the same narrow face, the same sharpness about the chin, the same shape of eyes and mouth, though Letitia's features were a finer, softer version of Daddy's, and their colouring was different. Letitia was fair, Daddy dark. Obviously this had always made her special to Gran, while Joan's appearance – well, just whom did she resemble? People were always comparing family members to one another, even with tiny babies, but there was no one to say whom Joan looked like. Only Gran, and she had never breathed a word. Had Joan's looks come from Estelle?

Was this . . . was this why Gran despised her?

The short conversation about Daddy's photograph was the only hiccup that occurred and since it happened when Gran wasn't present, there was no harm done. Joan relaxed, looking forward to the rest of the evening.

It was fun to go to first aid together. She, Mabel, Lizzie

and Letitia hung up their things and helped to set out the rows of uncomfortable wooden chairs. When the session began, Mr Bennet, who was in charge, took his place in front of the class, carrying a lidded bucket. Miss Lloyd, his assistant, laid an oil-cloth on the floor, whereupon Mr Bennet announced, 'You have to be prepared for anything, including blood and guts.' He removed the lid and upended the bucket over the oil-cloth, spilling out a quantity of offal to accompanying shrieks from his audience, and two ladies fainted clean away.

'At least it gave us the chance to see some real first aid in action,' said Mabel when they left at the end of the evening.

'What I want to know,' said Letitia, 'is where that oil-cloth came from and where it's going back to. I hope he didn't pinch it off Mrs Bennet's kitchen table.'

The others groaned at the thought, then laughed.

'Well, this sounds jolly.'

Lizzie smiled round at the little group. 'This is Mrs O'Grady from up our road. We're going home together.'

Mrs O'Grady nodded to the girls. 'Got plenty of home-work, have you?'

'I'll say,' said Mabel. 'Loads to learn by heart.'

Joan was glad that Letitia was doing first aid as well. It was easier to learn things together; they would test one another on how to treat primary shock so it didn't lead to secondary shock, and the different types of war gases.

'That's scary,' said Joan one evening. 'We've been carrying gas masks around all this time and now I truly understand why.' It was a sobering thought.

'Some men never recovered from being gassed in the last war,' said Letitia. Another sobering thought.

When it came to the final session, which was when they

were due to be tested, a gentleman attended, whom they hadn't seen before. The atmosphere was taut with anxiety as the group sat on chairs in a semi-circle. One fellow rubbed the back of his neck; a lady bounced her foot up and down; another couldn't stop looking around the room. Joan knew how they felt. She was nervous too.

'Good evening, ladies and gentlemen,' the new man greeted them. 'My name is Haslett and I'm the area organiser for the first-aid parties that are going to be added to those we've already got trained. Those of you who pass the test tonight will be invited to take part in an afternoon event, and those who do well in that will be assigned to first-aid parties in first-aid depots. At the afternoon event, there will be folk from other first-aid training groups like this one, as well as some men from the emergency services, who are already trained in first aid.'

Letitia nudged Joan. Steven was going to attend the afternoon event they would be at if they passed.

'I know from experience,' went on Mr Haslett, 'that occasionally someone puts themselves forward for this duty in the mistaken belief that a first-aider's duty won't commence until the all-clear sounds, so I want to make it plain to you that, if you are appointed to a first-aid party or station, you will be working throughout the air raids – and they will come, believe me.'

Dread clenched inside Joan's tummy, but she sat up straighter, aware of Letitia on one side of her and Mabel on the other doing the same.

'One final thing, before you take your test,' said Mr Haslett. 'Many people volunteer for this with their brother or their cousins or some other family member. Suppose that two brothers pass both this test and the afternoon one. They won't be assigned to the same first-aid party. That's against our rules.'

Letitia put up her hand. 'May I ask why? I'm here with my sister.'

'And naturally you had hoped to work together. That's understandable,' said Mr Haslett. 'To be blunt, young lady, the reason we separate family members is that it will reduce the chances of both of you being killed.'

Chapter Fifteen

Mabel felt bewildered by her growing friendship with Joan and Lizzie. How could she have got herself into this position? She had never expected to find friends again. She hadn't been looking for any kind of closeness. In fact, she had deliberately held herself aloof from it. Yet closeness seemed to be developing whether she wanted it or not – and she didn't want it.

Oh, but she did. In her heart, she did. Losing Althea had left a gaping hole in her life and Joan's innate kindness and Lizzie's irrepressible good cheer had worked their way into a corner of that hole. So had Letitia's common sense and wry humour. And Dot's cosy good nature. Even Cordelia's polished civility had come to mean something to her, because of the consideration behind it.

Guilt swarmed through her, making it hard to breathe. She tugged at her collar. It wasn't right to find companionship with others. What sort of person was she? The beating of her heart sent self-loathing pounding around her body. Althea could have answered that question. In fact, she had answered it with piercing clarity just before . . .

She huffed out a tight breath. She had come here to escape from all that, from the memories, the guilt. Stupid idea. As if she could ever leave them behind. But at least here she wasn't surrounded by people who knew what she had done. Mind you, the folk back home knew only a fraction of what had really happened. The only person left who knew everything was herself – the one person she couldn't escape from.

No, that wasn't true. There was somebody else left who knew. But there might as well not have been, because they would never see one another again.

The enormity of what had happened pinned her to her armchair. It was an actual weight inside her chest. If she moved, it might clog her windpipe, stop her heart.

Except that it wouldn't. Goodness knows, she had wanted it to enough times, back at home in wind-blown Annerby, with little to do other than boggle at what she had brought about.

Was this – was this the first time the black weight had clobbered her since she left home? That in itself was something to be ashamed of.

Was it possible to be too busy and too tired to feel like that? Toiling long hours on the permanent way, lifting heavy sleepers and shovelling ballast, was back-breaking work. Her body had toughened and grown stronger and she slept like a log. She ought to lie awake every night, crippled by grief, as she had night after night on her feather-bed at home, but instead she slept deeply and probably snored like a pig.

Her hands clenched around the studded arm of the old leather armchair. Her bedroom at Mrs Grayson's house looked as though there had been an explosion in a wool shop. A vast patchwork bedspread knitted in every colour under the sun was so huge it touched the floor on both sides of the bed. Inside the dumpy little wardrobe, the coat hangers had been padded and covered with knitted sleeves, while mats knitted in fern lace stitch adorned the dressing-table and the top of the chest of drawers; the lower half of the tiny wash-stand in the corner boasted a knitted curtain in dandelion stitch. The only thing not knitted was the rag rug beside the bed.

It was quite possibly the most ghastly room in the whole

of Lancashire, if not the whole of England. Mabel hadn't minded much, to start with. She seemed to remember finding it quaint. Quaint! Anyway, she had been too eager to escape from Darley Court and the Honourable Persephone to care much where she ended up. This was the place Cousin Harriet had found for her and she had grabbed it with both hands.

She was allowed to call Mrs Mitchell 'Cousin Harriet' now that she had moved out of Darley Court. She visited Cousin Harriet once a week. To begin with, this had been to keep Mumsy and Pops sweet so that they didn't worry about her being cast adrift in a strange place and come racing down here to haul her home, but now Cousin Harriet was part of the routine and . . . yes. Mabel sighed. Cousin Harriet's blunt, no-nonsense attitude had wormed its way into the vast hole left by Althea's loss.

One person she was in no danger whatsoever of coming to care about was Mrs Grayson.

'I've found you a place to live,' Cousin Harriet had informed her a few weeks back, during an hour together in her private sitting room below stairs. Cousin Harriet was busy darning. Mabel hadn't been doing anything, unless you counted hiding from Persephone.

'You're an angel,' Mabel had exclaimed. 'Where?'

'Not so far from here. Well, what did you expect? The folk I know are hereabouts, and, anyroad, what would your mum and dad say if I sent you off miles away? You'll be lodging with a Mrs Amanda Grayson. You'll have your own bedroom with wash-stand – use of bathroom to be negotiated – and all meals provided.'

Mabel had imagined Cousin Harriet writing those very words in a letter to Annerby. Maybe she had already written them. Maybe Mumsy and Pops had already consented – now there was a thought.

'It sounds splendid,' she said.

'I don't know about splendid, but it'll do.' Cousin Harriet did a few swift over-stitches to finish off, then snipped her thread and thrust the garment at Mabel. 'Fold that, will you?' Her other hand was already reaching over the side of her armchair to delve into the mending basket for the next piece. 'You and Mrs Grayson will be doing one another a favour.'

Mabel examined the darn. The cardigan's elbow was as good as new. 'Doing favours? How so?'

'She'll give you a roof over your head and you can do the shopping. Mrs Grayson doesn't leave the house.'

'Why? Can't she walk?'

'Aye, she can walk, but she doesn't go out. She used to send messages to the butcher and the grocer and have her foodstuff delivered, same as lots of folk, but now that rationing's here, everyone has to go and fetch their own.'

'And that'll be my job?'

'That'll be your job.'

So Mabel moved in with Mrs Grayson and spent some of her spare time traipsing round the local shops. She didn't mind, in the sense that she wasn't stuck up about it, but she quickly came to mind very much the sheer inconvenience. Her respect for Dot and all working wives and mothers knew no bounds. How did they manage full-time work as well as running a home and feeding a family? Belatedly, she realised that it must be the same for Cordelia, though Cordelia was so composed, it was difficult to imagine her impatiently bouncing on her toes in the queue at the butcher's.

Why couldn't Mrs Grayson do the shopping? Why couldn't she leave the house? There didn't appear to be anything wrong with her. It seemed to Mabel to be more a case of *wouldn't* than *couldn't*. In which case, what had she

179

got against doing her own shopping? Maybe she could ask when they knew one another better.

No. Absolutely not. She wasn't going to cultivate her landlady. Apart from meals, she was going to keep to her room. It was better that way. Safer. The closeness she was in two minds about developing with her fellow railway girls was one thing. She could explain that away by recognising its usefulness, and the fact that she lived separately from them automatically set limits on it. But if she once permitted any kind of closeness with Mrs Grayson, it would be impossible to escape.

'I'm sorry, Mrs Grayson.' Mabel had put her foot down early on. 'I know you want me to go round the shops every day, but I simply haven't time.'

'But that's how shopping is done,' said Mrs Grayson. 'That's how you get everything fresh.'

She was around Mumsy's age, but where Mumsy was expensively dressed and perfectly corseted and had her hair done every week, Mrs Grayson had a look of the genteel poor about her. Her clothes had once been good, but that had been some time ago, and she wore her hair in a bun, which Mumsy said was ageing. A hair-cut by a stylist who knew what she was doing would have tidied up Mrs Grayson no end.

'Shopping every day isn't feasible,' Mabel declared. 'I'm happy to help out, but you'll have to give me shopping lists to cover several days.'

Mrs Grayson wasn't pleased, but she agreed. She was an excellent cook, for whom the sugar rationing was merely a spur to finding sweetness in other ingredients, though when Mabel realised she was enjoying the meals, guilt stormed through her. Her appetite, which had fled in the wake of Althea's death, had returned. What a rat she was. She couldn't even manage to be indifferent to the savoury tang of mince and onions or the welcome sweetness of coconut and raisin pudding. It was just another way in which she was betraying the friend she had lost. Was that stupid of her? Possibly. Probably. But it was how she felt.

'Stop wallowing,' said Grandad's voice inside her head, so clearly that she gasped.

Goodness, that was an old memory. She couldn't remember now exactly what had happened, only that Mumsy and Pops had made a terrific fuss over her for something and she had let them, even though, really and truly, she'd felt better and was just revelling in the attention.

Then Grandad had come along, summing up the situation with a single glance. 'Don't encourage her. She's wallowing,' he said firmly.

Well, yes, fair enough, a daft little girl feeling sorry for herself and letting her parents coddle her, might have been wallowing, but that didn't apply now. The situation now bore no resemblance to that one.

Besides, if anyone was wallowing, it was Mrs Grayson. Whatever her reason for living her life entirely indoors, it wasn't a physical infirmity. She had no trouble keeping the house clean or cooking meals. She spent all her spare time knitting – garments, doilies, cushion covers, you name it. Dear heaven, the only thing in this house that hadn't been knitted was the bricks and mortar. That was another of Mabel's jobs – buying the wool, either from the shop or at the market in the form of old knitted clothes that could be unravelled and knitted up as something else.

'I'm now on passing-the-time-of-day terms with the local shopkeepers and the couple who run the second-hand clothes stall.' She made a point of sounding cheery about it when she was in the buffet. She didn't want the others thinking she was a crosspatch who didn't like helping out in her digs.

And she was happy enough in Mrs Grayson's house. It was better than being stuck in Darley Court.

Not that she had left Darley Court behind altogether. As well as visiting Cousin Harriet, she also called on Miss Brown from time to time. That was good manners. As far as was feasible, she steered clear of Persephone on these visits. It would be too horrid for words if the worst happened and the Honourable Persephone recalled having seen her in London, during the Season Mabel had found so excruciatingly difficult. Sometimes, though, they were bound to run into one another. On these occasions, Persephone was charm itself, but Mabel couldn't afford to let her guard down.

Even so, in spite of the hot flutters of embarrassment she felt when in Persephone's company, it was impossible to ignore that she had a certain admiration for her. For all her high-born pedigree, Persephone was courteous and kind to all, regardless of station. In different circumstances, Mabel would have liked her.

Should she stop going to Darley Court? No. As well as becoming fond of Cousin Harriet, she truly liked the mistress of the house. She might be elderly, but she was as sharp as a tack.

'Plenty of manor-houses have been commandeered by the powers that be.' This was one of Miss Brown's favourite subjects. 'But over my rotting corpse will that happen here.'

'I know,' Mabel agreed. 'That's why you let the cellars be used for storing valuable collections.'

'I'm doing more than that, my dear. Now that the cellars are full, I've invited all the local Civil Defence groups to hold meetings and training sessions here – Air Raid Precautions, Auxiliary Fire Service, Gas Decontamination and all the rest, not forgetting the WVS.' Removing her spectacles, Miss Brown jabbed the air with them, as she often did when she wanted to emphasise a point. 'If the powers that be intend to nab Darley Court for themselves, they'll have to push a lot of noses out of joint to achieve it.'

'No one's going to get the better of you.' Mabel couldn't help chuckling.

'I've had to be clever,' replied Miss Brown. 'It comes of being plain. Now then, tell me about your first-aid test. When is it?'

'Day after tomorrow.'

The test turned out to be pretty stiff. True to form when faced with an examination, Mabel's brain froze solid and she would have made a real pig's ear of treating a broken forearm if Joan hadn't casually touched a newspaper lying on the table beside her, which prompted Mabel to use the paper to make a splint, which she had fastened in position with bandages. Was that cheating? Mabel didn't care if it was. It would be horrid if the others passed and she didn't. It surprised her how much she wanted to pass, and not just so she would be able to help the injured, but because she was coming to value the others' companionship.

Could it be that after turning her back on everyone following the tragedy of losing Althea, she was now turning back to people again?

She hadn't come here to find new friends. But even so, was that happening?

At the end of the first-aid test, Mabel, Joan, Lizzie and Letitia clustered together near the church hall door. The routine was that everyone left together once the lights were extinguished. They slung their gas-mask cases over their shoulders and delved in handbags and pockets for their torches, for all the good they did, given that the beam had to be covered by layers of tissue paper. The lights clicked off and the door opened.

'You never get used to it, do you?' Mabel remarked. 'The

darkness is so dense. It always comes as a shock, or is it just me?'

'No, it's not just you,' the others assured her.

Lizzie's neighbour, who usually accompanied her home, wasn't working this evening, so, rather than send Lizzie home alone on the bus to Whalley Range, she had been invited to spend the night with the Fosters.

'You'll have to top 'n' tail with Letitia and me,' Joan said. 'It'll be a squeeze, but we'll manage for one night.'

Mabel hadn't exactly pretended not to hear, but she had poked about inside her handbag and even feigned a relieved smile as she 'found' something. Did the others think she should invite Lizzie back to her digs?

The four of them walked arm in arm through the black-out, torches poking out in front of them, giggling helplessly when they walked straight into a barrier of sandbags. By the time they had queued up at what they thought was the bus-stop, only to realise it was a lamp post, they were in near hysterics.

'You wait till I tell my mum,' said Lizzie. 'She loves me going out with my friends.'

Next to Mabel in the linked line, Lizzie squeezed her arm warmly. Mabel felt a small thrill of surprise, then alarm. These girls really did see her as their friend.

Maybe they wouldn't be so keen on her if they knew the shabby way in which she had betrayed her last friend.

It was time to take the weight off her feet. Dot perched on a tan-coloured leather steamer trunk and gazed at the scenery as the stopping train made its way to Leeds. She had been on this route for a couple of days now, thanks to the sickness that had resulted in several porters being shunted about. Heavy, purple-edged clouds hung low over a rain-darkened landscape, but she couldn't have felt any more carefree if it had been a day of glorious sunshine and she was looking out on chocolate-box villages in pretty valleys. She shook her head. What a dafty she was. But being free of Mr Bonner for a few days was a real pleasure, the more so because the guard on the stopping train to Leeds, Mr Emmet, who had come out of retirement for the duration, had welcomed her aboard and was proving to be cheerful company. Once his duties were taken care of, he was happy to sit in his captain's chair by the circular handbrake and have a chat about the places he had visited over the years, using his privilege tickets.

How long before the staff who had caught the sickness bug returned to work and she was plonked back on Mr Bonner's train? She couldn't afford to wait any longer. She wanted to ask, and she knew just how to do it an' all. A white lie? Maybe. But it was something she needed to know.

'Mr Emmet, would you explain Rule 55 to me? I don't know what it is, only that it's important, and I'd like to understand it. I'm sure my young grandson would be interested to hear about it.'

'Aye, they love trains, do young lads. You're right, it is important, possibly the most important thing a guard is called upon to do. It's about keeping the train safe if it has to make an unexpected stop between signals, in dense fog, say, or if there's been an accident. You have to make sure you aren't ploughed into from behind.'

Dot shuddered. It didn't bear thinking about. Something crumpled inside her. Then she pulled her spine as straight as it would go. All the more reason for her to know about it.

'In fact, I'll do better than tell you, lass. I'll show you – well, as much as I can without doing it for real, if you get my drift. There'll be time when we're at Leeds.'

'Thank you,' said Dot. Oh, to work alongside a charming old boy like this every day. Wouldn't that be grand?

Later, Mr Emmet showed her the procedure.

'Before you start, Mr Emmet.' She took her pencil from her pocket and reached for an old luggage label. 'I'll write it down if you don't mind, so I don't forget when I tell our Jimmy.'

'Fair enough. Here, see. This is the hand-brake. You put this on, like so, and then open the vacuum-brake valve, and that means the train can't move off. Then you need three of these – see?' He held out some small round discs, about the size of a half-crown. 'These are the detonators. You climb out and walk back along the track five hundred yards or so and use these little straps to fix the detonators to the top of the track, ten yards apart from one another. Then you come back to the train and tell the driver you've carried out Rule 55. If another train comes along, there'll be three loud bangs as it goes over them, and the driver knows he has to stop. See?'

'Thanks. Our Jimmy will love hearing about that.'

She hadn't asked about Rule 55 for Jimmy's benefit, but it was true that he would relish hearing about it, just like he had lapped up her description of the train passing fields scattered with wooden posts, vast cross-sections of pipe and even old motor cars, all put there to prevent enemy troop carriers from landing. Eh, what was it about lads that made them so keen on all the details of the war?

But when she arrived home, she was hardly through the front door and reaching for her pinny when Sheila flew in through the back door, her coat flapping open and Jimmy in tow. It couldn't be that much of a panic, though, as she had obviously found a minute to touch up her powder and lipstick – or was that Dot being cynical? She had no business being cynical. Harry loved Sheila and that was good enough for her. As she reminded herself from time to time, it was a wise woman who loved her son's choice of wife.

And Dot had found herself being very wise indeed over the years.

'Look at this!' Sheila pulled a piece of paper from the pocket of her jacket – and was that tighter than it used to be? Fashions for coats and jackets were getting more fitted and it looked like Sheila had taken in her old semi-fitted garment. 'Jimmy brought it home from school. Actually, I caught him about to stuff it down the drain.'

'Jimmy!' Dot exclaimed. She moved to take the paper, but Reg, at the table with his newspaper in front of him, held up his hand.

'If there's any trouble, it's for the man of the house to sort out. Give it here, Sheila. "Dear Miss Culpepper, our Lucy was absent from school on Tuesday on account of she had the trots." What the heck is this, Sheila?'

'The other side.' Sheila was busy lighting a cigarette. 'They're saving paper by turning over absence notes and writing on the back.'

'What's the trots?' asked Jimmy.

'Never you mind,' said Dot.

'Not a word out of you.' Sheila blew a stream of smoke across the kitchen. 'You're in trouble.'

'Gippy tummy,' said Reg. 'The squits.'

Jimmy hooted. 'Lucy told us she was looking after the baby while her mam was busy.'

'Hush up, Jimmy,' said Dot. 'Don't encourage him, Reg.'

Reg sniffed and turned the paper over. 'Our Jimmy's been playing tricks in class.'

'It must be bad if they've written home about it.' Sheila shook Jimmy's shoulder. 'What have you been up to?'

'Nowt,' said Jimmy.

Dot crossed her arms over her front and clamped her hands beneath her armpits so as not to snatch the note from Reg. 'Does it say what he's been up to?' A spider in the desk? Chalk smeared on the bench for some unsuspecting soul to sit on?

'Flicking ink pellets,' said Reg.

It could have been a lot worse. 'Oh, Jimmy,' Dot said in a voice of disapproval.

'At Mr Evans.' Reg eyed Jimmy. 'Come here.' He landed a sharp clip round the back of Jimmy's head, making Jimmy's cap fly off. 'And don't do it again.'

'Listen to your grandpa,' Sheila ordered Jimmy before turning to Dot. 'Can you have him tonight? Only I've got the chance to go to the flicks with the girls. Thanks, Ma.' A quick kiss on the top of Jimmy's head and she was gone.

'Can I get out the aeroplane-spotter book?' Jimmy asked.

'No,' said Dot. 'I think Grandpa's got summat else to say to you.'

Reg looked up. 'What about?'

'Flicking ink pellets at Mr Evans.'

Reg shrugged. 'I've chastised him and said not to do it again. That's all there is to it.'

Dot squeezed her lips together. You couldn't disagree with the head of the household. It wasn't respectful. But she couldn't leave this be. She took Jimmy into the parlour.

'So you've been flicking ink pellets at your teacher, have you?'

That poor old bugger. He hadn't been fetched out of retirement so much as dug up out of the grave. The last thing he needed was a live wire like their Jimmy ragging him.

Jimmy wriggled and wouldn't look at her. Giving him a talking-to was a job and a half. It was in one ear and out the other unless you came up with summat good to say, summat startling.

'I'm that ashamed of you, our Jimmy. What would your dad say? There's him, away fighting for his country, and here's you, mucking about.'

'It were only a few ink pellets,' Jimmy muttered.

'Correct me if I'm wrong, but don't you make an ink pellet by dunking a bit of paper in the inkwell? Aye, I thought so. Which means that while the rest of us are busy saving tin cans and cardboard and rags and everything else we can, for the war effort, including paper, I might add, there's *you* wasting paper by making ink pellets. D'you know what, our Jimmy? That's as good as helping Hitler, that is, and that's summat I never thought I'd say to one of my own.'

'Helping—' Jimmy opened and shut his mouth like a goldfish.

'You heard. It so happens I know where Mr Evans lives, so we're going round there for you to say sorry and promise never to do it again.'

The colour had leached from Jimmy's face at the mention of Hitler. Dot felt a pang of regret, but she hardened her heart. Jimmy had to stop mucking about in the classroom, and a thick ear from Reg wasn't going to achieve that. She knew him too well. Quick to bounce back, that was their Jimmy, but she could see in his eyes that he wasn't going to bounce back from this at his usual speed.

The incident roused a deeper concern in her that had been bubbling away beneath the surface.

'It worries me, all these dads being away from home,' she said to Reg later, after she had kissed Jimmy goodnight and come downstairs to make the Horlicks. 'Children need a dad, especially boys.'

'Are you still harping on about those ink pellets? You can't leave well alone, can you? I've dealt with it.'

And that was that. The wider issue of dads losing their relationship with their kids, and children forfeiting a father's guidance, was just being a busybody as far as Reg was concerned. And if the matter of Jimmy's conduct at school had been successfully dealt with, that was down to her, not Reg, but she would never be able to say so.

Didn't it occur to Reg that she worried about things? No, it didn't. If she expressed a concern, that was her sticking her nose in. And it wasn't just Reg. She didn't mean to sound whiney, but it seemed that nobody expected her to have worries of her own. She was the one you took your bothers and worries to, not the other way round. If you needed tea and sympathy, a helping hand or a dollop of sound advice, Dot Green was your woman, which had always suited her just fine, but wouldn't it be nice if once in a while someone realised she had something on *her* mind, instead of her having to be the capable one all the time?

Like Mr Thirkle. He took an interest in her, not in a nosy or inappropriate way, and very probably he took the same sort of interest in lots of other folk an' all, because that was the sort of chap he was. Kindly. Gentle. Sensitive, if you could call a man that, without it being demeaning. Reg would hoot with derisive laughter at hearing a man described that way, but Dot knew in her heart that it was just the word for Mr Thirkle.

The two of them had taken to having a chat now and then. She didn't much care for going into the mess unless there was a substantial number of other girls and women in there, because of the snide remarks from some of the men, remarks about going home and doing your knitting, or faffing about with parcels when you should be peeling the potatoes. She couldn't be doing with that. It wasn't polite. She ought to ignore it, but it nettled her. It was easier to stay away, less taxing on her nerves. She got enough snippy comments from Mr Bonner without putting up with derogatory remarks when she was meant to be enjoying a cup of tea. She and Mr Thirkle often joined forces in a quiet corner of the platform and had a bit of a natter if their breaks coincided.

Mind, it was only during her break-time that she did this, not after work. Having a chat with a colleague was one thing, but you only stopped and talked after work with real friends, like when she went to the buffet. Mr Thirkle wasn't a friend as such, more of an agreeable acquaintance. A darned sight more agreeable than many of the men working there.

The next time she saw him, she mentioned her worry about all those dads in the services who were missing out on their children's growing-up years.

'And it will be years,' Mr Thirkle said, 'if the last war is owt to go by.'

A gratifying warmth crept through Dot. She had been right to share her concern with this man. He understood. He didn't brush it aside.

They talked for a while about fatherless children, then moved on to the evacuated children and the mothers who were missing them so sorely.

'I'm glad my daughters-in-law brought their two home,' said Dot, 'though now that things are hotting up in Europe, I wonder if they should be sent away again, even if it would break my heart to see them go.' She told Mr Thirkle about Jimmy and the ink pellets. 'I know I did the right thing by saying he was helping Hitler, because that really gave him summat to think about, but I still feel guilty. Fancy telling anyone they're helping that man. I once washed our Archie's mouth out with soap for swearing, and now I feel like I should wash my own out an' all, for saying summat so shocking.'

Mr Thirkle thought for a moment. 'I can see you've taken it to heart. You want to do right by Jimmy's dad by looking after the boy in his absence. For what it's worth, I think you've done just that. Wait and see. I bet if young Jimmy sees other children wasting paper, he'll use the same argument on them. What about your other grandchild? Is he or she another handful?'

'She.' Dot felt a little burst of pride. 'Jenny. She's no trouble at all, is our Jenny. She's in the Girl Guides, working to earn her War Service badge.'

'She's got you to look up to as a good example, if I may say so, Mrs Green. It must give your sons comfort to know that you're here, keeping an eye on their families for them.'

'Have you got children, Mr Thirkle?'

'A daughter. She's always been the apple of my eye. It's funny, isn't it? It doesn't matter how grown-up they get, they'll always be our little boys and girls.'

'I don't think my boys would thank you for saying that,' laughed Dot. 'Look at the time. I'd best be getting back.'

'Thank you for your company,' said Mr Thirkle.

He never said anything like 'Shall we do this again?' or 'See you tomorrow,' nothing that might put her under an obligation to meet up with him again. She liked that. It felt comfortable. Everything about Mr Thirkle made her feel encouraged, supported and safe. It was like – it was like having a true friend.

Could a man and a married woman be friends with one another – just friends?

Of course not. It wasn't right. It wasn't moral.

But even so – could they?

Chapter Sixteen

Joan blew out a breath, trying to ignore the fluttery feeling in her tummy as she, Mabel and Lizzie walked up the steps into the big old house where the first-aid simulation test was to take place. The hallway was quite large, though it didn't feel much like it today with so many visitors arriving. A lady and gentleman sat at a table, ticking names off lists.

'Mabel Bradshaw,' said Mabel.

'Thank you.' The man put a tick against her name. 'The introductory talk will be through those doors on your left, starting promptly at two. Are you three young ladies together?'

'Yes,' said Joan. 'Joan Foster.'

She glanced around while Lizzie gave her name. Steven and Letitia were walking through the door, Letitia laughing at something Steven had said, and Joan's tummy fluttered for a different reason.

'They make a good-looking couple, don't they?' Mabel murmured.

'If they get married, their children will be proper little bobby-dazzlers,' Lizzie added.

'Lizzie!' Not just Joan's face, but her whole body seemed to be on fire.

'Sorry,' said Lizzie, 'but they are courting, aren't they? So it's not such an awful thing to say.'

Joan's heart thudded as she pretended to laugh it off. 'Shall we find seats?'

She ushered the other two ahead of her, but couldn't help glancing back at Letitia and Steven. Mabel was right. With her smooth skin and friendly smile, those captivating blue-grey eyes, and her fair hair showing through her open-mesh cotton snood, Letitia was a true English rose. Though his build was slim, Steven was muscular and assured, his light brown eyes clever and kind in his narrow face.

Joan turned away and followed Mabel and Lizzie into the room where the introductory talk was to be held. There were lots of chairs, but not enough, and most of the men stood at the back or at the sides, leaning against the walls. Letitia plonked down into a chair beside Joan, leaning forward to see round her and say hello to Mabel and Lizzie.

Mr Haslett, the man who had come to their first-aid test at the end of their course, entered the room in a purposeful way that made the men standing down that side of the room shift aside without being asked to make way. He positioned himself at the front and looked round.

'Can you hear me at the back? Good afternoon, everyone. My name is Haslett. Some of you have seen me before. We're here this afternoon to participate in a simulation that will test your first-aid knowledge and skills. We're grateful to the Conservative Association for the use of the building, and also to the volunteers who are obliging by acting as our wounded. As you know, we need civilian first-aiders to join our first-aid parties – people who know their stuff and can keep their heads.'

A suggestion of movement passed through the room. Joan pushed her shoulders back.

'There are haversacks in the next room, containing a selection of bandages, splints and so on. Pretend emergencies will be taking place all over the building, including in the, um, conveniences. An emergency is no time to be bashful.'

'I'm not going in the Gents, not for any money,' Letitia whispered.

'Some emergencies will take place outside,' Mr Haslett continued. 'We're going to jumble you up, so you won't be working alongside anyone you know. There's no knowing whom you'll be with when the real thing happens, so please pipe up if we partner you with your next-door neighbour or a member of your darts team.' He paused and there were one or two polite chuckles. 'Of course, you could find yourself in an emergency situation on your own, so that's what some of you will face this afternoon.'

A tiny ripple of cold breathed over Joan's flesh. Please let her have a partner.

'Others will be in twos, threes or fours. Each group will be called to one of the tables, where you'll be told about your emergency. Please deal with it promptly. All activities will be timed. I suggest you leave your jackets and hats in here, though naturally you must keep your gas masks with you at all times.'

A bustle followed while everyone was matched up. When her name was called, Joan swung her gas-mask case over her shoulder, said 'Wish me luck' to the others and headed back into the hall, where she presented herself at the table. The lady and gentleman were busy with their lists, looking efficient and important.

'Miss Foster, you'll be with . . . Mr Hubble.'

The lady glanced up and beyond Joan as she spoke, making Joan look round to see her partner. Mr Hubble was a few years older than she was, with a boyish face and thick, dark hair.

'How do,' he said, smiling. 'Bob Hubble.'

'Joan Foster.'

'Fetch a haversack,' said the lady, 'and report to the table by the grandfather clock.'

195

'I'll get the haversack,' said Bob. 'You save us a place in the queue.'

He was back in a minute. Joan felt self-conscious, having him by her side, but other girls had been paired up with men, and at least hers was young enough for her to feel she would be listened to instead of being swept along by a fatherly chap who felt he ought to be looking after her as well as their injured person.

'Do you go out to work?' Bob asked.

'Yes.' She lifted her chin. 'I'm a railway girl, though I only work in an office,' she added before he could ask for specifics.

There was that smile again. 'How's that for a coincidence? I'm on the railways too. I'm a signalman. My mum's a railway girl an' all. She's on the permanent way. I'm that proud of her. Have you been here before? And that wasn't a chat-up line, however it sounded.'

'Once or twice. They sometimes put on amateur shows here. How about you?'

'Never. We don't live round here, though my old man did when he was a lad. He remembers when they had a rifle range in the basement. He joined up early in the last lot, thinking that being handy on the rifle range would stand him in good stead.'

'Names, please?'

The trio ahead of them had moved away and they were in front of the desk. Two men sat there, one with an alarm clock in front of him.

'Hubble and Foster,' said Mr Hubble.

The official looked at his paperwork. 'Upstairs. Mother and baby.'

'Whereabouts upstairs?' asked Joan.

'You'll have to find them. Air raid in progress. Your time starts . . .'

'Now,' said the man with the alarm clock, making a scribble on a piece of paper – the time, presumably.

They headed for the staircase, dodging a group going outside. Ahead, a group of four was hurrying up the stairs, but a man standing at the bottom stopped the two of them.

'Names?'

'Foster and Hubble.'

'Sorry. Staircase unsafe.'

'But they've gone up,' Joan objected.

'Different emergency. In yours, the stairs are unsafe.'

'There must be back stairs.' She tried to look round, but all she could see was other people.

Bob swung the haversack onto his shoulder. 'Fire escape.' He headed for the front door.

They hurried up the fire escape, the metal steps delivering a hollow clang with each footfall, together with a vibration that Joan could feel humming inside her. Bob tried the door at the first-floor level.

'Locked,' he said. 'They're determined to make us work, aren't they, Miss Foster?'

The window to the side of the door was open at the bottom. Bob threw up the sash, pushed the haversack through and bent to climb in, immediately applying himself to throwing open doors. Joan was miffed that he didn't wait for her. On the other hand, it saved him being treated to a flash of leg as she slipped over the window ledge.

In the first room she looked in, a man was lying on the floor. Instinctively, she made a move towards him, but Bob stopped her.

'Mother and baby,' he reminded her. 'Chin up, mate,' he said to the supposedly injured man. 'Help is on its way.'

They tried all the rooms. In one, a man was sitting propped up against the wall, reading a newspaper.

'Smoke inhalation,' he said helpfully and they withdrew.

In another, an old lady was flirting spiritedly with two young men attending to her wrist; and in the next, four fellows were playing cards, which they attempted to hide as the door opened.

'We're the broken limbs,' one offered and Joan glimpsed the cards coming out again as she and Bob backed out.

The next door opened to reveal two groups clustered around their respective victims, the next a group of school-boys rolling on the floor, howling theatrically when they weren't sniggering their heads off. There was no sign of the mother and baby. A group of two girls and a man came trotting up the staircase that had been denied to her and Bob.

'Right,' said the man. He was in the lead. Why must men always take the lead? 'Boys with burns.'

'Follow the sound of the banshees,' said Bob. He looked at the stairs and then at Joan. 'Best not, I suppose.'

'Definitely not,' said an official, stepping forward, 'if the staircase in your emergency has been declared unsafe. Set foot on there and I'd have to declare you casualties and then you'd have to wait for rescue.'

'Go on, Hubble,' came a new voice and Joan looked round to see a jolly-looking group of two men and two girls. 'Try the stairs. We'll rescue you.'

'You most certainly won't,' the official began.

'It's got to be easier than the severe haemorrhoids we're looking for.'

'Haemorrhages,' chorused the girls, laughing.

'Very amusing,' snapped the official. 'Meanwhile, your patients are bleeding to death.'

'There's an attic stairway over here,' said Joan, as an old boy with his arm in a sling emerged from an alcove, escorted by a lad who didn't look old enough to be out all night in a first-aid party.

'You may use that,' said the official.

'Just as well,' murmured Bob, 'since the fire escape doesn't reach to the attics. This real-thing lark is all very well, but I draw the line at shinning up the ivy.'

Joan made a point of going upstairs in front of him to prove that she was capable and confident. The attics smelled of old floorboards and stale air. The walls were sharply angled, with a pair of narrow sky-lights up above that probably hadn't been cleaned since the day they were fitted. Illumination, such as it was, came from a couple of hurricane lamps. One casualty moaned with horrible realism each time one of his rescuers attempted to touch him. Perched on a trunk, another casualty had apparently bandaged his rescuer – Steven, no less – and was saying, 'That's how you do it, son. Now you do that on me.'

There were two or three girls whom Joan made a beeline for, one after the other, only to fall back when she realised each was spoken for by another first-aider. Where was their mother and baby? The only other female up here was a plump, middle-aged woman with rosy cheeks.

'Well, I don't know,' this lady announced cheerfully to the world at large. 'Me and my baby could have starved to death by now, the amount of time we've been waiting.'

'You're the mother and baby?'

'There's no need to sound so surprised, love. Don't be fooled by appearances. I'm not a day over twenty-one. I just forgot to put my beauty cream on last night. Now you're here, you can rescue me and Myrtle. My baby – Myrtle.'

Joan looked round for a doll.

The woman scooped up a rolled-up yellow blanket and rocked it in one arm. 'Myrtle. I named her after my old nan.'

'She looks a bit jaundiced to me,' said Bob.

A laugh escaped Joan before she could prevent it. She pulled her face straight and assumed a professional air. 'Are you injured, Mrs . . . ?'

'Mrs Parker. Not as such, but I've just given birth so you needn't kid yourselves I'm going to trail down all them stairs on my own two feet.'

'How about a fireman's lift?' suggested Bob.

'Ooh, I say! Are you a fireman?'

'Just a humble signalman.'

'That'll do for me, love.'

Joan frowned. Was she the only one taking this seriously? 'You can't perform a fireman's lift on a lady who's just given birth.'

'Then how about a signalman's arms, Mrs P?'

'Ooh, hark at him.' Mrs Parker chortled with pleasure. 'You'll have to carry me careful, though. I'm not having next week's washing on show.'

'It's a bit late for modesty when you've just given birth surrounded by all these people. Let's be having you.' Bob scooped her up and settled her in his arms. 'How's that? Comfy? My name's Bob, but you'd best call me Bobby like all my girlfriends do, seeing as how we're snuggled up close.'

'Just wait till I tell my sister about this,' said Mrs Parker. 'What a lark.'

Joan was about to pick up Myrtle when a voice shouted, 'Attention, everyone! Part of the roof has collapsed and the way down is blocked. Work together to clear a passage and assist your casualties.'

Steven, now free from the bandages his casualty had applied on him, strode to the top of the narrow staircase. 'There are cardboard boxes all down the stairs.'

'Pieces of roof,' the official corrected him.

'It won't take us long to shift them.'

'And there's an air raid in progress,' said the official. 'I'll let you know if a bomb lands on you.'

'Listen up, everyone!' Steven stood by the top of the

stairs. Joan glowed with pride to see him taking charge. He wasn't the oldest first-aider present, but he had a natural authority. 'I don't know what they've put in these boxes, but they're jolly heavy, so they'll need to be moved carefully. It's a squeeze on the stairs, so we'll need a human chain to bring them up. If the casualties can be helped over here to this side, we can stack the boxes over there.'

The party atmosphere had disintegrated. Joan's heart thumped. This might be pretend but it suddenly felt serious. Bob lowered Mrs Parker to the floor and went to help clear the stairs. Joan picked up Myrtle.

'Come along, Mrs Parker.'

But Mrs Parker slumped. 'Sorry, love, I need help. I've just had a baby, you know.'

Joan had no option but to put Myrtle down and assist Mrs Parker across to where the casualties were being made as comfortable as possible. Was it her imagination or were the casualties suddenly playing up?

'Ooh, I've gone all peculiar.' Mrs Parker grasped Joan's arm in a vice-like grip.

'Here, sit on this trunk.' Joan manoeuvred her into position. 'Lean forwards. Get your head as far down as you can.'

'Is your casualty stable?' asked a chap with an ARP band on his arm. 'If you assist with mine, I can help free up the stairs.' He bounced to his feet and was gone, leaving Joan with no option.

'Will you be all right for a minute?' she asked Mrs Parker. 'Breathe steadily. Tell me if you feel worse. I'll be right behind you with someone else.'

Would Mrs Parker take the opportunity to topple to the floor? No. Relieved, Joan stationed herself beside her new patient, a pretty girl about her own age, who was lying down while her leg was secured in a splint by a spotty young man whose bottle-bottom glasses proclaimed he was safe from being called up.

As Joan worked with him, she kept glancing at Mrs Parker.

'Keep your eyes on the patient,' snapped her new partner.

'I'm trying to keep an eye on my own patient as well.'

When the splint was secured, the young man hurried off to where there was a small commotion over a heart attack.

'Thank goodness he's gone,' said the girl. 'Just my luck to get Mr Unfit For Service. I only volunteered for this because I was told there'd be young men in reserved occupations.'

'Bombs dropping,' shouted the official. 'Explosion . . .' Everyone paused. '. . . in the vicinity.'

Joan looked at the growing mound of boxes. How many more to come? The ARP chap she had relieved was struggling with a box. Another man helped him heft it onto the pile. Next moment, the space at the top of the stairs filled with men coming up.

Steven appeared, looking flushed. 'The stairs are clear. Let's get everyone down. Walking wounded first.'

'Bombs dropping. Explosion . . . closer than the last one.'

Not quite able to believe her eyes, Joan saw the official lift a bucket and chuck its contents into the air. A cloud of dust floated free, prompting indignant exclamations, most of which subsided into coughing. Joan bent over the girl to protect her face.

'Come on,' Steven ordered. 'Let's get moving.'

Guided and supported by their rescuers, the first casualties were helped towards the staircase and disappeared.

'Who's your casualty?' Steven appeared at Joan's side.

'This lady over here – Mrs Parker.'

'I'm waiting to be carried down by a handsome signalman,' Mrs Parker declared. 'Here he is now.'

'Could you take over from me in my group?' Steven asked Joan. 'There's three of us and four casualties. Then I can stop up here till last.'

'Explosion . . . closer still.' The official extinguished one of the lights and pushed a couple of boxes from the top of the mound onto the floor.

'He's enjoying this a bit too much,' muttered Steven.

Assigned to Steven's group, Joan was given a blind man to look after – and he really was blind, not pretending. Was the main staircase still out of bounds to her? But Steven's group was going down that way, so, what the heck, she followed.

It felt odd to step outside into the calm afternoon sunshine after the pretend emergency in the attics. Seeing Letitia, she wanted to go straight over to her to tell her how marvellous Steven had been, but Letitia and another rescuer were talking to a man with a clipboard while another official was examining the treatment they had given their casualty.

'Do you mind if I leave you here, Mr Lynsky?' Joan placed the blind man's hand on the arm of one of his designated rescuers. 'I should get back to my own casualty.'

'Lost your casualty, have you, miss?' enquired an official, bearing down on her with a gleam in his eye.

A bolt of dread speared through her. 'Of course not.' She all but sagged with relief as Bob came striding out of the building with Mrs Parker clinging happily to his neck. 'Here's my partner with her now.'

'Casualty's name?'

'Mrs Parker.'

He consulted his clipboard. 'She's on my list. Bring her over here. I've got questions for her and for you and your partner. Is there a problem?'

Joan swallowed. 'No, sir. I'll be right back.'

'What's up, Miss Foster?' Bob set Mrs Parker on her feet and steadied her.

'I've left Myrtle behind.' Joan glanced round to make sure she hadn't been overheard. 'I'll have to go back.'

'They won't let you back inside.'

Disappointment sliced through her. Anger, too. How could she have been so stupid? Some first-aider she was. Who in their right mind would put her forward for a first-aid party now? She had probably scuppered Bob's chances as well.

'I'll go back up the fire escape.'

'Myrtle!' Mrs Parker exclaimed.

Joan just about managed to contain a groan. More histrionics from Mrs Parker – that was all she needed.

'It's what I'd do for a real baby.' Joan lowered her voice, willing Mrs Parker to keep her noise down. 'I'd go back for her.'

'Don't be daft, love. You'd never have left a real one behind,' said Mrs Parker. 'The very idea that you're supposed to take a blanket seriously – what tommyrot. Anyroad, I only meant, look, there she is.'

Turning, Joan saw Kathleen, a girl from her first-aid class, escorting a casualty with a yellow blanket draped around her shoulders. Myrtle! She sped across.

'Did you find that blanket in the attic? Could I have it, please? It's meant to be a baby.'

'A baby?' Kathleen looked at her as if she was mad.

'Yes, when it's rolled up. I know, you'd have expected them to use a doll, but they didn't.'

'Be a sport,' said Kathleen. 'My casualty's in shock, so let us hang on to it for two minutes while I get my rescue signed off, then you can have it back.'

Leaving nothing to chance, Joan hovered as Kathleen and her casualty answered questions. The moment the official turned away, she whipped the blanket from the woman's shoulders and scurried back to Bob and Mrs Parker, hearing them laugh out loud as she dived behind a shrub to restore Myrtle to her former rolled-up glory.

'Myrtle!' Mrs Parker threw herself back into her role. You had to hand it to her. She had certainly given her all this afternoon. 'What's your name, love?'

'Joan Foster.'

'Joan Foster – did you catch that, young man?' Mrs Parker demanded and Joan realised their official had appeared. 'Miss Foster has been splendid. In fact, I'm naming my baby Myrtle Joan after her for rescuing us both in our hour of need. Mind you, her nickname's going to be Bobbie, though only me and this here handsome signal-man know the reason for that.'

The official soon excused himself, looking relieved to escape.

'This your young man, is it, ducks?' Mrs Parker asked Joan.

'No.' Joan prayed that Bob hadn't heard, but of course he had.

'Footloose and fancy-free, that's me.' Bob made light of the moment, but Joan's toes had curled up with embarrassment.

'Well, it's no good you asking me out, dear, on account of Mr Parker doesn't like me having boyfriends, but you could do a lot worse for yourself than ask Joan here. Oh, look – there's the fishmonger's daughter, Lorna. I must have a word. Give us a shout if I'm needed.'

'First-aiders, inside, please,' called a man from the front steps.

There was something of a squash as they went indoors. They couldn't go straight in, but had to give their names to the officials, who were sending some people – most people, it seemed – into the big room where Mr Haslett had given his introductory talk.

'They're separating the passes from the failures,' whispered a voice behind Joan, and her heartbeat quickened. She badly wanted to pass. Directed into the room where they had all started off, she looked round and felt a moment's relief. Pass or fail, at least she was in the same boat as Letitia, Mabel and Lizzie. Steven, too, and Bob Hubble. They couldn't all have failed, surely? Steven couldn't have, after the way he had taken charge up in the attics. Then again, he must have made a botch of putting that bandage on his casualty, because the casualty had had to show him how to do it properly.

Mr Haslett came in and resumed his place at the front. The room fell silent without his having to ask. He looked round at everyone, then lifted his chin and nodded crisply.

'Congratulations, ladies and gentlemen. I am pleased to inform you that you have all passed the test. We'll write to each of you shortly to tell you where your first-aid party will be based and when to report for duty.'

There was relieved laughter around the room, accompanied by some hand-shaking. A couple of the men slapped each other on the back. One of the officials opened the door and the successful candidates began to leave. Spotting the downcast expressions on the faces of the folk leaving the other room, Joan felt a rush of sympathy, understanding their need to pick up speed as they crossed the hall.

Outside, the spring sunshine felt warmer than before, young leaves shimmering in the brightness of the afternoon. A small crab-apple tree formed a mound of pink and white blossom. How come she hadn't noticed it before? She must have been more nervous than she had realised. She and Letitia hugged one another and Lizzie took Joan by surprise by giving her a hug too. Gran wouldn't be impressed by such spontaneity, but Joan hugged Lizzie back, though all she and Mabel did was smile at one another.

Joan spotted Mrs Parker. 'Excuse me a minute. I must say goodbye to my casualty.'

She arrived at Mrs Parker's side just as Bob got there.

'I hope you both passed,' said Mrs Parker. 'You deserved to, after the way you took care of me.'

'And Myrtle,' Bob added.

'We both passed,' said Joan.

'Good for you,' said Mrs Parker. 'Here.' She lifted her cheek and tilted it at Bob, tapping it with one finger. 'You're not leaving without giving your best girl a kiss.'

Laughing, Bob bent down and planted a smacker. 'Any time you need a signalman's lift, Mrs P, I'm your man.'

'Ooh, you are a one. What would Mr Parker say?'

Bob winked. 'I won't tell him if you won't.'

Chortling delightedly, Mrs Parker went on her way. Bob and Joan turned politely to one another.

'Goodbye, Mr Hubble,' said Joan. 'Thanks for being my partner. I couldn't have managed Mrs Parker on my own.'

'She had a whale of a time, didn't she?' His smile faltered. 'Well, I'd better say goodbye.' He shifted a little from foot to foot. 'Goodbye, then.' In a rush, he added, 'Actually, I wanted to ask you . . .'

'Yes?' Joan asked when he stopped.

'Do you ever go dancing?'

She went hot and cold. She had never been asked out before; had never wanted to be asked out, because the one man in the whole world whom she wanted to be with wouldn't dream of asking her. Now she had been asked out in front of a crowd of people. A few were openly watching, smiles on their faces. Others weren't looking, but that didn't mean their ears weren't flapping. Please let Letitia and the others be far enough away not to be aware of this. If only the ground would open up and swallow her.

'No.' Her voice sounded hollow. 'No, I don't.'

He nodded. 'Oh well. Thanks for being my partner today.'

He held out his right hand and as she took it, a painfully sweet tingle jolted through her.

Chapter Seventeen

With talk that the Norwegian government might move to London setting everyone on edge with worry, was it tacky to ask about Bob? But Joan couldn't think of any other way to track him down other than through Cordelia, whose job as a lampwoman meant she had met some of the signal-men. Then again, even if Cordelia was able to tell her the location of Bob's signal box, what precisely did she think she was going to do with the information? March up the permanent way and loiter at the foot of the steps? Of course not. But at least the information would be a starting point. Although knowing where his signal box was wouldn't lead to finding out where he went dancing, which was what she really needed to know.

Lord, what a mess. She had gone from one hopeless, yearning attraction to another. Steven – well, her feelings for him had changed in an instant, in a heartbeat, the same heartbeat that had thumped good and hard when Bob Hubble took her hand.

She should have said something then, should have said, 'Actually, I do go dancing,' but instead, with her breath caught in her throat, she had shaken hands – and then watched him walk away. If he had looked back – if he had only looked back . . .

But he hadn't, and the next thing she knew, Lizzie had linked arms with her and she was drawn away in a tri-umphant group with Mabel, Letitia and Steven. As they left the premises, Letitia and Steven had parted company with them for Steven to walk Letitia home, and she, Mabel and Lizzie had headed for Wilbraham Road, walking Lizzie to her tram stop.

For once, in fact for the first time ever, she had seen Letitia and Steven on their way together without her heart tying itself in knots. Her feelings for Steven had already shifted into a new position. Already they had cooled and she felt a sharp annoyance at herself for having entertained such inappropriate feelings. Life would be easier and a lot less embarrassing if she never had to see him again. Could love change as swiftly as that? One touch of Bob Hubble's hand and she had outgrown her girlish infatuation for her sister's boyfriend. About time, too.

She had walked to Lizzie's tram-stop in a kind of daze. She was in a state of acute self-awareness, to the point of feeling distanced from her companions. Thoughts of Bob caused tiny pin-pricks of delight inside her, little sparks of consciousness and need.

She had tried to join in with the conversation, but couldn't have managed very well, because Mabel had said, 'You're miles away.'

She had laughed it off. 'Just thinking about passing the test.'

'It's such a relief,' Lizzie burbled. 'My mum's going to be so proud. I hope the three of us get put in the same first-aid party. That would be perfect.'

Joan's heart had executed a little flip that sent the blood rushing through her veins. Might she and Bob be assigned to the same party? Would he still want to take her dancing? What would Gran think? She approved of Steven because he was a policeman, but what would she make of a railway signalman? She was snobby about social rank. Not that the Fosters were anything special, far from it, but she might not be keen on a working-class chap. She certainly wouldn't have tolerated one for Letitia, but would it matter so much for second-best Joan?

Joan had wafted her way through Saturday evening and Sunday more in a daydream than in the real world. Now, on Monday after work, she was in the station buffet with Mabel, Cordelia, Lizzie and Alison. They were talking about the first-aid test and she had entertained the others with the tale of Mrs Parker and Myrtle, though she knew full well that she would have enjoyed telling the story a great deal more if she hadn't been so anxious to steer the conversation towards Bob.

'Your Mrs Parker sounds a hoot,' said Alison. 'I wish I lived nearer, so I could have done first aid with you. I'll ask my sister if she wants to do it.'

'I didn't know you had—' Cordelia began.

Joan felt a flash of panic. She had to prevent the conversation from moving on to Alison's family. Leaping in, she said, 'My first-aid partner was someone you might have met.'

'Really?' If Cordelia was taken aback at being interrupted, she was too well bred to show it.

'Oh yes,' said Lizzie. 'You had that handsome signalman, didn't you?'

'Well, I don't know about handsome . . .' Was she blushing?

'He was certainly strong. He carried that Mrs Parker all the way downstairs from the attic.'

'His name's Bob Hubble.' Joan addressed Cordelia. 'Have you come across him on your travels up and down the permanent way?'

Cordelia shook her head. 'I'm afraid not.'

Oh well, it had been worth a try.

'Did you say Hubble?' Mabel put down her cup. 'And he's a signalman? I wonder if he's . . .' Her voice trailed off.

Joan pressed herself into her seat so she couldn't lean forwards. 'He's what?'

'The foreman – forewoman – of my gang is Bernice Hubble. I know her son works on the railways.'

Alison laughed. 'He must be Joan's Bob.'

'Mrs Parker's Bob, you mean,' said Lizzie, inadvertently sparing Joan's blushes.

'What a coincidence,' she said. But how would it help her? It wouldn't, any more than it would have helped her if Cordelia had come across him on her travels. Even if Mabel had been her very best friend – and the reserved Mabel was far from being that – Joan could never have asked her to pass on a message via Bob's mother. Not his mother!

'Have you heard anything about the upper age of conscription being raised?' Mabel asked. 'That's a depressing thought, the idea that they need more men to join up.'

'I believe it's due to take effect in the next few days,' said Cordelia.

There was a silence around their table. Even the background hum of voices and clinking of teacups against saucers seemed to quieten as the railway girls looked at one another. Joan knew that the expression in her own eyes must be as sombre and thoughtful as those of her friends.

If the war was becoming more serious, wasn't it trifling and superficial of her to be fretting over a man she barely knew?

Or – if the war really was becoming more serious – wasn't this exactly the time when ordinary people, leading ordinary lives, should be making the most of what they had?

Wasn't this exactly the time when she ought to have the chance of . . . something . . . with Bob?

'We need to put old net curtains over these young cabbages,' said Letitia, 'or they'll end up full of cabbage white butterfly eggs. The baby carrots have to be protected as well, in case the nights are cold. Does it show that Steven's dad gave me a gardening lesson?'

'I feel sorry for the butterflies,' said Joan.

Letitia grinned. 'I feel sorry for Gran, having to sacrifice one of her old net curtains.'

Joan sat back on her heels, rolling her shoulders to ease out the knots after an hour's weeding, which was another thing Steven's dad swore by. She and Letitia were perched on top of the mound that was the Anderson shelter in their back garden. Steven, his dad and various neighbours had all helped to prepare the shelter and cover it with earth, which, in common with the roofs of many air-raid shelters, now did duty as a vegetable plot. The flower beds had been turned over to veg as well.

As she took a breather from weeding, Joan's tummy churned. She wanted to ask – but at the same time, didn't want to. Oh, blow it. She couldn't help herself.

'Do you remember Bob?'

'Bob?' Letitia's trowel stopped moving and she looked at Joan.

It took Joan a moment to realise. Drat. She had used Bob's first name without thinking. Or rather, she had thought about him so much that his first name was now lodged firmly in her consciousness. What a slip!

'Bob Hubble.' She glanced away, tried to be casual. 'He was my partner when we did the first-aid test in the Con Club building.'

Letitia made a sound that could have been the beginning of a laugh, instantly stifled. 'There's no need to ask why you've mentioned him. That "Bob" says it all. I thought you weren't keen. He asked you to go dancing – I heard him – and you said no.'

'I wish I hadn't.'

'Still thinking about him? Oh, Joanie.' Letitia leaned over and gave her a hug.

'I had hoped we might be assigned to the same first-aid party.'

'But now we've had our letters,' said Letitia, 'and he's not on your list. Nor mine, unfortunately, or I might be able to help.' She shook Joan's arm in loving frustration. 'And you seemed so pleased to be in a group with Mabel and Lizzie.'

'I was. I am. It's what we wanted. I just wish you could be with us.'

'We knew that wouldn't be allowed. Anyway, Bob wouldn't have mentioned dancing if he wasn't a dancer himself, so we need to visit every dance hall we can find.'

Joan laughed, heartened. 'I wish I'd told you before.'

'You've told me now and that's what matters. I want to hear every detail of that first-aid afternoon.'

'I've already told you.'

'Ah, but this time I'll pay special attention to the Bob bits.'

What a wonderful sister she was. Joan's heart swelled with love and appreciation. Letitia encouraged her to rattle on about the afternoon she had spent in Bob's company and she was only too happy to indulge in the memories. Or was she just setting herself up for a bigger disappointment later, should she never see him again?

That night, they lay whispering in the bed they shared. Even in the dark, the blackout left its mark, the darkness deeper and more intense than it ought to be. Would the night be as black as this even when they reached the height of summer?

'Do you remember that thing in the papers you told me about?' Joan asked softly. 'About girls in wartime who don't get married not really trying.'

'Goodness!' Letitia exclaimed. Her voice dropped to an urgent hiss. 'You're not thinking of you and Bob?'

'No, of course not. You and Steven, actually.'

For a moment, she thought Letitia might keep her own counsel, but then she spoke.

'Steven would get engaged like a shot, I'm sure, but I don't want to. If we got married, there'd probably be a baby and I'd have to stay at home and look after it.'

'Don't you want children?'

'Of course I do, but there's plenty of time for all that.' Letitia turned onto her side and the bedclothes shifted as she propped herself up on one elbow. 'Shall I tell you a deathly secret?'

'Go on. I've told you about Bob.'

'I'm enjoying the war. There: I've said it. I adore working at the munitions. I love feeling that what I do is helping the war effort and making a difference. And the work's so interesting. I was a wages clerk before. They wanted me because I'm good at maths, and the work was all right. I had to calculate hours worked and rates of pay and deductions and what have you, and I had to pay attention, but let's face it, when you've totted up one week's wage slips, you've done 'em all.'

'But then, surely, when you've checked the maths on one shell . . .'

'No, you're wrong, because it matters so much.' Although Letitia's voice was quiet, there was an intensity in it that sent a shiver through Joan. 'When this war is over, I want to be able to say, "I helped win it," not "I spent it changing nappies and wiping snotty noses." I know there's more to motherhood than that, and I've every intention of loving my children to distraction, but they're not here yet and I am.'

'You could get engaged and not get married until later.'

'It isn't like that these days. It's down on one knee, followed by a quick sprint to the registry office. I can understand why couples do that, I truly can, and maybe if Steven was in the forces, I'd be the same. But he's not, so we can have time together, which is a luxury most young couples don't have these days. Maybe something will change at some point and I'll want to get married at once, but for now I like things as they are. I have a hugely responsible job, which in the normal run of things would never have been given to a woman, no matter how capable or experienced she was, and certainly wouldn't have been entrusted to a girl my age. I'm younger than the daughters of the engineers whose work I double-check. I don't want to sound big-headed, but I'm proud of that and I don't want to give it up. Not yet, anyway.'

'You're not big-headed,' Joan assured her. 'You're amazingly clever and I'm proud of you.'

It was true. She had never begrudged Letitia her brains or her grammar-school education. As for her position as Gran's favourite, that sometimes made Joan feel miffed with Gran, but never jealous of her sister.

Letitia soon dropped off to sleep, but Joan stayed awake, staring into the darkness. Letitia had spoken of enjoying the war. It had brought challenge and opportunity into her life, but all it had given Joan was a typewriter to sit behind. Was it small-minded to wish for more? Was it . . . unpatriotic?

In the darkened cinema, Letitia's hand crept into Joan's and Joan squeezed it tightly as they gazed at the screen, unable to look away from the Pathé newsreel. There had been so many important days, so many significant events, but yesterday, Friday, the tenth of May 1940, seemed important like no day had before. Even though the change of prime minister had occurred yesterday and they had already heard about it on the wireless, seeing it on the cinema screen this evening endowed it with even greater consequence.

On Joan's other side, Lizzie huddled closer. Joan reached out her free hand and, after some flapping in the darkness, Lizzie found it and held on. Mabel was on Lizzie's other side. Was Lizzie hanging on to her too? Joan couldn't be sure. There was something stand-offish about Mabel. No, that wasn't the right word. It sounded cold and unfeeling. Just because she was less open to the casual arm-linking that the others did, didn't make her uncaring. Oh, she never refused you if you took her arm, but she never linked first. Maybe she had been brought up to keep her hands to herself. But there was nothing inappropriate in girl chums linking arms, was there? It wasn't like a girl straightening a chap's tie, say, if she wasn't engaged to him, or a girl smoking in public. Anybody would know exactly what to think about a girl who did either of those things.

No, there was just something reserved about Miss Mabel Bradshaw. As cordial as she was towards the others around the buffet table, she seemed to hold something of herself back.

Joan hoped for Mabel's sake that she had a hand to hold right now as the words swept over them, sharing the chilling news that the Germans had invaded Belgium and the Netherlands. Moreover, Mr Chamberlain had resigned and their new prime minister was Mr Churchill. Was that a good thing? Did changing prime ministers make the country look weak? Ripe for invasion?

At the end of the evening, after Errol Flynn and Olivia de Havilland had agreed to head for Virginia City, which was as deeply in need of taming as Dodge City, Joan rose with the rest of the packed house, sensing that nobody moved a muscle while the national anthem was played.

When they got home and had their bedtime Ovaltine,

Joan dared to voice her uncertainty about changing prime minister, but Gran wasn't having any of that.

'Mr Chamberlain is a decent enough gentleman, I daresay, but it's the job of the prime minister to make every single person in this country feel they can win this war and Mr Chamberlain would never be able to do that.'

And Mr Churchill would? How could anybody possess such personal strength and determination that they could inspire and embolden every single person in the country?

But, two days later, when she heard Mr Churchill's speech on the wireless, when he offered 'blood, toil, tears and sweat', she knew that Gran was correct. Mr Churchill was the right man, the only man, for the task, a true leader to whom folk would give their trust and be proud to follow. His words made her want to spring to attention, as if standing for the national anthem. She might not be required to give up any blood, tears or sweat in her office job on the railways, but she had other wartime toil to offer as a first-aider, and the news from the Continent made it a certainty that her toil in that capacity would be called upon sooner rather than later.

'You'll never guess what I've bought.' Lizzie's eyes sparkled.

'That sounds exciting,' said Joan. 'Do you want to wait for the others before you say?'

She and Lizzie were the first to arrive in the buffet. By unspoken consent, whoever arrived first chose a table by the wall, if possible, because it felt more private, but today all those tables were already occupied, and Joan had come into the buffet to spy Lizzie at a table in the middle. For once, Lizzie was wearing a lightweight mac over her uniform, so she didn't have to stand.

'No, you already know about them,' said Lizzie.

'Know about what?'

'The red shoes. D'you remember the red evening shoes I showed you the day we sat our tests in Hunts Bank?'

It took Joan a moment. 'You've never bought them?' Something chilled inside her, but she merely said, 'They must have cost a pretty penny, coming from a shop on Deansgate.'

'Not those actual shoes. Another pair. I found them in our local shoe shop. They're not exactly the same, but they're just as swish. They're bright red and shiny.' Lizzie gurgled with the laughter that came so easily to her. 'My mum says I look like I should dance down the Yellow Brick Road.'

'Your mum doesn't mind?'

'Mind what?'

Ah. And there it was – the difference between the Foster family and everybody else in the world. How did you say, 'Doesn't your mum mind you having shiny red shoes, when red is for tarts?' Well, of course you didn't say it, even if that was what you meant. Something inside Joan struggled to comprehend this new reality. Lizzie was not, absolutely not, a tart. She was warm and vibrant and took everyone on trust. She said what she thought and she was one of those rare people who always thought nice things. She was a real tonic. Anyone less like a tart would be hard to imagine. And her mother sounded so sensible and caring. Yet Lizzie had bought shiny red shoes and her mother, apparently, didn't mind.

Gran would throw forty fits if one of her girls dared to buy such a thing.

Red was for tarts. Red was for girls who were no better than they should be. Red shoes were for the likes of Estelle.

'Mind what?' Lizzie asked again.

Joan improvised. 'Your mum doesn't mind . . . you buying something so frivolous?'

'Not in the slightest. She said I work hard and I deserve

a treat.' Lizzie extended her leg to place her foot alongside Joan's. 'What size shoe d'you take? It looks like we're the same. I'll lend you my red shoes if you like.'

'There's just one thing wrong with that,' Joan teased. 'We go dancing together, so you'll be wearing them.'

Lizzie laughed at herself. 'There's Dot ordering her tea – and Mabel's joined the queue.' She leaned forward. 'What does your gran think of this first-names business? Especially calling proper grown-up ladies by their first names?'

'I haven't told her,' Joan confessed. 'She'd be outraged. 'It's fine for me to be on first-name terms with you and Mabel, but I'd never dare tell her about Dot and Cordelia. To be honest, I still don't feel comfortable using their names. I avoid it if I can.'

'Me too.'

'Have you told your mum?'

'Oh yes, I tell her everything.'

'Even about using Dot and Cordelia's first names?' Joan experienced a frisson of shock. Gran would hit the roof.

'She doesn't like it, but I explained about Miss Emery and sticking together and she said that, as long as Dot and Cordelia don't object, I'm allowed to do it, but only around the buffet table, never in public and never in the workplace.' Lizzie glanced at Dot, who was heading in their direction. 'I'm the same as you. I never use their names if I can help it.' Lizzie beamed at Dot, half-rising to pull out a chair for her. 'Have you had a busy day? Come and sit down.'

Joan smiled to herself. She hadn't met Lizzie's mum, but presumably that was where Lizzie's warm-hearted behaviour came from.

Soon Mabel joined them.

'Look!' Lizzie exclaimed. 'Mabel, isn't that your friend in the queue?'

Joan turned to look. Oh yes, the violet-eyed stunner from their first day as railway girls. Persephone, that was her name, though Joan couldn't recall her surname off-hand. She expected Mabel to signal to her, but it was Lizzie who waved.

Carrying her tea, Persephone headed towards them. Did the volume lower as this beauty made her graceful way across the buffet? If it did, Persephone appeared unconscious of it.

'Miss Cooper,' she said, 'how perfectly sweet of you to remember me.'

'You remember my name,' breathed Lizzie.

'Naturally,' said Persephone.

Everyone looked at Mabel as she performed the introductions. The Honourable Persephone Trehearn-Hobbs – that was Persephone's full name and rank.

'Take the weight off your feet,' said Dot.

'Are you sure?' Persephone glanced round the table. 'I don't want to barge in.'

Again, everyone looked at Mabel.

'Have a seat,' she said.

Persephone sank onto a chair, popping her cup and saucer on the table.

'What brings you to Victoria?' asked Joan.

'I accompanied a friend of Miss Brown, the lady I live with, to catch her train. I've just waved her off in the company of some handsome young soldiers.'

'Lucky her,' laughed Dot.

'What job do you do on the railways, Mrs Green?' Persephone asked.

They chatted for a while. If Joan had expected sitting with an Honourable to be somehow different to being with a plain Miss or Mrs, she was agreeably surprised to find that Persephone slotted in with ease.

'I remember that the first time we saw you,' Lizzie said to Persephone, 'you mentioned writing an article.'

'I'm interested in journalism,' said Persephone. 'I had a few pieces published before the war, but they weren't serious pieces, and, frankly, it was my social position that got them into print.' Her eyes sparkled. 'I used to write for the society column – you know, who danced with whom, things like that. But what I want to do now is write about the experience of war from the point of view of the people at home.'

'I'm sure you're clever enough,' said Dot.

'That remains to be seen. Let's just say, my hopes of writing something publishable have so far come to nothing.' Persephone came to her feet. 'If you'll excuse me, I ought to go. It's been a pleasure to meet you all.' She looked at Mabel. 'I expect we'll see one another again shortly, and I don't mean at Darley Court. I've signed up as a railway girl, passed the tests and everything.'

'Congratulations,' said Joan.

'When do you start?' Dot asked.

'Monday the twenty-seventh. It was hearing bits and bobs from Mabel that inspired me.'

Lizzie's delight was transparent. 'You're going to be one of us.'

Joan felt a little flush of delight at the thought of all the dances Letitia was insisting they go to in her determination to reunite her with Bob Hubble. Usually, the two of them went with Mabel and Lizzie, and, of course, Steven came too if he wasn't on nights.

'Doesn't he mind going out with a crowd of girls?' Joan asked.

Letitia laughed. 'Find me the man who'd say no to escorting a group of girls.'

Whatever Steven thought of it, he certainly appeared perfectly at ease with the arrangement. There were never enough male partners these days and often girls danced with one another. Sometimes Steven would dance with two girls at once, the second girl positioned behind the first with her left hand resting lightly on the girl in front's shoulder and her right hand under the first girl's elbow, while Steven led the pair of them through the steps of the dance. It wasn't unheard of to dance like that these days, but it still turned heads.

Joan felt easier in Steven's company now. She no longer felt that edgy annoyance with herself for her old love. After all that time keeping her feelings for Steven a secret, sharing her interest in Bob with Letitia seemed to have loosened something inside her that had been wound up tight. Now she felt warmth towards Steven – and it was a safe, sisterly warmth.

'Is everything all right, Joan?' Steven asked as he waltzed her expertly round the crowded floor of the Palais in Chorlton. Joan had been smiling to think of how Letitia seemed to be bent on taking her round every Palais in Manchester, until Steven's question put her on her guard.

'Of course. Why wouldn't it be?'

'I mean between you and me. I – well, I thought I'd offended you not so long ago, though things seem fine now.'

'Things have always been fine between us.'

'Good.' Steven negotiated the corner and plunged her back into the throng. 'You're my little sister.'

Just days ago, those words would have crushed her, but now she could embrace them and hold them to her heart. Steven's sister was precisely who she wanted to be, for Letitia's sake, which enabled her to say in all sincerity, 'Then I'm pleased to have a brother who's so light on his feet.'

Steven laughed and twirled her round, laughing again

when she called him a show-off. 'It's a good job I'm competent on the dance floor. That sister of yours has always
loved to go dancing, but I have to say she seems even more
keen these days.'

Joan hugged her secret to her. She was glad that Letitia
hadn't confided in Steven. The search for Bob was something just for the two of them.

'It seems hopeless,' Joan said that night as she and Letitia
were putting their rollers in before bed. In her heart, she
didn't really mean it, but it wasn't so very wrong to seek
reassurance, was it?

'Maybe,' said Letitia, 'but it's a lot of fun looking,' which
wasn't quite what Joan had wanted to hear. 'We'll go to the
Ritz next.'

'I love the Ritz.'

'Me too. See if Lizzie and Mabel want to come.'

But the night that Letitia suggested wasn't suitable for
Lizzie.

Sitting in a corner of the buffet, she groaned. 'That's
Mum's and my evening for mending club. Never mind.
There'll be other times.'

'What about you?' Joan asked Alison. She hadn't seen
Alison in a while and didn't want her getting the idea that
doing first aid with Mabel and Lizzie, and also going dancing with them, meant she wasn't interested in being
friends. 'You and your boyfriend could come, couldn't you?
It would only be a matter of coming into town, same as us,
but from a different direction.'

'Thanks for asking,' said Alison. 'We'd love to, I'm sure,
though I'll have to check that Paul hasn't made other plans
for us.'

'Is he very attentive?' asked Lizzie. 'Is he all protective
and loving, like Colette's husband?' She wriggled her
shoulders. 'I hope my husband looks after me like that.'

'I'm very lucky,' Alison murmured.

On the day of the visit to the Ritz, Joan was leaving the office when she heard footsteps flying along behind her. Turning, she found Lizzie in her porter's uniform, running full tilt, clutching a cloth bag. She blew out a huge breath as she reached Joan.

'I've caught you. I was worried I wouldn't get here in time. Here.' She thrust the bag at Joan. 'For you for tonight.'

Even before she opened the bag, Joan knew what would be inside. The red shoes. She felt torn up one side and down the other. The red shoes. They were stylish, with a heel the perfect size to lift you a little and make you taller, but without in any degree compromising your ability to dance, and they were pretty. Not tarty, not vulgar, not in bad taste. Just pretty dancing shoes.

Could she wear them? They were just shoes. They weren't going to turn her into something she wasn't.

Just pretty dancing shoes.

Chapter Eighteen

Entering the foyer of the Ritz Ballroom, Joan blinked to adjust her eyes. Coming indoors from the blackout, the light in here seemed brilliant. Steven went straight into the ballroom to see if there was a table to be had. Mabel and Letitia headed towards the cloakroom to hand in their coats and hats, but Joan hung back, perching on a chair to change her shoes. After a moment, Letitia came back.

'I thought you were beside me. What are you doing? Oh my goodness.'

Joan kept her head bent over to hide the blushes. 'Lizzie lent them to me.'

'But . . .'

'But what?' Joan looked up at her sister. What was that in her face? Censure? No, just concern. 'But Gran would be angry? I'm perfectly well aware of that.' She stood up, dropping her own shoes into the cloth bag. 'It's just a pair of shoes. I'm not doing any harm.'

Letitia blew out a huge breath. 'As long as Gran doesn't find out.'

'She won't. Why would she? You aren't going to say anything and I certainly shan't. It's just this once and I do love them.' She almost asked, 'Don't you?' but it wasn't a fair question.

'Come on, then.' Letitia led the way to the cloakroom, where Mabel was waiting. They handed in their things in return for tickets. 'Let's see if Steven has bagged a table.'

'I wonder if Alison and Paul are here yet.' Joan looked

around. She was so aware of wearing such stylish shoes that she almost felt embarrassed by the pleasure. It was only a pair of shoes, for heaven's sake – but a pair of shoes that made her feel special and beautiful. As they walked into the ballroom, she could have sworn that the red dancing shoes responded with a little lift of their own as they trod on the sprung floor.

The ballroom was packed. This was among the most popular venues in town and people flocked from miles around, especially now, when, in spite of the blackout and the grim news from the other side of the Channel, an evening of music and dancing, fun and companionship, beneath sparkling chandeliers, could make you feel happy and hopeful and blissfully alive.

Steven had found them a table right beside the dance floor. Letitia gave Joan a secret nudge. If Bob Hubble went whirling by, he would be easy to spot. Letitia and Steven took to the floor in a waltz. They always had the first few dances together and were so accustomed to being partners that their steps were perfectly fluid. Now that her infatuation for Steven had dissolved, Joan could watch the two of them *one*-two-three, *one*-two-threeing around the floor with admiration instead of with her bones tightening with envy.

She danced a couple of times with fellows whom she knew slightly from having danced with them before. She was happy to sit out a few as well, so she could scour the dancefloor for any sign of Bob. As for Mabel, she could dance every dance if she so chose. She wasn't the most beautiful girl in the room, but she had such poise and was so well-groomed that she always drew eyes to her. And did that slight air of reserve add to her appeal? Or was that Joan's imagination getting overactive?

Alison and Paul arrived and joined them at their table.

They had met Paul before, when they had all gone to La Scala on Oxford Road to see *Mr Smith Goes to Washington*. The orchestra began to play 'Pennies From Heaven' and Alison hauled Paul up for the foxtrot.

'You don't mind?' she asked.

'Go ahead.' Joan was happy to stay put and sip her lemonade while listening to the hopeful lyrics.

She glanced around the dance floor, but there was no sign of Bob. She had been in this position plenty of times before and made a point of not letting it spoil her evening. An evening of dancing was fun and uplifting, from getting ready right through to humming a favourite tune under your breath as you walked up the garden path to the front door when you arrived home. And tonight she was wearing Lizzie's red shoes. She glanced down at them, a warm glow of confidence filling her. She hadn't worn proper evening shoes before and it was wonderful to feel elegant.

Glancing up again, she saw – oh no. Toby Collins. The chap Letitia and Steven had tried to match her up with. There was nothing wrong with him, but if he noticed her sitting alone and came over . . .

She rose and casually threaded her way between the tables, smiling and saying 'Excuse me,' as if she was on her way to a particular table. She looked over her shoulder to find Toby looking in her direction. Good manners forced her to smile in recognition, but when several couples heading to the dance floor blocked the line of vision between them, she darted away and hid behind a pillar. With luck, Toby would be no keener to see her than she was to see him, but you never knew. Her heart was beating quickly. Was it safe to look?

'Hello. What are you doing, lurking behind a pillar?'

She turned – and now her heart really did speed up. Bob Hubble had come up behind her. The evening's dancing had got the better of his Brilliantine and his dark hair had loosened into a floppy bit, in an Errol Flynnish kind of way. Other than that, there was nothing Errol Flynnish about him. He wasn't suave or debonair. His jacket, though smart enough, was clearly not new, but it was a man's shirt and collar Gran had always told her girls to look at, and Bob Hubble's was pristine. Here was a young man whose mum made sure he went out looking pressed and spotless.

She had found him at last – or rather, he had found her. Lurking behind a pillar, he had called it. Lurking. What could she say to that?

'You look like you're hiding from someone,' he added.

What could she do but laugh it off? 'I am. There's a chap I don't want to see.'

'How about hiding from him in the throng on the dance floor?'

She was breathless and tingly all over as they stepped onto the floor. She moved into Bob's arms and all those hopeless evenings spent not finding him, all those yearning daydreams, slipped away in a silent sigh as she took her place naturally in his arms. She turned her face up to his as he caught the correct beat and swept her into the dance. As the music ended, he lifted one dark eyebrow in enquiry. She nodded and that was all it took for them to stay in hold for the next dance. The familiar introduction to 'Lovely Lady' soared into the ballroom, the signal that the Ritz's famous revolving stage would shortly begin to turn and the band currently behind the stage would gradually be revealed, playing in time with the one in front as it disappeared from view, so that the music and the dancing never stopped.

The mellow notes of the trombone's introduction gave way to the singer's warm baritone as Joan waltzed in Bob's arms. Would this be their special piece of music, to be treasured and remembered? Was he, like the words of the song, falling madly in love with her? Oh, don't be daft! Just enjoy the moment.

They danced a third dance together and as it drew to a close, Letitia and Steven appeared by their side.

'I'm Joan's sister,' said Letitia. 'I remember you from the first-aid afternoon.'

'Bob Hubble.'

'Letitia Foster, and this is my boyfriend, Steven Arnold. Would you like to join us at our table?'

Bob glanced Joan's way, seeking consent. She nodded and, simple as that, Bob was absorbed into their group. Joan poured a thousand blessings on Letitia's head for making it happen. Steven and Paul went to get fresh drinks while the others chatted. On their return, encouraged by Alison, Bob and Joan regaled Paul with the tale of Mrs Parker and Myrtle, which quickly broke the ice.

'Where do you live?' Alison asked Bob.

'Stretford.'

'We're in Chorlton,' Letitia told him, 'so we're not far from you.'

Joan felt a moment's unease. Was Letitia being too obvious? But if Bob liked her, and he must do or he wouldn't have wanted to see her again after the first-aid test, then he would be as keen to know where she lived as she was to know where he did.

'There's me and my parents and my three sisters, all crammed into a two-up two-down,' said Bob, 'and I wouldn't have it any other way.'

A two-up two-down? Gran wouldn't like that. If Gran had cause to utter the words 'two-up two-down', her tone of voice was such that it was obvious what she was really saying was 'poky'.

'Three sisters?' said Alison. 'I have just the one. Lydia.'

'I have just the one as well,' joked Letitia, slipping her arm through Joan's. 'We live with our gran. Our parents died a long time ago.'

'I'm sorry to hear that,' said Bob. 'My family means everything to me.'

At the end of the evening, Letitia said to Bob, 'We'll be here again on Saturday. Shall we see you?'

Again Bob glanced towards Joan. 'Yes,' he said.

'Good,' said Letitia. 'If you get here first, grab a table, won't you?'

'Do you always organise everybody?' Bob asked with a smile.

'You'll get used to it,' said Steven, standing close by Letitia, his face showing how proud he was to be her boyfriend. A tiny shiver rippled through Joan. Would Bob one day be proud of her in that way?

Goodbyes were said in the foyer, then, with torches at the ready, they slipped outside into the blackout. Alison and Paul set off to walk into town to catch a tram or bus to take them north; and the others went their separate ways, Mabel insisting she didn't need seeing home by her friends.

Joan felt fluttery and self-conscious all the way home. At the front gate, Letitia and Steven paused to let her reach the porch before they said their goodnights. Then she and Letitia would go inside together. Less chance of breaking the blackout that way. Not that a single glimmer was ever permitted to escape from the Foster household. Their local ARP warden was famous for taking delight in banging on doors and threatening locals with fines because he had spotted a tiny sliver of light, but he had never had cause to knock on the Fosters' door.

Standing beneath the overhanging porch, Joan usually tried to fix her mind on other things so as not to be aware of the tender embrace going on just feet away, but tonight she had no trouble ignoring it, as she was completely wrapped up in a daydream of tender embraces to come. With a sigh, she leaned her back against the wall, lifting one foot to rest the sole against the bricks – and froze.

The red shoes.

Hell's bells, she was still wearing Lizzie's red shoes. Gran would go mad. Why had she ever imagined she could get away with it?

Letitia joined her, key at the ready. Joan grabbed her arm.

'I never changed back into my own shoes. The shoe-bag must have got separated from my coat in the cloakroom – and I forgot. I clean forgot. Gran will kill me.'

'Oh, Lord. You can't go indoors wearing them. Take them off and hide them.'

'Where?'

'I don't know. In the coal-bunker.'

'Don't be daft. They'd get spoilt.'

'You're in shoes Gran would slaughter you for wearing, and you call *me* daft? Put them somewhere, then we'll go in. You run straight upstairs and put your slippers on while I make a bee-line for Gran and keep her talking.' Letitia gave her a push. 'Go on.'

Joan switched her torch back on, using the muted beam to help her find her way up the passage at the side of the house. She lifted the latch on the side gate and slid through. The coal-bunker was opposite the back door. They were growing lettuces in boxes on the top. She placed Lizzie's shoes in the space behind the boxes. It would be the work of a moment to retrieve them in the morning – wouldn't it?

Behind her, the snap of a bolt being unlocked sent fear cascading through her. Had Gran heard? She slid back through the gate, latching it slowly to maintain silence, then hurried to the front door. She and Letitia slipped inside and Joan ran upstairs, leaving Letitia to lock up.

When she came down again, she went to the kitchen, where Letitia turned round to pull a face of exaggerated worry at her. Gran, in dressing-gown, rollers and hairnet, was in the act of shooting the bolts on the back door.

'I told you there was nobody there,' said Letitia. 'It must have been a cat. Watch out – the milk's about to boil over.'

Crisis averted, they made the Ovaltine and took it into the parlour to tell Gran about their evening. She always wanted to know whom they had seen, not to mention what sort of family they came from. It was a kind of retrospective spying, but if they didn't go along with it, Gran wouldn't let them go out so much, so it was worth it.

Letitia, bless her, dropped in Bob's name. 'He was at that first-aid test. He was Joan's partner, do you remember?' Without pausing for breath, she moved seamlessly to something Mabel had said.

'You two go on up,' said Gran. 'I'll wash up.'

After they put their rollers in and climbed into bed, Joan gave Letitia a hug.

'You're the best sister ever.'

Steady breathing soon showed that Letitia had dropped off. Joan felt excited and alert enough to stay awake all night, but presently, soothed by the shared warmth, she felt her limbs grow heavier as she dozed off.

Shock – cold – she jerked awake – a dream? No, cold water. Real water. Wet hair, wet face. She struggled to sit up, blinking – shock, wet, light. Beside her, Letitia stirred, mumbled, then raised herself on an elbow.

'Gran?' said Letitia.

Gran held a jug aloft. More water poured over Joan. She squealed and spluttered, tried to scrabble her way out of bed.

Gran clutched the jug to her chest. 'There! Has that cooled you down?'

'Gran . . .' It came out as a croak. It should have been an exclamation, a cry, but it barely emerged at all.

'Well, has it?' Gran demanded. 'Has it cooled down all those steamy, hot feelings rampaging around inside you? Has it? You're a tart, Joan Foster. A slut, a loose woman – just like your mother.'

Fear and bewilderment almost made Joan crumple.

Letitia flung aside the bedclothes and swung her feet out. 'Gran, what is this? How could you?'

'How could I? I know when the wool's being pulled over my eyes, that's how. A cat in our passage – as if! That was you, Joan, sneaking around looking for somewhere to hide your streetwalker's shoes. God knows, I've done all I can to bring you up decently, but blood will out. You're Estelle all over again, you are. Proud, are you? Proud to be like your tart of a mother, who ran off with another man and abandoned her husband and her baby girls, leaving your poor father to die of a broken heart? You make me sick.'

Letitia pushed herself to her feet. 'Joan is nothing like Mother. She's kind and good and she knows right from wrong. She would never, ever behave like . . . like that.'

'Wouldn't she? She already has. She's got herself a pair of floozy's shoes. What's next, eh? French knickers and her skirt slit to her stocking tops?' Gran's mouth twisted into an ugly line as she eyed Joan. 'You may well cower in that bed, lady. You're a nasty piece of work, rotten to the core, just like your mother, pretending to be all good and clean and decent when really you're a slave to your lustful feelings.'

'Gran!' Remorse clogged Joan's throat and turned her eyes to grit. 'I'm not like that, I'm not!'

'Not like that, she says.' Gran's voice rose, then suddenly dropped. 'I've seen your shoes, lady. Shiny enough to reflect up your skirt and show the boys what's on offer. Oh aye, I've had my eyes opened to the real you. Maybe you should get out of here, leave home and go in search of your slut of a mother. Not that she'll want you, oh no, not her. Couldn't wait to get shot of the pair of you, she couldn't, when her fancy man came along. Upped and left, she did, and your poor father, poor dear daddy, was left behind to pine away. My poor boy, my poor boy, dying of a broken heart.'

Gran raised the jug in her hands. Joan caught her breath. Was Gran about to chuck it at her? She lifted her hands instinctively to protect herself, but Gran hurled the jug at the wall. It crashed and broke into several pieces that landed on the candlewick bedspread. Joan was shaking on the inside, but on the outside, she couldn't move.

Gran stared down at her, her mouth a slash of disgust. Above her dressing gown's embroidered collar, her stringy neck had tightened into cords and her jaw was clenched. Rage hung in the air, years old, and as thick as pre-war stew.

Turning on her heel, Gran marched from the room. The door slammed behind her.

Chapter Nineteen

For the third day running, Dot raced home after her day's work. She threw tea on the table, barely stopping for a bite to eat, then flew upstairs to change her clothes and dash back into town. It was unbelievable. Heartbreaking. The BEF, those dear men of the British Expeditionary Force, all of them sons, husbands, fathers, sweethearts. The man who bought two ounces of Golden Virginia for his pipe, the chap with the biggest cabbages on the allotment, the young husband who had held his firstborn in his arms, the proud father who hoped for nothing more than to walk his beloved daughter up the aisle – the BEF was in retreat. Worse, they had been cornered on the beaches. Even now, at this very moment, hundreds of thousands of men were trapped at Dunkirk. Sunday, the 26th of May 1940 would be engraved on Dot's heart for ever. She prayed to God they would survive as they were shot at from the air, waiting to be rescued by the navy. And not just the navy. Dot's heart soared with pride, resolve and hope. 'The little ships', they were calling them. The little ships – sailing barges, pleasure cruisers, fishing boats, RNLI lifeboats – were chugging to and fro across the English Channel to assist in the extraordinary rescue.

And she, Dot Green, mother of two brave lads, was doing her bit, along with hundreds of thousands of other civilians across the country. The concourse at Victoria Station had been more or less taken over by the Women's Voluntary Service. Tea-urns, milk, sugar. Mugs, cups, spoons – hotels and restaurants had sent supplies. Mountains of sandwiches and buttered cakes. Bakeries and shops had provided the wherewithal. Worn-out old men, who had run their corner shops since the dawn of time, had turned up with boxes of jars of fish paste.

Dot had spent the past two nights, in between the troop trains arriving, filling milk churns with lemonade to ease parched throats, and writing scores upon scores of 'I am safe' postcards on behalf of shattered servicemen who had given their addresses to the WVS. When the trains pulled in, her job was to help direct those men who were being moved on elsewhere to the right platforms for their next trains. God bless the railways. All those hundreds of thousands of men who were in the process of being lifted from the beaches at Dunkirk, once they were returned to Blighty had to be sent home or to hospital. How could that ever be achieved without the railways? And God bless dear old Mam an' all. It was her work as a railway girl in the last war that had inspired Dot to sign up for the railways this time around, enabling her to be a part of this massive national effort.

She wasn't the only one with half an eye on the past. Last night, she had opened the door to the mess, only to spot several of the older porters and ticket-office clerks and ticket collectors, all of them old enough to have served in the last lot, Mr Thirkle among them, sitting together and looking – well, stricken was the only word for it. She had withdrawn, quietly closing the door, hoping she hadn't been spotted. No man wanted his moment of weakness to be witnessed by a woman, even if she understood his feelings and shared them. Some of those old soldiers were the fathers of men serving in the current conflict; sons who might or might not come home. Pray to God they would come home.

Glancing across towards the mess a few minutes later, Dot had seen the door open and the men come out. Old wounds and fresh fears might have surfaced, a tear or two might even have been shed, but now they pinned back their thin old shoulders and set to.

They would all be there again tonight, Dot had no doubt, working round the clock doing their bit to bring the boys home.

Would Archie and Harry come home tonight? Pray to God, pray to God, pray to God.

Dot's heart all but cracked open in anguish at the thought of her two boys. How was she to carry on if they . . . ? She mustn't think like that. Be strong. She was the one everybody relied on. Catching sight of her reflection in the looking-glass on top of the chest of drawers, she stilled. Was this the face of the mother of two living, breathing boys? Pray to God, pray to God, pray to God.

Dressed in her comfortable linen skirt, with a blouse and cardigan, she went downstairs. What she really wanted to do was ease off her shoes and soak her feet in a bowl of hot water, but there was no time for that. At the bottom of the stairs, Reg was putting on his homburg. That was a sign of summat important, that was.

'I'm coming with you,' he said.

'To the station?'

He didn't say, 'Where d'you think, you daft bat?' He said, 'Aye. I can help blokes get home. I can carry kit-bags. I've got my shaving tackle in my pocket. I bet they haven't shaved in days. I might be too old to be called up this time round, and I don't know what I can do, Dot, but I'm ruddy sure I'm going to do it.'

So that was that, then. Homburgs didn't just mean church, funerals, the annual prize-giving at the bowls club. They meant national emergencies an' all.

At the station, one train-load of men had been more or less dispersed and they were preparing for the next one. More tea urns, more plates of sandwiches. The WVS worked steadily. Every woman was competent and concerned, and no matter how tired she was, she was inexhaustible. In Dot's opinion, the WVS was fast becoming the backbone of the nation.

Aye, and didn't that one over yonder know it? Among all the women whose attitude was heads down and get on with it, she alone, who had been blessed with a bosom you could serve afternoon tea off, was fussing about from here to yon and back again, doing her bit, no doubt, but doing it in a way that said she knew she was doing it and wanted the rest of the world to know it an' all.

'There's always one, isn't there?' said a soft, cultured voice beside Dot. Persephone. She was one of them now, one of the railway girls, as hard as it was to believe that someone so upper class would muck in like the rest of them. Yet why should it be hard to believe? Why shouldn't a lass out of the top drawer do war work, the same as ordinary folk? When you thought about it, it was only right and proper, because oughtn't the upper classes set a good example? All that wealth and privilege meant they were supposed to be the best of the best. Give Persephone her due, here she was, working as hard as any of them.

She had done some war work in Darley Court, apparently. Dot had heard of Darley Court, a posh place down Chorlton way. When that job had finished, Persephone had applied to the railways – inspired by Mabel, so she said, though Mabel's mouth had tightened when she said it. Persephone's first day at work should have been Monday the 27th, but instead she had pitched up on Sunday, as soon as the news broke. She had charmed her way into the ranks of the WVS and started making sandwiches as though born to it – which you could tell from her posh voice and smooth hands, she definitely wasn't. She had one of those double-barrelled surnames an' all, complete with a hyphen. You had to be proper posh to have a hyphen.

Dot glanced at Persephone. She was hyphenated, all right. That dress – and it was a dress, even though at first sight it appeared to be a two-piece costume – was wool crepe, if Dot's eyes weren't mistaken. Eh, what she wouldn't give to be able to dress their Jenny like that when she was older. The knee-length skirt had a slight flare to it and the sleeves were three-quarter-length, which, let's face it, was sensible, if you were going to be up to your elbows in bread and marge. But it was the hat that caught most of Dot's attention, though she didn't let it show. On anybody else, a hat like that would look like an upside-down flowerpot, but on Miss Persephone, it was natty and stylish. That feather sticking out of the hat-band looked as jaunty and casual as if Persephone had stuck it there on her way out of the door, as a way of thumbing her elegant Roman nose at Jerry.

Dot turned her critical gaze back to the WVS volunteer. 'Look at her, scurrying about.'

'Conspicuously helpful.' Persephone said it with a smile. 'Well, she doesn't warrant a mention in my article, that's all I can say.'

Aye, and that was another thing about Persephone. She fancied herself as a writer, a journalist no less. Did that mean she was clever or just big-headed? Dot was reserving judgement on that one. Or maybe it just made her upper-class and born with the sort of confidence that said you could do whatever suited you.

'Have you had any sleep?' Persephone asked.

Oh Lord, did that mean she had bags the size of dinner-plates under her eyes? 'I grabbed a bit here and there. You?'

'Likewise. No one will get any proper sleep, no one will want any, until this is over.'

And afterwards, after Dunkirk, would they stay awake to prepare for invasion?

'Here comes my husband,' said Dot. 'He has a mad idea he's going to help some lads get home tonight.'

'What's mad about that? I think it's a wizard idea. Will you introduce me?'

Dot called Reg over. 'Reg, this here is Persephone . . .'

'Trehearn-Hobbs.'

'Trehearn-Hobbs,' finished Dot. She remembered too late that you were supposed to introduce the man to the woman, not the other way around. 'This is my husband, Reg Green.'

'How do you do, Mr Green?' said Persephone, while Reg gawped, possibly at her beauty, possibly at the cut-glass accent. He didn't merely raise his hat to her, he actually removed it from his head and held it in front of him, like a yeoman in the presence of the lady of the manor. 'I gather you intend to help some brave lads get home tonight. May I offer my services? I haven't been resident in these parts for long and I know absolute squat about the lie of the land, but I do have a motor parked outside, so if you'll be my navigator, I'll gladly serve as chauffeur – for as long as the petrol lasts, that is.'

'You've got a motor outside?' Reg repeated.

Persephone delved inside her capacious, tapestry handbag and pulled out a contraption Dot had never seen before. 'Here's the rotor arm to prove it.'

Dot exchanged a glance with Reg. Was the girl doolally?

'The family seat is in Sussex, you see. Daddy said we must always remove the rotor arm when we leave the motor anywhere, in case Jerry parachutes in and tries to get the car started. I don't know whether that applies up here in quite the same way, but better safe than sorry and all that.'

The smile Persephone gave them had probably knocked the socks off dozens of young baronets. She had the loveliest violet eyes. Really unusual.

Reg cleared his throat. 'We'll get some local lads home in style tonight, then.' He looked at Dot. 'Let's hope us own lads are among them, eh?'

She was pierced by pride – in Reg, of all people. Talk about unexpected. Old, long-forgotten love echoed through her. Blimey. Was the national catastrophe of Dunkirk going to bring her and Reg back together?

Mabel had heard the expression about being asleep on your feet, but she had never taken it literally. She thought it just meant dog-tired, but now she knew that it really was possible to fall asleep standing up. Propped up against walls, against one another, some men were well and truly in the depths of slumber. They were the lucky ones, the ones who had escaped from this nightmare for a while – though who was to say that their dreams were any better? Some of them were so deeply asleep that their mates had to give 'em a prod now and then to make sure they were still alive.

The sight of all those exhausted soldiers, waking, sleeping, all of them on that station, wrenched at Mabel's heart. They were grimy, unkempt, as tattered as beggars and probably covered in lice and goodness knows what else. But they were here; they were home. They had been plucked from the catastrophe that was Dunkirk and brought home. That was all that mattered. The air was enough to knock you off your feet. The salt tang of seawater, the sour smell of unwashed bodies, the tinny aroma of blood and the musty whiff of despair all mashed together into a substantial pong that seared the backs of your eyes.

But these weren't the men Mabel was here for. These were the so-called able-bodied. She had been assigned to a hospital train. Along with other volunteers, she had been sent from Victoria to London Road Station, over the far side of Piccadilly Gardens in the middle of Manchester, to join the main line down to London. There were nurses and doctors on the hospital trains, of course. The volunteers were there to do – well, whatever they were told.

'And do it quickly but calmly,' one of the nurses had instructed Mabel. 'No matter how difficult it is, no matter how distressed you are, and you will be distressed, believe me, it mustn't show in your face.'

Mabel had nodded. She had thought – then – that the worst thing that could possibly happen to her already had. She had thought that losing Althea was her own personal worst thing and should have given her a kind of immunity to any other events, no matter how tragic. But it turned out life didn't work like that. It wasn't neat and predictable. It could rip your heart open from right to left one day, and from left to right the next, and there wasn't a single damn thing you could do to prevent it.

Since then, she had travelled up and down in the hospital trains, submerging her tiredness, her emotion, her fears and, in some cases, her gut-churning nausea, beneath an overwhelming determination to do the best she possibly could for the injured men in the bunks. What if someone she knew was on this train? What if she had to change his dressings? What if . . . what if he died and she knew before his parents, before his neighbours and friends? It could be a man she knew by sight from the streets of Annerby; a man from the factory; the son of a hill farmer. Most of the hill farmers had stayed put, but she had heard of a couple of muscular sons who had thrown their reserved occupations to the winds, or, more accurately, to the land girls.

Bobby Thornley, whose snobby mother looked down on the Bradshaws, had joined the navy. Althea's cousin Dennis had joined the army. So had Andrew Cooper-Jones. So had Gil and she had said, 'Go, then,' because it was immediately after Althea's funeral and she hadn't cared about anything other than the terrible loss she had caused.

'Miss . . . miss . . .'

Some of them called her 'miss', others called her 'Nurse'. She answered to both.

'Is there any . . . water? Please.'

God, look at this lad. Half his face in bandages, both his arms in splints, but he still remembered his manners. 'Please,' he said. Please.

'Here, sip this. I'll hold it for you.'

'Thanks, miss.'

She didn't want to rush him, poor blighter, but she had to keep one eye on the primus. Keeping that going was one of her jobs. She had to jiggle the little pump on the side in and out every so often, or their carriage wouldn't have heat for the water. They needed hot water for soaking off filthy, blood-caked bandages. Fly-ridden bandages, in some cases. Crikey, they had turned her stomach at first, but it was surprising what you could get used to. After all these journeys, all these trains filled with lines upon lines of bunks with injured soldiers, what was one more fly-ridden bandage? Nothing. Compared to what these men had been through – nothing.

A cry went up from along the carriage. 'Mum! Mum!' Mabel's heart turned over. She hadn't understood the first time she heard it, back on that first train. But now, after – how many trains? Now she knew what it meant.

'You'd be surprised how many of them call out for their mothers in their last moments,' Nurse Spooner had told her.

Mabel looked along the aisle down the centre of the

carriage, but a nurse was already there, beside the man who had called for his mother. Poor beggar. Was he in his final moments? Was he to slip away here, now? Having survived Dunkirk, was he going to die on a train halfway to Manchester? Life was cruel. Death was crueller.

At least she was on a hospital train, not a coffin train. Dear heaven, she had seen coffins being loaded onto a train. An entire train filled with dead bodies. And not just that one train, either. She didn't want to think about how many of those there might be.

'Ta for looking after us, Nurse.'

She looked down before realising the voice had come from the upper bunk. A young lad. No, he must be her own age, early twenties. Not a lad at all, though he looked like one just now.

'I'm not a nurse,' she told him. 'I'm a volunteer.'

'Me too. I mean, I joined up proper, I weren't called up. My dad said I'd learn a proper trade in the army. Been in since '37, but I won't be in after this. Too badly mangled. I'm not complaining, mind. I'm lucky to be here. A couple of hospital ships got sunk, you know. They're meant to be safe from that, but they got sunk. That's plain wicked, that is.'

'Best sight I ever saw was the White Cliffs of Dover,' said the chap on the bunk underneath. 'It was like a miracle.'

'Well, aren't you two the chatty ones?' came Nurse Spooner's voice from behind Mabel. 'Stay as perky as that and I'll have you on your feet, taking care of the men with real injuries. Let me have a look at that arm. The primus needs attention, Miss Bradshaw.'

She joined Mabel a minute or two later.

'The lad at the far end has passed away, I'm afraid.'

'The one who called out for his mother?'

'Yes, poor chap – and poor mother. Dr Williams has pronounced life extinct. Can you help me lift the stretcher off the bunk and carry it through to the mortuary carriage? It's less of a fuss if we do it. Send for a couple of orderlies and the men will know the reason why.'

Unable to speak, Mabel nodded.

'He's right down the end, so only a couple of fellows will see him being removed. You've gone rather white. Will you be able to do this? Say if you won't.' There was a bracing note in Nurse Spooner's voice. 'Say if you're going to faint,' had been her very first instruction to Mabel.

Mabel inhaled deeply and focused on the kind of determination that had seen Pops pull himself up by his bootstraps from being the son of a wheeltapper, in a small cottage near the tracks, to the owner of Bradshaw's Ball Bearings and Other Small Components, and the master of a handsome house overlooking the whole town.

'It's a good thing we're next door to the mortuary carriage,' said Nurse Spooner.

A good thing? A horrible thing, a tragic thing. But good, too, because it meant they could transfer their dead with minimum bother.

When Private Carbury had been laid down in the mortuary carriage, Nurse Spooner gently covered him with a sheet.

'Not his face,' said Mabel. 'Not yet.'

Nurse Spooner looked at her. 'Don't be long. It's the living that need us.' She turned to go, her body swaying with the movement of the train as she headed for the connection between the two carriages. Once there, she looked back. 'Don't forget to cover his face, will you?'

Nurse Spooner probably thought she wanted to say a prayer, and maybe she did, but she hadn't prayed over any of the men who had died during her journeys. She had whispered poems over them. Was that wrong – disrespectful? They had done a lot of poetry at school, had been required to learn masses of the stuff by heart. She hadn't known she'd remembered any of it, but somehow, here, in the mortuary carriage of this hospital train, the poems had risen to the surface of her mind.

Over her first deceased soldier, she had murmured the one about the night mail crossing the border; over the next, the one about the sweet bells over the bay, and the sea beasts and the salt weed. Another time it was Portia's 'quality of mercy' speech. This time, what came to mind was her favourite Thomas Hardy poem, which had inspired her, in numerous English compositions, to have characters brushing the boughs of trees and releasing scents, and wishing the idea had been her own in the first place. What would Private Carbury's mother or his wife think if they knew that these were the words that had been spoken over his body? Would they think she had taken a liberty in reciting a poem instead of saying a prayer? Or might they be comforted to know that she had simply made the time to do it, to be with him, to stand beside him in the early moments of his passing from this life into the next?

Or was she just doing it for herself? For the greater glory of Mabel Bradshaw?

Lifting the sheet, she covered Carbury's face. Already you could see that he wasn't there any more. Whatever it was inside him that had made him Private Carbury had departed. Mabel moved her face about, shifting her jaw, stretching her mouth, blinking. Whatever expression she had worn these past few minutes must be eradicated. She had to look cheerful and competent when she returned to the men in her hospital carriage. It was all too easy to give the game away by having the wrong expression on your face. She huffed out a breath and forced a smile.

More hours of keeping the primus going. More icky bandages to be soaked off. 'Will you write a postcard for

my folks, miss?' ... 'Will you write a note to my mum?'
More blood and vomit to clear from the floor. More brows
to dampen, more sips of water to give. More bedpans and
bottles to hand out. God, it was staggering what you could
get used to.

'Ma!'

Mabel looked round, met Nurse Spooner's eyes and saw
the answer to her unspoken question.

'Nurse!' called the doctor. 'Over here – now!'

Nurse Spooner immediately scuttled further along the
carriage. Mabel headed for the man who had called out.
She didn't go right up to him. She kept her distance.

'Ma!' His eyes were blurry, his features contorted with
pain. One hand snaked out, wafted around uselessly.

Mabel caught it, clasped it tight inside both her own.

'Ma, is that you?'

'Don't be afraid,' she managed to say through the con-
striction swelling inside her throat. 'I'm here.'

Chapter Twenty

'... and when he said that about fighting on the beaches, I was ready to grab a milk bottle in one hand and the poker in the other and march all the way to Fleetwood to take on Jerry and give him a good bashing, and I don't suppose I was the only one.'

Dot looked round the buffet table. She still felt fired up when she thought about it. The catastrophe of Dunkirk had been turned into a triumph, the single greatest part of which was that both her boys had come home safely. Filthy, stinking and covered in blood, but other men's blood, and God forgive her for being grateful for that. They were both fast asleep now, had been since yesterday, when she had stood looking down at each of them in turn, in their own beds in their own homes, and the years had fallen away, as if they were little boys asleep in bed at home. All she had wanted was to protect them and fetch them up to the best of her ability, in spite of Reg's slapdash ways. As she had watched them sleep yesterday, her heart had swelled with gratitude and fear until she could scarcely breathe.

'Come away now, Mother,' Pammy had said. Pammy hadn't liked it when Dot had raced straight up the stairs to look at Archie. It probably wasn't good manners. It hadn't bothered Sheila when Dot had done the same thing to see Harry, to see him with her own eyes, so that she could know for certain that he really had come back in one piece.

Presumably they would wake up today. She couldn't

wait to get home and see them properly. More than anything she wanted to hold them, hug them, hang on to them and never let go. Her skin was squirmy with the need to touch them. It would tear her apart when they had to leave again, but she would have to keep her anguish to herself. It would be worse for Sheila and Pammy. She had to remember that. As their mother, she must remember that she didn't come first any more.

'The LMS is starting up a prisoner-of-war fund,' said Cordelia. 'We're all going to be asked to contribute a penny a week.'

'That's hardly anything,' said Lizzie.

'Ah, but all those pennies put together will add up,' said Cordelia. 'Think how many people are employed on the railway.'

'I think the plan is to send parcels every so many months,' said Mabel. There was a strained look about her. She had been on one of those hospital trains, so goodness only knows what she had seen in recent days, poor girl. 'Clothes and tobacco and things.'

'I'll gladly put in my penny every week,' Dot declared. 'I'll do it out of gratitude for the safe return of my boys.'

'We're all glad your sons have come home,' said Cordelia, and the others echoed her words.

Dot couldn't speak. They had come home this time. What about next time?

She pushed back her chair. 'I must get home. You understand.'

'Of course,' said Mabel. 'You're dying to see them again. It was good of you to pop in here and make sure we knew they were safe.'

It was tempting to fly straight round to Archie's or Harry's, but she made herself go home. She had to let the boys have their family time with their wives and kids. Plenty

of time for them to see Mum and Dad afterwards. *Mum* –
oh, wasn't it the best word in the world? It certainly was,
when your boys had been snatched from the jaws of death
and had come home safe. There were plenty of mothers
today who would never be called Mum again as long as
they lived. Dot's heart ached for all those bereaved women.
Pray to God she would never suffer as they did.

She all but ran along Heathside Lane. Maybe the boys
would have come round. Maybe they would be in there,
waiting, jostling each other aside to be the first to pull her
into a giant hug. She flung open the door.

There was no cry of delight, no shout. Stupid to be disappointed. She plastered a smile on her face. She was going to
see her boys this evening. She still had boys to see. She was
one of the lucky ones.

'That you, Dot?' called Reg.

She bustled into the kitchen. There he was, sitting at the
table with his newspaper. Same as always.

And just like that, they were back where they always
were. Never mind the pride she had felt when he'd marched
off with Persephone to find some local lads and help get
them home in that motor. Never mind that he had spent
hours giving directions to get soldiers home. And when the
petrol ran out, never mind that he had carried kitbags, handed
out cigarettes, helped keep one of the mobile canteens outside the station stocked up with provisions, fetching and
carrying, rushing to and fro like a fellow half his age.

Dot had grown into a bigger person during those Dunkirk
days. She had been more than plain old Dot Green,
with her housewifely cares and responsibilities. She had
been someone who mucked in and made a difference to
the war effort. Oh, she wasn't blowing her own trumpet. It
was just that she had been a part of something vast and
important and ultimately magnificent. She had answered

the call and so had her husband. Shouldn't that have some sort of lasting effect? Shouldn't it have brought them back together?

Reg's actions throughout the days and nights of the Dunkirk evacuation had touched her heart in a way she hadn't experienced in years. She had been ready to burst with pride at the thought of her husband doing his bit, making a difference.

She had been proud of every citizen in the whole ruddy country, but that didn't mean she wanted to be married to them.

And now it was over and Reg was back at the kitchen table.

'What time's tea?' he asked.

'Bugger the tea. Put your cap on.'

She nipped upstairs to get changed, then came straight down again without bothering. With wings on her stout black lace-ups, she ran to Pammy's, and whether Reg could keep up was his business. As she barged through the kitchen door and into the sitting room, her heart was beating fast from running, but the sight that greeted her set it drumming in pure elation. Her boys, her two boys, were both here. They came to their feet as she rushed in, their beloved faces – pale, older, but still the faces of her two little 'uns – creasing into grins.

She surged forwards and so did they, the three of them joining together in a gigantic hug in the middle of the room. They towered over her. She couldn't see out. Her face was squashed against a chest – Archie's. He smoked a different brand to Harry. She wanted to push free and gaze at them both; she wanted to stay put for ever in the cosy darkness of their embrace. This was what she had prayed for every night since they'd gone away. Thank you, God.

'My turn,' said Harry, and the group shifted so that now

she was crushed against Harry's chest, though Archie didn't let go.

Tears gushed from Dot's eyes. She had sworn she wouldn't cry. Tears were for wives. But here she was, soaking Harry's shirt and making a right ninny of herself.

The boys stepped away from her. Her arms ached to grab them and hold on. It was like being a brand-new mum all over again. Protectiveness, pride and overpowering love poured from her heart into her bloodstream, coursing round her system and transforming her into a better person.

'Nan's crying,' said Jimmy.

'That's because she's happy,' said Jenny.

Knuckling her tears, Dot tried to laugh, but it came out as a strangled croak. Her darling grandchildren were here too. After all these months without her sons, now her whole heart was in this room.

Compulsory overtime was increased in the charging office. Joan felt a chill inside her chest at the sight of several empty chairs. Miss Clayton was absent because her brother had died during the retreat to Dunkirk, and Mrs O'Brien was at home taking care of her daughter, who had collapsed upon hearing, from a family friend who'd made it back, that her husband had been lost at sea. He was on the *Grafton*, which had been torpedoed by a Jerry sub when she stopped to pick up survivors from the stricken HMS *Wakeful*. Miss Hoskins, the girl for whom they had all been saving the tiny paper circles from their hole punchers to use as confetti, was on her way down south to see her fiancé, who was in a bad way in a hospital in Kent.

If she was honest, it wasn't just to support her absent colleagues that Joan was happy to work the extra hours. It gave her a genuine reason to be out of the house. Even though Gran hadn't been able to maintain her level of fury in the face of the crushing blow that had been delivered to the nation, the atmosphere at home was distinctly icy. No further mention had been made of Estelle, but it was as if she was hovering in the shadows and if you turned round quickly enough, you might catch a glimpse of her. Yes, all right, that was downright fanciful, but Joan had felt unsettled and watchful ever since that frankly scary scene in the bedroom.

'I've never seen Gran worked up like that before,' she had whispered to Letitia afterwards. 'Do you think – do you think . . . ?'

'That you deserved it? That – that you're like Mother? No.' Letitia's voice, though quiet, was fierce. 'She left Daddy for another man and abandoned us. You're not like that. You're good and loyal and decent.'

Was she? In her heart, she was sure she was, but maybe Estelle had thought so too . . . until temptation came her way.

'Gran losing her rag like that was just horrible, but she had her reasons, as we both well know,' said Letitia. 'Whatever happens, don't let it stop you seeing Bob.'

And Joan hadn't. It was the strangest thing. At a time when she was persona non grata at home, she found herself being warmly welcomed into Bob's family. She had always been second best in Gran's eyes, not just because of Letitia's cleverness but also because of Letitia's resemblance to Daddy, whereas at Bob's house she felt welcome and wanted. Even the thought of it took her breath away. She had never felt . . . accepted before. Gran accepted Letitia. Gran adored Letitia, but she didn't adore Joan. She never had and Joan knew she never would. But the Hubbles all loved one another, and they loved Bob, and if he liked her, and liked her enough to bring her home, then they liked her too. Might they be willing to go further than liking her? She didn't doubt it for one moment.

Bob's sisters, Maureen, Petal and Glad, treated her more or less as another sister, and, of course, Mrs Hubble, Bob's mum, was the Bernice who worked with Mabel. Not that Joan called her Bernice to her face. This first names malarkey had shaken up the proprieties a bit – more than a bit – but there were still rules to be followed. First names around the buffet table was one thing, but the rest of the time, in front of other people, they Miss'd and Mrs'd one another, as was right and proper.

Joan was fascinated by Bob's dad. The father was the most important person in the family. Even in the Foster household, where she and Letitia couldn't remember Daddy, he was hugely important. Gran had trained them to aspire to live up to his expectations and Joan couldn't look at Daddy's photograph – and she knew it was the same for Letitia – without experiencing a sense of longing for what they had never had, as well as a sense of the reverence in which fathers were held.

So she was taken aback, to say the least, by the casual way the young Hubbles teased their father. Take that business of the blackout frames. The Hubbles didn't have blackout curtains. Mr Hubble had made lightweight frames that slotted into place over their windows, and these Mrs Hubble had covered with several layers of blackout fabric.

But when Joan made an admiring remark, she prompted gales of laughter from Bob and the girls, who practically tripped over one another to tell her how Dad had laid the pieces for the frames on the floor to construct them – only to discover, when he came to pick up the finished articles, 'that he'd gone and nailed them to the floor!' cried Glad in between howls of glee.

Joan's hand flew to her chest in anticipation of the

harsh reprimand that was certain to follow from the angry lips of the head of the family. But no, Mr Hubble roared with laughter along with the rest of them. Joan's heart had pitter-pattered. Gran would never have permitted anyone to laugh at her, still less at Daddy. And yet here were the Hubbles all enjoying the joke at Mr Hubble's expense. She wouldn't have believed it if she hadn't seen it with her own eyes. She hadn't known a father could be like that.

The Hubbles' blackout was a sight to behold, for Mrs Hubble and the girls had sewn silver stars all over the inside of the black fabric.

'We like to make the best of things,' said Bernice Hubble.

They had gone to town over the anti-blast tape on their windows as well.

'They have one window with the usual criss-crossed tape,' Joan told Letitia and Gran, 'but they actually cut up little bits of tape to form noughts and crosses and turned the window into an actual game. The kitchen window is a cat's face and another is a flower. They've even got a desert island.'

'It sounds fun,' said Letitia, but Gran snorted.

'It sounds irresponsible,' she declared.

Joan wanted to say she knew this wasn't the case, but she was scared of setting Gran off again.

Mrs Hubble had said to her on her first visit to their house, 'War is a serious business. Believe me, love, I lived through the last one and I know. I lost three brothers, I did. But just because it's serious doesn't mean you have to be glum all the while. That's not the Hubble way.'

No, as Joan had soon learned, it wasn't the Hubble way. Their house was filled with laughter and that was a revelation to her. There might be the occasional joke in the Foster household, but that was as far as it went, whereas the

Hubbles' two-up two-down was awash with good humour and affection.

She tried to explain it to Letitia and was taken aback when Letitia laughed.

'What's so funny?'

'You. Are you sure it's Bob you're interested in?'

A cold sensation washed through her. Surely Letitia hadn't somehow discerned her old attraction to Steven? 'What do you mean?'

'You're obviously so taken with Bob's family. Don't get me wrong. I think it's lovely. But is it Bob you're in love with, or the whole Hubble family?'

The gateway to Alexandra Park was bare of gates these days. Joan cycled through the empty space, her tyres crunching on the path. Her insides felt crunchy too, all her hopes jangling against one another as she headed for the park-keeper's house. Here at last was her chance to do some work for the war effort that was likely to be tough and risky, unlike her office job. Of course, she hoped with all her heart not to be called upon to do it. She didn't want there to be air raids. But if there were – and after Dunkirk, it seemed increasingly likely – then here she was, ready, willing and . . . Would she prove able?

Hope got tangled up in her throat and she had to drag in a breath. What if, after all that training, not to mention the frustration of being stuck behind a typewriter day after day, she turned out to be a complete dud, who fell to pieces at the first sound of an ack-ack gun? She was untested, that was the trouble. Mabel had spent the Dunkirk days and nights on a hospital train, but all Joan had been called upon to do was wash up endlessly so that the returning men could be offered tea.

Outside the park-keeper's house were a few bicycles and

a couple of motor cars. That was good. Some first-aid parties were to have motor cars so they would be able to reach stricken areas more speedily – as long as the roads hadn't been blasted full of bomb craters.

She ran up the steps through the open door, dancing out of the way of a young man carrying two wooden chairs by their backs. Another man carried a stool and a third was manoeuvring a big wicker chair.

'Coat pegs behind you. We're meeting in there.' The man with the wooden chairs tilted his chin to indicate an open door across the hall.

Turning to hang up her things, Joan bumped into a small table that stood by the stairs, jiggling the telephone that stood on it.

'Clumsy!' said a gruff voice behind her. 'Telephones aren't installed in first-aid depots just to get broken by silly girls.'

Silly girls? She bridled, but the men were too busy with chairs to pay any attention. She went into the room to find a parlour dominated by a cast-iron fireplace with two overmantel shelves topped by a vast mirror. Furniture had been pushed against the walls to make space for the additional chairs that had been squeezed in. Just inside, a man with the same kind of well-bred good looks as Leslie Howard was sitting on a chair, one knee thrown across the other and a clipboard resting on his thigh, fountain pen in his left hand, cigarette between his right index and middle fingers.

'Joan Foster, reporting for duty.'

What on earth had made her say that? What a twit she sounded.

But the man smiled. 'Good to see enthusiasm.' He put the cigarette to his lips, inhaled and blew out a stream of smoke before ticking off her name. 'Take a pew.'

'Room here for a little 'un,' offered a middle-aged woman from the sofa.

'Over here, Joan,' called Lizzie from the window-seat, but the woman on the sofa had already budged up, so Joan felt obliged to join her and found herself squashed into the corner.

'I hope the park-keeper doesn't mind us invading his house,' she said.

'He's been called up,' the woman told her, 'and his wife and children have gone to Wales, so this place is ours for the duration.'

A man who had the same sort of broad forehead and wide-set eyes as Sir Anthony Eden introduced himself as Mr Turnbull, who was in charge of their unit.

'Thank you for turning out early this evening. When our duties commence, the overnight hours will be ten till six and we'll be using a system that came in handy in the last lot. We'll deal with minor injuries on the spot. Others will be sent or taken to first-aid posts, each of which will have its own doctor and some nurses. Those most seriously injured will go to hospital. Now then, first things first. We need to set up shop. We'll keep our supplies in the boxroom at the top of the stairs, so the stuff that's in there has to be stowed elsewhere. Can you organise that, Atkins?'

The man with the fountain pen and the cigarette nodded.

'That will be our main business for tonight.'

The rumble of an engine had those nearest the window turning to peer between the lines of criss-crossed tape. From her corner of the sofa, Joan could make out the top half of a van with *Dickinson's Bakery* painted on the side in fancy writing.

'That'll be our supplies,' said Mr Turnbull. 'Let's get ourselves sorted, then we can practise loading the cars. They have to be loaded every evening and unloaded at the end of the night for return to their owners. Atkins, if you're ready . . . ?'

Mr Atkins came to his feet, not exactly jumping to it, but in a relaxed, fluid movement. His hair was the colour of runny honey and his eyes were light brown in a face that was clever but reserved.

'These people, upstairs to clear the boxroom.' He rattled off names. 'These, unload our stuff from the van.' More names. 'Mr Harrison and Mr Preston, check the lists to make sure we've received everything, and Mrs Marshall . . .' He turned to the woman who had made room for Joan on the sofa, '. . . if you wouldn't mind bunging the kettle on, I'm sure it would be taken as a great kindness by one and all.'

It wasn't long before the boxes of supplies were indoors. Judging by the occasional bang followed by a short silence and then laughter coming from upstairs, it wouldn't be long before work up there was finished too. Presently everyone was squashed back into the parlour, Joan perching on a chair this time. There was a matey feeling in the air.

'Each first-aid party will have five members,' said Mr Turnbull. 'Each person will carry a metal bottle for water and a small rucksack with essential supplies. Six is the magic number. Six dressings in each size, six triangular bandages, six labels, but four splints, please note, not six.'

'What are the labels for?' Lizzie asked.

'Good question. Any ideas, anyone?'

Joan recalled the news reels at the pictures last year, showing all those children being evacuated, but before she could speak, someone else piped up.

'To label the casualties.'

'Good man. Yes, indeed. We'll use code. T for tourniquet, I for internal injuries, and so on. You shall have to learn the full list of initials. We have two cars, each of which will carry a large rucksack with extra supplies, as well as blankets and stretchers; so our next job tonight is to sort out how to fit all the equipment plus the chaps into the motors. Atkins?'

'These are the first-aid parties.'

Mr Atkins read from a list. The first party was all men, as was the second, and the third. Joan exchanged a glance with Mabel. Weren't any girls' names to be read out? Or maybe there would be an all-girl group?

'And then we'll have a four-man party.' Mr Atkins read out the names and sat down again.

'Jolly good,' said Mr Turnbull. 'We'll fill the personal rucksacks, then load the motors.'

'Excuse me,' said Mabel. 'What about us girls?'

'Good question – Miss Bradshaw, isn't it? Good question, Miss Bradshaw. You girls can fold the blankets.'

'I meant, what about us being in first-aid parties?'

Mr Turnbull blinked. 'You girls won't be going out. You'll take care of things here. I don't know why you thought any differently.'

'Possibly because we had to go through the same test,' Mabel said mildly.

Mr Turnbull's gaze slid away from her. 'Atkins?'

'If the first-aid parties wouldn't mind moving outside, let's get the stretchers fastened to the roofs of the motors, then we'll see about the rucksacks. Mrs Marshall, could you and the young ladies get all the rucksacks filled?'

'In the normal run of things,' said Mr Turnbull, 'each man will keep his own rucksack kitted up, so make the most of the help of our little ladies-in-waiting this evening, gentlemen.'

There was a rumble of masculine laughter. Joan narrowed her eyes. The men set off to bag cars and probably vie with one another as to who could get their stretchers attached the quickest.

'Don't take it personally,' Mr Atkins advised, then left the room.

'Did you hear that?' Mabel asked.

'It's not Mr Atkins's fault,' said Lizzie.

'Not that. I meant the old boy next to me. I swear he said, "The ladies, God bless 'em," under his breath.'

'Mr Fitzpatrick,' said Lizzie. 'I know him from our church.'

'Mr Fitzpatronising, more like,' said Mabel.

'This really isn't what I was expecting.' Joan's heart felt as though it was shrinking.

'It's not what I expected either,' said Mrs Marshall. 'Being landed with a bunch of whining girls isn't my cup of tea. War work isn't about picking and choosing. I suggest you pull your socks up.'

Colour stung Joan's cheeks. 'Let's get the rucksacks ready.'

She led the way out of the room. It felt important to lead. She was jolly well going to do her best, even if all that was asked of her was to fill rucksacks. She smothered a sigh, practically had to chew and swallow it. Would she never get the opportunity to do proper war work? Would she never get the chance to prove herself?

She counted out some blank labels. T for tourniquet, I for internal injuries.

How about U for useless?

Chapter Twenty-one

That was it, then. Archie and Harry had set off. But the wrench Dot felt was nothing compared to what Pammy and Sheila must be enduring, she reminded herself firmly. She couldn't bear to be one of those clingy mothers who carried on as if no other female was good enough to have the care of her sons. She had seen it enough times in others and thoroughly disapproved. She felt sorry for those mothers, at the same time as rather despising them for not letting their sons have lives of their own. She sympathised with the daughters-in-law, who were probably perfectly good wives. What must it be like for the young men, caught in the middle?

Did other women feel sorry for her? Even rather despise her? Not if she could help it. Her heart might beat for her sons, but that was her business. It was a strain to hold her heart together in one piece when Archie and Harry returned to their units, but she focused her energy on the ache that Pammy, Sheila and the children were feeling and thrust her own pain aside.

'Not that our Jimmy seems to feel the pain of parting from his dad,' she said to Reg afterwards. 'He's too busy being excited and proud.'

'Quite right too,' said Reg. He looked at her. 'What?' he demanded, as if she had raised a loud objection, which she had, but only inside her head.

'I suppose it'd be worse if he had any real idea.' She

pushed her way through conflicting thoughts. 'But for him to be so cheerful about it . . .'

'Oh aye?' There was a sneer in Reg's voice. 'You'd have him skriking like a babby, you would.'

'I would not.' Would she? Did she want their Jimmy to be upset? Of course not. The fierce protective fire in her heart proved that. 'It's only that—'

'Shut it, Dot. You're making summat out of nowt, as usual. Harry and Archie have gone and that's hard on all of us. Jenny cried her eyes out because she's a girl and Jimmy pinched the label off the tinned peaches and drew a Union flag on it because he's a boy. That's all there is to it, so stop trying to make things worse.'

'Make things worse?' Her jaw practically hit the floor in shock. 'Is that what you think I'm doing?'

'You can't leave well alone, that's your trouble.'

Was that what he thought of her, her own husband? Oh, they had grown apart over the years, but the criticism stung even so.

'I was proud of you,' she said, 'for what you did while Dunkirk was on.'

His shoulders moved. A shrug? Or a proud straightening? They went back to normal before she could decide.

'I didn't do much,' he said.

'You did.'

'It didn't feel like it, though I don't know what more I could have done.'

'That was what it took, wasn't it? Umpteen folk all doing what they could added up to a country doing a massive amount. And you were part of it, Reg.'

This time it was definitely a shrug. 'I did it for our lads.'

'I felt I was a bigger person during Dunkirk,' she ventured.

'You what?'

'I felt that – I don't know – I rose to the challenge. Something was asked of me and I did it with all my heart and soul and I wasn't about to stop until it was over.' She gazed at him. Would he understand?

'What the ruddy heck are you blathering on about, you daft bat?'

And that was that. No expression of pride in her. No effort to understand. No attempt to . . . reach out. That admiration, that fellowship, that glow of old remembered love she had felt for him during the dark days of Dunkirk had just been her being stupid.

The girls dropped in. The four of them sat around the kitchen table, Sheila puffing away like a chimney. The children were playing outside. Posh Pammy didn't like her Jenny to play in the street, but since the alternative would be for Jenny not to have any friends, Pammy had to grin and bear it . . . though grinning was the last thing Pammy would do. A polite smile was more her line.

Right now Pammy's smile was sympathetic. 'You look tired, Mother. You were such a marvel all through Dunkirk—'

'Don't tell her that,' Reg cut in. 'Her head's swollen enough as it is. She was telling me earlier what a heroine she was.'

'I never said that,' Dot objected.

'You said—'

'I said that I hope I rose to the occasion, just like everybody else in the country. That's not big-headed. It's patriotic.'

Reg struck a match and lit a Woodbine. After much encouragement – yes, all right, nagging – he had painted the kitchen for her last year. Already the white ceiling had a circle of yellow above his place at the table.

'As I was saying,' Pammy went on, 'you look tired, Mother.'

'I'm fine, love.'

'You do such long hours on the railway,' said Sheila, 'and some of it is shift work.'

'You two work long hours an' all,' Dot pointed out.

'We do,' said Pammy. 'And we have the worry of child care.'

'You know our Jenny and Jimmy have friends they go to after school,' said Dot, 'and they come here regular.' Especially Jimmy.

'The summer holidays start next month,' said Sheila. 'If you hand in your notice now, you can look after our two horrors full-time.'

'Jenny isn't a horror,' Pammy said stiffly.

'It was a joke.' Sheila rolled her eyes, then narrowed them. 'Mind, I notice you don't deny that our Jimmy is.'

Sheila blew out a final stream of smoke and Dot thrust the ash-tray across the table before she could grind out the spent cigarette into her saucer.

'You want me to pack in work and look after the children.' Dot kept her voice flat, though her heart took a few beats at a rush.

'Your grandchildren,' said Pammy.

'I like my job.'

'But you're only doing it because of the war,' said Pammy, 'the same as the rest of us. In an ideal world, we'd all be at home, taking care of our husbands.'

Oh aye, stuck inside these four walls, looking after Ratty Reg. Lucky her.

'Not all women are expected to do war work, Ma,' said Sheila. 'Not women your age, not grandmothers.'

'Thanks very much,' Dot said mildly. 'There's nothing like being reminded of your age.'

'Sheila didn't mean it like that,' said Pammy. 'You've seen the posters. *If you can't go to the factory, help the neighbour who can.* That could be you, helping us.'

'It would be such a weight off our minds,' said Sheila. 'You'd like to have the kids here all the time, wouldn't you . . . ?' Dot expected her to say '. . . wouldn't you, Ma?' but Sheila was looking at Reg '. . . wouldn't you, Pa? You don't want a stranger looking after them all summer long, do you?'

'I hear it's been fun and games on the trains now that the station names have been removed,' said Mabel, smiling at Dot across the buffet table. The others smiled at her too. There were five of them crushed around a table for four, plus young Lizzie standing in the corner.

'Fun and games is one way of putting it,' said Dot. 'It's all well and good for folk on a familiar route, but passengers new to the line haven't a clue where they are and are constantly asking for help. It takes me twice as long to walk through the train now. What it'll be like come winter, travelling in the dark, I daren't imagine. There'll be folk getting off at the wrong stops all up and down the line.'

The others laughed.

'All I can say is,' remarked Alison, 'that if it causes confusion for us, then it'll certainly do the job if Jerry parachutes in.'

'God forbid,' Cordelia murmured.

There was a moment's silence. Dot felt like gathering up the group and giving them all a big cuddle, even the cool, well-spoken Cordelia. Could she confide in them? Would it be disloyal to her family? But she wanted to talk and they had all promised on their first day that they would stick together, hadn't they?

'My daughters-in-law want me to give up my job.'

All eyes turned her way and her skin prickled.

It was warm-hearted Lizzie who spoke first. 'You're not going to, are you? You're one of us. We don't want you to go – do we, girls?'

'Why do they want you to leave?' Trust Cordelia to get straight to the point.

'They're both in the munitions and, with the school holidays coming up, they want me to have the children.'

'Oh.' Lizzie's face fell. 'Your family needs you. Well, that's different.'

A chill swept through Dot. 'You think I should leave?' She looked round the table. 'Is that what all of you think?' She saw Alison, Mabel and Joan exchange uncomfortable glances.

'It's what mothers do, isn't it?' said Alison. 'They do what's best for their children.'

'This is my grandchildren.' Dot could have ripped out her tongue. Now she had made it sound like she didn't care about Jenny and Jimmy, when really the sight of Jimmy's inquisitive blue eyes and the sound of Jenny's bubbly giggles could melt her bones. Anyroad, Alison was right. You did everything you could for your children. Wouldn't the best thing for Archie and Harry be for her to give Sheila and Pammy what they wanted? That was what had kept her awake last night. If Harry and Archie were her world, shouldn't she give in to Sheila and Pammy? Wouldn't the boys expect her to?

But she didn't want to give in. She wanted the very best for Jimmy and Jenny, but . . . but she didn't want to leave her job and look after them. So how could she claim to want the best for them? And the dismayed expressions on the faces of the four young girls around the table said the same. Something inside Dot withered – a piece of her self-respect.

'It's easy to make rules for other people,' said Cordelia.

She looked elegant, as always, in her two-piece suit with its pleated skirt, her stylish felt hat trimmed with silk braid, and her suede gloves. Had she been provided with a uniform yet? There was no knowing, since she had made it clear from the start that she never intended to wear a uniform outside work. Would anybody dare put the lofty Cordelia in a uniform? It was all too easy to imagine her cleaning the lamps in crêpe de Chine and pearls.

Now everyone gazed at Cordelia, who took a moment to look at the girls one by one. There was something very middle class about that. If a working-class woman wanted to say her piece, she had to get it in quick before everybody else barged in with their own opinions, as Dot well knew from her own kitchen table, and her mam's kitchen table before that.

'You young girls,' said Cordelia, 'your only experience of wives and mothers comes from your own mothers, or in your case, Joan, from your grandmother. Your mothers have devoted their lives to you, or for your sake I hope they have, and so that is your expectation of mothers. But this is wartime. Doesn't it occur to you that by working on the railway, Dot isn't just serving her country, she is also serving her family? What better thing can she do for her grandchildren than help win this war?'

'I hadn't thought of it like that,' said Joan.

'Think of it now,' said Cordelia. 'Do you recall my advising you young ones to embrace the opportunities that come your way in wartime? Did you imagine that opportunities are only for the young? The government wants women to work, remember.'

Dot had an innate respect for the middle class, but she couldn't let Cordelia do all the talking for her, especially if she was about to deliver a lecture.

'Aye, the government needs us all at work, and then we're expected to go home and do everything there an' all – and we do, because it's what's needed, but by crikey, when do they expect us to get our shopping done? That's what I want to know.'

269

'It's because the country is run by men,' said Cordelia. 'The inclusion of a few women among the powers that be would be a great help.'

'Happen you're right.' For the first time, Dot felt a kinship with Cordelia. Never mind her cool manner and her educated voice, Cordelia too agonised over finding time to buy a couple of fillets of fish. 'But we're wandering off the point. What about my grandchildren?'

'Do you want to leave work and look after them?' asked Joan.

'No,' she answered honestly. 'I love 'em to pieces, but I love my job an' all. Only, if I stop on as a parcels porter, it might look like I care more for portering than I do for my grandchildren, and of course I don't. So maybe I should give up work – but I don't want to. I keep going round in circles.'

'There's plenty of women looking after other women's children these days,' said Alison. 'It's war work in its own way.'

'It's war work, full stop,' said Cordelia.

'Here's an idea,' said Mabel. 'Why don't you find someone to look after the children? One of your neighbours, someone you've known for years. Then you'll know they're being looked after properly and you'll have saved their mothers the trouble of sorting it out themselves.'

Dot looked at Mabel. So did the others. Then they looked at her.

'Clever old you,' she told Mabel.

Sheila and Pammy couldn't argue with that, surely. Not that there had been arguments as such. The thumbscrews of emotional blackmail, yes, and a scattering of grouchy remarks courtesy of Ratty Reg, but no actual arguments.

Eh, it wasn't plain sailing being a working mother and grandmother, let alone a working wife. But the thought didn't get her down. Actually, it gave her a boost. She was going to carry on doing her bit and if that caused difficulties, so what? Overcoming difficulties was what women did best.

As well as her wages, Mabel received a generous allowance from Pops, so she could easily have afforded a brand-new bicycle, but she had bought herself a second-hand one as a new one might have looked showy-offy. As she cycled to Alexandra Park, she felt a little breathless, not because cycling was a strain but out of excitement. Tonight was her first night on duty at the first-aid post – hers, Joan's and Lizzie's.

'I'm so glad the three of us have been put into the same group,' said Lizzie as they sat together in a corner of the park-keeper's parlour, waiting to be given their instructions.

'You're welcome,' Mabel murmured, trying to hold back a smile as the other two turned to her with frowns.

'Did you have something to do with it?' asked Joan. 'I thought it was just our good luck.'

'I wasn't going to rely on luck,' she said. 'I had a quiet word with Mr Atkins at the end of the other evening. He'd assigned all the men to groups, but it hadn't occurred to him to assign us girls.'

'Not important enough to go out on emergency calls,' said Joan.

'So I more or less snatched the clipboard from his hand and wrote down all the names.'

'And we're all together,' Lizzie said happily.

'And the odious Mrs Marshall is with another group,' said Mabel.

Soon the parlour was full and Mr Turnbull walked in.

'Welcome, everyone,' he said. 'I'm here because it's your first night on duty, but this will be the last you see of me for a while. One or two points of order. This house is our depot and this room is our ops room. Supplies are kept in the store. Please use the correct terminology. That way, should you be detailed to a different depot, you'll know what people are talking about.'

'As long as we all know the correct names of the kitchen and the tea pot,' a wag remarked.

'First job tonight, and every night, is to prepare the motors and check that the rucksacks are ready, so let's set to.'

For a time, there was a bustle of activity – for the men, anyway. The girls checked the contents of the large rucksacks and that seemed to be it for them. They stood outside, watching the men loading their kit into the motors.

'We'll have to sit on the blankets,' said Mr Atkins. 'It's the only way they'll fit in.'

Once the motors were ready, everyone came indoors and double-checked the blackout.

'What happens next?' Joan asked.

Mr Atkins gave a faint shrug. 'We wait.'

'Play cards, have a chin-wag,' said another of the men, whose moustache could do with a trim. 'Grab some shut-eye.'

'The lady of the house has crammed the master bedroom full of personal possessions and locked the door,' said Mr Turnbull, 'but there's the children's room, with two single beds. I propose setting it aside for the ladies' use.'

'We don't want any special treatment,' said Lizzie.

'Don't turn down the opportunity of a proper bed,' said Mr Harrison.

'You young ladies need your beauty sleep,' said Mr Fitzpatronising.

'All of you must grab what sleep you can,' said Mr Turnbull.

It felt odd, being trained and ready – with nothing to do. At last it was time to head up the wooden hill. The children's room was small, just two beds with a mat in between, a small cupboard at one end and the window at the other.

'Should we take turns to sleep on the floor?' Lizzie suggested.

'What about taking turns to sleep alone while the other two share?' said Mabel.

'I'm used to sleeping with my sister,' said Joan, 'but our bed is bigger.'

'Then you can have first dibs on sleeping alone,' said Mabel.

She and Lizzie settled themselves top to tail, not the most comfortable arrangement, and Mabel didn't sleep awfully well. She worried about disturbing Lizzie, but when she woke early next morning, Lizzie was wrapped round her legs.

When Mabel disentangled herself, Lizzie sat up and yawned. 'Morning. What time is it?'

'Half five.'

They patted down their appearance and combed their hair.

'You've got the right idea, putting your hair in a snood,' Mabel said to Joan. 'At least yours is tidy.'

'Tidy but flattened,' said Joan. 'Normally I sleep in rollers, but Gran would lock me in the cellar if I tried to leave the house wearing them.'

'Plenty of girls are wearing their rollers all day underneath turbans,' said Lizzie.

Mabel laughed. 'Don't let the chaps hear us talking about our hair. Imagine what Mr Fitzpatronising would say.'

That first night set the pattern. When she was on duty, Mabel cycled to Alexandra Park for ten o'clock, where she settled down to get as good a night's kip as she could before cycling back to Mrs Grayson's at six. But it wouldn't be like that indefinitely. The news was getting more serious. Germany had invaded the Channel Islands, the shock of which held Mabel frozen in her cinema seat as she watched the newsreel. A Welsh city had been bombed. The newspapers didn't say which, but it made sense for it to be Cardiff because that was by the sea, so presumably had docks. Besides, how many cities did Wales have?

There were other attacks too, on both land and sea. Night raids on aircraft factories felt horribly close to home. Not only were they a promise of air raids to come, but the thought of factories being attacked made Mabel worry for her parents and everybody in Annerby. They didn't build planes in her father's factory, but his ball bearings and small components were vital to the war effort. Might Jerry find out about Bradshaw's and add it to the list of buildings for destruction?

'I've taken down the desert island from my front window,' said Bernice when the four women lengthmen had downed tools to have their morning cup of tea.

'You what?' said Louise.

'I told you ages ago. We made pictures on our windows out of our bomb-blast tape. Anyroad, we had a desert island in us front window, complete with palm tree, and I've took it down now that the Duke of Windsor has upped sticks and headed off to the Caribbean or the Bahamas or wherever he's gone. I wasn't having anyone looking at my desert island and thinking I supported him, thank you very much.'

'I don't think he's upped sticks exactly.' Mabel spoke cautiously. Bernice was pretty het up and she didn't want to make her worse. 'I think he's been appointed Governor.'

'Oh aye? You reckon, do you? The road I see it, either he's buggered off because he's a coward or he's been sent away for being too friendly with Herr Hitler. Either way, we're better off without him. When I think how I cried when he abdicated . . .'

'You and me both, Bernice,' said Bette. 'But we've landed on us feet with the King we've got now, I reckon.'

'And the Queen,' added Louise, taking the words out of Mabel's mouth – words she wouldn't have been able to utter in that moment, because her throat had tightened with emotion.

More attacks in the Channel were reported and that dashed Lord Haw-Haw crowed over the destruction of British shipping, though whether he was telling the truth was another matter.

'Loathsome little creep,' was Mrs Grayson's opinion of him. 'The day he is hanged for treason, the world will be a better place.'

And at last, after all the months of waiting, one night at the end of the month, bombs were dropped on Salford. A transport time-keeping office was hit, though whether it had survived in a recognisable state or had been blown to smithereens depended on which rumour you listened to.

The next night, there was a sharpened edge to the atmosphere in the first-aid depot. Would the next lot of bombs fall closer to home?

In the event, the next thing to be dropped on the Manchester area was – leaflets.

'Ruddy cheek – pardon my French,' raged Dot. Mabel had never heard the good-natured woman sound so indignant. 'Dropping leaflets on us – I ask you.'

'"A Last Appeal to Reason", or some such tripe,' said Alison. 'My father says it's a disgrace.'

'My concern,' said Cordelia, 'is that the German plane was able to fly here without the sirens sounding a warning.'

'I know,' said Joan. 'That's scary. It's a good thing it was just leaflets that were dropped.'

Mabel felt a twinge of sympathy. Bernice had told her about the 'coffins' in the signal boxes. Each signal box had a metal cabinet made of boiler plate that was big enough for one man and served as his air-raid shelter. The idea of being unprotected if all those windows blew in wasn't something Mabel wanted to think about, especially now that this Jerry plane had somehow got through. Did Joan know about the signal-box 'coffins'? Best not mention it.

As infuriating as it was that Hitler had dared to drop leaflets on them, was the 'Last Appeal' a warning that what came next wouldn't be made of paper?

Chapter Twenty-two

Joan walked down the corridor in Hunts Bank, along with a stream of other clerical and administrative staff. It was Saturday, which, before the war, would have meant everyone would have done a morning's work and then gone home, but now they were required to work the full day. There were a few long faces, but Joan's wasn't one of them. Yesterday she had spent a blissful evening in Bob's arms, dancing. Had she slept on her own, she would have snuggled down to sleep cuddling her pillow, but you couldn't do soppy things like that when you shared with your sister.

Miss Emery was coming towards her. The assistant welfare supervisor had meant it when she had said back on their first day that they wouldn't see much of her. She was responsible for railway girls all over the North and spent much of her time travelling from place to place.

She greeted Joan with a smile and a narrowing of the eyes. 'Good morning, Miss . . . don't tell me . . . Franklyn?'

'Foster.'

'I knew it began with F. I'm sorry to get it wrong, but there are so many of you. Miss Foster: charging-office clerk, yes? I don't always remember names, but I do remember jobs. How are you getting on?'

'Fine, thank you. It's interesting, and, being clerical, it leaves me free for night duties.'

'Fire-watching? ARP?'

'I'm in a first-aid party stationed in Alexandra Park.'

'Jolly good. I don't suppose you've had anything to do thus far.'

'We get set up just in case and then bunk down for the night.'

'Long may it continue. Excuse me. I'm on my way to a meeting. Someone – not a woman, I hasten to add – has raised concerns about whether it's respectable to have a woman signalman working alongside a signalman. What gossip might there be if they are obliged to work together in the dark? Oh well, no rest for the wicked.'

Miss Emery hastened on her way. Either she was a naturally rapid walker or else she was permanently in a hurry. The latter was easy to believe. Joan made her way to the charging office and took her place. Seeing Miss Emery had bucked her up, but she still experienced the now customary dip as she faced a day of typing. It was extra important to concentrate today because she'd been on duty last night. Admittedly, the duty had mostly involved sleeping, but at best she only snoozed and generally felt a little tired the following day – tiredness that wasn't helped by the repetitive nature of her work.

At twelve thirty, the other clerks started tucking their chairs under their desks and heading off for the canteen or a quick dash around the shops.

'Are you coming?' asked Miss Bligh. She had had her hair cut and restyled and now wore it loose but demure, like Myrna Loy in *Too Hot to Handle*.

'In a minute. I need to finish this and then do another or I won't meet my score today.'

The silence after the others had left made her realise how accustomed she was to the clatter of their machines. All on its own, her typewriter made an almost tinny sound.

She had almost finished when the door at the far end

opened and Mr Clark appeared. He looked down the office, then headed for her desk.

'All alone, Miss Foster? Would you kindly come through? I need a word.' And she must have looked uncertain, reluctant or downright alarmed, because he added, 'I'm doing you a favour, Miss Foster. I assume you would prefer not to be reprimanded when your colleagues return.'

Reprimanded? She stood up. Mr Clark retraced his steps, leaving her to follow. Walking between the rows of desks was hard, but how much harder would it have been had the desks been occupied? Mr Clark held the door for her and she walked through into another empty office.

Mr Clark walked past her and sat behind his desk. She stood in front of it.

'No, no,' he said. 'Come round here or you won't be able to see.'

An invoice lay on his blotter. She walked round the desk to stand beside him – well, no, not absolutely beside him, obviously, but near enough to see the invoice.

'This is one of yours from this morning, Miss Foster. These are your initials, are they not?'

'Yes, Mr Clark.'

'You've made an error. Here – see?' His finger touched the paper. 'You do realise this is a sackable offence?'

Cold gushed through her and ended up swooshing sickeningly in her stomach. Sacked?

'Or, if you prefer . . .' He looked up at her. 'I could smack your bottom for you.'

Dot watched the guard walk the length of the train along the platform, slamming doors that had been left open and checking those that were already shut as the train prepared for the off. Mr Thirkle appeared by her side and she gave him a polite smile, to which he replied by indicating with a nod of his head that she should look behind her. Down at the far end of the platform, the signal changed, its horizontal bar rising to give the train permission to proceed. The guard blew his whistle to claim the driver's attention, then he stepped up into the guard's van, leaning out to wave his green flag. In response, the driver blew the train whistle. Then came hissing as clouds of steam were forced out of the lower part of the front of the engine. A thrill passed through Dot as, with a rushing sound, a vast puff of steam burst from the funnel and the familiar and beloved *puh . . . puh . . .* started slowly, gradually building up. As the train began to move, there was some creaking as the couplings that held the coaches together stretched and shifted before the train gained momentum and, accompanied by its regular chuffing sound, pulled away.

'Shall we take the weight off our feet now the platform is empty?' Mr Thirkle suggested, and they settled on a bench. 'What mischief has your grandson been up to recently?'

'What makes you think he's been up to owt?' Dot replied.

'Yon lad o' yours has always been up to something.'

Dot laughed. It was true that things hadn't been so good in the wider world recently, but in spite of everything, she had felt lighter of heart ever since she had sorted out the problem of a childminder for the children. After years of doing the right thing for her family, she had done something that was right not just for them, but also for herself. She ought to feel guilty. If she had a decent bone in her body, she would feel guilty. But she didn't. As a matter of fact, her bones felt really rather good.

'Go on, then,' said Mr Thirkle. 'What's he done now?'

'Jimmy's school used to use the local rec as its playing field,' she told Mr Thirkle, 'but it's been given over to growing veg now, so instead of PT, the kids are doing first aid and ping-pong. Our Jimmy only went and snaffled all the ping-pong balls and set up races in the playground.'

'That's not so bad.'

'It is when you're peeing on the ping-pong balls to shift them along.'

Mr Thirkle threw back his head and laughed. His laughter had a rich sound that was surprising coming from such a thin fellow.

Confusion coloured her cheeks. 'Oh, I'm that sorry.'

'What for?'

'For saying . . . that word I said. Only a hard-faced fish-wife would say a word like that in mixed company.'

'You mean the word about . . . the manner of making the ping-pong balls move?' Mr Thirkle lifted his chin, pulling his neck taut. He gazed into the distance. 'Some women are ladies because they grow up with money and education and all kinds of folderols. Then there are other women, who don't have any advantages and who work hard all their lives, but they have something that's born in them, something right and decent that makes them ladies even though they aren't out of the top drawer. You're one of them, Mrs Green, a real lady, and never let nobody tell you different.' He looked at her. His brown eyes were concerned. 'I hope I haven't spoken out of turn.'

'I take it kindly, Mr Thirkle.'

'It was kindly meant, Mrs Green.'

Kindly meant. Aye, there was a lot to be said for that. Ratty Reg could learn a thing or two from Mr Thirkle.

'I don't know about being a lady,' she said, 'but I do know I see myself differently these days.'

'In what way?'

'It's working on the railway that's done it. It's given me a new sense of who I am. Not Mrs Reg Green, not Harry and Archie's mother, not the kids' grandmother, but just me. It's like I'm a real person in my own right.' She chewed the inside of her cheek. 'Does that sound daft?' Worse, did it sound like she was fishing for another compliment?

'Nay, Mrs Green. You've confided in me, so I'll confide in you. My late wife, God rest her soul, was a dear woman, but she wasn't best suited to domestic life.'

'I'm sorry to hear that.' She was an' all. She didn't like to think of Mr Thirkle being lumbered with another Sheila the Slattern.

But he didn't mean that. 'Don't get me wrong. She loved me and she adored our Edie and she kept our house like a new pin, but she found it dull. She wanted to get a job in the corner shop, but I couldn't have that, could I? It would have looked like I couldn't support my family, so I told her no. I wasn't one for putting my foot down over a lot of things, but I did about that.' His chest rose and fell as he expelled a sigh. 'Now I look round at all you ladies working here and thriving on it and it makes me wonder . . .'

'I'm sure you made your decision with the best of intentions at the time.'

'What other decision could a self-respecting husband and father have made? But it still makes me wonder, when I see all these lady porters and lady ticket collectors. There are even lady welders and lady steam-hammer operators in the engine sheds.'

And quite right too. Women were just as good as the men they had replaced and were proving it every single day. Did all those other women feel the same as she did? That they were more than the providers of meals and clean clothes, that they were more than the family dogs-body? Working on the railway gave her – eh, it sounded daft, but it gave her a sharper sense of who she was. Was that big-headed? Disloyal to her family? She wouldn't swap her boys or her grandchildren for all the tea in

China, but, by the stars, it was grand being Dot Green, parcels porter.

'I'll let you mull it over,' said Mr Clark. Rising from his chair, he picked up the invoice with the mistake, folded it unhurriedly and placed it in the inside pocket of his jacket. One final smile in her direction, a quick all-over glance, and he walked from the room. He closed the door softly behind him, leaving her feeling as if a prison door had banged shut on her.

She stood there like an idiot, shaking violently on the inside, though her outer body was frozen solid. What an oaf she was. Why had she let him speak to her like that – although how could she have stopped him? Did he make that disgusting suggestion to every girl who made a mistake? Was he serious? She couldn't bear to lose her job, but nothing on earth would ever make her let him do what he had suggested.

Her legs felt wobbly. She might have crumpled into the chair, except that it was Mr Clark's and what if he came back and found her sitting there? A sudden rush of energy sent her beetling back into the typing room. What was she to do? She could never breathe a word to anyone. She was too ashamed. Mr Clark had admired her legs after she'd shortened her hems. Did he think that was a come-on? Was Gran right? Had she inherited Estelle's tarty nature?

She forced herself to go to the canteen, not because she could face eating anything, but simply to be away from her desk if Mr Clark came back. Afterwards, she more or less pushed her way into a crowd of girls from her office and was the life and soul of the group as they made their way back to their desks. The afternoon felt as if it would never end, but on the few occasions when the interconnecting door opened, it wasn't Mr Clark who appeared. Was it too much to hope that nothing more would happen? But Mr Clark wouldn't have said such an outrageous thing if he hadn't meant it . . . would he?

Or, if you prefer, I could smack your bottom for you.

Horrid man! He was old enough to be her father. Not that it would have been in any way acceptable for a young man to speak to her like that, but coming from a middle-aged man made it worse. Her flesh crawled.

It wasn't until the end of the day that she thought of Miss Emery. Could she confide in the assistant welfare supervisor? She thought of the meeting Miss Emery had mentioned. It showed that working relationships between men and women were an area for concern. But Miss Emery's meeting had been about potential gossip, not an actual complaint. What would she think of Joan for being involved in something like this?

When she reached the women's welfare office, Miss Emery wasn't there.

'You've just missed her,' said the secretary.

'I'll come back on Monday.'

'You won't see her, I'm afraid. She's set off on her travels again. She has such a large area to cover. Would you like to leave a message? I can get in touch with her if it's urgent.'

'No, thank you.'

She trailed home, feeling disorientated. Was this something other girls would tell their parents about? Then the mother would cuddle the girl and make her feel better and the father would go to the office and have stiff words with the man in question, possibly even sock him one on the chin.

But she didn't have parents. Daddy was dead and Estelle was heaven alone knows where, living it up with her fancy man. And Joan could never confide in Gran. She was already the hard piece who had worn red shoes. This incident would seem like something that was inevitable for Estelle's daughter.

After an endless evening, they went to bed. Letitia soon fell asleep, but Joan felt as though she would never sleep again. She managed to doze off, but in an uncomfortable way that kept dragging her back to the surface, until she was jerked awake by the sound of an eerie wail. She sat bolt upright. The air-raid siren! Letitia tumbled out of bed and stood up. Joan scrambled after her.

'Are we going to take out our rollers first, before we go down the Andy?' she asked.

'No. We'll have to do it in there. It'd be pretty gruesome if we got blown up standing in front of the mirror.' Letitia grabbed her dressing gown, thrusting her feet into her slippers.

The door banged open.

'What are you two dithering about for?' Gran demanded. 'Get downstairs.'

The three of them hurried down, getting tangled up together at the bottom of the stairs when they stopped to pull on mackintoshes over their night things. Joan strained to hear the sound of aeroplane engines, but all she could hear was the soft rush of their footsteps and the thud of her own heart. Letitia ran into the kitchen and grabbed the air-raid box. Joan unbolted the back door.

'Where's Gran?'

Gran appeared, clutching Daddy's photograph – of course. They would have to keep it in the air-raid box after this.

Armed with a torch, its beam dimmed by a couple of layers of tissue, they stepped outside. The night air was cool. Beneath the wail of the siren, the sounds of neighbours' voices could be heard, including a rude exclamation as the man next door stubbed his toe. In the back garden,

Letitia opened up the Andy and held the torch to guide the others inside. Joan held the air-raid box and Daddy's photograph as Gran disappeared inside. It was a full three feet to the floor and the single step, which would double as a shelf once they were inside, was an uncomfortably long way down. Joan passed their belongings to Gran, then she and Letitia followed her inside. Letitia closed the door behind them, pulling the heavy cloth across it.

After the race to get here, Joan experienced a strange, disjointed feeling. Here they were, in their shelter . . . and there was nothing to do but wait. She glanced at the couple of small suitcases tucked in the corner, packed ready in the event of the house being blown to kingdom come or, worse, their having to make a quick escape, should Jerry invade. Her chest felt heavy, as if it carried a lead weight inside it.

She felt Letitia's expert fingers starting to undo her rollers.

'What are you playing at?' asked Gran.

'We made a pact,' said Letitia. 'We're not going to die with our rollers in.'

'The point of the Anderson shelter is that we don't die at all,' said Gran.

'It's a matter of principle,' said Letitia, carrying on unwinding and dropping the rollers into Joan's lap.

'You won't be fit to be seen in the morning, if you sleep with your hair loose,' Gran prophesied.

Sleep? That would have been a fine thing.

'It's like trying to settle on the wooden staging in Steven's dad's shed,' Letitia complained later on from her position on the top bunk.

Anyway, they were too wound up to sleep. They talked on and off for a while, but between keeping one eye on the alarm clock on the shelf and straining her ears for the sound of planes, Joan wasn't much use to the conversation.

At last, the all-clear sounded.

'So much for that,' said Letitia.

'Better a false alarm than a real raid,' snapped Gran, picking up Daddy's photo and hugging it to her.

They trailed back inside and upstairs, the girls with their dressing-gown pockets stuffed with rollers. They put them back in their hair and tumbled into bed.

'What do you think a real raid will be like?' Joan whispered.

'Bally scary, I should think.'

'I wonder what it'll be like when we're on duty.'

'Don't worry about that,' advised Letitia. 'We'll be run off our feet, far too busy to worry. Now let's try to get some shut-eye, shall we? Night night.'

Letitia soon drifted off. Joan tried to relax but all the nerves in her body were wound up tight. She would be safe tomorrow, but what would happen when she went back to work on Monday?

Chapter Twenty-three

Dot was about to do the one thing she had sworn she would avoid. She was going to play mother hen. How could she not? Poor Joan looked like she could do with a big hug, and had for the past couple of days. Come to think of it, she had skipped joining the group in the buffet on Monday, which wasn't like her. Dot had spotted her from a distance a couple of times and had been struck by how wan she looked. One of those times, Joan had been chatting to another girl and Dot had been pleased to see her smile, but the moment the other girl walked away, Joan's face had fallen. Did she have something on her mind?

That settled it. Dot might want to leave her maternal instincts at home, but it hurt her to see her young friend unhappy.

When she got back from Southport, she popped into the buffet and asked at the counter for the group's notebook, checking to see if Joan had put herself down for today. Yes: good. So had Cordelia. That was good an' all. Having two women old enough to be her mother taking a sympathetic interest was just what Joan looked to be in need of. Dot wasn't worried about not being able to speak to Cordelia in advance. She had no doubt that Cordelia would cotton on sharpish.

Dot's shift was such that if she got a move on, she could dash over to Hunts Bank and meet Joan coming out. Let the girl try to wriggle her way out of coming to the buffet!

It went according to plan. Dot scooped Joan up as she

emerged and Joan was too well-mannered to give her the brush-off. Dot linked her arm through Joan's and didn't let go until they were in the queue.

Mabel waved to them from a corner.

'Save my place,' Dot told Joan, then hurried to have a quick word with Mabel. 'Do us a favour, Mabel, love. I need a private word with Joan, so do you mind excusing yourself after a few minutes?'

Mabel looked startled, but she nodded. 'Is something wrong?'

Dot ducked out of answering by hurrying back to the queue. As she resumed her place beside Joan, the door opened and Cordelia appeared. It had come as a surprise to Dot when she'd realised that Cordelia wasn't much taller than herself. Cordelia's elegance made her seem taller. Dot had never felt anything other than dumpy.

The four of them chatted at the table for ten minutes. Having told Mabel to push off pronto, Dot made a point of paying attention to her.

'You've caught the sun, love.'

'Has my nose gone red?'

'You just have a healthy glow.'

Mabel slipped down an arm of her jacket to reveal a sleeveless blouse. 'It's jolly hot shifting ballast in this weather.'

'Can we expect to see you muffled up like an Eskimo in the winter?' asked Cordelia.

When Mabel had gone, Joan made a move to leave as well.

'How's that young man of yours?' Dot asked and Joan's taut features softened as she spoke of Bob and his family. It was good that she liked his folks so much.

'Now then, love,' said Dot. 'Me and Cordelia need a word with you.' Ignoring Cordelia's raised eyebrows, she looked intently at Joan. Was that fear in the girl's eyes? 'It seems to me you've got summat on your mind. You could do a lot worse than discuss it with us. I assume it's nowt to do with Bob, as you sound so happy talking about him. Is it work?'

The look on the girl's face, coupled with her fiery blush, confirmed Dot was right. But Joan pressed her lips together as if she might never open them again.

'Tell us, chick,' said Dot.

Silence.

'You have an obligation to tell us,' said Cordelia. 'May I remind you that on our first day, we all agreed to support one another? If you don't permit us to help you now, how can we ever turn to you, should we need to?'

Gradually, with her gaze fixed firmly on the table top and her fingers twisting in her lap, Joan told her story. Dot's blood boiled.

'. . . I keep looking at the other girls and wondering if he has ever said the same thing to them. Then I think it's my own fault for not standing up to him at the time – but I was so shocked . . .'

'It's not your fault,' said Cordelia.

'I don't have a daughter,' Dot fumed, 'but if I did and a man tried it on like that with her, I'd clock him so hard he wouldn't know if it was this week, next week or school sports day. This wants reporting, this does.'

'I went to Miss Emery's office, but she's away.'

'I'm not sure what she could do, anyway,' said Cordelia. 'Think about it. Were there witnesses?'

'Of course not,' snapped Dot. 'You don't say summat like that in front of a room full of folk.'

'Precisely,' said Cordelia. 'So it's Joan's word against Mr Clark's, the word of an employee of a few weeks against that of a man who has probably worked there all his life. And it's taken Joan from Saturday till Wednesday to speak up.'

'That's because she was too ashamed,' said Dot.

'Some might say that had she been truly upset and inno-cent, she would have poured it out immediately.'

'Whose side are you on?' Dot demanded.

'Joan's, naturally. But if she reports Mr Clark, there will be repercussions.'

'I should flaming well hope so. He deserves to lose his job.'

'But he won't, will he? That's the point. Joan might or might not be believed, and Mr Clark might or might not get into hot water; but whatever happens to him, it won't go well for Joan. Girls get talked about and it isn't pleasant. If she isn't believed, she'll be labelled as a troublemaker of a certain sort; and even if she is believed, there will be those who'll say she must have done something to deserve it, that she must have led him on.'

The colour fled from Joan's face. 'I never . . .'

'Of course you didn't, love,' said Dot. 'But Cordelia's right. Girls do get talked about. The world is very unfair.'

'What can I do?' Joan whispered.

Dot made up her mind. 'Keep out of Mr Clark's way and make sure you aren't alone with him. Leave the rest to us.'

The eerie moan of the siren lifted into the night. Mabel's skin prickled. This was it – an alert while she was on duty. She, Lizzie and Joan had filled the metal water bottles earl-ier on. Without needing to be told, they hurried to the little kitchen, banging shoulders in the doorway. The bottles wobbled on Mabel's tray as she made for the array of tables that now lined the hall, bearing the men's rucksacks. The girls placed a bottle beside each one.

'Let's get the cars loaded,' said Mr Atkins.

Mabel stood aside. It was rather galling, having to keep out of the way. When the men had grabbed the equipment and trooped outside, she followed, standing just outside the door, next to the row of buckets of earth and water that were lined up, ready for emergencies. When they came back indoors to wait, Lizzie was seated at the telephone table, which now lived just inside the cupboard under the stairs. Manning the telephone was a job that had been entrusted to the girls.

While Lizzie listened on the telephone and made notes on her pad, Mr Atkins hovered in front of her as if it was all he could do not to snatch the receiver. Didn't he think a girl could take a message accurately? When Lizzie hung up, he leaned forward, placing his hands on the table.

'Well?' He listened while she spoke. Did he keep his back to everyone else so they couldn't hear? 'I see.' He turned round and addressed everyone. 'The area is a couple of motors short tonight, so we may be called upon to go further afield than our own neck of the woods. In the meantime, down to the cellar, please – not Miss Cooper, of course.'

'Shall we stop up here with you?' Joan whispered to Lizzie, who was looking rather pale.

'You as well, ladies, please,' said Mr Atkins, and they had to leave little Lizzie behind. It was a surprisingly hard thing to do.

The cellar was cold and smelled damp, but a table and a few chairs had been brought down, so at least there was somewhere to sit.

'Welcome to the Ritz,' said Mr Preston.

A distant boom made everyone freeze.

That was it, then. It had started. Joan squeezed Mabel's hand and, for all her determination not to get close to her fellow railway girls, Mabel returned the pressure.

'Poor Lizzie, under the stairs on her own,' said Joan.

'She's no coward. She's got a job to do and she'll do it.'

There was the sound of planes and firing and Mabel

discovered why people used the word 'crump' to describe the noise when a bomb landed. Heavy ack-ack guns started up.

'Are they getting nearer?' asked Mabel.

'It's when the plaster dust lands on your head that you have to worry,' said Mr Atkins.

From above came the sound of the telephone bell. Mr Atkins, who had seated himself at the top of the cellar steps, sprang up and disappeared. In the cellar, the men began to stand in readiness. Mabel and Joan stood as well. Mabel felt edgy and her heart was beating fast. Things were about to kick off and it was hard to accept she wasn't actually going to do anything.

Mr Atkins appeared at the top of the steps. 'Time to move.'

Everyone clattered upstairs. There was no 'ladies first' about it.

'Switch off the light,' Mr Atkins ordered.

The hall was plunged into darkness. The front door opened and the men bustled out. Instinct told Mabel to watch them on their way. Standing in the doorway, she felt an odd sense of surprise that nothing had changed. Had she really thought she would be looking out into a battlefield?

She shut the door.

'What now?' she asked.

'We wait,' said Lizzie. 'There may be more telephone calls. And you could have a cup of tea, if you like. Before the phone call came, while you were all down in that cellar, I was thinking how uncomfortable you must be, so I nipped out of my hidey-hole and put the kettle on. I thought you could all do with a cuppa. I was going to bring a tray to the top of the cellar steps . . .'

'And then go back to your post,' finished Mabel. She and Joan looked at one another. 'I think I may have underestimated you, Lizzie Cooper. Here you were, the one person obliged to stay up here during the raid, and you took the time to think of the rest of us slumming it in the safety of the cellar.'

'You thought of everyone else instead of yourself,' said Joan.

Lizzie gave a little shrug. 'My mum puts other people first, so I try to as well. Anyroad, you two should go back down to the cellar.'

'And leave you alone up here?'

'I'll be quite safe under the stairs.'

'We'll sort out more supplies,' said Joan. 'They'll need them ready if they come back and have to go out again in a hurry.'

They ran upstairs.

'If we make a separate pile for each rucksack,' suggested Joan, 'they can tip out what they've got left and stick in the new lot.'

'Good thinking,' said Mabel.

Six of everything, except four splints, and don't forget the labels. She forced herself to concentrate while a different part of her brain listened to the ack-ack gunfire, the aeroplane engines and the howl and crump of the bombs.

Downstairs, she and Joan placed the piles of supplies on the tables. She looked round at Lizzie in her cupboard.

'Maybe I'll bring my knitting next time,' said Lizzie.

What now? They looked at one another.

'What time did the siren go off?' asked Joan.

'Half ten,' said Lizzie.

They all looked at their wristwatches. It was coming up to half-past eleven now. How much longer – and how much nearer?

'You should go back to the cellar,' said Lizzie.

Mabel glanced at Joan. Lizzie was right.

'I feel rotten leaving Lizzie up there on her own,' said

Mabel as they reached the foot of the cellar steps. 'It feels like we're skulking down here in the safe bit.'

'Cupboards under the stairs are safe places,' said Joan. 'The government says so. But I know what you mean.'

'My landlady uses her cupboard under the stairs.'

'There you are then. Is that where you were when we had the false alarm on Saturday night?'

'No,' said Mabel. 'When I moved in, the neighbours told me I could use their Anderson shelter if need be, though I felt a complete bounder leaving Mrs Grayson behind.'

'Presumably she wanted to be left.'

'Yes. She's a funny soul. Refuses to leave the house. I have to do all our shopping.'

'Why won't she go out?' Joan asked.

'I don't know.' Hadn't asked, more like. Should she have taken more of an interest in Mrs Grayson? 'What did Dot want to say to you in the buffet?'

'Oh . . . nothing.'

Gradually the noise lessened and died away. Finally, at quarter to midnight, the all-clear sounded. Mabel and Joan went back to the hall.

'Put the kettle on,' said Lizzie. 'I bet the men will want a cup of tea when they get back.'

'I'm not sure they deserve that consideration,' said Mabel, 'after leaving us girls behind.'

'Someone has to man the fort,' said Lizzie.

True – but did it have to be the girls?

It was ages before the first car returned – nearly quarter to four. Mabel expected the men to trail in, shocked and exhausted, but instead they came hurrying indoors.

'We were right in the thick of it,' exclaimed Mr Preston. 'Right in the middle! A bomb dropped on an oil and petrol store – went up like a Roman candle – still be blazing tomorrow, I shouldn't wonder. Tomorrow? Hark at me. It's tomorrow now, isn't it?' His face was shining with pride and excitement. He couldn't shut up. 'Plenty of casualties – plenty – but we coped. Followed the drill and coped, by Jove. Splendid show, everyone!'

They stood there, laughing and clapping one another on the back. Surely what they had seen should have sobered them, but they were bursting with energy.

'Come and tell us about it,' said Mabel, drawing the triumphant warriors towards the ops room, which suddenly seemed very much a sitting room, and a rather poor one at that. 'We've got the kettle on.'

'Tea?' burbled Mr Fitzpatronising. 'Well, I suppose in the absence of a whisky and soda . . .'

At Mabel's side, Joan murmured, 'I feel I'm never going to get the chance to do proper war work.'

It wasn't hard to find out which church Mr Clark attended. Dot had always been a great one for nattering and she could strike up a conversation with anybody – one of her less appealing characteristics, according to Ratty Reg.

'It takes double the time to get anywhere when you go out with Dot,' he complained. 'If she sees someone she knows, it isn't enough for her to say "How do" and carry on walking. Oh no, she has to stop and find out everybody's business. A right nosy parker, she is. She'll talk to complete strangers, given half a chance.'

What was nosy about taking an interest in folk? It was part of being a good neighbour, part of what kept communities together. As for passing the time of day with strangers, where was the harm in that?

And why did Reg have to run her down? No wonder she talked so much to people outside the home when Ratty Reg was the company she got when she was indoors.

Anyroad, she had found out Mr Clark's church,; and

Cordelia, in her self-assured way, had walked into the charging office as if she owned it and asked to have Mr Clark pointed out to her. Dot could imagine everyone falling over themselves to assist the elegant Mrs Masters, who had probably looked like the wife of one of the company managers, in her smart linen dress with stylish top-stitching, lacquered straw hat, gloves, clip-on earrings and leather clutch bag.

Now it was Sunday morning and Dot had met Cordelia on a leafy street in Fallowfield at nine o'clock, so they could nab Mr Clark when he came out of church. The service ended about a quarter past and there was no sign of him.

'The next service starts at ten,' said Cordelia. 'I suggest we go in and sit at the back. Then at least we shall have fulfilled our Sabbath obligation.'

'If you can call it that,' said Dot, 'given that we're here to sort out a dirty old man.'

They went into the church to wait for the next service. Every time a member of the congregation walked in, Cordelia looked at who walked past and Dot looked at Cordelia, on tenterhooks for a sign of recognition. At last, Cordelia gave her a discreet nudge and glanced towards a couple in their Sunday best. Dot just had time to grab an impression of ruddy cheeks and a pot-belly before she was looking at the man's back as he walked beside his wife up the aisle.

Dot and Cordelia slipped out shortly before the end, stationing themselves beside where the church gates would have been if they hadn't been carted off to be melted down for the war effort. As the congregation spilled outside into the August sunshine, Dot took a step forward. What if they missed him? No, there he was, tipping his trilby to a pair of elderly ladies who looked like sisters.

They had already agreed that Cordelia would make the first move. Neither of them had said so, but obviously the well-spoken Cordelia would fare better in the initial approach. With a shared glance and a nod, the two of them stepped into the Clarks' way.

'Mr Clark – good morning.' Cordelia spoke in a friendly voice that all but made Dot grind her teeth. Even the pretence of being pleased to see this vile man made her want to spit in his eye.

'I'm sorry,' said Mr Clark. 'Do I know you?'

'How foolish of me,' Cordelia murmured. 'Of course you don't.' She smiled at Mrs Clark. 'Do excuse the intrusion, but my friend and I both work for the railway. Your husband is a gentleman whom we know by sight – and by reputation. He runs the charging office with such efficiency.'

Mrs Clark beamed. 'You don't attend here regularly, do you? Or maybe you come to a different service normally?'

'Nay, we don't live over this way,' said Dot. 'We're out looking for my young scoundrel of a grandson. He's kicked a ball through next door's window and run away.'

'Boys will be boys,' murmured Mr Clark.

'When I get hold of him,' said Dot, 'I'll . . . smack his bottom.' She looked straight at Mr Clark. His eyes popped wide.

'Mrs Clark – it is Mrs Clark, isn't it?' said Cordelia. 'I've been admiring your costume.'

'Thank you. I made it myself.'

'Did you really? Could you possibly explain to me how you managed the box-pleats? I've never got the hang of them. Would you mind awfully if we stood over there in the shade? I find this sunshine rather dazzling.'

Mrs Clark happily toddled off with Cordelia. Dot gave Mr Clark the evil eye.

'This is nice, isn't it?' she said. 'Or aren't you so keen to spend your time with an old bag like me? Like 'em young, so I've heard. Oh, I know all about you, Mr Clark.'

'I don't know what you're talking about.' He made a move to go.

'Feel free to walk away, but I'll be obliged to shout after you, and don't kid yourself I won't. I'm a common or garden fishwife, me. Not like my friend over there. A real lady, she is. Now then, you and me are going to have a nice little chat all about bottom smacking.'

'Keep your voice down!' Mr Clark's gaze was all over the place. 'I don't know what you mean, madam.'

'Let me give you a bit of help, then. You made what's called an improper suggestion to a young lady in your charging office. My guess is that she's not the first, neither.'

'This is ridiculous. How dare you?'

'I dare, all right, matey. You're known for being a dirty old man.'

'I don't have to listen to this—'

'Suit yourself. I'll take myself over yon and have a word with Mrs Clark, shall I? Are you feeling all right?' she asked, as Mr Clark made a spluttering sound. 'You don't sound in right fine fettle, I must say.'

'Mrs – whoever you are—'

'Mrs Decent, that's who I am, a working woman what is spitting feathers because you've been taking advantage of girls in your office. That's who I am. And who are you? A dirty old goat. There – now we've been properly introduced, so let me tell you what happens next. Me and my friend, we have eyes and ears all over Hunts Bank, and if you ever – ever – so much as breathe the wrong way in a lady's presence again, you'd best keep your eyes open when you next walk out of church, because you never know who you might bump into, do you?'

She waved to Cordelia, who came back with Mrs Clark.

'It's been such a pleasure to meet you, Mrs Clark,' Cordelia was saying.

'Aye, and I've had a nice chat with Mr Clark an' all,' said Dot.

'Oh, Mr Clark,' said Cordelia, 'I meant to ask you. Have you met my husband? Kenneth Masters, he's a solicitor.'

'Can't say I have.'

'How foolish of me. I was sure he'd mentioned your name. I thought maybe he'd been in correspondence with you.'

'Not me,' snapped Mr Clark, then forced a smile for his wife's benefit.

'No one wants to receive a solicitor's letter, do they?' laughed Mrs Clark.

'Very true, I'm afraid,' said Cordelia.

'We'd best push off and get us dinners on.' Dot nodded to the Clarks. 'Nice to meet you.'

With swift goodbyes, they left the Clarks and walked along the road, past a line of houses that had turned their front gardens over to veg.

'What did you say to him?' asked Cordelia. 'Did you succeed?'

'I think I got my point across,' said Dot, 'and if I didn't, then the mention of your husband was a master-stroke – no pun intended.'

'I think we did what we came to do,' said Cordelia.

'Aye, happen we did.'

After a moment, Cordelia asked, 'Would you care to link arms?'

Dot breathed in, savouring the moment. Not so long ago she had acknowledged that, had things been different, she might have been the elegant Cordelia's daily. Very likely, Cordelia had thought so an' all. But look at them now. Their railway jobs had brought them together and the determination of their group of railway girls to stick like glue and support each other had overcome their differences of class.

Never mind Hitler and the war. Never mind rationing. Right here, right now, her world was a good place, because she had made a true friend.

'Aye,' she said, slipping her arm through Cordelia's. 'Happen I would.'

Chapter Twenty-four

There was another hum and a wallop and the building trembled. The vibration entered Joan through the soles of her feet and travelled up through her body and out of the top of her head. Plaster dust drifted down from the ceiling, shimmering in the reverberating air. Everyone froze, then started moving again, the men dumping their remaining supplies and thrusting the new sets into their rucksacks.

'All set?' asked Mr Atkins.

He nodded to Joan. She switched off the light with one hand, throwing open the front door with the other. The men streamed past her. They smelled of the smoke and dust. A rucksack bumped her and she tried to step back but hit the wall. Then there was empty air in front of her.

The ack-ack guns were at it full tilt. The sound of aircraft engines filled the night, a droning backdrop to the whistle and crump of the falling bombs. Last night, Baguley and Brooklands had copped it. Now it was their turn – the Alexandra Park area, and Platt Fields not far away. Moss Side and Hulme were also getting their share, according to a telephone call Lizzie had taken from HQ.

Letitia was on duty as well tonight. Was it safe over Didsbury way? What about Gran and their house?

There was a glow of fire in the sky – more than one glow, more than one fire. The night was warm, yet there was a chilling prickle in the air. She shut the door and Mabel flicked on the light. With the blood singing through her veins, Joan helped Mabel gather the discarded supplies and take them upstairs. They started collecting together fresh sets, which they took downstairs. They worked well together. Joan appreciated having Mabel by her side. Mabel knew what to do and did it without fuss. But it was more than that. When she was on duty, Mabel seemed to unbend, losing that sense of separateness that characterised her in social situations. She became positively good-humoured, even funny, sometimes. If only she would be like that all the time.

'You'd better get down into the cellar now,' said Lizzie from her place in the cupboard under the stairs.

Before they could move, there was an enormous bang. Did the building shift on its foundations? Instinctively, Joan reached out to steady herself against the wall.

'That was close,' said Mabel.

'They sound closer than they are,' said Lizzie. 'My auntie lives in Brooklands and she came round today and told my mum that when they were in their Anderson shelter, they were convinced a bomb had landed practically in the garden, but it turned out to be four streets away.'

There was a clatter as the door flew open and a man rushed in.

'Thank God you're here. This is the first-aid post, isn't it? We need help. My girl's trapped. Come on!'

Mabel slid behind him and shut the door, but he whirled round and yanked it open, almost dancing from foot to foot.

'Come on!' It was an anguished yell.

Calm descended on Joan. 'I'll go.'

'We're supposed to stop here,' said Lizzie.

'I'll dash upstairs and fetch some stuff.'

'Stuff? Look at all this stuff.' The man waved his hand at the tables. 'What good is it doing? It looks like a ruddy market stall.'

Tempting as it was to grab a set, Joan ran upstairs, leaving the poor father to his desperate tirade. It was second nature by now to reach for the right selection. She thrust everything into a spare rucksack and grabbed a folded blanket. As she swung her way out of the store, she collided with Mabel.

'I'm coming too.'

'We can't leave Lizzie on her own.'

'I'll be more use with you. How many people does it take to answer the telephone?'

Joan bounded downstairs. The man was already racing across the grass. She and Mabel raced to keep up, plunging through the darkness. Where in blazes had the man gone?

As she left the shelter of the trees, she skidded to a dead halt. Over the road from the park, flames shot into the sky from the roof of a house, while the house next door seemed to be crumbling away, its roof gone, along with the upstairs front wall and much of the side wall. In the glow of the fire, Joan could see the cabbage roses on a quilt, the pictures hanging skew-whiff.

A pile of rubble blocked the downstairs and men were working away at it, a chain of them passing bricks and wood away from the scene. The sight of the girl's father running across the road galvanised Joan into action. She ran across the final stretch of grass to the wall, very low these days now that it didn't have railings on top, sprang over it, twanging her ankle as she landed but carrying on running anyway, arriving breathlessly at the father's side.

He grabbed her shoulders. 'There – she's in there – underneath all that.'

'Please stay back, Mr Darrell,' said an ARP warden. 'We'll get her out, never fear.'

'She needs help now. I was talking to her before you lot

pitched up, but then her voice faded away. This girl is one of those first-aid bods from over yonder—'

'Us wardens are trained in first aid—'

'But you can't get through that hole and my Margaret needs help right now. This girl . . .'

The ARP warden eyed Joan, sizing her up. 'Aye, she might be small enough at that, though she's hardly dressed for it.'

'They don't give uniforms to us girls.' Joan lifted her chin, refusing to sound apologetic. The blouse and cardy were just about all right, but the skirt – well, she would be wearing slacks on duty from now on, no matter what Gran said.

'Watch it!' said the warden as Mabel raced up behind them. 'You can't go clodhopping about on this rubble. I've got one of my blokes seeing to the folks from next door. You go and relieve him and send him back here.' Turning his back on Mabel, he nodded to Joan. 'Come on, miss. Mind your feet.'

Joan picked her way up the crumbled remains of the front of the Darrells' house. The smells of smoke, dust and, bizarrely, wood polish swarmed up her nose. Atop the rubble lay a couple of books, wide open, a brass candlestick and a plump little padded stool with a frilly apron around it.

The warden stopped. A couple of men were working right at the front of the building, with plaster and brick dust falling on them from above, not to mention the possibility of loose floorboards and chunks of brickwork hurtling down on them. One man was lying flat, reaching into a hole; the other knelt beside him, taking whatever was handed to him and passing it back to the fellow at the head of the chain.

'Down there.' The warden indicated the hole with a jerk of his chin. 'She's in the cellar. There's a small window there, at ground level. That's the only way in at this stage. The kitchen floor came down and blocked the cellar steps.'

'How did Mr Darrell get out?' Joan splayed her hand across the rough fabric of her rucksack, telling herself everything she needed was here.

'He was never in. Came hurrying home from his sister's when the raid started. If we break the window, can you crawl through?'

Joan swallowed. They had a tiny window like that in the cellar at home, letting in a trickle of light. What if she got wedged? What if she got in but couldn't get out?

She nodded. Her heart settled to a steady thump.

'Good girl,' said the ARP warden.

The kneeling man got up and backed away. Joan inched forward and peered into the hole. She could make out the window. It was every bit as small and impossible to get through as she had feared. The chap who had cleared the hole had a stick – no, a piece of metal pipe. He pushed it down the hole, angling it at the window. He tapped – tapped again, harder. There was a sharp crack. He hit again. The pane shattered and Joan heard the distant sound of pieces tinkling to the floor.

'Are you there, love?' he called. 'Can you hear me?'

No answer.

He looked over his shoulder at Joan. 'I'll clear it a bit more, then you can go in.' He tapped away as much as he could of the pieces clinging to the frame. 'Be careful. The last thing we need is the first-aid girl getting cut to ribbons.'

Putting down the rucksack and blanket, Joan climbed into the hole, trying not to cause a miniature avalanche. When he passed her things down to her, she unravelled the blanket and wound it round her body and legs for protection, though there was nothing to stop her arms and hands being slashed to pieces.

'Have you a torch?' she asked and he handed one down to her.

She stuffed it under the flap of her rucksack. The whistle of a strip of bombs descending was followed by a series of ear-splitting explosions that shook the world. The house trembled above her. Clouds of dust lifted; she covered her face and held her breath, panic streaking through her at the thought of suffocation. The rubble beneath her shifted and brickwork fell from above. She curled as small as she could, wrapping an arm around her head. The vibration passed through her in a series of tiny jolts and her teeth clicked.

What had she agreed to? Suppose another bomb fell and the front of the house came crashing down, blocking this hole and trapping herself and the presumably injured girl underground. She drew a breath to stop herself feeling shaky but coughed on the dust.

Thrusting her rucksack through the empty window, she let go. Her turn now. It was a devil of a job to sit down and wriggle into position. The rubble around her moved. She stopped while it settled, but as soon as she moved again, so did her surroundings. She just had to get on with it and force herself through the gap. For one stomach-chilling moment, she was stuck, then she managed a wiggle and inserted herself in further.

Her legs, encumbered by the blanket, were through, leaving her waist pressed hard against the ledge. She pushed further backwards, trying to kick her legs for help. Now her cocooned ribs were on the ledge. Next would come her arms, protected by nothing more than a cardy and a thick layer of dust.

She let out a hiss of pain as something sharp stabbed her flesh through her sleeve. Her fingers scrabbled, trying to find purchase, but slipped. Her heart leaped, her stomach whooped and she plunged to the floor, glass crunching beneath her as her legs folded. Crumpled inside the blanket, she pushed free and scrambled up.

The darkness swooped on her, almost locking her in position. After the noise, activity and urgency outside, it felt alien to be thrust into this world of black stillness. It was like plunging into the deepest cave, not into a cellar beneath a house.

Crouching, she waved her hands around until they made contact with the rucksack. Hauling it to her, she fumbled with the fastening, grabbing the torch before it could tumble from beneath the flap. Looping the rucksack over her arm, she stood up and flicked on the torch – was this place so dark that light couldn't penetrate it? Of course: it was an outdoor torch, the lens covered with layers of tissue. Using her nail, she picked a hole in the tissue and tore it off, allowing a beam of white light to pour out. It danced across a couple of camp beds, a table and chairs, a whopping great armchair – how the heck had they managed to get that down here?

But where was – oh, Jiminy, the poor girl was lying in a corner. Joan played the torchlight around, assessing the situation and trying to make sense of it. Part of the ceiling had come down, but why would Margaret have been over there when she had the furniture to keep her comfy? Ah, yes, of course – there was a wire rigged up, with a blanket hanging from it, no doubt to conceal the bucket in the corner.

With grit crunching beneath her shoes, she made her way across and dropped to her knees beside the girl.

'Margaret – may I call you Margaret? Can you hear me? I've come to help you.'

Margaret was lying on her back. She had thrown her arms out as she fell. One leg was bent sufficiently that it had escaped, but the other was pinned beneath fallen brickwork. This was Joan's first casualty. Her first real casualty, and she had to deal with her all on her own. Margaret's face was caked in grime. Her eyelids fluttered.

'Can you hear me?' Joan asked again.

'Joan . . . is that you?'

Startled, Joan bent closer. 'Goodness!' It was Margaret from Ingleby's, with whom she had sometimes shared fire-watching duty through a long, hard winter.

Margaret uttered a little gasp.

'Don't try to move,' said Joan. 'Can you tell me where it hurts?'

'Every . . . where.'

But there was the tiniest flicker of a smile and Joan recognised pluck when she saw it. Carefully, she checked Margaret for bleeding and broken bones, swallowing hard when she came to where Margaret's leg vanished under the rubble. What damage might be under there?

'Let's see about making you comfortable first.'

She fetched a couple of blankets and a pillow from one of the beds. Gently, she raised Margaret's head and eased the pillow underneath before she tucked one blanket around Margaret's body and another around her free leg.

'I'll be back in a mo.'

'I'm not . . . going anywhere.'

Guided by torchlight, Joan went to stand beneath the window. It showed up as a paler patch of darkness.

'Hello?' she called.

She had to call a couple of times before she heard a scratchy sound and some dust came floating down. She coughed and ducked her head.

'How are things?' came a man's voice. 'Is she all right?'

'As far as I can tell, but her leg's trapped. I'm going to see if I can shift the stuff on top of it.'

'Be careful.'

She returned to Margaret. 'I'll have a bash at freeing you. Yell if it hurts.'

Margaret nodded. Joan knelt by her legs and ran the torch's beam over the rubble before, with infinite care and one brick at a time, she started to lift it away. She froze as she part heard, part felt a distant wallop and the pile of rubble gave a tiny shiver in the torchlight. The ceiling crackled and another layer of dust descended. Grey powder covered Joan's arm and the brick in her hand.

Would another tremor bring down the rest of the ceiling?

'We'll look like a pair of statues if much more plaster dust falls.' She forced a cheery note. 'Have you any water down here? Oh yes, and a primus stove. I'll fix us a brew when I've got your leg free.' She dampened a bandage with water from the kettle. 'Here, wipe your face.'

'Thanks.' Margaret chewed her lip, her brow creasing, eyes shutting briefly.

'What is it?'

'Nothing. Just a spot of stomach-cramp. It's gone now.' But her eyes told a different story.

'How's your foot? Can you feel it?'

'Hurts like billy-o.' Margaret's glance flickered. 'That's good, isn't it?'

'I'll have another go at freeing it.'

The bricks rasped against Joan's fingers as she shifted them. She made good progress and managed to uncover most of Margaret's leg, which she cleaned up, revealing purple bruises and long, deep grazes, but no blood loss and no apparent fractures. She rolled her shoulders before applying herself to freeing Margaret's foot.

'Soon have you out now.'

Margaret made a convulsive move, accompanied by a strangled gurgle.

'Try not to move,' said Joan. 'Did I hurt you?'

Margaret curled round, attempting to pull herself into a ball. Something cold and clammy unfurled itself inside Joan's stomach. Laying her hand on Margaret's shoulder, she dropped her head almost to the floor to speak to her.

'What is it? Tell me.' You weren't supposed to scare the casualties, but it was impossible to keep the alarm out of her voice.

'It hurts . . .'

'Your foot – I know. Maybe it's broken—'

'Oh my goodness . . . oh my goodness . . .'

'Margaret, what is it?' Joan's mouth dried out. What had she done wrong? What had she missed?

Margaret moaned and made as if to rear up. Joan scooted sideways on her knees, putting down a hand to steady herself, then picking it up immediately because it felt sticky. She shone the torch on the floor, her heart delivering a great thump at the sight of a pool of blood spreading from between Margaret's legs.

Margaret moaned again and clutched her stomach.

'Is it your monthly?'

'I hope so. It must be.'

'You're flooding. Are you always this bad?'

'No . . . no . . .'

Lord above, was she haemorrhaging? 'Do you have another injury? Are you sure it's just your foot?'

'Positive. It can't be anything else.'

A memory swirled into Joan's mind of scandalous words whispered at Ingleby's about a girl who had gone off sick and then was never seen again on the shop floor. The words popped out of her mouth. 'Margaret, are you expecting a baby?'

Margaret's eyes opened wide. 'No – no, I can't be.'

'I'm so sorry to ask. I can't apologise enough.' She cringed. How could she possibly have said such an appalling thing?

Grabbing Joan's hand, Margaret burst into tears. 'I can't be – I can't. Oh please, it was only once.'

Joan looked at the fingers wrapped around her own. There was no sign of a ring. Her heartbeat slowed to a sluggish thud. 'Do you mean you might be?'

'You can't get caught your first time – everyone knows that – and it was only the once.'

Joan braced herself to withstand panic, but what she felt was a deep calm. She got to her feet and started to head towards the window, then veered across the room and brought a wooden chair to stand on.

'Are you there?' she called.

'Have you got her free?'

'Not quite. Is there a doctor or nurse, by any chance?'

'Aye, lass. The fire brigade has arrived next door and there's an ambulance with a doctor. I'll fetch him up to have a word once he's done with next door.'

'It can't wait. I need advice – now. Please fetch him. It's important.'

'Hang on. I'll ask our gaffer.'

Damn the ruddy gaffer. 'The young lady is – is in the family way and there's a lot of blood. You have to get me that doctor.'

'Blimey O'Reilly, that's all we need. Give us a minute.'

She climbed down and returned to Margaret.

'Let me see if I can staunch the flow.'

She lifted Margaret's nightie, revealing slender legs at the top of which was a mess of blood. Margaret groaned and turned her face away. Joan tucked several triangular bandages between Margaret's legs, the metallic smell of blood mingling in her nostrils with the musty smell of plaster. She couldn't have her casualty bleeding in this filthy corner. She renewed her efforts to free Margaret's trapped foot.

'Hey, down there! What's going on?'

Joan jumped up and hurried to stand on the chair. 'I'm here.'

'I'm Dr Phillips. What's wrong?'

'I'm not sure, but I think my casualty is losing a baby.'

'Stomach-cramps?'

'Yes, and – and blood.' She wanted to say 'lots of it', but couldn't with Margaret in earshot. She willed the doctor to understand.

'Other injuries?'

'Her foot's trapped, but I've nearly got it free.'

'Do that first, then, and quick about it. Any hot water down there?'

'Yes, and linen.'

'Keep her warm and clean. That's all you can do. What's that?'

Joan could make out some shouting.

'Get him away from here,' roared Dr Phillips.

'What's happening?' asked Joan.

'I think one of the wardens has just informed the father he's going to be a grandfather. Well, that remains to be seen. When the firemen have dealt with next door, they'll dig you out. With luck, the baby will hang on till then. If not . . .'

'If not?'

'Not squeamish, are you? If the worst happens, you've got to keep everything. Understand? I'll need to make sure everything's been expelled.'

Joan could have beaten her knees with an egg whisk.

Dr Phillips said, 'I'm counting on you.'

First things first. She put the kettle on. Next: Margaret's foot. It didn't take long to uncover it. With a sideways glance at the girl, who had got her lips clamped together, Joan lifted away the final bricks. There was no doubt Margaret's ankle was broken. For one appalling moment, Joan's mind went blank, then her knowledge came flooding back and she pulled the rucksack closer and set to work on the injury.

That done, she wanted to get Margaret away from the rubble and filth. The camp beds had thin mattresses. She put one on the floor alongside Margaret and, with encouragement and a helping hand, persuaded her onto it, carefully supporting the injured ankle on a pillow. Then she lugged the mattress across the floor to the furnished part of the cellar.

A *Daily Mirror* was lying folded on the table.

'Can you raise your hips?' asked Joan. 'I'll slide this underneath you.'

'You can't. Dad'll go mad.'

'After what's happened to your house tonight, I doubt he'll notice. Come on – lift up.'

She slid half the pages into position; they crackled as Margaret lay on them. She uttered a whimper and closed her eyes. Determined to make this ordeal easier for her, Joan had a look round and spotted a bottle of cordial. She filled the beakers and tipped the rest away, then poured hot water from the kettle into the bottle, wrapping it in a blanket before she gave it to Margaret, who pulled it to her tummy.

'Thanks.' After a pause, Margaret said in a rush, 'You won't tell him, will you? My dad. You won't tell him I'm in the club.'

'I won't breathe a word.'

'If I lose it, he need never know.'

Joan kept quiet about the ARP warden who had already blabbed. 'What does it feel like?'

'Not all it's cracked up to be and on top of that, it turns out you *can* get caught the first time.'

Joan's cheeks burned. 'Not that. What sort of girl do you

think I am? Some girls might be using this war as an excuse to forget their morals, but I'm not one of them.' God, she sounded just like Gran.

Tears spurted and Margaret smeared them away. 'Neither am I, whatever you might think.'

Joan swallowed words of disbelief. Whatever she thought of Margaret's behaviour, she had no business upsetting her patient.

'When I asked how it feels, I meant . . . what's happening now.'

'Imagine the direst monthly you've ever had. Times it by ten and that's what it's like.' Margaret caught her breath, then released it in a sound halfway between a snort and a groan. She swallowed. 'It feels like my insides are being dragged out.'

'Is it getting worse?'

Any desire to be judgemental vanished. This was her patient, her casualty, her responsibility, a girl in pain – twice over, not forgetting her ankle – and the how and why of it were none of Joan's business. She was a first-aider and it was her duty to assist in every way she could. Not just her duty, either. It was her simple human wish to help this frightened, suffering girl.

'The doctor wants us to . . . um . . . save what comes out.'

'Oh my godfathers.' It looked like Margaret was going to refuse, then she gave in. 'There's a po under the bed.'

Joan helped her onto the chamber pot. Margaret cried out. One hand flailed and grabbed Joan's, practically crushing her bones to powder. Margaret's eyes were shut tight, but that didn't stop tears squeezing out and streaming down her face. The smell of warm blood encircled them.

Margaret slumped against Joan, who sank down to provide better support, the fine layer of grit that covered the floor thrusting a thousand tiny shards into her knees, but that was nothing compared to what Margaret had been through. Joan concentrated on being strong for her.

'Come on,' she whispered at last. 'You need to lie down. Can I let go for a minute?'

Margaret gave a watery nod. Joan screwed up the sheets of blood-sodden newspaper, then pulled the mattress from the other camp bed and threw it on top of the one on the floor. She spread out the remaining newspaper on it before throwing a sheet over the lot, with pillows at either end for Margaret's head and ankle.

She cleaned Margaret as best she could and wadded the last of her bandages to improvise sanitary towels before wrapping Margaret in a clean blanket and helping her lie down. White-faced and exhausted, Margaret fell asleep. Or possibly fainted. It was impossible to say which.

God, what a night. At long last, the hole was large enough and men appeared in the cellar. Margaret was awake again and clutching Joan's hand.

'You'll be in hospital soon,' Joan whispered.

It felt odd to have to stand back and let the men do their job. One of them was Dr Phillips. He crouched beside Margaret, but Joan couldn't hear what was said. He took the sheet of newspaper off the top of the chamber pot into which Margaret had miscarried her baby and had a brief look by the light of a torch. Joan's stomach twisted, but she sucked in a breath and stepped forward, expecting to be asked questions, but Dr Phillips merely thrust the chamber pot into her hands.

She hovered while Margaret was lifted through the hole. At last it was her turn to climb out. At least somebody took the chamber pot off her at that point. But instead of emerging into fresh air after the staleness of the cellar, she found an atmosphere that smelled thickly of smoke and brick dust. Gas as well – her insides gave a swoop of nausea as the cloying aroma streamed down her throat and up inside her head.

Margaret's hand snaked out towards her, but other hands intervened, gently batting Margaret's out of the way. All Joan could do was stay close by and hope her presence provided support. The men laid Margaret on a stretcher, strapping her onto it, fastening her arms by her sides. Then they proceeded to carry her down the heap of rubble towards the waiting ambulance.

A man erupted from nowhere.

'Is that my girl you've got there? How could you, our Margaret? How could you? I've heard what you've been up to. Getting yourself in the pudding club! Didn't I tell you that some girls' morals were bound to go out the window when war broke out? But I never thought – I never imagined . . . How could you?'

Tears poured down poor Margaret's face as her father not just washed their dirty linen in public, but starched and ironed it too. She couldn't even wipe the tears away because her arms were strapped to her sides. If any of the neighbours had had their suspicions beforehand, her father had given them fodder with bells on for their gossip. Poor girl.

In the early-morning light – not the usual pearly light of a summer dawn, but a sulky, ashen gleam that hadn't shaken off the horrors of the night – Joan crossed the road and slipped over the wall into the park. It was like being in a dream. She felt distanced, though whether this was the result of everything she had had to contend with or pure exhaustion, she couldn't tell and didn't care.

Mabel appeared from among the trees and came towards her, running a few steps, then walking, then running again.

Her hair was flattened beneath a layer of brick dust. Joan realised – and knew it should have surprised her, only any reaction seemed beyond her just now – that Mabel was crying. Her eyes were huge and dark and tears were streaming from them, glistening on her face and dripping onto her collar.

She held out her hands to Joan. Joan responded likewise, but Mabel took just one of hers in both her own, one hand holding it to lead her along, the other stroking it. They walked through the trees. How good it felt to walk on grass after the cellar's gritty floor. Joan breathed in, but instead of grass and fresh morning, all she could smell was smoke.

Mabel stopped and turned to her. Joan waited for her to speak, but all Mabel did was touch her face, cupping her cheek tenderly, then pressing her fingertips against it as if to make sure Joan was real.

Mabel walked on, taking Joan with her. Mabel held one hand out in front, indicating something—

They emerged from the trees and there, where the first-aid depot should have been, was – nothing. Just a huge crater in the ground, a gigantic dip filled with rubble.

Chapter Twenty-five

The smell of smoke was heavy in the air, but it wasn't the smell that made Mabel's head feel swirly. It was the shock, the sheer disbelief. How could this have happened? Poor Lizzie, manning the telephone, doing her duty – it was unbelievable.

It could have been them as well. It might so easily have been her and Joan. If that man hadn't come for help – if she hadn't insisted on following Joan into the night . . .

I'll be more use with you. How many people does it take to answer the telephone?

Dear Lizzie. Good-natured, chirpy Lizzie.

Gone.

For ever.

People . . . people at the site of the – of the crater. Men with ARP arm-bands and tin helmets. Mabel stood there, her hands tangled up with Joan's. The bones in her legs felt watery, but somehow she stayed upright.

'Have they come here to gawp?'

The voice was sharp enough to penetrate the woolly sensation that prevented Mabel from thinking properly. She might have looked round to scowl at the people who had come to get an eyeful of the tragedy, but she didn't have full command of her body or her senses.

'Nay, lad. Leave 'em be,' said another voice. 'They're part of the first-aid depot.'

The words slurred around in Mabel's head, like a fairground visitor stumbling about on the cake-walk. Then the words slotted into position and her head reared up in shock. Joan and herself – the men were talking about Joan and her. The first man had thought that she and Joan – that she and Joan . . .

Massive fury burst inside her. How dare anyone imagine that they had come here to stare, to find something to gossip about, something to share over the garden fence in hushed voices? How *dare* they? She wanted to grab the first man by his lapels and – and . . .

It wouldn't bring Lizzie back.

Oh, Lizzie . . .

'Go home, lasses. Go home. There's nowt you can do.'

Their bicycles weren't there any more – wait, yes, they were. They had parked them under a tree and the – the blast had picked them up and dumped them a distance away, but, yes, they were there. Why couldn't Lizzie have been picked up and dumped elsewhere? But even if she had . . .

Mabel didn't want to go home. She didn't want to stay here either – she couldn't bear to. She didn't know what she wanted. She wanted – she wanted it not to have happened.

Was it wrong to think of how close she and Joan had come . . . ?

'I . . .' Joan shook her head, as if trying to free up the words. 'I ought to go home. Gran will be worried.' She stared at the crater. 'I can't believe it . . . I can't believe it . . .' She wrenched her gaze away, swinging round to look Mabel full in the face. Joan's eyes were huge. Instead of their normal blue, they were dark as ink. 'We need to inform HQ – only we haven't got a telephone.' A burst of laughter escaped her lips. She gasped and, pulling free from Mabel, clapped a hand across her mouth. 'I'm so sorry.'

'It's all right, it's all right.' Mabel's words were no more than a whisper. Her throat was filling with tears. 'The ARP men will . . . do whatever is necessary. Go home. Your grandmother needs to know you're safe. So does Letitia.'

'What about you?' asked Joan.

'I'll go as well. I can't stay here.'

Even so, it was a wrench to leave. This was the last spot where Lizzie had been. How could they turn their backs and push their bicycles away? It was a betrayal.

But they did. They did.

Somehow Mabel managed to cycle home. It was as if her body remembered what to do and where to go. Her mind certainly was of no help. Her thoughts were blurry, but at the same time there was a jagged edge to her consciousness.

As she approached Mrs Grayson's house, she braked, stumbling from the bike and pushing it onto the pavement. All at once, her eyes were swimming. She thrust open the rickety wooden gate and shoved the bicycle through.

A figure reared up in front of her and she shrieked.

Bob. It was Bob. Joan's Bob, Bernice's Bob. And he hadn't reared up. He had been sitting on the doorstep and had stood up when she appeared.

What are you doing here? She meant to say the words out loud, but she wasn't sure they had come out of her mouth.

He came towards her. His face was a mask of shock and sorrow. Probably hers was the same.

'I heard,' he said. 'Word came to our depot about . . . about the Alexandra Park depot. Is it true?' He shook his head. 'That's a stupid question. I know it's true. I couldn't bear to go to Joan's house in case . . .' His words trailed off. Then he shook his head and lifted his chin, pressing his lips tightly together. A deep breath, then he said, 'Please – just tell me.'

Mabel dropped her bicycle, leaving it to clatter onto the path. She went to him and caught his hands. 'Joan's safe. She wasn't in the house. She's safe.'

Bob pulled his hands free, turning away as he covered his face. He breathed out a huge sigh that sent a shudder through his body before he scrubbed his face and dropped his hands to his sides. He shook his head and pushed out a sharp breath.

'She's safe,' Mabel repeated. 'But . . .' Could she say it? Should she? What if she said it and then it turned out to be a huge mistake?

'But what?'

'Lizzie . . .' Her voice dried up.

'Lizzie?' He frowned. He understood – she could see it in his eyes. He shook his head, rejecting the idea – well, she knew how that felt.

'Joan and I . . . we'd gone to an emergency, but Lizzie . . . Lizzie was inside the depot.'

Bob slumped against the wall of the house. 'Lizzie . . . poor girl. I came here frightened of what might have happened to Joan and – and it was Lizzie.'

Mabel smeared away tears. 'Go to Joan. Go now.'

'I'm sorry. I'm stopping you from going indoors, aren't I?'

'No.' In that instant, she made up her mind. 'I'm not going in. I'm going round to Lizzie's house to see her mum. There's no Mr Cooper, no brothers and sisters. I have to go.'

'I'll come too.' Bob stood up straight. 'I can't let you go on your own. Joan's safe. She has her family.'

'I'm fine on my own, honest Injun. You should go round to Joan's.'

'Not until I've seen Mrs Cooper. It's the right thing to do.'

He really was his mother's son, wasn't he? Mabel had liked Bernice from the start. She was straight-talking but kind and compassionate.

'Are you all right to cycle there?' asked Bob.

All right to cycle? She didn't feel all right to cope with

anything – oh crumbs, what an unutterably feeble thing to think. However bad this was for her, she had to be strong now for Mrs Cooper. It was something she could do for Lizzie.

Dear little Lizzie. Such good fun, everyone's friend.

Bob picked up her bicycle from where she had dumped it. His own was propped against the side wall of the house. He snapped on his bicycle clips. They wheeled their bikes out onto the road and set off. Mabel wobbled dangerously before she got going properly. After the damaged buildings she had seen near Alexandra Park, it gave her the oddest feeling to cycle through streets that remained untouched. Did the people who lived here know how lucky they were, how close they were to the destruction?

They arrived outside Lizzie's house, which was midway along a long row of red-brick terraced houses with front doors opening straight onto the street. They propped their bikes against the wall and exchanged glances that spoke of determination.

Bob took a moment to remove his bicycle clips, but even so he made a point of overtaking her before she reached the front door. 'I would say "Ladies first", but . . .'

Mabel's heart turned over. He was protecting her. He was going to speak the first words to Mrs Cooper so that she wouldn't have to. What a good chap he was, solid and kind. Joan was a lucky girl.

Impulsively, she said, 'I work with your mother. I know how proud she is of you.'

About to knock, Bob let his hand fall back. 'Thanks. It's kind of you to say so. Mum and Dad are proud of all four of us. They worry like crazy when we head off to do our war work, but they're chuffed to bits at the same time.'

'None taken.'

Imagine having such love and support from your

parents. Mumsy and Pops loved Mabel, of course they did. She had never doubted it, but she had always been aware of their expectations. Her father's ambition for her to make a grand marriage by parading her round London had come to nothing, while Mumsy, always a slave to her book of etiquette, was constantly on the alert to make sure that Mabel wouldn't slip up. Cycling through the early-morning streets with Bob probably constituted a social blunder of the first water, something that a real lady – like Persephone – could get away with, with a shrug and a laugh, but which would spell social death to a nouveau riche pretend-lady.

Bob knocked on the door. Mabel's heart thudded and her mouth went dry. What did you say to a mother whose daughter had just been killed in the most horrific circumstances? God, it was like – it was Althea all over again. Except that she hadn't had the guts to go to Althea's parents, hadn't even written them a letter of condolence.

The door opened and it wasn't Mrs Cooper. It was, of all people, Mrs Marshall, the woman from their very first meeting in the park-keeper's house, whom they had all been glad to see sent off to another depot while the three of them stayed together in Alexandra Park.

'This isn't Mrs Cooper,' Mabel said before Bob could say anything. 'Do you remember me, Mrs Marshall? Mabel Bradshaw from the Alexandra Park depot. We've – we've come to see Mrs Cooper.'

'I don't think this is the best time—' Mrs Marshall began.

'Who is it?' came a voice from behind her – Mrs Cooper's – and Mrs Marshall stepped aside.

Mrs Cooper was a bird-like little woman with faded fair hair. Her eyes were unnaturally bright, almost glassy. She bustled forward, for all the world as if this was a social call.

'Mrs Cooper,' said Bob. 'We're Lizzie's friends.'

'Oh, come in, please, I insist.'

Mrs Marshall didn't look best pleased, but Mabel ignored that. Did Mrs Cooper know about Lizzie? Her friendly fussing suggested possibly not. Yet why would Mrs Marshall be here other than to break the bad news?

Mabel and Bob followed Mrs Cooper into her small parlour. Standing by the fireplace with a cup of tea in his hand was Mr Turnbull – so Mrs Cooper must have been told. A couple of women sat on the settee, neighbours presumably, in spite of the early hour – yes, one was Mrs O'Grady, who used to collect Lizzie from first-aid class. The hushed atmosphere was overlaid with strain and horror.

'These are Lizzie's friends,' trilled Mrs Cooper. 'Aren't they good to come? Everyone is so kind.' Her face crumpled, then sprang back into an intent eagerness that was painful to behold.

'Mrs Cooper,' said Mabel. 'I'm Mabel Bradshaw and this is Bob Hubble.'

'Mabel . . . Mabel. Yes, dear, I've heard your name. And don't you look smart.'

Smart? She must have misheard. But, no, she hadn't.

'My Lizzie said you were always beautifully turned out and she was right.'

Mabel's body heated up. She had just come off duty after a night of helping ARP men and ambulance men, and she was beautifully turned out. She had just lost a friend and colleague, and she was beautifully turned out. She didn't feel beautifully turned out. She felt as if she had been ripped to shreds. Everyone was looking at her. If – if she looked perfect, might they think she didn't care?

'Are you from Lizzie's first-aid depot an' all?' Mrs Cooper asked Bob.

'No, Mrs Cooper. I'm – I walk out with one of the girls from there. Joan.'

'Joan! Oh, you're *that* Bob. My Lizzie liked you. She said

you had nice manners. She said – she said you were top-notch at the waltz, but your foxtrot left something to be desired.'

'That's about the sum of it.' Bob's Adam's apple jerked.

'Well, you make sure you improve your foxtrot, and think of my Lizzie when you do it.' Mrs Cooper lifted her chin and pressed her lips together. 'Now then, who's for a cup of tea? I don't know what it is about times like this, but everyone wants a cup of tea.'

Mrs O'Grady stood up. 'You should have a seat, Mrs Cooper, and let us look after you.'

'It's no trouble.' Mrs Cooper bustled from the room, leaving everyone looking at one another in dismay.

The other neighbour got to her feet as well. 'We'll go and lend a hand.'

That left Mabel, Bob, Mr Turnbull and Mrs Marshall looking at one another. Mr Turnbull put down his cup and saucer on the end of the mantelpiece.

'A very sad business,' he said. 'I'll have to write a report and . . . well, I gather you and Miss Foster weren't present when . . .'

'No,' said Mabel. 'We—'

'I don't think this is the time,' said Bob.

'No, no, of course not,' said Mr Turnbull.

An awkward sorrow filled the parlour. It was an old-fashioned room – and wasn't that a snobby thing to think? If you were rich, your old stuff was called traditional.

'You'll receive notification as to the location of your new depot,' Mr Turnbull murmured, not looking at Mabel.

She went cold. The new depot. The old one had been blasted to bits, but, heigh-ho, let's find another and carry on. Without Lizzie.

Mrs Cooper came back, carrying a tray, her neighbours fluttering behind her.

'Here, allow me.' Bob took the tray from Mrs Cooper's hands and placed it on a low table, where the neighbours swooped on it and started pouring, leaving poor Mrs Cooper wringing her hands, which suddenly didn't have a job to do. She rubbed her palms down the front of her skirt.

'We've only just finished saving up for the headstone for Lizzie's dad.'

Mabel's fingers tightened into fists. 'Mrs Cooper, I just want to say . . .' She stopped. The correct thing to do was to say how sorry she was. Instead she said, 'Lizzie was such a lovely girl, an absolute darling.' Lord above, she sounded like Persephone. 'We were all fond her, all of us who started work on the same day. She was a real breath of fresh air.'

'That's my Lizzie,' said Mrs Cooper.

'She was funny and so kind-hearted,' said Mabel.

'And she was a good dancer,' Bob added.

'Oh, she loved her dancing,' said Mrs Cooper. She looked at Bob. 'What are you doing here, young man? That's what I'd like to know. You should be with your Joan, not hanging around an old thing like me. I mean it,' she added as Bob glanced uncertainly round the room. 'Off you go, and mind you give my best regards to Joan's granny. She was hospitable to my Lizzie and I'm not the sort to forget that.'

Stepping forward, Bob took Mrs Cooper's thin hands in his. He looked down into her face, then he lowered his head and dropped a gentle kiss on her cheek. Emotion jampacked Mabel's throat all the way down to her chest.

With a flutter, Mrs Cooper pulled away. 'Oh, get on with you! And make sure you give your Joan a big hug. I hugged my Lizzie before . . . before she went out last night.' Those busy hands of hers made shooing motions. 'Off you go.'

Bob nodded to the occupants of the parlour. Mrs Cooper made to follow him as he went into the hallway, whereupon everybody moved, reached out a hand, said she wasn't to bother and they would see him out, but Mrs Cooper waved them away.

'Nay, you all stay put. I'll see him out.'

A dark silence fell on the room. Despairing glances were exchanged. Mrs Cooper could be heard trilling her farewells.

'There now, what a nice young man,' she said as she came back. 'My Lizzie always said so.'

'She always had a good word for everyone,' said Mabel.

'Yes, she did. She had a heart of gold, did my Lizzie. I'm grateful to you for coming.' Then Mrs Cooper crumpled, simply dropped like a stone onto the settee. 'Oh, my poor Lizzie, my darling girl. She was all I had left. What am I to do without her?'

Dot didn't know how she had got through the day, but she had. What choice was there? This was wartime. Folk were bound to get killed. Oh, but for it to happen to Lizzie, sweet little Lizzie, so young and so lovable. Distress shimmered through Dot's frame. That poor mother. Her shoulders tightened. One day she might be 'that poor mother'. She had to stop breathing to keep hold of the anguish that sliced through her.

She was on the afternoon and evening shift today. Her break between trips to Southport fell at the same time as her group of friends would normally meet in the buffet. A meeting hadn't been arranged for today – today, the very day when they most needed one another. Dot found her feet taking her across the concourse towards the station buffet. She opened the door, quivering on the edge of disappointment, because of course no one was going to be there – but there they were. The railway girls. Her friends. Gratitude made her heart swell. They were all there, all of them – even Colette. Something clobbered Dot on the inside. The sight of Colette made it real. Colette never joined them in the buffet because she was always rushing off to meet her husband, but she was here now and that could mean only one thing: that it was real and Lizzie, dear little Lizzie, had been taken from them. Of course, she had known all along that it was real, but at various times during the day, pure disbelief had overwhelmed her, a powerful sensation that it simply had to be a hideous mistake. But not any more, not now that she had clapped eyes on Colette.

'Dot,' called Cordelia. 'Budge up, girls. Make room for a little one.'

They had pushed two tables together. Chairs scraped as they made a space for Dot, Mabel pulling over a free chair from another table. Dot's eyes were drawn automatically towards the corner behind them. That was where Lizzie should be. She hadn't been allowed to sit down in public while wearing her uniform. Now there would always be an empty space beside their table when they met up. Oh, Lizzie.

'It feels as if everywhere I go today,' said Alison, 'people are talking about Paulden's taking a direct hit.'

'It's understandable, I suppose,' said Cordelia. 'Everybody has shopped there at one time or another.'

'But it feels so wrong,' said Alison. 'As if a building matters more than people.'

'Put like that, it doesn't, of course,' said Cordelia, 'but if a building is well-known, everyone feels as if it belongs to them. It's something they have in common.'

The buffet door opened and Persephone walked in. Her natural grace and confidence seemed to have been knocked. She glanced across at the rest of them, but didn't head their way. As a latecomer to their group, did she feel she wasn't quite one of them? Well, Dot wasn't having that. Today of all days, the group needed to be stronger than ever.

She waved. 'Persephone!' She addressed the couple on the next table. 'Excuse me, but may I take this chair for my friend?'

Receiving nods of consent, she drew the seat across amidst more shuffling round by the others. Persephone came over, placing her handbag on the table. It was a clutch bag of soft leather, with a folded-over, triangular flap, like an envelope.

Dot looked across at Mabel and Joan. It was the best thing for them, being here among friends. They looked exhausted. Their faces were drawn, their eyes haunted. Never mind not wanting to be the mother figure. Her arms ached to hug them both.

'Can you bear to talk about it?' she asked.

Joan and Mabel looked at one another. Would they say anything?

'Joan was a heroine,' said Mabel.

'No, I wasn't,' said Joan.

'She climbed through a tiny hole to get into the cellar of a damaged house to give first aid to an injured girl,' said Mabel.

'I didn't do much, just helped the ambulance men. And while we were out doing that . . .'

No one spoke. In the busy buffet with its chattering voices, there was a sensation of profound silence around their table.

'If you hadn't gone out,' said Persephone. 'If that house hadn't been damaged, if that girl hadn't been trapped . . .'

'How can you say that?' Alison demanded. 'Do you mean we're supposed to be grateful it was "only" Lizzie who was killed?'

'I didn't mean that.' Persephone looked startled.

'Stop it this minute, the pair of you,' Dot cut in. 'This is no time for bickering. We're all shocked and desperately upset. Losing our Lizzie . . .' A lump of emotion clogged her throat. She had to stretch her jaw to get her voice working again. 'Lizzie is such a sweet soul – was – was.'

She could say no more. Her heart was full but her mind was clouded. She wasn't even sure what she had meant to say, other than to express her sense of loss. Was there comfort to be found in shared loss? Or did that make the loss seem worse? Bigger?

'Have you seen Bob?' Alison asked Joan.

Joan nodded and some of the tension seemed to ease out of her. 'He came to our house this morning after he heard.'

Alison shivered. 'Did he already know you were safe?'

'He'd seen Mabel and she told him.'

'Eh, he must have been that relieved to see you safe and sound,' said Dot.

'Yes, he . . .' A small breath erupted from Joan's lips, a mixture of relief and . . . and an almost-laugh? 'My gran answered the door, but she wouldn't let him in, because of how early it was in the morning. If she'd let him in, and then the neighbours had seen him leaving at breakfast-time, well . . . So I ran to the doorstep and straight into his arms, and she pulled him indoors pretty sharpish after that, I can tell you.'

Smiles flickered round the group in a moment of gratitude for something good. Then the moment crumpled and they all looked at one another.

Joan sat up straighter. 'Mabel and Bob went to see Mrs Cooper.'

'They did? What, first thing?' asked Alison, and everyone looked at Mabel.

'How was she?' Colette asked softly.

Mabel took her time answering. 'She was being very strong.'

Strong, aye. Shocked, disbelieving, desperate, heartbroken, ready to lay down her own life if it would bring her child back – but strong for other folk. That was mothers for you.

Colette sat up a little straighter. 'I'd like to say something, though I'm not sure whether I should.'

Along with everyone else, Dot looked at her. Colette glanced down at her hands.

'Why not?' asked Cordelia.

Colette looked up. 'I've hardly seen any of you since starting work. I don't feel I have the right to speak.'

'Eh, lass,' said Dot, 'we'll have none of that, thanks very much – will we, girls? You're one of us and having to rush off regular to be with that loving husband of yours makes no difference to that.'

'Thank you,' said Colette. 'I truly wish I could come now and then to the group meetings, but – well, anyway, I might not be here usually, or hardly at all, but I do think about you. But after this, there'll always be an empty space, won't there? The group will never be complete again.'

Chapter Twenty-six

Being with her friends gave Joan a comfort of sorts while it lasted, but all too soon the group had to split up. Dot had another train journey to make; Colette's husband appeared, standing just inside the buffet door. With a heavy heart, Joan headed for home. On the bus, she sat behind a couple of headscarfed women who were talking about Paulden's. She wanted to bang their heads together and pour out what had happened to Lizzie. Instead she alighted two stops early and marched home, her feelings all over the place.

When she arrived, Gran thrust a piece of flimsy paper at her.

'Telegram for you. It says where your first-aid group is to meet.'

'You opened it.'

'Of course I did. This is wartime. Telegrams have to be opened immediately.'

'When are you to report?' asked Letitia.

'Tonight at ten.'

'Not today, surely,' said Letitia. 'Not after . . .'

Joan shrugged, though she felt anything but dismissive. 'We're in the middle of the Battle of Britain. I don't think anyone gets a night off. And – and I wouldn't want one.'

'Where are they sending you?' asked Letitia.

'Withington.'

'Pity. I thought they might send you to Didsbury with me.'

'They wouldn't do that,' said Joan. 'They don't put family members together, remember.'

'I wouldn't want you in the same place.' Gran's shoulders shifted. 'Not after what happened to that girl.'

The muscles jumped beneath Joan's skin. 'Don't call her that girl. Her name's Lizzie.'

'Pardon me for breathing, and since when did you start talking back to your elders?'

'I'm sorry, Gran.'

'Let's get that awful brick dust out of your hair,' said Letitia. 'I'll help you wash it.'

'It needs a good brush first,' said Gran. 'You're not doing that inside the house.'

Joan's scalp had felt claggy all day, though she'd felt guilty each time she noticed it. Her snood hadn't afforded her hair much protection last night. Letitia ran upstairs, returning with Joan's hairbrush, and they went outside into the passage. Removing her snood, Joan sucked in a breath as Letitia proceeded to hack away with the brush.

'Do you have to tug so hard? It's worse than when Gran combed our hair when we were children.'

'Keep still or it'll never come out.'

By the time Letitia had finished, Joan felt as though her scalp had been sandpapered. Upstairs, she hung over the bath while Letitia hefted a jug over her head, trickling water through her hair and into a bowl in the bath so it could be used again, having fresh for the final rinse only. Letitia insisted on using some of their precious Amami, N° 5 and as Letitia massaged her head, working up a lather, Joan closed her eyes, feeling her shoulders start to loosen.

'Will you be all right going on duty tonight?' Letitia asked as she rubbed Joan's hair with a towel. 'You look done in.'

'Not as done in as Lizzie.' Joan caught Letitia's hand. 'I'm so sorry. That was a horrid thing to say. I've been thinking about her all day. It's hard to believe.'

'I've spent the day thinking how easily it could have been you. Come into the bedroom and I'll do your hair.'

As Letitia expertly twisted the rollers into place, Joan couldn't keep her eyes off her reflection. She looked the same. She didn't feel the same, but she looked the same. It wasn't right. Lizzie deserved more than that.

'I didn't even say goodbye to her. I just grabbed what I needed and dashed out.'

Letitia's hands stopped mid-air. 'It was an emergency. You don't go round bidding everyone a fond farewell in a situation like that. You did a splendid thing last night, entering an unsafe building to help that girl who was trapped.' She wrapped the end of a lock of hair around a roller and coiled it towards Joan's head. 'I'm proud of you and I'm going to be prouder still when you go back on duty tonight, because I know you're going to do your best, same as you always do. We can't afford to let anything knock us back. Today's been unbearable, I know, but tomorrow will be a tiny bit easier and so will every day after that.'

'Stop it.'

Letitia's hands froze.

'Not that,' said Joan. 'Yes, actually – that.' She stood up and faced her sister. 'How can it possibly matter what my hair looks like? Lizzie is dead, and you're doing my hair, and I'm letting you. How can it matter?'

Letitia tried to draw her towards the bed. Joan resisted, then gave in, but when she might have tried to leave a gap between them, the mattress dipped and slid them together. Letitia put her arm round Joan and kissed her forehead.

'What's this about, Joanie? And I'm not talking about your hair.'

Joan rubbed the back of her neck. 'I don't want to be told you're proud of me. I don't want to hear that eventually I'll feel better.'

'Both those things are true,' Letitia whispered.

'I know.'

'Then what do you want to hear? What do you need me to say?'

Joan sprang to her feet. 'That you're sorry about Lizzie, that you're shocked, that you can't believe you'll never see her again. That you liked her and cared about her . . . and she was so cheerful and friendly . . . That's what I want to hear. About Lizzie. Not about me and how I'll get over it eventually. About *Lizzie*.'

Joan batted aside the net curtains so she could see properly out of the bedroom windows. She hated nets. She wasn't going to have them when she got married and had her own home, and Gran could say what she liked about it – probably some nasty remark about Estelle. Did neighbours and passers-by really gawp through your windows if you didn't have nets to protect your privacy? Joan certainly didn't go round peering through other people's un-netted windows.

Through the mesh of anti-blast tape, she looked down at their back garden, where their wigwam of runner beans boasted a pleasing crop among the small, bright red flowers. Over the fences to either side, the next-door gardens looked like theirs – a socking great mound in the middle beneath which was the Anderson shelter, with vegetables on top and more veg in the old flower beds along the sides of the gardens.

Her eyes were raw from weeping. People called it having a good cry, but what was good about it? Her eyes felt as if they had come off worse in an encounter with the cheese grater.

'Here, have this.'

She turned round as Letitia appeared with a hanky she had dampened in the bathroom.

'Thanks.' Joan gently patted the tender skin round her eyes.

'Love you, little one,' Letitia whispered.

'Love you too, big sis.' With a deep breath that came out on an 'oo' sound, Joan went to the wardrobe. 'I need to get ready for tonight.'

Aware of Letitia's eyes growing round in surprise, Joan removed the pair of trousers she had made at Ingleby's from the drawer at the bottom of the wardrobe. When she had stopped working these, she had brought them home and hidden them.

'What are you doing?' Letitia's voice was a whisper.

'Climbing through that cellar window showed me that there are more important things than dressing in a lady-like way.'

'Good luck telling Gran.'

'Now that I've slithered through a window, she'll be worried about me flashing my knickers.'

Letitia grinned. 'Shall I pave the way for you?'

'Would you?'

'Never say I don't do my best for you.'

Joan left off unfastening the belt on her short-sleeved rayon dress to catch Letitia's arm as she made to leave the room. 'Thanks for looking after me.'

Not feeling quite as brave as she might have sounded when speaking to her sister, she changed into a plain blouse and her trousers, sliding the narrow self-belt through the loops below the high waist. Then she went downstairs, pausing outside the parlour to lift her chin and brace herself.

Gran was sitting on the edge of an armchair, back straight, ankles together but one foot tapping. She gave Joan a glassy stare, her eyes travelling from Joan's head to her feet and back again.

'You look very . . . workmanlike. You know my opinion of slacks. They're called slacks because they're for slack women. I expect your mother is wearing slacks, wherever she is.'

'Gran, please.'

'If this is what comes of letting you turn up your hems, I wish I'd never agreed.'

'It's nothing to do with hems, Gran.' Joan used her politest voice. 'It's to do with climbing into a hole to slide through a cellar window, in front of a load of men. It's best to wear something practical.'

'Well, if you're going to come home in the state you were in this morning . . . It took me all day to soak the bloodstains out of your blouse.'

'At least she came home,' Letitia said softly.

Gran tilted her face to the ceiling. Blinking furiously, she sniffed and pulled her hanky from her sleeve. 'I've been frightened out of my wits all day. Ridiculous, isn't it? You come home safe and I spend the day all churned up. That poor girl.' Her voice wobbled and she pressed the hanky to her mouth.

Which poor girl? Lizzie or Margaret?

Joan's vision blurred as she crossed to kneel in front of her grandmother. She caught Gran's hands, hanky and all, and administered a gentle shake. 'Don't, or you'll start me off.'

'And me.'

Letitia appeared beside Joan, reminding her of how, as small children, they had sat at Gran's feet, leaning against her legs as she told them fairy tales and stories about Daddy. For the first time since she had stood transfixed, staring into the crater, Joan felt a glimmer of warmth trickle into her heart.

'My girls.' Gran reached to put her arms round them. Leaning into the embrace, Joan bumped heads with Letitia. 'I've always done my best for you. You know that, don't you?'

'Of course we do,' said Letitia, and Joan felt her sister's slender arm slip round her waist.

Gran gave an extra squeeze, then sat up, releasing them. Joan smeared away a few tears. The others did too, and they all laughed shakily.

'I want to hear about last night,' said Gran. 'All you said this morning was that a girl was trapped in a cellar, but I want to hear everything about what you did to help her. It saved your life, doing that.'

Joan began to tell the story. Was it really less than twenty-four hours ago that Margaret's distraught father had appeared at the park-keeper's house?

'Your first casualty,' said Letitia when Joan described Margaret's leg being trapped. 'I wish I'd had mine. I'm scared I won't remember what to do.'

'My mind went blank, but then my hands took over.'

'So her leg was trapped under the rubble,' prompted Gran. 'What was wrong with her?'

'Broken ankle.'

'Then where did all the blood come from?'

Joan went very still. She could blame it on the rubble. That was what she would have done, if Lizzie hadn't died. But Lizzie's death had shifted everything into a new perspective.

'She was having a baby . . .'

'She had a baby?' said Gran. 'You said she was your age.'

'Plenty of girls our age are married,' said Letitia.

'I don't mean she gave birth,' said Joan. 'She was expecting a baby, but she lost it. She had a miscarriage.'

'And you had to deal with that?' said Letitia. 'All on your own in that cellar?'

'There was a doctor outside who told me what to do.'

'You shouldn't know about things like that, not at your age, and you an unmarried girl,' said Gran. 'They should never have sent you into that cellar. That's not decent.'

'They didn't know,' said Joan. 'Margaret hadn't said a word to anyone. She had barely admitted it to herself. And even if they had known, it wouldn't have made any difference. I was the only one small enough to fit through the window. And just imagine if it had been a man.'

Gran's eyes narrowed, with a gleam that had nothing to do with the emotion of a few minutes ago. 'Why hadn't she told anyone? Do you mean to say she wasn't married?'

Joan remembered Margaret's ringless finger.

What sort of girl do you think I am? Some girls might be using this war as an excuse to forget their morals, but I'm not one of them.

While she was busy passing judgement, Lizzie had been blown to kingdom come.

'No, she's not married.'

'Bloody disgraceful.'

Joan's eyes pinged open. 'Gran, she needed help. First-aiders can't pick and choose. You wouldn't mind if she'd been a married lady.'

'But she wasn't, was she?' Gran pushed her away and Joan had to slap her hand onto the carpet to keep herself from toppling over. 'She was a flighty piece, a common little tart, who couldn't keep her knickers up.' Gran's mouth turned down at the edges. She pushed her hands onto the arms of the chair as if about to spring up. 'The dirty little slut.'

She didn't say the rest. She didn't need to.

Like your mother.

A great wave of grief rushed through Joan. What she wanted, what she had yearned for all day, was for people the whole world over to think about Lizzie and mourn for her, share their memories and weep in one another's arms. That was what she wanted.

But what did she get? A reminder of her mother.

Bloody Estelle.

Chapter Twenty-seven

Was it good or bad to be buried on a day of glorious sunshine? Rain would feel more appropriate, but it would make the day a lot drearier for those attending the ceremony. Dot heaved out a sigh, but it failed to lift the weight from her heart. Lizzie was to be buried beneath wide skies of sapphire blue, with that special sunshine edged with gold that you sometimes got in September. It might be the ninth month of the year, but it always brought a sense of new beginnings for Dot, and had done ever since her lads were young and September meant the new school year. What a time to be saying a final farewell to your young daughter.

The service was to be held at English Martyrs. Blimey, that wasn't much more than spitting distance from Alexandra Park, where Lizzie had died. Dot's heart turned over. Lizzie's poor mum. Oh, it didn't bear thinking about. But she had to think about it. Her mind couldn't think of anything else. Besides, it would be disrespectful not to. She gave Jimmy a clip round the ear when he said summat about her going to 'English Tomatoes" but it was an automatic gesture. She didn't really want to make anything of it, didn't want him to glimpse the scale of her grief.

She was on the afternoon and evening shift today, so she was able to go to the funeral service. Cordelia was going to be there as well, as were Joan and Mabel, who had been given the time off. Dot had an idea Persephone was also attending, but she wasn't sure.

She set off in good time, trying not to feel that the it was an odd piece of work, like two buildings stuck together, with two long parts, one double the height of the other. The taller one had a tower or a steeple, whatever the right word was, while the other contained the arched front door, above which was a circular stained-glass window.

Dot was early. She had told herself she was setting off in good time, but the truth was that she hadn't been able to stop indoors a moment longer. She felt all itchy under her skin at the thought of the funeral. Now she hovered by the gates and was relieved when Cordelia came walking towards her. Her slender figure looked elegant in black, though it didn't do her complexion any favours. Mind you, Dot probably looked like an old crow in her ancient black overcoat, so she shouldn't throw stones.

After they had exchanged greetings and made a few sorrowful remarks about the occasion, Cordelia said, 'I'm glad to catch you on your own. I want to speak to you. I've been to see Miss Emery about what happened to Joan.'

'What for?' Whatever Dot might have expected Cordelia to say, it wasn't that.

'When we went to Mr Clark's church that Sunday, I told my husband where I was going and why.'

Dot's mouth dropped open. She snapped it shut before her jaw could land on the pavement. She had never breathed a word to Reg and he hadn't asked.

'Fancy telling a man something of that nature,' said Dot. 'That's distasteful.'

Cordelia's eyebrows rose beneath the brim of her hat. 'So it's acceptable to confront Mr Clark and threaten him, but not to inform a solicitor?'

'Aye. You tell a solicitor, next news things get out in the open, and then that's Joan's reputation ruined.'

'How else is Mr Clark to be stopped?'

'I thought we'd already stopped him,' said Dot, 'by making threats. I thought you knew that an' all.'

'Dot, please listen.'

Dot was getting hot under the collar. How could Cordelia be so dratted calm all the time? Didn't she have any feelings?

'I confided in my husband, as between husband and wife,' Cordelia continued, 'not as solicitor and client, but it was as a professional solicitor that he advised me to inform Miss Emery, without going into detail. As my husband pointed out, were Miss Emery to be furnished with details, she would be obliged to follow up the matter, which could, as we know, go badly for Joan.'

'Then why tell her at all?'

'By making Miss Emery aware, we have added to Joan's armour. It means that should she ever be in the position of having to make a complaint, Miss Emery will know that it has happened before. Moreover,' and surely the middle classes were the only folk on God's green earth to use words like *moreover*, 'should another girl go to her with a similar problem, Miss Emery will have ammunition.'

'You know as well as I do,' said Dot, 'that even if it was sung from the rooftops, Mr Clark would get away with it. It'd be the girls that would suffer.'

'I'm not suggesting anything that puts the girls' reputations in jeopardy,' said Cordelia.

Jeopardy! Blimey. Dot had never used that word in her whole life and here was Cordelia dropping it into the conversation as if she used it three times a week and twice on Sundays.

'So what did Miss Emery have to say for herself?' Dot demanded.

'She thanked me.'

Annoyance flared. 'She thanked you? What the ruddy heck use is that supposed to be? There! I've only gone and sworn, and us about to set foot inside God's house an' all.'

'I apologise,' Cordelia murmured. 'I know we should concentrate on Lizzie today, but when else would I get you on your own?'

'I know,' said Dot. 'We have to grab us moments. But today is for Lizzie.'

A vast, gleaming motor car drew up at the kerb. Mabel and Joan emerged from the rear of the motor, holding the door open for an elderly lady, at the same time as Persephone climbed from the driver's door on the far side of the vehicle.

Once again, Dot had the sensation of scooping her chin off the pavement.

'Good morning.' Persephone walked round the motor's long bonnet.

'Does this belong to your family, Persephone?' Cordelia enquired.

'It belongs to the lady I live with.'

'And is this . . . ?' Dot asked, though the elderly lady didn't look the sort to own a socking great motor like this, or indeed any motor at all. That tweed coat with the patch pockets was ten years old if it was a day.

'This is my grandmother, Mrs Foster,' said Joan. 'Lizzie came to our house, so Gran wanted to be here today. Gran, this is Mrs Green and this is Mrs Masters.'

'Pleased to meet you,' said Dot. So this was Joan's nan. She wasn't Dot's idea of a nan – not a besotted nan with a box of sticking-plasters in one hand, leaving the other arm free for a cuddle; not a rushed-off-her-feet nan with a thousand and one things to do, who would instantly cast 'em all aside if her little ones had need of her. No, Mrs Foster was a grandmother through and through. A tight-lipped creature with judgemental eyes and a poker up her bum to keep her spine straight.

'My sister wanted to be here as well,' said Joan, 'but she couldn't get the day off work.'

'That goes for a lot of folk,' Dot said. Alison and Colette were both at work, though they had dearly wanted to attend. Eh, wartime was worse than the cruellest of Victorian factory owners for keeping your nose to the grindstone.

'I'm sorry I didn't offer lifts to you two ladies as well,' Persephone said to Dot and Cordelia. Dropping her voice, she murmured, 'I thought Mabel and Joan might be more in need.'

'Of course,' said Cordelia. 'This will be quite an ordeal for them.'

'Mabel doesn't look too good.' Dot felt a twist of concern. 'She looks rather flushed.'

'She's caught the sun from being outdoors all day long on the permanent way,' said Cordelia.

Persephone turned with a smile to Mabel and Joan. 'We're just saying, Mabel, that you'll be brown as a berry before long.'

But Dot couldn't get rid of that uneasy feeling. 'Are you sure you're all right, love?'

'I'm fine, thanks,' said Mabel.

'Excuse me,' said Persephone. 'I must go and collect Mrs Cooper.'

Dot smiled. She hadn't expected to smile today, but here she was, smiling. 'That's a kind thing to do.'

'Not really. One wants so badly to be of service, doesn't one? Yet what is there to do, in the face of such appalling tragedy? Miss Brown, the lady I live with, said we must put the petrol to good use while we've still got it, so I'm driving Mrs Cooper and her sister and brother-in-law here, then to Southern Cemetery and back home again. Mrs Cooper was most reluctant to accept, but I said we must do Lizzie proud.'

As Persephone climbed into the vehicle and drove away, Cordelia looked at Mabel. 'Are you sure you're up to this?'

'She's uncomfortable,' said Joan. 'Her arms are sun-burned and they've blistered.'

'Only a little bit,' said Mabel dismissively.

Dot nodded approvingly. 'You might not be feeling quite the thing, love, but you're setting it aside in honour of Lizzie, and that's how it should be. Today is all about our Lizzie.'

Churches were meant to be cool inside, weren't they? Mabel had been banking on that to make her feel better. How lousy to feel ill today of all days. There was something dis-respectful about it. She ought to concentrate on Lizzie and her mother, but she felt shaky and her heart was fluttering about and beating quickly. It must be the sunburn. She was a trifle woozy – more than a trifle. When she had applied fresh nail varnish this morning, her eyes had drifted in and out of focus, so heaven knows what sort of a hash she had made of the job. Seated in the wooden pew, she shifted, try-ing to ease her discomfort. The plasters she had applied to the burst blisters on her arms rubbed against the lining in her jacket sleeves. Ha! So much for being brown as a berry.

Persephone, of course, had pale, smooth skin. You could drop her down a mine-shaft and she would climb up again, utterly unblemished. She had a perfect complexion, too. During her London Season, Mabel had heard that Pond's, the face-cream people, had approached the Honourable

Miss Trehearn-Hobbs in the hope that she would consider appearing in an advertisement for them, though presumably Persephone, or possibly her parents, had turned down the offer, as Mabel had never seen any such advertisement. Mabel had had kittens at the time in case a similar approach was made to her – which sounded horribly big-headed, but it was just the dread of what Pops might shove her into, regardless of Mumsy's precious etiquette book. Mind you, if the likes of Persephone could be asked, then Mumsy might have considered that the requirements of etiquette had been met.

Why were her thoughts rambling like this? She'd had trouble concentrating this past day or two. She had put it down to shock and distress about Lizzie – or she had tried to. She did feel unwell, and not in an upset-about-Lizzie kind of way. Was she coming down with something? She felt ill all over. But she had to hold on, whatever happened. She mustn't be taken ill, or even look unwell, at Lizzie's funeral. That would be the worst possible disloyalty to Lizzie and a resounding insult to Mrs Cooper's bereavement.

Beside her, Joan leaned closer. 'Are you quite sure you're well?' She peeled off a glove and touched Mabel's forehead. 'You feel warm. Maybe you've got a temperature.'

'I'm fine,' Mabel whispered, but her heartbeat hadn't slowed, even though she was sitting down.

And now it was time to stand up. The coffin was brought in, followed by Mrs Cooper, leaning on a man's arm, another woman following closely behind. The coffin had a simple posy on the top – a dainty bunch of white roses, their stems tied together. Perfect for Lizzie, perfect for a young girl. God, not yet eighteen, and gone for good.

The pall-bearers set down the coffin with care. What was inside it? Mabel had thought – had thought . . .

Had she been wrong to think – to think that Lizzie had

been blown to smithereens? That there was nothing left of her? She couldn't breathe.

She had never looked for Lizzie's body. She and Joan had stood there like a pair of idiots, hanging on to one another, when they should have been searching for dear little Lizzie's broken body.

And yet – and yet . . .

What was in that coffin? Lizzie's body? Her earthly remains? Or – nothing?

No, it couldn't be nothing. There must be something. That was clear from the way the pall-bearers had handled it. But in Alexandra Park that frightful morning, Mabel had known, she had *known*, that there was nothing left of Lizzie.

So what was inside the coffin? Sandbags? Meticulously weighted to represent a girl of seventeen, spread evenly along the inside of the coffin?

Oh, dear heaven. Did Mrs Cooper know?

The priest invited the congregation to be seated. Mabel experienced an odd swaying sensation as she sat down, but at least she managed not to miss the seat. Perspiration bloomed across her flesh. She silently inhaled a long, slow breath. The priest was speaking, but his words were a blur in her ears. She just had to hang on for the duration of the funeral, then she could get outside for some fresh air and that would set her up to attend the burial. Mr Mortimer had said she could take the whole day off, so afterwards she could go home and lie down.

'Our opening hymn is going to be Elizabeth's old school song,' said the priest.

Elizabeth? Hadn't anybody told him she liked to be called Lizzie? Or wouldn't he sully the proceedings by using a pet name? Oaf.

'Some of the children from school are here to sing it,'

continued the priest, 'as well as some of Elizabeth's old friends from school.'

Thank heaven for that. At least the congregation could remain seated.

'The school has lent its hymnals. The school song is number one hundred and two. Please rise and join in with the singing once you are familiar with the music.'

Mabel swallowed her disappointment; actually swallowed it. There was a sourness in her mouth. Joan handed her a tatty hymnal and she fumbled through it, struggling to find the number, her eyes not working properly. The music started and, all around her, people came to their feet, which meant she had to as well. She didn't so much stand up, as lurch upwards, and the movement didn't stop there. She surged upright, wavered, then tipped over, simply tipped over, and crumpled.

In the corridor, as they headed for the charging office, a few of the girls said quietly that they hoped the funeral had gone well yesterday – 'you know, as well as these things can' – and Joan nodded, murmuring something meaningless in return. She had no desire to tell them that Mabel had collapsed and had had to be carted off to hospital by Persephone in a grand motor car, with Cordelia in attendance. That would turn Lizzie's funeral into a piece of gossip and she couldn't bear that.

Yesterday evening, not knowing how else to get any information, she and Letitia had cycled over to Darley Court. Under any other circumstances, it would have felt the most frightful cheek to cycle up the long drive towards the mansion, but as things were, who cared? Persephone welcomed them with her usual grace and good manners, introducing them to Miss Brown, an elderly lady with clever eyes.

'I'm waiting to hear from Cordelia,' Persephone had explained. 'She stayed with Mabel at the hospital and she promised to telephone here this evening after she got home. I expect she has to get her husband his meal first. You're welcome to wait.'

Presently, the telephone bell had sounded.

'Excuse me if I answer it right away instead of waiting for the maid,' Persephone said to Miss Brown, 'but our friend will be in a telephone box.' She disappeared, returning a few minutes later, looking rather ghastly. She sank back into the chair she had vacated. 'Suspected blood poisoning. Good Lord. But the good news is, they think they've caught it in time.'

Now, heading into the charging office, Joan wondered how Mabel was feeling this morning. Had she – had she survived the night?

If Joan had said one word about it to her colleagues, she might have ended up howling the place down.

She entered the charging office and took off her jacket, putting her hat on the shelf and giving her hair a quick fluff up before she walked across to her desk and sat down. Miss Bligh, who had given up on the Myrna Loy hairstyle in favour of what would have been a cascade of Scarlett O'Hara waves had her hair been longer, placed a neat handful of charging sheets in the wire tray on the right-hand side of her desk. By the close of this morning's work, the sheets were required to be in the wire tray on the left-hand side.

She took the first sheet and glanced at it. Then she wound two invoice sheets, with carbon paper in between into her typewriter. She lifted her fingers above the keys, but instead of typing, they remained poised mid-air. She glanced around. Everybody else was already busy. No one coming in would have known they had only just this minute got started. They might have been there since daybreak. Joan looked again at her typewriter keys. She flexed her fingers, but didn't type. Once she started, it would be like everything had gone back to normal, that life without Lizzie was right and natural.

She felt disconnected from what was happening around her. Was this what it had been like for Daddy after Estelle ran off with her boyfriend? Did he have to go to work the next day and conduct himself as if everything was right and normal? Yes, he must have done, because he had two little girls to support.

Well, she had to get started. Life went on. That was the old saying, wasn't it? Look at Gran. Ever since before Joan's first birthday, Gran's life had been a testament to getting on with it. Her daughter-in-law had run away, her son had died of a broken heart, and she had been left with two tiny children to bring up.

The door opened and Miss Emery walked in and headed towards the other door, leading to where the men worked, doing their calculations. She disappeared inside.

'Miss Foster,' said a voice close by.

Joan glanced round. It was a quiet reminder from Miss Bligh to stop gawping after the assistant welfare supervisor. She looked once more at the work in front of her. It was time to get started – no, she wasn't going to sigh. She was going to get on with it – like Gran had.

Checking the charging sheet beside her, she began transferring its information onto the blank invoice. She had worked her way through several invoices before the door at the other end of the room opened and Miss Emery reappeared. As Miss Emery walked along the room between the rows of desks, Joan couldn't help but be aware of her. So much for trying to concentrate.

'Good morning, Miss Foster.' Miss Emery stopped beside

her. 'When you have finished that invoice, please will you report to Mr Mortimer's office? Thank you.'

A brief smile and she was gone. Joan felt a flutter of panic. Was she about to be dismissed? Had Mr Clark spilled the beans about that mistake she had made? Hadn't Dot and Cordelia sorted out the trouble after all?

Hauling her thoughts back under control, she finished the invoice and turned the knob to remove it from the typewriter, putting the top copy on one pile and the carbon copy on another. Images of what might be about to happen darted through her mind. Outside Mr Mortimer's office, she paused to pull herself together before she knocked.

'Come,' called Mr Mortimer.

He looked up from where he was seated behind his desk. Miss Emery, seated in front of the desk, turned round, giving her a smile. Not a warm, friendly one, but then they weren't friends. A professional smile? Was there such a thing? Or was she reading too much into something that was nothing more than a common courtesy?

'Thank you for coming, Miss Foster,' said Mr Mortimer. 'Please sit down.'

She sat next to Miss Emery – no, not quite next to. Miss Emery's chair was at an angle so that she could look comfortably at both Mr Mortimer and Joan. What was going on?

Mr Mortimer clasped his hands together and placed them in front of him on the desk. 'Such a sad business about Miss Cooper.'

'Yes.' Sad? Pathetic word.

'As you know, Miss Cooper worked as a lad-porter. We have to replace her, and Miss Emery has suggested you, Miss Foster.'

'Me?'

'Yes,' said Miss Emery. 'You will leave the charging office immediately and take up your new duties.'

'I'm going to have Lizzie's job – Miss Cooper's job?'

'You shall be paid more,' said Mr Mortimer. Miss Cooper is – was – under eighteen and therefore a lad-porter. You are nineteen, going on twenty, I believe, if you'll pardon me for mentioning a lady's age, so you shall train as a porter and shall be paid accordingly. You shall receive a further small amount when you turn twenty-one.'

Joan stared at him. 'You think I care about the salary?'

Miss Emery cleared her throat. 'We realise that this has come as a surprise to you, Miss Foster, and clearly you're still upset about Miss Cooper. But we can't do without our porters, so kindly return to the charging office and collect your things.'

'Don't I have to finish this morning's work?'

'No. Just hand in what you've done.'

'Thank you, Miss Foster.' Mr Mortimer gave her a nod of dismissal.

She stood up. Miss Emery accompanied her to the door.

'I hope you'll find your new position more agreeable,' Miss Emery murmured so softly that Joan's ears took a moment to hear her properly. Before she could respond, Miss Emery shut the door.

She stood in the corridor, trying to take in what had happened. She had been given Lizzie's job. She had raged inwardly for so long about being stuck behind a typewriter in an office – and now she had been given what she had wanted all along.

Thanks to Lizzie's death.

She didn't want it – not like this. Absolutely not like this.

Back in the charging office, Joan picked up her completed invoices, taking what felt like a hideously long walk between the desks. She knocked briefly and opened the door. She couldn't help but notice that the odious Mr Clark was at his desk at the other end of the room. The weedy Mr Hargreaves was at his desk close to the doorway. Thank goodness.

She went to him. 'May I give these to you, please?'

Mr Hargreaves frowned. 'This is rather irregular.'

'Please will you see that they get to whoever needs them? I – I shan't be working in the typing office any more. I'm going to be a porter.'

'I hope it suits.'

'It can't be worse than this.' She couldn't help glancing down the room.

'You mean because of . . . ?'

She didn't pretend not to understand. She nodded.

'We were all surprised when you did that, when you sat down with Mr Clark, I mean.'

'I . . .' She floundered. 'But . . . you all let it happen. No one said a word. What was I supposed to do?'

Mr Hargreaves shrugged, but colour flooded his cheeks. 'You didn't seem to mind. We were all taken aback, if you must know, because you didn't look like that sort of girl.'

Chapter Twenty-eight

Each time Mabel had woken from a troubled sleep, she had been aware of what seemed like acres of polished surfaces punctuated by perfect hospital corners. Now, at last, she felt properly awake and the acres had reduced to the length of a ward. Her bed was halfway along one side – the shadowy side. The windows were behind the beds on the other side. That side of the ward looked a brighter place. What barmy thoughts she was having. With luck, it would be the medication causing them, rather than whatever was the matter with her. She felt rough still, but she felt confident too, confidence that came from knowing she was in the right place.

She had a dim memory of being in the back of the motor, with Cordelia's voice saying from a long way away, 'Huddle down and rest your head in my lap.' She hadn't wanted to; she was mortified enough already at having disrupted Lizzie's funeral, but in the end, what choice had she had? It was a case of obeying Cordelia or running the risk of passing out again, or, worst of all, throwing up all over the smart interior of Miss Brown's Bentley.

Her memory of what had happened when they arrived at the hospital was dimmer yet. Had Persephone had to dash off again at once? That would make sense, because of her promise to ferry Mrs Cooper around. Somebody had asked questions, but Mabel's head had been full of mush by that time. Had Cordelia answered the questions?

Next thing she knew, she had been tucked up in bed,

with Cordelia sitting beside her. Cordelia had talked to her. She had tried to listen, but her concentration had wavered, rather like when the signal wandered off when you were listening to the wireless.

'I've told them what job you do ... and about the blisters ...'

Dear heaven, Cordelia had told the hospital staff about the blisters, of all things. Now they would think her a complete banana for fussing over something piffling.

'I've given them your name, but I don't know where you live.' Then, once more, as if a long time had passed, Cordelia said, 'Are you able to give me your address?'

'Don't tell my parents ...' The words had slurred out of her.

'I know they live elsewhere. The hospital needs your current address. As do I.' And Mabel must have provided the information, because Cordelia went on, 'I'll inform your landlady. What's her name? Will she be in at this time of day?'

'Bound to be. Never goes out.' Weird woman. Had she said 'Weird woman' out loud?

'Oh, good, you're awake,' said a young voice now and a nurse appeared at Mabel's side. 'How are you feeling?'

'A bit strange.'

'That'll be the medication. They've had you on it since yesterday.'

'Yesterday?' Mabel made a move – or tried to, but the sheets were tucked in so tightly that she couldn't. Her bedding was stronger than she was.

'You were admitted late morning yesterday and it's now late morning today. We tried waking you to give you something to eat, but you've been out for the count. Doctor said you would be and to leave you be. But it's Doctor's rounds soon, so Sister sent me to wake you.' She smiled and leaned

357

closer. She had a cheeky face. 'You can't sleep through Doctor's rounds.'

'What should I call you?' asked Mabel.

'I'm Nurse Watkins.'

'Is there any chance of a quick bite to eat?'

'You'll have to wait for dinner-time, like everyone else, but I'll ask Sister Medical if you may have a sip of water.'

'Sister Medical?'

'Sisters are known by the kind of ward they run, so we have Sister Surgical, Sister Paediatrics and so on. There are two wards for women's medical, so we have Sister Medical Bellchambers and the other one is Sister Medical Melrose. I'll be back in a mo.'

She returned after a few minutes to say, 'Sister says you may have a sip of water and can you sit up, please?' Mabel had a feeling that the 'please' had been added by Nurse Watkins. 'Everyone who is able to has to sit up when Doctor comes.'

She wriggled her way upwards in the bed. Her head went swimmy, but then settled. The moment she was in position, Nurse Watkins swooped and tidied the bedclothes.

Before Doctor arrived, the nurses lined up at one end of the ward and a nurse in an impressive head-dress, presumably Sister Medical Bellchambers, walked along the line, like a sergeant major inspecting the soldiers' appearance before a dignitary arrived. The door opened and Doctor walked in, a small, tubby fellow, who didn't look anything special except for the fact that he had a train of young doctors following respectfully in his wake. He talked with Sister, then began on his round of the ward, stopping at the foot of each bed. Sometimes he spoke to Sister about the woman in the bed; sometimes he asked questions of the young doctors.

When it was Mabel's turn, he looked at the clipboard of notes that Sister handed him.

'The patient works on the railway lines, Doctor,' said Sister. 'She had sunburn blisters which burst and which we think got grit in them.'

Doctor pinned down one of the young men with a single glance. 'Early signs of blood poisoning. Symptoms?'

Blood poisoning! Mabel's heart bumped. She sat up straighter.

The young doctor blinked a few times. Mabel willed him to find the answer.

'Rapid rise in temperature, rapid pulse, flushed skin.'

'Anything else?' demanded Doctor.

Mabel wanted to say, 'Confusion.'

'Drop in blood pressure,' said another young chap.

'Complications when untreated?' asked Doctor, his gaze picking out another young man.

'The patient can go into shock.'

'What else?' Doctor clicked his tongue. 'Who can tell him, please?'

'The infection can overwhelm the patient's system and lead to death.'

'Crikey,' said Mabel.

Doctor glanced in her general direction, but removed his gaze before it could actually land on her. With the grace of an orchestral conductor, he returned the clipboard to Sister, who gave Mabel a look that said she wasn't pleased, then went on his lordly way.

Mabel watched him go. Was she allowed to lie down now? But none of the other women Doctor had seen had settled back, so she didn't either.

At last it was time for dinner, though she wasn't given as much as the other patients. More than anything, she relished the cup of tea. She started to feel dozy again, though she stirred when a bell rang and the door opened to admit visitors, some with concerned looks on their faces, others with smiles. A handsome young man walked in. Was he aware of the admiring glances he received from women of all ages up and down the ward? He was carrying his hat, so it was easy to see his broad forehead and slicked-down short back and sides with the suggestion of a widow's peak. His eyes were dark, his nose straight, his mouth generous. Who would be the lucky girl? Or maybe he had come to see his mother. Mabel watched, but only because she had no visitor of her own. With a smile, the man headed for a fair-haired girl on the opposite side of the ward.

Not that Mabel expected anyone, but she felt a dip of disappointment when no one came for her. Then the door opened again and Lizzie's mum walked in, accompanied by Persephone.

Mrs Cooper plonked herself down on the chair beside Mabel's bed, settling a handbag that had seen years of use on her lap, and holding its handles in both hands. Persephone magicked up another chair from somewhere and sat beside her. One thing Mabel had learned during her brief stay in London was that girls of breeding could do anything, simply by expecting it to happen.

'Well, my lovely, how are you feeling?' asked Mrs Cooper.

'I'm so sorry, Mrs Cooper. I can't apologise enough for collapsing when I did.'

'Don't be so soft. It's not as though you did it on purpose. My Lizzie would have laughed – except for the fact that you were poorly, of course – but she would have had a good old chuckle at the way you turned things upside down.'

'Well, I'm still very sorry.'

'Aye, well, how are you feeling now?'

'A lot better, thank you.'

Mrs Cooper lifted a thin eyebrow that owed more to pencil than it did to natural growth. 'Mmm, why don't I believe that? This young lady . . .'

'Persephone,' murmured Persephone with a smile that suggested she had already tried and failed to get Mrs Cooper to address her by her first name.

'This young lady tells me that she had it from that nice Mrs Masters that it was blood poisoning. I wasn't sure about coming to visit you, but Miss Persephone here turned up with that great monster of a motor car to take me to Southern Cemetery so I could have a chat with my Lizzie, and then she said why not come and see you an' all? But I said your parents would probably be here.' Mrs Cooper looked round vaguely, as if Mumsy and Pops might spring out from behind a screen.

'They don't know,' said Mabel, the startled look in Mrs Cooper's eyes making her feel unexpectedly guilty. 'I don't want to worry them.'

'Trust me,' said Mrs Cooper. 'They'll want to be worried.'

'I'm sorry,' said Persephone. 'I know we've been here only a few minutes, but I do need to get back to Darley Court. Do you mind?'

'Of course not, miss,' said Mrs Cooper, getting up. She started to bend over Mabel, then pulled herself upright again. 'Silly me. I'm that used to giving my Lizzie a kiss goodnight that I just leaned over the bed automatically. I'm sorry, love. Get well soon.'

'Thank you for coming.' Did the simple words convey the depth of her appreciation, not just for the company but also for Mrs Cooper's bravery?

As her visitors walked away, leaving her with a warm feeling squirming pleasantly inside her, the handsome young man stood up on the opposite side of the ward.

'I'll see if I can find out,' he told the girl he was visiting. 'I won't be a jiffy.'

As he passed by the foot of Mabel's bed, he looked at her and winked.

Cheeky blighter.

Cheeky handsome blighter.

'Well, it sounds to me like you've been demoted.'

Shock thudded inside Joan's chest. Was she really hearing this? She had, as a matter of course, told Gran before anyone else about her change from charging typist to station porter. Even though she had gone to the buffet after work, she had hung on to her news and not mentioned it to her friends. It had been a rocky day, filled with emotion, mostly raw guilt. How many times had she longed for a 'proper' railway job? And now she had one – but what a terrible price to pay. How was she ever to come to terms with it? She had betrayed Lizzie. That was how it felt. And to be given the job the day immediately following the funeral – what was everyone going to think?

Now she was home, and Gran, instead of understanding how hard this was for her, instead of being kind, had to do her down because of it.

'It isn't a demotion,' she said.

'It looks like it from where I'm standing,' Gran retorted. 'From a respectable desk job to a measly porter, fetching and carrying for all and sundry. You need the three Rs to be a clerk. Any damn fool can be a porter.'

'Gran!'

'Don't look at me all shocked,' said Gran. 'You've come down in the world, my girl. I thought you'd made something of yourself when you were appointed to that clerking post, but no, you didn't suit, so they've made you a porter. You might as well go back to running a sewing-machine at Ingleby's. I wonder what Daddy would make of this. Do you think he'd be proud – or ashamed? I think we both know the answer to that.'

*

Had the buttons always been this fiddly? Joan's fingers shook as she fastened the white blouse patterned with tiny forget-me-nots that she had run up a couple of summers ago. Forget-me-nots: how appropriate. She would never forget Lizzie. But they were hideously inappropriate too – hypocritical, in fact. She had stolen Lizzie's job.

Letitia understood – up to a point.

'It's hard on you, being given Lizzie's job. It would have been better if they had hung on a week or two at least before offering it to you.'

'They didn't offer it – they just gave it to me.'

'I suppose they couldn't hang about. Porters must be kept jolly busy, and imagine them having to cope, being a man – or girl – down.'

'I suppose so.' Could she share how she felt?

But then Letitia said, 'I know it's unsettling, but you'll have a lot more fun being a porter than being stuck in an office,' and that made Joan feel worse. Hadn't Letitia talked about how she was enjoying the war? Was she going to end up enjoying it too? And all because Lizzie had been blown to kingdom come. Talk about betrayal.

Her shoulders had gone rigid and were practically under her ears. She rolled them, trying to unwind the tension. Bob would be here soon. She closed her eyes, letting her feelings for him wash through her. An evening in his company was what she needed. She was proud of him for going with Mabel to Mrs Cooper's so soon after Lizzie copped it. Plenty would have shied away from that, but not her Bob. He was decent through and through, a man with a heart and a conscience, and no wonder when you thought about the decent, loving family he belonged to. And after seeing poor Mrs Cooper, he had turned up on Joan's doorstep, bringing joy and relief to contend with the shock and grief that had threatened to overwhelm her. He might be 'only' a signalman in Gran's judgemental eyes, but he was steady and capable and she loved his family for taking her to their hearts so willingly. Cherished, that was how Bob and his folks made her feel. Cherished.

'You look pretty,' said Bob when she opened the door to him.

'Thank you, kind sir.' She dipped her knee in a pretend curtsy. 'Come in and say hello before we go.'

They went into the parlour. Gran looked up from a piece of darning.

'Good evening.' Gran never said just 'Evening' or 'Morning', the way most people did. It was always the full greeting. 'Are you two off, then? You'd better make the most of it.' It wasn't said with a smile. Oh Lord, she wasn't about to be sarky, was she? 'Now that Joan's a porter, she'll be working all kinds of funny hours.'

'That's all right,' said Bob. 'I work funny hours myself. We'll manage.' He smiled at Joan. 'As long as I can see my girl regularly.'

'Don't be late back,' said Gran.

As they left the house, Bob said, 'I want to hear all about being a porter.'

Joan's heart sank. Was she supposed to take it on the chin and be cheery about it? But she couldn't lie to Bob. Stopping on the path, she turned back to face him as he shut the front door behind them.

'It's hard.'

Concern sprang into his eyes. 'You mean it's heavy work?'

'No, I mean because it's Lizzie's job. I feel rotten, if you must know. I've been given something I should never have had, because Lizzie should never have died.'

It was a moment before Bob answered. 'I'm trying to think of the right thing to say. I'm not that good with words. I'm better at doing than saying. I thought you'd want a quiet evening, just a walk, perhaps, but now I think maybe we should take our bikes and go to Southern Cemetery, pay Lizzie a visit. I can't do anything to take away the bad feeling you have about being given her job, but I know how much you liked her, so what do you say we go and see her, eh?'

He understood. There was something right about being close to Lizzie.

Bob's bicycle was parked in their side-passage. He fetched Joan's bike from the little shed in the back garden, snapping on his bicycle clips before they walked their bikes through the gate and onto the road. They cycled all the way down Barlow Moor Road until they reached the vast cemetery that served the south of Manchester. The walls were low – lower than they used to be, now that the railings had been removed.

'We mustn't be too long,' said Bob as they dismounted from their bikes beside the stone-clad gate-posts. 'The opening hours are shorter now than in the summer.'

They walked down long, quiet paths. How peaceful this place was, with its handsome old trees and rows upon rows of headstones. Should they feel comforted to think of this as Lizzie's last resting place? Would Mrs Cooper draw comfort from it? Or was it all a load of nonsense, just something to cling to when you were at your most desperate?

They halted beside the grave where Lizzie was at rest with her dad.

'Poor Mrs Cooper,' Joan murmured, 'losing both of them inside a year.'

'She said that she and Lizzie had recently finished saving up for the headstone,' said Bob.

'And now there'll be two names to go on it.'

How shallow she was, to be obsessed with her own upset, when things were so grim for Mrs Cooper.

They stayed at the graveside for some time. The light of the September evening was edged with brilliance. This time last year, war had not long been declared. Now, here they stood, paying tribute to the first casualty whose death had true meaning for them.

'We'd better make tracks,' Bob said. 'We don't want to get locked in.'

They retraced their steps, heading to where they had left their bicycles.

'I suppose you must come here quite often,' said Bob.

'Why?'

'To see your parents, of course. They're buried here, aren't they?'

The sorrowful, loving sense of calm from standing by Lizzie's resting place was obliterated by the streak of panic that flashed through her. 'No. We're not from here originally. Gran brought us here after Mother and Daddy died.'

'I didn't realise.'

'Tell me what you've been up to today.'

Doing what she had been brought up to do. Changing the subject. Deflecting interest from the Fosters' past. Practically the first lesson learned in childhood.

After Mother and Daddy died.

After Mother died.

She couldn't lie to Bob. She couldn't lie to the boyfriend who meant the world to her.

She just had.

Chapter Twenty-nine

The oddest thing had happened yesterday evening. As soon as the door had been shut firmly after the last of the patients' visitors, two nurses had appeared by Mabel's bed and wheeled it across the ward to a space on the other side, so now she was one bed over from the cheeky blighter's friend, on the sunny side of the ward. Well, maybe sunny was an exaggeration, but it was certainly brighter over here, where the tall windows were. Mabel was feeling brighter today too. She must be shaking off the infection – the blood poisoning. She gave a little shudder. Scary.

But she wasn't going to dwell on that. She had lived to tell the tale and what more could she ask? She certainly wasn't going to make a three-act drama out of it, not after what had befallen Lizzie. Poor kid. She felt a twinge of guilt for having disrupted the funeral. How kind of Mrs Cooper to come and see her in hospital. How brave. Lizzie's mum was one in a million, that was for sure.

Grateful to be feeling more like herself, Mabel was content to lie up in bed, alternately drifting off into her own thoughts and watching the workings of the ward. The amount of cleaning that was done took her breath away.

'Is this done a couple of times a week?' she asked a nurse, impressed.

The nurse treated her to a glance that had plenty of meaning in it. 'It's done every day.'

Everybody who was capable sat up straight when Doctor

was due on his rounds, and there was a repeat performance of yesterday.

When he reached Mabel's bed and Sister Medical Bellchambers handed him her notes, Doctor frowned.

'Wasn't this patient over there yesterday?' He glanced behind him.

'Yes, Doctor.' Sister Bellchambers murmured something.

Doctor lifted his eyebrows, then used them to frown impressively at Mabel. 'I hope you appreciate that it was a piece or pieces of grit getting into your system via your sunburn blistering that made you so ill, young lady.'

'Yes, Doctor.'

'I heartily recommend that a well-bred young lady such as yourself would be better employed in a less menial position.'

He waved the clipboard in the air and let it go. Fortunately, Sister Bellchambers was blessed with admirable reflexes and caught it as neatly as if he had pressed it tenderly into her grasp.

Shortly after Doctor's rounds, a new patient arrived and was installed in the bed next to Mabel's. Mabel looked across, ready to smile a welcome, but the woman was lying back with her eyes shut. She must feel pretty awful, poor thing. Mabel knew all about that. She hoped the woman would respond to treatment as quickly as she had.

Might she have a visitor this afternoon? The other railway girls would very likely all be at work and who else did she know? Nobody. Only Mrs Grayson and she wouldn't stir herself to leave the house. Was it her own fault for wanting to keep her distance from others when she came here? Now, that was enough of that. What had become of being cheerful and grateful after what had happened to Lizzie? She had her reasons for wanting to keep other people at arm's length ... or did those reasons no longer apply?

Those reasons had been tangled up with her grief and guilt over Althea and now—

Oh, hell. So much had happened since then. She might have come here to Manchester to escape from the tragedy she had caused, but in doing so, had she moved on? No. Absolutely not.

Oh, hell.

The bell rang to signal the start of visiting time and the doors opened. Several people walked in, some with the confidence that came from having been before, while a couple hesitated, looking up and down the rows of beds. Then a black man walked in. Mabel had never seen a black man before. She couldn't take her eyes off him. He walked past her bed to the newcomer's. She greeted him with an outstretched hand and he bent over to kiss her.

Realising she was staring, Mabel looked away and promptly noticed how many others were looking at the couple. Then, as if the ward had given itself a shake, everyone started paying attention to the people they were with, though the lowering of a few voices left Mabel quite certain of what they were talking about and she felt a twinge of discomfort.

She glanced up the ward in the other direction. The cheeky blighter was here again. Their glances clashed and she looked away. Goodness, it was tricky when you didn't have your own visitor on whom to focus. She couldn't look to her left for fear of being caught looking by the cheeky blighter, who was seated beside the next bed but one, and she couldn't look to her right in case she appeared to be staring at the black man and his white wife. Were they used to being stared at?

'Excuse me.'

She looked round. It was the cheeky blighter.

'I'd like to apologise.'

'For what?'

'For winking at you yesterday. I don't want you to think I was taking liberties.'

Aware that the woman in the bed to her left and her visitor both had their ears flapping, Mabel said coolly, 'It's all right.'

She expected him to go away. She wanted him to, with these others listening. But he smiled and moved his head in a little pantomime of relief.

'Thank you. You're very gracious.'

'Hadn't you better get back to your girlfriend?' Mabel made a point of saying 'girlfriend' to show the listeners she wasn't in the market for being picked up.

'She's my friend's sister.' And there was that smile again. Did he think she had been fishing for the girl's identity? 'I'll get back to her.' He nodded to the listeners. 'Ladies.'

And off he went. Determined not to watch, or to catch the listeners' eyes, Mabel turned her head away.

'Well, look at you. You don't look so bad, I must say.'

Mabel turned her head, her heart lifting at the sound of the familiar voice. It was Cousin Harriet from Darley Court. 'How did you know I was here?'

'That's charming, I must say.'

'Don't be daft,' said Mabel. 'I'm delighted to see you, but how did you know where I was?'

'Miss Persephone, of course. So I've come to see for myself, and I'll write to your parents tonight to let them know how you are.'

'Please don't. I don't want to worry them.'

'Your dad sent you down here into my care, in case you've forgotten, and I take my responsibilities seriously, even if you have moved out, so come on then, let's have all the details.'

'You're incorrigible.'

'I've been called worse.'

It did Mabel good to spend time with Cousin Harriet. She felt herself perking up.

When the bell rang to signal the end of visiting time, Cousin Harriet delved in a large handbag that wasn't much smaller than a carpet bag.

'Here's the latest *Vera's Voice* for you. You can pass it on to one of the other ladies on the ward when you've finished with it.'

As Cousin Harriet walked away, Mabel snuggled down in bed to make sure she couldn't see either the cheeky blighter or the black husband as they left. When all the visitors had gone, she wriggled back up again, aware of how she had mussed up her bedclothes – and look, here came not one but two nurses to tuck her in properly. No, they went past her to the bed on her right. A minute later, Sister Medical Bellchambers arrived. She spoke quietly to the woman in the bed, who covered her face with her hands. Sister Bellchambers stood aside and the nurses wheeled the bed across the ward into a new place. The patient's hands still covered her face. Then she removed them so as to wriggle down in the bed and lie flat on her back, making it impossible for the other patients to see her expression.

Nurse Watkins was going past. Mabel called to her.

'Is anything the matter?' asked Nurse Watkins.

Mabel spoke quietly. 'Why do beds get moved around? I started off over there and was put over here, and now that lady has gone the other way.'

'Oh, that. Sister wanted her moved because she was on the wrong side.'

Mabel frowned. 'What's the difference?' It must be something to do with how unwell you were. She had started off on the shady side when she wasn't very well, and now that she was on the mend, she was on the side with the windows. Maybe her erstwhile neighbour hadn't been chipper enough to be over here. No wonder she had put her face in her hands, if Sister Bellchambers had delivered bad news.

'You saw her husband, didn't you?' asked Nurse Watkins.

'What's that got to do with anything?'

'You see that patient over there?' Nurse Watkins discreetly tilted her head to indicate a patient on the other side of the ward.

'You mean the Indian lady?'

'Can you see any Indian women on this side of the ward?'

'No,' said Mabel, 'but then that lady is the only Indian in here.'

'Well, if she was one of a dozen, they'd all be over that side. That's how Sister Medical Bellchambers runs her ward. Anyone of the coloured persuasion goes over there, and that includes Mrs Nicholls, who was next to you, because of who she's married to. Unmarried mothers are put over that side too. And it's why you started out over there an' all.' Nurse Watkins was warming to her theme. 'All we knew about you was the job you did and you have to admit, working on the railway tracks does make you sound pretty rough.'

'So I was put over there.'

A cheeky grin fluttered across the young nurse's face. 'It's a good job you'd painted only your fingernails.'

'What's wrong with nail varnish?'

'Nowt – so long as it's not on your toes.'

'What d'you mean?' asked Mabel.

'You know what ladies of the night are?'

'You mean shift workers?' There were plenty of those on the railway.

Nurse Watkins glanced round to make sure no one could hear. 'Prostitutes,' she whispered so softly that Mabel practically had to lip-read. 'You know what they are, don't you?'

Heat burned Mabel's cheeks. How had she ended up in

the middle of a conversation about the kind of creatures whose job couldn't be named in mixed company, and preferably not in unmixed company either?

'If you have painted toenails, the hospital takes it for granted you're one of that sort and automatically tests you for certain diseases. It's the same for men with tattoos. They're sailors with a girl in every port. So now can you understand why you want to be on this side of the ward?'

'Yes, but – how . . . ?'

'Sister found out who you are – I mean, who your father is – and she had us put you over here quick sharp. She doesn't like it when patients are on the wrong side.'

'So that's what she said to Doctor,' Mabel realised, 'and why he said to me that well-bred young ladies shouldn't work in menial jobs.'

'Did he say that?' The young nurse's eyes twinkled. 'I hope you consider yourself thoroughly told off.'

She toddled on her way, apparently oblivious to Mabel's shock. But then, in the world of Sister Medical Bellchambers and her minions, everything was as it should be.

As the evening visiting bell rang and the doors opened, the black husband walked in, only to pause in confusion when his gaze fell on the spot where his wife ought to be. Then he saw her discreetly waving to him from the other side of the ward. As he arrived by her side, she leaned forward to whisper to him, no doubt telling him of the humiliation, and Mabel's heart ached for the pair of them. She tore her gaze away. Leave them in peace. Don't make it worse by watching.

When she looked the other way, there was the cheeky blighter coming in. She didn't want to see him either. She looked away.

'Mabel, love, how are you?'

'Dot! It's good to see you.'

'You an' all, chick. You gave us no end of a fright, fainting like that, but you're looking a lot better now.'

'Thank you for coming.'

'Think nothing of it. Me and the others have sorted it so that you'll get a visitor every evening. Shifts permitting, you'll get an afternoon one an' all.'

'You're so kind, all of you. Thank you.'

Dot shrugged. 'If it was one of the rest of us stuck in hospital, you'd visit, wouldn't you?'

'Of course.'

'Well then,' said Dot.

'It's more than that,' said Mabel. 'Since I arrived in Manchester, I've – well, I've deliberately tried to hold back from being friends with the rest of you, but now Lizzie's gone and I've missed the chance to be a proper friend to her. I feel rather a cad about that.'

'Can girls be cads?' asked Dot. 'I thought it was just men.'

'You know what I mean.'

'Losing Lizzie has hit us all hard, one way or another. There must be lots of regrets floating around. Why did you want to keep us all at arm's length?'

Should she explain? Could she? 'I lost my best friend and it made me feel – well, I suppose it made me feel I didn't deserve more friends.'

'Nonsense,' said Dot. 'You'd have to be a very bad sort not to deserve friends.'

Ah, but she was a bad sort, wasn't she? 'There's more to it than that.'

'There always is. Life is complicated. Spare Joan a thought. She's got Lizzie's portering job.'

'Never!' Mabel exclaimed.

'Aye, so you can imagine how churned up she's feeling at the mo. She told us today in the buffet that, all the time she was a typist, she longed for what she called a "proper" railway job.'

'And now she's got one . . .'

'Lizzie's, to be precise, and she feels right guilty about it.'

'Poor girl. What did you say to her?'

Dot sighed. 'What could we say? We said she's got nowt to feel bad about – though when did hearing that ever stop a body feeling guilty? We told her Lizzie wouldn't mind. We said lots of things, but I'm not sure we did much good. All we can do is keep an eye on her and make sure she knows we're on her side.'

Mabel felt even more of a cad. She had kept her distance from Joan and now that Joan needed support, she wished she hadn't. The others in the group were true friends, with one another's best interests at heart, and most of all, they cared for each other – while she had deliberately held herself aloof, enjoying all the benefits of the others' companionship without committing herself to intimacy and familiarity. She had been their acquaintance up until now, but henceforth she wanted to be their friend.

'You look thoughtful,' said Dot.

'I'm sorry. I was miles away.'

Dot stood up. 'I wish I could stop longer, but I have to pick up my granddaughter from Guides. They're busy collecting waste paper and silver paper at the minute. And cotton reels – I ask you. What are those for? Anyroad, I'll love you and leave you.'

'Thanks for coming, Dot. I know how busy your family keeps you.'

She watched Dot walk down the ward – until her view was interrupted by a man standing up. It was the cheeky blighter, no less – and he was coming this way. Well! She wasn't sure what to do. Would it be rude to turn away? But looking at him might seem like an invitation. She glanced away, cursing her pulse for speeding up. Embarrassment, that's what it was.

'Good evening.' He had a pleasant voice, she had to give him that.

A nod and the faintest of smiles. That was what it said in Mumsy's etiquette book in the section about acknowledging an acquaintance whom you didn't wish to encourage.

'I believe army signallers wind wires round them,' he said gravely.

'I beg your pardon?'

'Cotton reels – though what the wires have to do with signalling, I couldn't tell you.'

Mabel surprised herself by laughing, and having laughed, it would be rude to snub him. Worse, it might seem coy and she couldn't bear coy females.

'You were listening,' she said. They hadn't been talking that loudly, had they?

'The young lady I've come to see is fast asleep.'

'So you amused yourself by earwigging on a private conversation.' What had he heard?

He held up his hands in surrender. 'I swear all I heard was what your friend said after she got up to go. Girl Guides and cotton reels – that's all. Am I forgiven?'

He was nearer to her than he had been on those other occasions. Yes, he had the rugged jaw and the dark eyes, but now he had a boyish look about him. Was he flirting with her? He wouldn't get far if he was.

'I suppose so,' she said crisply. She shifted herself in the bed, turning her face away, dismissing him.

He laid his hand on the back of Dot's chair. 'It's an awful cheek, but would you mind? My patient is in the land of nod and you haven't got a visitor. We can help one another out.'

'I don't think so.' Please let everyone else be busy with their visitors. Don't let anyone be watching.

'Fair enough.' He removed his hand from the chair. 'Harry Knatchbull.' He waited. Then he grinned. 'You're not going to tell me your name.'

She didn't answer.

'I'd be a lot less conspicuous if you let me sit down.'

'You'd be even less conspicuous if you went back to your friend.'

'If you insist. By the way, that's your cue to say, "Please don't go." Are you going to say it?'

'No.'

'Fortunately for me, I have a thick skin.'

'A thick head, more like.'

'Ouch. Are you sure I can't sit down?'

'Thanks for telling me about the cotton reels, but now it's time for you to go.'

'On one condition. When you're better, you let me take you out. You're the loveliest girl I've ever seen, and you've got a sense of humour, and you haven't chucked your glass of water at my head, so you must have the patience of a saint. What d'you say?'

'Mabel! Darling, how are you?'

Mumsy and Pops came hurrying towards her.

Joan walked along Bob's road towards the little house where his family lived. He wasn't going to be there, but she didn't mind. As important as Bob was to her, and as much as his smile made her heart turn over, she was fond of his family too and loved the time she spent with them. Also, she treasured the thought that she was welcome among them when Bob wasn't there.

She had run up a dress for one of his sisters and this evening Maureen was going to try it on before Joan committed the tacked seams to the sewing machine.

'It's perfect,' said Maureen, doing a twirl. 'You're so clever.'

'Just look at all those tiny pleats in the front panel of the skirt,' said Petal. 'And the pretty neckline. You certainly know how to add a touch of flair to a garment, Joan.'

'I had a lot of experience of it at Ingleby's before I ended up sewing blackout curtains and WVS uniforms.'

'Make the most of the pleats, girls,' advised Mrs Hubble. 'It won't be long before there are rules about not using unnecessary extra fabric.'

'Don't be daft, Mum,' said Glad.

'Just you wait and see,' said Mrs Hubble.

'Thanks for doing this for me,' Maureen said to Joan. 'I do appreciate it. It's like having another sister.'

'A very useful sister,' Petal added with a grin.

'Lucky for us Bob found you,' said Glad.

'Pay them no heed, love,' said Mrs Hubble. 'You're here because you're part of the family.'

It was true. Joan could feel it. They had accepted her as one of them. It wasn't just Bob's sisters she liked. She enjoyed his parents' company as well. What would it have been like to have been brought up by Daddy and Estelle? What if Estelle hadn't run off? Would she have been dreadfully unhappy, had she stayed? But how could a mother be unhappy if she was with her children? You didn't have to be in Mrs Hubble's house for five minutes to know she would never turn her back on her family, not for anything or anybody. Estelle must have thought her boyfriend was worth it, but she was wrong.

What could be more important than family? And, oh, the sheer bliss of being part of a happy, fun-loving family under a roof where there was laughter and messing about. Not like Gran's house, where everything had to be just so. Joan loved Letitia as much as ever, but that didn't stop her feeling she now had three more sisters.

Maureen was a beauty, tall and slender with masses of

chestnut-brown hair, brown eyes and fine cheekbones. She was in the WVS and was currently on a warning for having doled out the sugar with too free a hand when making tea for the survivors of the air raids in August. Petal was just as lovely, though in a different way, with her fair hair and greenish eyes. She had ditched her one true love when he announced he was a conchie. Since then, she had, according to her mother, been going through boyfriends like a dose of salts. Joan didn't dare mention Petal's chequered love life to Gran. The combination of a conscientious objector and a succession of admirers afterwards would have set Gran saying all sorts of unpleasant things that Joan had no wish to hear.

Then there was Glad, the youngest. With her mid-brown hair and hazel eyes, she wasn't at all bad-looking, but she wasn't anything special either – as Joan wasn't, compared to Letitia. Joan identified strongly with Glad. Each of them was a sister to a breathtaking beauty, without being jealous. Not that this made them goody-goodies. It just meant they loved their sisters and were proud of them.

'Penny for them, Joan,' said Maureen. 'You were miles away.'

Joan laughed it off. What would this loving family think if they knew about her mother?

'Let's get you out of that dress, Mo,' said Mrs Hubble, 'then you girls can skedaddle and me and Joan can have a chat while she finishes off the sewing. I've got the machine ready.'

The girls put on jackets and hats and disappeared in a flurry of chatter and goodbye kisses.

'Now then, love,' said Mrs Hubble, 'I wanted a private word about your new job. Bob says you feel bad about getting it off that poor Lizzie what got killed, God rest her soul.'

'Well – yes.' Crikey, what was coming next?

'I don't want to speak out of turn, because I know you've

got your gran and your sister to talk to if you need guidance, but you're part of our family now an' all. We care about you, not just because you're Bob's girl, but also for yourself. I don't like to think of you eaten up with guilt. It's not your fault you've been given that job.'

'I know that, but I still feel bad.'

'Have you spoken to Lizzie's mother?'

Joan's heart executed a little flip. 'Briefly, at the funeral. You know, just to shake hands and say a few words. Everyone wanted to speak to her.'

'In other words, you haven't, not really. Have you called round to pay a condolence visit? I take it from the look on your face that you haven't. Maybe you should.'

'How can I, when I've been given Lizzie's job?' It came out as a whisper.

'How can you not?' Mrs Hubble replied in her matter-of-fact way. Not the harsh, judgemental matter-of-fact way of Gran, but sensible and compassionate. 'However hard this is for you, it's a heck of a sight harder for Lizzie's mother.'

'I know that.'

'Of course you do, love. Never mind Lizzie's job. You were there the night she died. The least you can do is call on her mum.'

'What if she slams the door in my face?'

'What if she does? You're a big girl. You can cope with that. But you ought to give her the chance to do that, if that's what she needs to do. Whatever happens, you'll be doing the right thing, believe you me.'

A sigh welled up inside Joan's chest and poured out. Was it the right thing to do?

'I'll tell you summat else an' all,' said Mrs Hubble. 'You could do a lot worse than devote yourself to Lizzie's job and do it to the very best of your ability – in her honour.'

*

Tucked up beneath a blanket and a jolly tartan car rug on the chaise longue, Mabel gazed through the window at the starry faces of the asters and the tall red-hot pokers in the flower bed. With a garden this size, the Bradshaws could give over a huge section to patriotic vegetables as well as keep a section purely for show. Mr Dale, their gardener, was busy deadheading the summer perennials that had finished flowering. It was strange to see how the old life was carrying on here in the old way, on the surface at least. There had been changes, of course – rationing, and the factories turned over to war work – but they hadn't suffered any air raids. She prayed Jerry wouldn't identify Annerby as housing factories that supported the war effort.

The news was grim. London was taking a mighty hammering. Mabel sucked in a breath. All you could do was remember those inspiring words, 'Never was so much owed by so many to so few,' and resolve to keep going.

Not that she was keeping going at present. After she had spent another couple of days in hospital, Mumsy and Pops had been permitted to bring her home on the strict understanding that she was to remain bedridden – which was just what her parents, especially Mumsy, who was desperate to wrap her up in cotton wool, wanted to hear.

Doctor had also made a remark about the unsuitability of her job – 'given that she is clearly a young lady'.

But while Mumsy was busy agreeing, Pops had made a stand.

'It's war work, man. My daughter has to muck in, same as everyone else. As for its being unsuitable for a young lady, I'll have you know my father was a wheeltapper and he for one would have been proud to know our Mabel has followed in his footsteps.'

Lumme! Pops must be riled if he was defending something unladylike, but that was Pops for you. He was happy to throw his weight around, but he didn't like being on the receiving end.

The journey home to Annerby had taken more out of her than she cared to admit, but she had still expected to need no more than a day or so under the covers. Mumsy wouldn't hear of her getting up, though; and, truth to tell, she knew she wasn't altogether up to it quite yet.

So here she was, with the gramophone close by and Tommy Dorsey, Gilbert and Sullivan and the comic songs of Flanagan and Allen to entertain her. She had raced through *Jamaica Inn* and *Rebecca* and had a stack of *Vera's Voice* and *Woman's Illustrated* to flick through.

But no amount of music or reading could stop her missing her railway friends. After being determined to hold them at arm's length all that time, you would think she could manage a bit longer without them. But she couldn't. She missed them, especially Joan – and Lizzie, of course. Oh, Lizzie.

She could do with a sister to alleviate her loneliness. Ah, but she'd had a sister, hadn't she, as good as, and see what had become of that relationship.

How she longed to walk across the tops on a blowy afternoon, with the rich, robust smell of the moors filling her senses. She wanted to walk down the hill as well, to visit her old haunts and call on dear Mrs Kennedy.

She'd had some visitors – Mumsy's friends.

'If they ask about your railway work,' Mumsy had ordered, 'be vague.'

And then – oh, and then Althea's parents had come.

'Mabel dear, you look surprised to see us.'

Surprised? Taken aback, more like. Guilt-stricken.

'Of course we've come to see you. You were our dear girl's best friend, right from the cradle. You've been like a second daughter to us.'

A second daughter. Through all these years, Althea had been her sister, as good as.

'That accident was the most terrible thing that has ever happened to us,' said Althea's mother, 'but it will never stop us caring for you, my dear.' Her voice faltered. 'That wretched accident!'

'Now then, Maud,' her husband said, his own voice gruff with emotion. 'Chin up, old thing.'

That wretched accident – but it had been so much more than an accident. Grief and guilt seemed to drop on Mabel from a great height, pinning her to the chaise longue.

After Althea's parents left, Mabel might have descended into a desperate gloom, but there was a knock at the door and the maid came in.

'There's a friend of yours here to see you, Miss Mabel, come all the way from Manchester.'

Who? Not the railway girls? But who else? Imagine them all piling into Miss Brown's Bentley and Persephone bringing the vehicle to a triumphant, weary halt at the foot of the stone steps leading up to the front door of Kirkland House. No, it couldn't possibly be her friends – and yet who else could possibly have come all the way from Manchester? Her heart lifted and she laughed in pure pleasure. She looked beyond Doris, a smile already on her face.

Looking devastatingly handsome in an RAF uniform, in walked Harry Knatchbull.

Joan didn't tell anybody where she was going as she wheeled her bicycle onto the road. She had agonised over whether to visit Mrs Cooper. What would she say? It was never easy to know what to say to someone who had been bereaved. They had a couple of Irish families in their road and when there was a death in anyone's family, you could guarantee that the two Irish mothers would go round, armed with a posy or a plate of home-made biscuits – 'for you to offer round when folk come calling'.

'That's the Irish for you,' Gran said scathingly. 'They can't leave a bereavement alone.'

But Joan loved them for it. How generous they were with their time and their compassion. She admired them too. It never mattered to them how well they did or didn't know the dead person's family. If you'd had a death, you needed support. Simple as that. And they were never stuck for the right thing to say.

Joan could do with a spot of Irish blood in her right now.

What if Mrs Cooper didn't want to see her? What if she thought Joan should be dead too? Joan and Mabel had cheated death by the skin of their teeth. They had defied protocol and abandoned their posts, leaving Lizzie under the stairs, manning the telephone. Would seeing Joan be too painful for Mrs Cooper?

But Mrs Hubble was right. She had to call on Lizzie's mum. It was the most basic of courtesies. But it wasn't just a courtesy. Visiting Mrs Cooper would be an expression of the regard and friendship she had felt for Lizzie. If Mrs Cooper chose to turn her away, so be it, but at least she would have tried.

She arrived outside Lizzie's house. Should she lean her bike against the wall or use one of the pedals to prop it up on the kerb? She smoothed her skirt, touched the collar of her forget-me-not blouse and made sure her hat was on straight, but when she patted her hair, she knew she was just killing time. You didn't have to worry about stray hair when you wore your hair tucked into a snood.

She knocked and waited, trying not to bite the inside of her cheek as uncertainty assailed her.

'Who's that?' said a voice behind her and she turned to

find Mrs Cooper, with a wicker shopping basket. 'Oh, it's you, Lizzie's friend. I remember you from the funeral. Joan, isn't it? How nice of you to come.'

Joan stepped aside so Mrs Cooper could open the door. Inside, Mrs Cooper took her basket through to the kitchen to unpack her shopping.

'There's so little of it,' Mrs Cooper remarked.

'Rationing,' said Joan.

Mrs Cooper looked at her. 'No Lizzie.'

She flitted about, putting things away, behaving as if she was unpacking the wherewithal for a feast. Just trying to keep her hands busy, Joan realised, and her throat tightened.

'There, that's everything' said Mrs Cooper, her voice bright. 'I'll put the kettle on and we'll go in the parlour.'

The parlour was small, its furnishings worn but clean.

'I'm glad you've come,' said Mrs Cooper. 'The house feels so empty without Lizzie. I'm sorry, love. I don't mean to make you uncomfortable. Things just pop out of my mouth sometimes.'

Determined to say the right thing, Joan screwed her courage together – only for Mrs Cooper to come to her feet.

'I'll see to the tea. The kettle will have boiled by now.'

'Let me help.'

'Nay, lass, you take the weight off your feet. It's good for me to keep busy.'

She bustled out, leaving Joan wondering if she should have followed. When Mrs Cooper returned with the tray, Joan waited for her to pour, then said her piece.

'I've got something to tell you and I'm worried over how you'll feel about it. The thing is, I've been given Lizzie's job.'

Mrs Cooper put down her cup and saucer. 'Sweetheart, did you think I wouldn't know? That nice Mrs Masters told me and so did young Mrs Naylor.'

Mrs Naylor? Oh yes, Colette.

'They called round to see me, which was so kind of them, and so did Mrs Green. Mustn't forget her. It's good to know my Lizzie worked with ladies who thought so much of her, but then she was a real ray of sunshine, wasn't she? That's what her dad always called her, his little ray of sunshine. That Mrs Naylor's a nice girl, isn't she? Quiet, though. She doesn't go out dancing with the rest of you, does she?'

'No.'

'Shame, and her with such a handsome husband. She'd be the envy of the dance-floor.'

'Mr Naylor came here too?' asked Joan.

'Nay. Men aren't so good in a situation like this, are they? But he came to collect her and that's when I saw him.'

This had wandered right off the point. Joan tried to haul the conversation back again.

'Mrs Cooper, I hope – I hope it hasn't hurt you, my being given Lizzie's job.'

'Someone had to get it, didn't they, and who better than one of her friends?'

'I'll never forget Lizzie,' said Joan, 'and I promise I'll do my best in her job, as a way of honouring her memory.'

'Bless you, you do feel guilty about it, don't you?' Mrs Cooper stood up. 'Come here and let me hug you. I think that's what you need, isn't it?'

It was.

Chapter Thirty

Mabel wound down the window of Harry's Austin Ten. It was her first venture out of the house and Harry had gone behind her back and persuaded Mumsy that a trip out in his motor would be less taxing for her than the walk she had been looking forward to.

'I pegged you for a cheeky blighter the first time I set eyes on you,' Mabel had chided.

'Ah – that wink.' Harry looked rueful. 'I've already apologised for that, but you can't blame me for finding you pretty, and it's not as though you were on the ladies' side of the ward!'

So out they went on the road that snaked across the tops. After days in her dressing-gown, it felt good to have been permitted to get dressed. When she'd moved to Manchester, she had taken her very simplest clothes – expertly tailor-made, of course, but in simple styles, so as not to set her apart from the other girls. But here in her vast oak wardrobe hung an array of stylish garments in the best fabrics, the sight of which almost startled her. Had she forgotten how beautiful her clothes were? Lord, she must keep that to herself or Mumsy would panic that she had lost her grip on her correct station in life.

From among the wool crepes and fine linens, she had selected a crepe dress in blue-grey, with a button-through bodice and knee-length flared skirt, which she teamed with an edge-to-edge lightweight wool coat, a hat of blue lacquered straw and blue gloves. The last time she had worn an ensemble such as this, she had been stick-thin owing to her dramatic loss of weight after losing Althea. She had filled out a bit now and was slender rather than thin, her cheekbones less pronounced. It was impossible not to see how much better she looked. She felt a stab of guilt. Poor Althea was dead and buried – and here she was, getting her looks back. It wasn't right.

But no amount of guilt could diminish the pleasure she felt in cruising along in Harry's motor – yes, Harry. Not Mr Knatchbull. Quite how they had instantly got on to first-name terms, she couldn't have said. Yes, she could. She knew precisely how and why. Well, she could hardly have introduced him to her parents as a man she barely knew, could she? That would have made her look fast, and, leaving aside the fact that poor Mumsy would have swooned in horror on the hearthrug, it could well have made Pops refuse to let her go back to Manchester. He hadn't got where he was today without knowing how to wangle things to his advantage; and if he wanted her back home, doing her war work under the roof of Bradshaw's Ball Bearings, then he would make it happen.

As it was, Mumsy and Pops had been proud to welcome the handsome RAF johnny to Kirkland House, especially when he explained he was a bomb aimer.

'Dashed dangerous job,' said Pops and marched across the room to shake hands with him.

Mabel, who had only seen Harry in civvies before, had been as swept off her feet as Mumsy by the sight of him in uniform.

'I thought it would give me a better chance of getting through the front door,' he'd told her in an undertone while Mumsy was busy informing Cook there would be one more for dinner and Pops had disappeared into the cellar to dig out a bottle of something disgustingly expensive.

Yesterday night, Mumsy had followed Mabel upstairs at bedtime and sat on her bed, smoothing the counterpane thoughtfully.

'Is there romance in the wind?'

'Heavens, no,' Mabel had exclaimed, reining herself in before she could add that she barely knew him.

'You can't blame me for wondering. After all, he's driven all this way and he's using an entire forty-eight-hour pass on you.'

'On me and the open road,' Mabel said blithely. 'Don't forget all those hours of driving.'

'Exactly.'

Mabel put her hands on Mumsy's shoulders. 'Don't read anything into it.'

And just what was she supposed to read into it herself? She lay awake into the early hours, her pulse flickering with excitement. Impossible not to be flattered. Impossible not to be intrigued. Harry Knatchbull had driven all this way to see her. Not only that, he had somehow found out her name and address. He must like her – as in, *like* her.

Yesterday afternoon, when he had walked in, he had taken her breath away, partly with surprise, yes, but also because he looked so dashing.

To cap it all, he had made her laugh. Blast his eyes, he had made her laugh.

'They're for coils for radios,' he said. No 'How do?' No 'How are you?' Not even an 'I say, I hope you don't mind my barging in.' Just 'They're for coils for radios.'

'What are?'

'The cotton reels. In the hospital, your visitor mentioned the Girl Guides collecting cotton reels and I said army signallers wound wire round them, but I didn't know why. Now I've found out. It's all to do with radios. I thought you'd want to know.'

And she had laughed. Surprise, of course. Delight too?

But she wasn't sure. Or maybe she was sure, but pretending not to be, because . . . because her life and her past and her guilt were all too complicated to allow her to embark on a new relationship. But if they hadn't been, would she want to?

If they weren't, her entire life would be different.

Following her directions, Harry had driven along the road that crested the tops, and picked a spot not far from the edge of the hill.

Mabel turned to look at Harry. 'Let's walk.'

'I promised your mother—'

'To take care of me. You can do that by following doctor's orders. Starting today, I'm allowed to be up and about, taking exercise.'

'Promise you won't race down the hill into the valley.'

'If I do, you'll have to carry me up again.' It was a joke, but there was truth in it. She bit her lip. Would Harry use it as an excuse to flirt? To say 'Race you to the bottom' or some such?

Harry got out and came round to her side of the motor to open the door. Mabel swung herself sideways on the seat to lift her legs out, ankles together. She wasn't the daughter of an etiquette fanatic for nothing.

Harry crooked his elbow. 'Do you need an arm?'

'No, thank you.'

She certainly wasn't going to hang on to him. It was better to keep her distance. She was good at that.

They walked towards the edge, where the ground fell away in a steep slope down to the valley floor. Mabel breathed in the crisp, lively air. Only the air of the moors could make you feel invigorated and peaceful at the same time.

'That's Birkfield down there. It's a market town. Over

there – can you see? – is Ladyfield, whose claim to fame is that it used to have the local workhouse.'

'They're small places compared to Annerby.'

'You're lucky my father's factory is in Annerby. If we'd lived in one of those places, you wouldn't have found a comfy hotel to stay in overnight.'

'Maybe your mother would have taken pity on me.'

'Don't.' She fixed her face forwards, not looking at him. 'I'm not interested in flirting.'

Beside her, he moved. She didn't look, but she sensed a gesture of backing down.

'I don't mean to offend,' said Harry.

'You haven't.' She swung round to face him. 'How did you know where to find me?'

'Ah.' Now it was his turn to glance away.

'Never mind "Ah." Tell me. The hospital wouldn't have handed out my name and address.'

'Not as such, no.'

Harry produced a packet of Player's. He twitched a couple a short way out of the box and offered her one, but she shook her head. He placed one between his lips and pulled out a lighter – a proper lighter, mind, not a Zippo. There was a small flare of flame, then the tip of the cigarette glowed.

'I asked one of the nurses where you lived.'

'Don't tell me. You winked at her.'

It was difficult to imagine any nurse under the sway of Sister Medical Bellchambers breaching confidentiality in such a way, but presumably the cheeky blighter's charm had prevailed. Yes, his charm. Harry Knatchbull could charm the birds out of the trees.

Could he charm Mabel Bradshaw?

The mere fact that she wondered about it was . . . scary.

'Thanks for bringing me out here. You've no idea how I've longed for it. Being laid up for days on end . . .'

'I can imagine. The breeze has put roses in your cheeks and a sparkle in your eyes. There's no need to glare at me. That wasn't flirting. It was simple observation.'

Was it? She wasn't going to question it, because that would in itself be a form of flirting.

'Thank you. I must admit I feel better.' God, did that sound as prim to Harry's ears as it did to hers?

'How much longer before you can return to work?' he asked.

'It depends. The end of next week, all being well, but they'll have to put me on light duties, to start with.'

'What's your regular job?'

'Are you sure you want to know? It's horribly unladylike.'

He smiled. Goodness, just when she thought he couldn't be any more handsome, his smile sent shivers cascading through her.

'You've got to tell me now,' he said.

She described her job as a lengthman.

'You're right,' said Harry. 'It doesn't sound at all ladylike. I'm surprised your parents allow it.'

'They had no idea until I told them.' And it came tumbling out, how she had gone to Hunts Bank, expecting to be employed as a bank clerk.

Harry laughed. It felt good to make him laugh. For a split second, she imagined the two of them in a crowded room, and making him laugh, and all the other girls screwing up their insides in jealousy. Lord, what was she thinking?

'We'd better get back,' said Harry.

'Did you promise my mother not to keep me out?'

'I did, but I also need to keep an eye on the time. It's a long drive back.'

'I'd almost forgotten you have to leave,' said Mabel.

'I'll take that as a compliment.'

'I'm sorry you have to go so soon.'

'Even more of a compliment.'

'I only meant I appreciate your coming all this way.' The prim voice again.

'I'd have travelled twice as far just for the pleasure of an hour with you,' said Harry, 'but I think you know that.'

He threw down his cigarette and looked at her. How dark his eyes were. Was he going to kiss her? Would she let him? What would it feel like?

'We'd best go,' said Harry.

He returned to the motor and opened the passenger door. It took her a moment to follow him. Her feet were glued to the ground. Had she wanted to be kissed? What was wrong with her?

Back at Kirkland House, Harry graciously refused Mumsy's offer of lunch. Amidst a blur of thanks and good wishes, he departed. The Austin Ten purred down the drive. Mabel and Mumsy stood on the steps, watching. Then Mumsy slid an arm around Mabel's waist and guided her inside.

Mabel went to fetch her Agatha Christie, which she had left beside the chaise longue. Her bookmark was sticking out. She opened the book and there, nestled in the pages, was a piece of paper with an address.

Mabel felt strong and healthy again, more than ready for her first day back on the permanent way. Was she ready for a hard day's physical labour, packing the ballast back under the railway tracks? You bet your life. A long day in the open air, with trains rushing past, taking her breath with them. She loved the trains, the rhythmic cadence of the wheels on the tracks, the puffing of the white clouds from the funnel. As well as the passenger trains with their maroon-liveried coaches, there were engines that pulled wagons, their contents covered by tarpaulins – lines of wagons that took for ever to pass by. Sometimes, the load was so great that it took two engines coupled together to haul the freight. It would be good to be back at work with the rest of her gang.

She checked the contents of her knapsack. A sandwich and a bun, a bottle of cold tea – it was surprising how good it tasted cold when you were gasping for a drink. Maybe they would be near enough to one of the lengthmen's huts to be able to heat up their tea today. She unscrewed the lid from the bottle of hand lotion, savouring the cucumber scent and smiling to herself. She was looking forward to sharing it with the other three. Thick gloves. And that all-important item, toilet paper. Your gas mask was meant to be the most essential thing you possessed, but that was a matter of opinion.

Her heart lifted at the prospect of returning to work with Bernice, Bette and Louise.

'We've been keeping your place warm for you,' Bernice had told her.

Mabel had enjoyed – well, up to a point – her sojourn in the station mess. Mumsy would throw forty fits, if she knew where her darling daughter had been put on light duties. She had undoubtedly imagined Mabel behind a desk, employing her gold-nib Parker pen to fill in forms in a thoroughly ladylike manner. Instead, Mabel had been behind the counter, pouring tea and dishing up pilchard pancakes followed by sultana roll.

She had liked it to start with. It was fun and she appreciated the opportunity to get to know some of the station staff by sight. The porters and ticket collectors were glad to see her each day, or maybe they were glad to see their hot meals. Either way, almost all of them had a smile and a thank you for her, and when some made remarks like 'It's nice to see a pretty face,' she took it in good part, seeing no harm in it.

She wasn't meant to do anything more than serve behind the counter, but after a day or two she had started clearing the tables, partly to test her returning stamina, partly because she wanted to muck in and do a proper job. She didn't want anyone saying she wasn't pulling her weight.

When she moved around the mess, loading her tray with dirty dishes, she overheard the occasional remark that pulled her forehead into a frown. If a railway girl made a mistake, some men took it as proof that women had no business working on the railways; and what she took to be a sensible conversation about the practicality of girls wearing trousers in certain jobs, turned out to be an excuse for the men to complain about not being able to see their legs – 'especially when they're up ladders'.

'Is that really the way the men regard us?' Mabel demanded in the buffet. 'No wonder you don't want to come into the mess much, Dot, if that's the kind of talk that goes on. It's enough to grind anyone down.'

'It's the way of the world, love,' said Dot. 'All you can do is go about your duties – oh yes, and taking that furious scowl off your face would probably be a good idea.'

She had heeded Dot's advice, though the day she overheard a porter say, 'They'll all fall to pieces in an emergency. You wait and see,' she gave in to temptation and nudged him with her loaded tray, sloshing water down his neck.

'You never!' cried Alison later that day in the buffet.

'Well, they do say revenge is best served cold,' Cordelia remarked, causing hoots of laughter.

Oh, how good it felt to be back among her railway friends. Something inside her had relaxed now that she knew she wanted to be proper friends with them. Holding back from them, maintaining that reserve, had felt right at the time, but now she realised what hard work it had been. Even so, guilt sometimes assailed her, dumping itself, hot and heavy, in her stomach. If she became true friends with the other railway girls, it would be a colossal slap in the face to the memory of Althea. Althea deserved so much better. Mabel had tried to honour her memory and assuage her guilt by separating herself from the rest of the world, but the plain truth was that she couldn't manage without other people, without friends and laughter and intimacy.

Picking up her knapsack and grabbing her gas-mask case, she ran downstairs. If her time at home with Mumsy and Pops had made her feel cosseted and special, there was nothing like living with Mrs Grayson to bring her back down to earth, what with having to fit in the shopping, a job that in her absence had been done by a neighbour.

She had wondered about finding another billet, but Pops had said she had to stay put. Moreover, she felt sorry for Mrs Grayson. Yes, she felt impatient and annoyed with her at times, but underneath that she was sorry for her – and puzzled. Mrs Grayson was fit and able, so why did she stay indoors the whole time? Mabel didn't ask. She might feel eager to drop the barriers between herself and the other girls, but there were limits. She had no desire to be drawn into her landlady's strange half-life. Was that horrid of her?

Maybe. Probably. But then, as Althea had found out, Mabel Bradshaw was a pretty horrid person.

By the end of her first day back on the permanent way, Mabel ached all over, just as she had on her first day, back in March. It was almost the end of September now. Thank goodness she wasn't due to be on first-aid duty tonight. She would be stiff as a board later.

How would she feel when she returned to duty? It would be strange without Lizzie. The war had stolen Lizzie's young life and now marched on relentlessly, dragging the rest of them with it. Lizzie was just a memory. Had she and Althea met up somewhere in the hereafter to compare notes?

Mabel abandoned her post, you know, leaving me to cop it.

You think she left you high and dry? Just wait until you hear what she did to me . . .

According to Joan, the assumption that the girls would all stay behind to man the fort had vanished.

'Quite right too,' Mabel had declared. 'I'm glad someone saw sense.'

'I'm not sure it was that,' was Joan's dry answer. 'I think it was more a matter of necessity.'

Arriving back at Victoria, normally Mabel's first act would be to nip into the Ladies to change back into her own clothes, but today she was desperate for a cuppa and a sit-down, so she went straight to the buffet, where she bagged a table. Persephone arrived next. Mabel felt a moment's disappointment. She didn't wish to be alone with Persephone.

To get round the rule that said they weren't allowed to sit in the buffet in uniform, Persephone wore a coat over her uniform, the same as Dot did, except that Dot's was an ancient overcoat and Persephone's a lightweight summer coat with a nipped-in waist and oversized collar that left Mabel acutely aware of her own appearance, in cord trousers and an old tennis blouse. Having learned her lesson about working with bare arms, she also had a substantial jacket, but at least she had removed that, chucking it on top of her knapsack on the floor.

Persephone sat down. 'How was your first day back on the permanent way?'

'Fine, thanks. Hard work, but fine. My poor body is crying out for a long, hot bath, but it'll have to wait until after the war, unfortunately.'

'I'm pleased it wasn't too taxing for you.' Persephone smiled. She was radiantly pretty and those violet eyes were pure heaven. Then the smile slipped and she leaned forwards. 'I'm glad to catch you on your own. I wanted to say I hope you didn't mind that I gave your parents' address to the sister in the hospital.'

Tingles scattered across Mabel's skin. 'You . . .'

'Not the address, exactly, because I don't know that, but I said your father owns Bradshaw's Ball Bearings somewhere up in Lancashire. The sister said that would be quite sufficient to contact him. And it must have been, because your parents came to fetch you.'

Oh crumbs. All this time she had assumed Mumsy and Pops had been sent for by Cousin Harriet; but now she thought about it, Mumsy and Pops had turned up before there would have been time for Cousin Harriet's letter to arrive in Annerby. It was the hospital that had sent for them, probably Sister Medical Bellchambers in person. But that wasn't the point. The point was—

The point was that the Honourable Persephone Trehearn-Hobbs knew who she was.

'I hope you don't feel I stuck my nose in,' said Persephone, 'but you seemed so frightfully unwell, and Mrs Cooper was upset that your parents didn't know, and I knew about your father's firm, so . . .' Persephone lifted one shoulder in an elegant little shrug.

'You know who I am,' said Mabel. 'You know about my family. You've known all along.'

And to think she had believed Persephone knew nothing about her. She had taken comfort from that, from not being recognised by the Honourable Persephone, with her ancestral home, her family portraits, her family crypt and her family retainers.

'You never let on,' said Mabel.

'Neither did you.' Persephone eyed her steadily. 'You pretended not to recognise me, so it seemed courteous to respond in kind.'

Mabel winced inwardly. 'You must think me a complete dope.'

Another of those graceful one-sided shrugs. 'I thought you must be fearfully chippy.'

'Chippy?'

'You know – with a chip on your shoulder.'

Mabel gawped. There, that was a good old Lancashire word if ever there was one. Her eyes widened and so did her mouth. How appalling that anyone would think that of her.

'I don't have a chip on my shoulder.'

'Don't you? When I knew you were coming to live at Darley Court, I was thrilled to bits. Some young company in the house, and I knew exactly what I was going to say to make you feel welcome: "We knew one another by sight previously and now we're going to be friends." But then you looked at me with that glassy, blank expression and allowed Miss Brown to introduce us as if we were perfect strangers. If I'd mentioned the London Season after that, you would have looked a dope. Your word, not mine.'

'So you went along with it.'

'And having started to, I couldn't very well change my mind, could I? That would have been too awkward for words.'

Mabel didn't speak. Her mouth felt clogged with cotton wool. But her mind was working at top speed. Idiot. Dolt. Ninny. All the words Persephone must have applied to her in recent months. Fathead. Sap. Dunderhead.

Chippy.

'I didn't mean to embarrass you,' said Persephone. 'I only wanted to apologise if I overstepped the mark by giving your details to the hospital.'

Mabel was determined to explain herself. 'Did you enjoy the London Season?'

'Didn't I just? I adored it. It was such fun.'

'I didn't. I loathed it. I was surrounded by girls like you, with generations of breeding and pedigrees as long as your arm, girls who were presented at court by their mothers because their mothers had themselves been presented years ago. My mother was never presented – well, of course not. We're new money. So my father paid a dowager viscountess to present me.'

That shrug again. 'It happens. Some hard-up Ladies with a capital L make something of a career of presenting girls whose mothers aren't permitted to. And before you say anything, it isn't always because of new money. New money is a far more respectable reason than some of the reasons why an outsider is required to do the honours.'

'It wasn't just that,' said Mabel. 'It was the whole thing. I never felt comfortable.' She clicked her tongue. 'Lord, now I do sound chippy.'

'No. Overwhelmed, possibly.'

'There's no need to be kind. I was there because my parents insisted, but, no matter how courteous everyone was, I felt out of place from beginning to end. When you and I met at Darley Court, it wasn't that I pretended not to know you – well, not exactly. I was horrified to meet someone who had possibly witnessed my distinctly inglorious Season and I froze. Then you didn't appear to recognise me and, goodness, the relief! I felt I'd had a lucky escape.'

'From what?'

'From all those fish-out-of-water feelings that came

rushing back the moment I saw you. It was cowardly of me not to acknowledge you, but there you are.'

Now it was her turn to do that one-sided shrug, though she doubted hers looked fluid and refined like Persephone's. And didn't that sum it up? She saw Persephone as her social superior.

She leaned forward. 'I want this sorted out once and for all. I want you to understand my point of view, so I look less of a twerp and so that – so that we can be friends.'

'I'd like to be friends,' Persephone said immediately. 'There's really no need to explain anything.'

'Yes, there is. You're everything my parents want me to be. They want me to marry the brother of someone like you. And it won't ever happen. I'm not – my family isn't cut out for it. You're out of the top drawer and we're not, but my parents think – hope – that because they've bought me a private education and a tailor-made wardrobe and a London Season, maybe I'll make a good marriage and they'll have real quality in the next generation. That makes them sound like the worst sort of social climbers, and they're not. They're decent people.'

'I'm sure they are, and they want you to get on.'

'And that makes me uncomfortable.' How to explain? 'Privilege is in the air that you breathe, Persephone. Everything I know about privilege comes out of my mother's etiquette book.' She pulled a face. 'Do I sound chippy again?'

Persephone laughed. 'Not one bit. Did you mean it about being friends? I'd like that.'

'So would I.'

'Splendid,' said Persephone. 'That's settled.'

'What's settled?' Joan was beside them, cup of tea in hand.

'We were discussing how the war brings one into contact with new friends,' said Persephone.

'Our group, you mean?' Joan sat down. 'Miss Emery was spot on when she advised us to stick together. How was your first day back on the permanent way, Mabel?'

'Fine, thanks. The others seemed pleased to have me back, especially Bernice – Bob's mum.'

'She would,' said Joan. 'She – well, let's just say she helped me with something important.'

'Are you seeing Bob tonight?' Persephone asked.

'No, he's on air-raid duty. When I was based at Alexandra Park, our shifts coincided, but now I'm at St Cuthbert's in Withington, we're out of step.'

'Shame,' said Persephone. 'Mind you don't drift apart because of it.'

'Never!' Joan sounded shocked. 'Nothing would do that to us.'

'Serious, is it?' asked Persephone.

Joan blushed and glanced away, but then she smiled and met their combined gaze. 'It's more than a wartime romance.'

'Lucky you.' Persephone turned to Mabel. 'You've gone quiet.'

Mabel's thoughts were in turmoil. Speak up? Or hold her tongue? If she intended to enter into real friendships, that could only be achieved if she opened up. Besides, wouldn't it be a relief to say something? More than a relief. A pleasure. The excitement of speaking about Harry Knatchbull.

'I've got something to tell you. There's a chap who's keen on me.'

'Do tell.' Persephone's violet eyes were alive with interest.

Out came the story of the cheeky blighter winking at her, then earwigging, then chatting. When she got to the bit about him turning up unannounced at Kirkland House, the other two caught their breath, then laughed in delight.

'. . . and there was his address, tucked inside the pages of my book.'

'He's definitely partial to you,' Persephone commented.

'What are you going to do?' Joan asked.

'I don't know. I'd like the chance to see if anything comes of it, but . . .'

'What are you waiting for?' Persephone demanded. 'This is wartime, sweetie.'

'It's complicated.'

'No, it isn't,' said Persephone. 'You like him and he likes you. It doesn't always happen that way.'

'Are you talking about yourself?'

'Don't change the subject,' said Persephone. 'What's stopping you? Are you worried about letting him down if you find you aren't so keen after all?'

'It's because . . .' Her blood was hot and thick, but she pressed on. 'I had a friend, a best friend, more like a sister, really – Althea. We did everything together. We were going to be one another's bridesmaids.'

Joan nodded and Mabel knew instantly that she and Letitia had made the same bridesmaid promise.

'Althea died last year; was killed, I should say. There was a horrible accident.' Her eyes burned as tears flooded them. 'I know all that stuff about life goes on, but – but I'm so aware that I still have my life and she doesn't. I can live my life on a day-to-day basis, and that's all right. I can go out dancing or go to the flicks, and that's all right too, because they are ordinary things to do and they're preferable to being holed up indoors. But if I do this, if I write to Harry, that's more than ordinary everyday life. That's me doing something extra . . . something that could make my life special. How can I face that?'

Joan spoke softly. 'If you and Althea were as close as you say, I'm sure she'd want you to be happy.'

That's all you know. Mabel held in a bitter laugh. Althea had died with no reason whatsoever to wish her a happy future.

And that was the problem with confidences, wasn't it? If you didn't confide the whole truth, you couldn't possibly hope for proper help or support.

But when you had done what she had done, half-confidences were all you had to give.

Chapter Thirty-one

'Here you are.' Joan walked across the school playground to meet Mabel as she arrived for her first night on duty in the St Cuthbert's depot. 'I'll show you where to leave your bike, then I'll quickly show you round the building before Mr Haslett begins his talk.'

They had been ordered to arrive an hour early so that Mr Haslett, their area organiser, could speak to them before they officially went on duty at ten o'clock. Joan showed Mabel round, introducing her to the members of the first-aid party, starting with Mr Wilson, who was in charge.

'I don't like him as much as Mr Atkins,' Mabel whispered afterwards. 'He's not so much in charge as very much in charge. I bet he watches over people's shoulders.'

'It's only while we're in here. Once we're out in the field, there's no time to be officious.'

Mabel grinned and nudged her. 'Hark at you. "Out in the field"! Seriously, though, have you been all right, doing this? I mean, after Lizzie . . .'

Pain twisted inside Joan's chest. 'You have to be all right, don't you?' She looked at her wristwatch.

'Time to see what the Lord High First-Aid Parties has to say,' Mabel murmured.

They entered the school hall, one end of which was set up each evening as their depot.

Mr Haslett took his position at the front and waited for silence.

'It's the start of October now and we had raids on and off throughout September. It's possible that some of our raids were an overspill, as it were, from the bombing on Liverpool. Amongst other incidents, HE bombs were dropped on Heaton Park and the water pipe to the hall was fractured. Just a few days ago, a flock of sheep were killed over Worsley way and incendiaries were dropped on Swinton and Stretford.'

The hairs on Joan's arms prickled. Bob's family lived in Stretford. They were safe. That was what she had to cling to.

'In spite of the damage,' said Mr Haslett, 'there were no casualties.'

'Apart from the sheep,' someone called out.

'There are two things I want you to bear in mind. Firstly, since the middle of September, it has seemed that Jerry is no longer concentrating on RAF targets; and secondly, the nights are now getting longer. Put these two together and I think it's safe to say we should be prepared for more raids.'

And, as if Mr Haslett had spoken the magic words, the siren's spine-chilling wail rose in the air.

When the all-clear sounded at eleven, Joan joined the rest of the first-aid party heading up the steps from the cellar beneath St Cuthbert's.

'That was dirty enough to be a coal-hole.' Mabel brushed her sleeves, glancing at Joan's snood. 'You've got the right idea, keeping your hair covered.'

It wasn't often Joan was grateful for the snood Gran insisted she wore in public. She was grateful for her slacks too – or trousers, as Gran persisted in calling them. They felt practical and appropriate and she didn't care how dirty they got.

'I didn't even want to breathe in down there,' said Mabel,

'for fear of what I'd suck into my lungs. I was on the verge of wishing for a telephone call from HQ.' She pulled a face. 'What a crass thing to say.'

'Be careful what you wish for,' said Joan.

And she turned out to be right. The respite was short-lived. At midnight, the siren went off again. This time, they had barely reached the foot of the cellar steps before, without a word being spoken, they all turned and went up again. Already the drone of enemy aircraft could be heard. The ack-ack guns sounded in sharp bursts and a distant *whump* made everyone freeze briefly before heading for the school hall to await orders.

Joan pressed her elbows to her sides, as if that would keep her nerves from spilling over, but she felt a certain anticipation too. As frightening as this was, she was determined to play her part to the best of her ability.

Letitia was on duty tonight as well. Joan threw out a silent prayer for her sister's safety, and Gran's too, all alone in the Andy. And Bob's safety, and his family's, and that of all her railway friends. So many people to care about, to worry about. How her life had expanded since she'd become a railway girl.

But now wasn't the time to dwell on that, no matter how important it was. Now was a time for single-minded concentration on what was required of her.

The telephone bell sounded and was cut off almost at once as it was answered. Glances flashed around the waiting first-aiders. Joan stood close to Mabel, ready to seize her knapsack the instant she received her orders.

Just as Mr Wilson appeared, a series of loud crumps boomed through the locality. In the school hall, the air vibrated. Mr Wilson touched a hand to the knot on his tie.

'Looks like we'll be taking a hammering tonight. As you can hear, the bombing is extensive.'

He paused as another crump, closer this time, spoke of damage and destruction. All around Joan, there was a collective intake of breath and a general flutter as everybody suppressed a shudder.

'HQ reports that Trafford Park is under attack. That's way outside our area, of course.'

Mabel shifted so that her arm pressed against Joan's. Joan understood and blessed her for sympathising. Trafford Park was where Letitia worked, along with so many others. How much of it would be left standing come the morning?

'Around us, Platt Fields, Fallowfield, Longsight and Moss Side have all been hit. There are reports of a fire at the rubber works in Audenshaw. We should prepare for our own call-outs, which are bound to follow.'

With a sense of unreality, Joan collected her knapsack. Some in the group had tin hats and she almost laughed at the thought of her oh-so-respectable snood. She bounced her knuckles against her mouth, then stopped in case she looked scared.

Again the telephone bell – again cut short. In the brief, anxious wait, a couple of people shuffled their feet, but Joan stood stock-still, preparing herself. Could you prepare yourself for this? For going out to face danger and destruction when the instinctive thing was to run for safety?

Mr Wilson returned.

'HE bombs have fallen at various points along and around Wilmslow Road. Group 1, reports have come in from the vicinity of Fog Lane Park, specifically Ferndene Road. Possible oil bomb, which has failed to detonate – so far. Group 2, you're going in the opposite direction. Moorfield Road, Morris Street, Davenport Avenue: reports of casualties. And, um, be prepared for fatalities. Off you go. Group 3.'

Joan stood taller. Here it came.

'Your turn will undoubtedly come in the next few minutes.'

It did.

It would have been quicker to have got out and walked. That was how it felt. Squeezed into the back of the Austin Seven belonging to Mr Mullins, between Mabel and Mr Stanwick, Joan willed the vehicle to go faster, even though she knew it wasn't possible, not in the pitch-darkness of the blackout with no headlights to guide them, just sidelights, and dimmed ones at that.

As they started to round a corner, a figure appeared beside the car. Mr Mullins wound down his window, though the man outside could have actually spoken through the gap at the top that had jerked down a tad each time the motor had gone over a bump.

A man with W on his tin hat stuck his face in. 'You can't come this way. There are flames coming up through cracks in the road. Gas main.'

Mr Mullins heaved the steering-wheel round and they carried on, heading up Wilmslow Road to the junction with Parsonage Road, where a bomb had dropped near the White Lion. Joan had an impression of arched windows and – was that a clock tower? On top of a pub?

The vehicle drew up and Joan scrambled out, following Mabel and holding her knapsack tight. The road was crunchy underfoot, covered in rubble, glass and bits of plaster.

An ARP warden appeared at a brisk trot. 'This way.' Beneath his tin hat with its 'W', his face was rigid with shock. 'Serious injuries – at least a dozen. And a lad has been killed.'

'Oh no,' Mabel breathed.

'A Civil Defence messenger boy. Killed outright.' No wonder the man's face was a mask of tension.

'Show us the way,' ordered Mr Mullins.

They crunched their way along the road, with Mr Mullins peppering the warden with questions about known injuries, the structural integrity of buildings and possible UXBs. The ARP man heaved his stiff upper lip into position and handed out the necessary information.

Mr Mullins stopped suddenly and the four behind had a job not to cannon into him. Ahead, a couple of casualties were being carried out of a house that had lost its entire façade, like a doll's house with a swing front.

'Stanwick and Hedges, see to these casualties,' Mr Mullins ordered.

With the girls hurrying behind, he strode across the street to where a house had been flattened, simply flattened. What remained was a mess of rubble not four feet high. Bodies had been brought out and laid on the pavement, but they hadn't been covered, so they were still alive.

Mr Mullins glanced at Joan and Mabel. 'You two – over there.'

Further along the road, neighbours were beckoning. Trying to swallow an ache of dread that had got lodged in her throat, Joan ran towards them, her stomach swooping as her feet skidded on roof-tiles that were scattered here, there and everywhere. The thrumming of aircraft engines grew louder and a thread of urgency ran through the scene, but, beyond casting anxious glances to the skies, no one gave up their desperate fight to rescue the trapped and tend the injured.

A policeman practically pulled Joan through a front door. 'Lady in the kitchen. We have to get her out, but I want her looked at first.'

The house creaked as Mabel and Joan hurried along the

hallway. The kitchen was inches deep in brick dust, plaster and glass, plus flour, rice and jam. The lady of the house had evidently taken shelter under the kitchen table, which had served her well, except that the Welsh dresser had taken a tumble, shoving the table across the tiled floor.

'It landed on her leg,' said the copper. 'We've lifted it off, but – well, see for yourself.'

Shock swam through Joan's head at the sight of the bones protruding through the skin. Dear heaven, she wasn't going to faint, was she? Deep breaths. Concentrate. You know what to do.

She and Mabel worked quickly, with the building sighing around them. Ambulance men arrived and took the girls' places, not pushing them aside but somehow appearing in front of them. The girls rose and stepped away.

'Come on,' said Joan.

Back outside, the night air roared with the sounds of planes and AA-fire, and was that the sickly smell of gas?

'Over here,' yelled a voice and they obeyed, tramping over rubble and plasterboard, a fallen door and heaps of bricks, skirting an upside-down rocking chair and a mattress.

Joan's brain split in half. Part of her was there, in the moment, concentrating, following her training, working alongside Mabel, drawing strength from Mabel's closeness and competence; but the other part of her was observing in shock and terror, boggling at the horror of it all, the damage, the way a house could be bashed down to fragments, the mangled limbs and blood and pain, guns thudding, grime and dust and chaos.

A hand landed on her shoulder and she all but jumped out of her skin.

'The ambulances have taken as many as they can,' said Mr Mullins. 'You girls help me take these walking wounded to the motor and I'll ferry them to hospital.'

411

The walking wounded were a man with a broken arm, another with a broken collar-bone and a woman with a head injury, who started off walking supported by an ARP warden, but when she stumbled and slumped, he picked her up and carried her, setting her down beside the car before disappearing into the night.

The scream of an engine – for a split second, Joan stared at the motor before she realised. Her heart swelled as if about to explode.

'Take cover!' Mabel yelled, scooping the broken arm around his waist and heading for the shelter of a wall.

Rapid gunfire. The sound ricocheted everywhere. Mr Mullins dropped like a stone. Joan ran to him. Mabel fell to her knees beside her and turned him over. Joan fumbled, trying to insert her fingers beneath his collar, then she pressed her ear to his mouth.

She and Mabel stared at one another.

A small disturbance behind them wrenched their attention elsewhere. The head injury had fallen forwards – fainted? Dead as well?

Dead. Mr Mullins was dead. Opening car doors one moment and flat on the ground the next.

The others – the broken arm, the broken collar-bone – moved to assist the head injury.

'Move aside.' Mabel came to her feet. 'Let us.'

Relief and gratitude poured through Joan. Good for Mabel. Now she must pull herself together and help. She dragged herself up. Her legs wobbled. Sheer will power held them up, so she could help with the head injury. Fainted. Not dead. Fainted. Thank the stars. Mr Mullins—

'These people still have to get to hospital,' she whispered to Mabel, 'especially the head injury. Does one of the other men drive?'

'There isn't time to find out,' said Mabel. 'A head injury

losing consciousness – that's serious. Get them in the motor.'

'But—'

'Help me get the head injury in the back.'

They assisted the head injury and the collar-bone into the back seat and the broken arm into the passenger seat in the front. Falling shrapnel crashed. Beside the motor, Joan instinctively shrank, covering her head. When she looked up, Mabel was – Mabel was behind the wheel.

'Get in,' Mabel ordered. 'Look after the head injury.'

'You don't know how to drive,' said Joan. 'You wouldn't learn. You were too scared.'

'Says who? Don't stand there staring. I haven't a clue where to go. I need directions.'

Joan slid onto the back seat, perching on the edge so as to give the head injury as much space as possible. There was a jolt and the motor pulled away. Disbelief fluttered in Joan's belly, but she mustn't show it in front of her patients.

'Don't be scared,' she said to the head injury. 'My friend will get you safely to hospital.'

'I think we've made quite enough fuss of Mabel for being a heroine,' Cordelia declared. 'Now it's time for her to answer the all-important question.'

All eyes turned to Mabel. She managed not to squirm. It had been rather awkward, actually, having praise heaped upon her for driving those injured civilians through an air raid to get them safely to hospital. It hadn't been so urgent for the broken arm and the collar-bone, but the head injury had lapsed into unconsciousness on the journey, so hospital was definitely where she needed to be.

'It wasn't just me,' Mabel had said, doing her best to fend off the admiration coming from all sides of the buffet table.

'Don't forget Joan. We worked together to look after our casualties.'

'But you're the one who drove through the streets in the dark,' Joan had responded immediately. 'She even managed to swerve around a socking great hole in the road,' she told the others.

Mabel had found all the praise hard to swallow. She had simply done her duty. If any courage had been required, it had been provided by the urgency of the moment. It didn't feel right to be given credit for it.

But if the praise had been uncomfortable, it was nothing compared to what was coming next. She sat straighter, bracing herself to answer the all-important question. And she was going to answer it before it could be asked outright, too. That was a matter of self-respect.

'I've told a couple of you about my friend Althea – my late friend, I should say. I said that, after losing her, it didn't feel right for my life to carry on in a normal way, certainly not in an enjoyable way.' She glanced at Joan and Persephone. 'I could see you were struggling to understand. After all, as hard as bereavement is, it isn't natural to hide yourself away for ever.' Nerves jangled beneath her skin. 'It's no wonder you didn't understand – because I didn't tell you the whole truth.'

Around her, she sensed the glances that flew round the group. Glances of concern? Censure?

'You don't have to tell us,' Dot said quietly.

'Yes, I do. You have to know what I did or you'll never understand why I refused to be a driver when we first came here.'

'Take your time,' said Cordelia.

'We're on your side,' said Alison, 'no matter what you tell us.'

Mabel looked from Persephone to Joan. 'Did I tell you

Althea died in a motor accident? What I didn't say was that . . . I was the driver. It was my fault.'

'Oh, Mabel.' The soft cry went up around the group.

'You mustn't blame yourself,' said Dot. 'It was an accident.'

'If you knew how sick I am of hearing that! I'm sorry, Dot. I know you mean well. I know everyone means well who has said that to me. But – I was driving.' She shook her head. 'I've never been behind the wheel since. The day I started work here and Mr Mortimer said I was going to be a delivery driver—' Her voice caught.

'And you refused the job,' said Joan, 'because you couldn't bear to drive again.'

'I know some of you were criticised as a result,' said Mabel, 'and I'm sorry about that, but I couldn't face it.'

'We thought you must be scared of learning,' said Cordelia.

Mabel almost laughed. 'I'd been driving for yonks. My father had even bought me my own motor. I used to love driving. I used to feel very dashing and modern. Used to.'

'How perfectly vile for you,' said Persephone. 'But you did the right thing last night. The lady with the head injury might have died if you hadn't got her to a hospital.'

The murmurs of agreement that followed might have been quiet, but they expressed unstinting support. Imagine if that was all there was to it. Imagine letting the others' friendship and unity wash over her and allow her to feel better. She had admitted to not telling the whole truth to Joan and Persephone, and she had told a fuller version now, but she still hadn't revealed everything. Oh, she couldn't. She was too ashamed, and what would they think of her? She knew the answer to that only too well, because it was what she thought of herself.

And yet, listening to the words of concern all around

her, she couldn't help wondering if maybe one day . . . After all, not so long ago she wouldn't have believed the time would ever come when she would publicly talk about having driven the motor that had seen off the dearest friend anyone ever had. Yet she had just shared that confidence.

Could she, might she, one day tell the whole truth? The real whole truth? If she ever did, then these were the friends she would tell.

'Let's leave Mabel alone for a minute,' said Dot. 'I'm sure she could do with a breather.' She produced the group's notebook and laid it on the table. 'I got this from under the counter.'

'Do you want us to agree on some dates?' asked Alison. 'It'd be a good idea to do it while we're all here – well, all except Colette. Better than leaving notes and hoping for the best.'

'No,' said Dot. 'I've put a new book under the counter for us to make our arrangements.'

'Then what's this for?' asked Cordelia.

'Lizzie's birthday is coming up,' said Dot. 'It's going to be hard on her mum, but I've thought of something we can do for her.'

'What's that got to do with our old notebook?' asked Alison.

Dot flicked through the pages. 'It's got Lizzie's writing in it. It's full of our messages to one another.'

'So what?' said Alison. 'It's only "Can't come on Tuesday. How about Thursday?" and things like that.'

'It's more than that,' said Dot. 'Not much more, I grant you, but little things like Mabel saying "Thanks for listening to me complaining about aching limbs" and a couple from me saying "Dratted shifts! Hope to see you soon." Things like that. There are one or two from Lizzie an' all.'

Cordelia nodded. 'You want to give the notebook to Mrs Cooper.'

'I do. It's a little piece of Lizzie and it shows she had friends. Lizzie's birthday falls on a Sunday. I think we should all go together to Mrs Cooper's in the afternoon and – well, show that we care. What do you think?'

'I think it sounds perfect.' There were tears in Joan's voice and in everyone else's as they added their words to hers.

'I think we should all take the notebook home,' Dot went on, 'and add our memories of Lizzie. It doesn't matter how tiny or insignificant they seem. Every single scrap will mean the world to her mother.'

'We must make sure Colette does it too,' said Alison.

In that moment, Mabel knew she was going to write Althea's parents a belated condolence letter – a horribly belated condolence letter. She had never been able to write one before, because what could you possibly say to the parents of the person whose death you had caused, even if it had been accidental? Goodness, was she telling herself lies now? The accident wasn't the real reason. The real reason was that Althea, her dearest friend, had died hating her – and with good reason. That was why she had never sent Althea's parents the letter of condolence they must have waited for.

To her surprise, Dot laid a hand on top of hers. 'We'll never forget our Lizzie and you'll never forget your friend Althea, but you can remember and move on at the same time. Moving on doesn't make the memory any less precious. It just means life goes on. Don't fight it, love. Let it happen. Make the most of it. Folk died last night, folk who lived not much more than a hop and a skip from my house. Live your life, Mabel. Don't be held back.'

Mabel looked round the group. They were a mixed

bunch, but, goodness, they provided solid support for one another. Warmth tingled in her limbs as gratitude filled her chest. These were her friends.

Beside her, Joan leaned nearer. 'Althea wasn't the only person you talked about to Persephone and me. There was Harry Knatchbull as well. He left you his address. He wants to see you again. Do think about what Dot said. Life is for living.'

Was the trap opening? Guilt had held her captive for so long. Was this the moment to squeeze her way out?

'You said you'd like to see if anything could come of you and Harry,' Joan reminded her.

Excitement bubbled inside Mabel's chest. She was going to take a chance. Take it? Grab it, seize it with both hands, more like.

'Harry Knatchbull might be a cheeky blighter,' she told Joan, 'but he's *my* cheeky blighter and I can't wait to tell him so.'

Chapter Thirty-two

One feature of working on the railway was that you worked alongside folk from all over Manchester. It was something that Dot treasured, but it had its darker side an' all. Like now. Coming from Withington, she knew which roads had been bombed these past couple of weeks, and even if she hadn't ever met the casualties personally, she queued up at the shops with women who had, and so she had learned their names.

That night when Mabel had driven the motor belonging to the first-aid man who had been killed, Mr Abbott and the Harrisons and Marjorie Wattleworth had all copped it in Moorfield Street, and the Brodericks had been injured, and that was just one road. There had been other dead and injured in Brown Street, Morris Street, Davenport Avenue and Allen Road. And that was just her own bit of Withington. Yew Tree Avenue and Laurel Avenue in Moss Side had been clobbered an' all. Three houses in a row had been hit in Laurel Avenue; please God let their residents survive their injuries – which was more than the Burleys of 28 Yew Tree Avenue, and their neighbours at number 26, had done.

All that in one evening. God, it had been hard this past couple of weeks, with air raids practically every night. Even when you got a night off from them, you didn't sleep soundly. Well, Dot didn't. Was that because of working on the railways? Hearing details of air raids further away was part and parcel of working in a place where people flocked in from all over to go about their daily duties.

'I'd know about the raids over in other places if I didn't work here, of course,' she confided to Mr Thirkle, 'but I wouldn't know so many details. I'd just know it was Old Trafford and Urmston and Northenden.'

'And Greenheys and Heaton Mersey,' Mr Thirkle added.

'But from talking to folk here, it isn't just the places, it's the actual roads and the people's names.' Dot shivered. 'Two families in next-door houses in Lincoln Street in Hulme; the Sands family and the Taylors. It doesn't bear thinking about. It's the only time I've ever felt any reservations about working here – well, aside from when I'm running round like a scalded hen, trying to fit the shopping in alongside my shifts.'

'That's your kind heart speaking, if I may say so, Mrs Green. It does you credit that you care so much about other folks' suffering.'

'It scares me, it really does, and that's the truth, Mr Thirkle. Every time I hear of another family . . .' She made a helpless gesture, not wanting to say the terrible words *being killed*. '. . . I think of my own lot. Our daughters-in-law and the grandchildren. I worry that the little 'uns should have stayed evacuated.'

'It's hard for everyone,' said Mr Thirkle. 'After the last war, how can it have been allowed to happen?'

'That's a question for cleverer people than us,' said Dot. 'We're just the ordinary folk who have to put up with it.'

'You do sound down in the dumps, and that's not like you, Mrs Green.'

Dot instantly plastered a smile on her face. 'I'm just tired.'

'No, you're not.' Mr Thirkle's voice was gentle. 'That is, of course you're tired. We all are after this spell of air raids.'

'That's what my husband said.' Or, to be accurate, what Reg had said was, 'Everyone's flaming tired after all the air raids we've had since the end of the summer, you daft bat.'

Then, later, he had said to the girls, 'Your ma thinks she's the only one what's been affected.'

Mr Thirkle shifted slightly. Did he take a small step away from her? 'You've discussed it with your husband, of course you have. Pardon me for sticking my nose in.'

'You'd never do that, Mr Thirkle.' Dot almost took a step to follow him. 'I appreciate your kind consideration.' Not least because it was summat she hadn't had from Reg in donkey's years. 'My husband . . .' She mustn't criticise Reg. That would be disloyal. 'You have a way of understanding folk, Mr Thirkle.' Did that make it sound as if Reg didn't? 'And you're right. I'm not just tired. I'm feeling a bit down at the moment. You remember little Lizzie?'

'The young girl from your group that all started on the same day?' Mr Thirkle sighed. 'Such a tragedy.'

'It's her birthday next weekend – or it would have been.'

'Ah.' Mr Thirkle pursed his lips in a thoughtful way. 'And you're putting yourself in her poor mother's shoes, I expect, knowing you, Mrs Green. No wonder you're feeling low.'

Such compassion. What a good man he was. Dot told him about the notebook and how they had all written in it, filling it with their memories, some trivial, some amusing, some touching. Joan had got her sister and her grandmother to write summat, and that nice Bob had added a few lines about what a nifty dancer Lizzie had been. Even Colette, who you might have thought would have had hardly anything to say, had written a whole page about Lizzie's sunny smile and cheerful nature and how she must have brightened the day of all those passengers she helped.

'We're all going to take the notebook round to Mrs Cooper's on Lizzie's birthday afternoon.'

'I think that's a splendid thing to do. Correct me if I'm wrong, but I wouldn't be at all surprised if it was your idea.'

'Since you mention it . . . but I didn't do it to put myself forward—'

'I never meant to suggest you did.' Mr Thirkle looked quite flustered. 'You did it out of the warmth of your heart, Mrs Green, and the lass's mother will bless the day her girl was taken under your wing.'

'Thank you.' Not that she wanted to be big-headed, and she certainly hadn't come up with the notebook idea in order to garner compliments, but how good it felt to receive a bit of appreciation. The most appreciation she got from Reg was when she added chopped onions to the gravy. She felt . . . well, was 'uplifted' a silly word? 'You've made me feel better, Mr Thirkle, and I'm sorry for saying what I said about having to put up with the war.'

'We all feel that way sometimes.'

'But there's so much more to it than just putting up with it, isn't there? Yes, there are all the inconvenient things that you have to tolerate – the blackout, the rationing, the telling-off from the ARP warden if you let the tiniest sliver of light show.'

'I think I know what you're getting at,' said Mr Thirkle. 'Yes, there's all the day-to-day things, but there's something bigger behind it all, and that's what matters: the sense of shared determination, the knowledge that everybody has a part to play.'

'Exactly.' Oh, how wonderful that he understood. 'Yes, we have to put up with all kinds of things, but I never doubt for one moment that, in our own way, us so-called ordinary folk are essential to the war effort.'

'We are indeed,' agreed Mr Thirkle.

Dot felt a warm glow of companionship, of closeness to this dear, kind man. Hey, steady on a minute. She was a married woman. But there was no harm in this friendship between her and Mr Thirkle. Yes, friendship. Real, true

422

friendship, a meeting of minds. She had heard that expression somewhere, probably on the wireless. A meeting of minds. There was nowt wrong with that, was there? It wasn't as though they were all over one another like rampant bindweed. It was friendship, pure and simple – pure being the operative word. A meeting of minds. And in these dark days, it felt like a precious gift.

Dot made sure she was the first to arrive at Mrs Cooper's. She didn't want one of the young girls getting here first and ending up all tongue-tied in the presence of the bereaved mother, who would undoubtedly be struggling to cope on her daughter's birthday. And she didn't want Cordelia arriving first either. No offence to Cordelia, but the last thing poor Mrs Cooper needed was to have to mind her Ps and Qs in the presence of a well-spoken, middle-class lady in her own parlour.

Changing her cloth shopping bag from one hand to the other, she knocked on the door, touching her felt hat to make sure it was on straight. She had considered sewing a decorative button onto the brim, just to smarten it up, but when she had mentioned it to the girls, Pammy had flinched.

'Don't you think that's a bit mutton dressed as lambish, Mother?'

And Sheila hadn't argued. Thank heaven the conversation hadn't been held in Reg's presence.

She was wearing her best costume in honour of the occasion. Did the square neckline and the skirt's box-pleats look dated? She had never felt anything but her Sunday best in the costume before, but these days she was more aware than was good for her of Cordelia's elegant appearance. Lord, she wasn't jealous of Cordelia, was she? No. At least, she didn't think so. But they were the only two members of their group who were of a certain age and so perhaps comparisons were inevitable. Mind you, Cordelia, as the mother of a schoolgirl, was presumably a few years younger than Dot, but her gravity made her seem older than she was. Dot huffed out a small sigh. There were times when she wished she had never uttered those words on their first day, about her being on a par with Cordelia's charwoman.

The door opened and she threw concerns about her own appearance to the winds. Crikey, but Mrs Cooper looked a wreck. That is to say, she had obviously made the effort to dress in her best and the tightness of her waves said that her hair hadn't long been out of rollers, but she still looked a wreck. Her eyes were reddened, and no wonder, given what today was, and there wasn't a peck of flesh on her. She looked like there was nowt but good manners and knicker elastic holding her up.

'Been crying, have you, love?' Dot said without preamble. 'I don't blame you. It's a hard day for you and there'll be more tears before it's over, I don't doubt, but me and the others will be here to help you through the afternoon.' She stepped over the threshold. 'I hope you don't mind, but I've brought along some extra cups and saucers in case you don't have enough.'

'Why would I mind? That's a neighbourly thing to do and I'm the last person to take it amiss. A bit of kindness here, a bit of thoughtfulness there, that's all it takes.'

'Very true. That's what you taught your Lizzie, wasn't it?' Good: she had wanted to get the first mention of Lizzie in at the earliest opportunity. That was what this afternoon was all about. 'It rubbed off on her an' all. I never met a cheerier, kinder lass, and that's the truth.'

'Aye.' Mrs Cooper's eyes misted. 'She were a little love, weren't she?'

'She was.' Dot bustled along the hallway. 'Kitchen this way, is it? I gave my crocks a wash before I came, but it'd be nice to rinse them again after being wrapped up. Eh, just look at your tea set. Isn't it pretty? Are those bluebells?'

'Harebells. I . . . I were saving it for my Lizzie to have one day.'

Dot slipped an arm around Mrs Cooper's shoulders. 'D'you know what my old dad would have said? He'd have said, "It's a reet bugger," and that's swearing, and I apologise, but even so, it is, isn't it?'

'Aye, it is that.' Mrs Cooper moved away, not rejecting the hug, Dot could tell, but so as to hang on to her self-control. 'Let's have a look at your tea set, then.'

Dot picked the pieces out of her bag and Mrs Cooper unwrapped them.

'Yours is pretty an' all,' said Mrs Cooper. 'We do like our nice things, don't we? Our keep-for-best things. My set were a wedding present from my mam and dad. Years later, my mam told me that she'd had a big falling-out with her sister, and this sister, my Aunt Leonie, had had a special cup and saucer with harebells painted on. Not a full tea set, mind, just the one cup and saucer. And then my mam saw this set in the pawnbroker's window and she bought it for me. After that, I were never sure whether she got it because she knew I'd like it or to spite my auntie.'

'I hope you didn't let that spoil it for you,' said Dot.

'Nay, she were a funny creature, my mother, full of moods, and she knew how to bear a grudge.'

'Not like your Lizzie, then.'

A smile crept across Mrs Cooper's thin features. 'She was her dad all over again, was my Lizzie, good-natured to a fault. Let's get your things rinsed, shall we? I'm glad you brought them or some people would have had to have mugs.'

'And we couldn't have that.' Dot fished a couple of twists of paper out of her bag. 'I've told everyone they must bring tea and sugar with them.'

'There's no need.'

'Nonsense. There's every need.' Aye, and not just to help

out in these days of rationing. After losing her breadwinner last autumn and her wage-earning daughter a few weeks ago, just how was Mrs Cooper managing?

A knock at the door heralded the next arrival. Dot busied herself with the tea-towel while Mrs Cooper let in Joan. Persephone arrived almost immediately afterwards, armed with a sponge cake.

'Just to add to the table,' she whispered to Mrs Cooper. Dot blessed her as Persephone added softly, 'We can pretend you made it, if you like. I promise not to tell tales.'

'Get along with you, miss.' Mrs Cooper flapped a hand at her.

And having enjoyed the joke, it was too late for Mrs Cooper to feel awkward about accepting the cake. Dot shook her head wonderingly. That Persephone was nothing if not charming. There was warmth beneath the charm and that was what counted.

Cordelia and Mabel arrived. Colette was dropped off by that handsome husband of hers.

'I hope you don't think you're coming in,' Dot teased Mr Naylor as she opened the front door. 'It's ladies only this afternoon.'

'I'll pick you up later,' he said to Colette.

'He looks after you summat beautiful,' said Dot as she and Colette watched him walk away. 'Now come in and take your coat off. Oh, is that the dress you made? Goodness me, it was ages ago that you showed me the material. Such a pretty blue.'

Colette swiped a hand down the front of the dress. 'It isn't really my colour.'

'Nay, love, it looks fine on you.'

Colette smiled, but Dot could see she was just being polite. What a shame, because she really did look lovely. With her fair colouring and blue eyes, the bluebell hue of the fabric was perfect. It was tempting to say so in the parlour, just so the others could agree and boost Colette's confidence, but Colette was such a quiet little thing. The last thing Dot wanted was to embarrass her.

Contenting herself with 'Well, I bet your husband likes it, anyroad,' she led Colette into the crowded front room. As another knock sounded, she pressed Mrs Cooper into her chair. 'You stop there, love. Let me be the butler.'

It was Alison at the door, her dark hair falling in a shining roll onto her shoulders.

'Was that Colette's husband I saw walking away?'

'Aye, love. He dropped her off a minute since.'

'My Paul would have escorted me, of course, but he's busy this afternoon.'

'Take your coat off. Have you brought your tea and sugar?'

'Yes – and a tin of shortbread that my mother has been hoarding.'

'Good girl. You go into the parlour and I'll put the kettle on now we're all here.'

But Dot's intention of spoiling her hostess was scuppered when Mrs Cooper came into the kitchen. She made it clear she wouldn't go back and be waited on.

'You're my guests. It wouldn't be right not to look after you.' She threw Dot a smile. 'But you can stay and help.'

Joan and Mabel came to help too, but Dot shooed them away. 'We'll have everyone out here if we're not careful.'

Before long, Mrs Cooper was pouring tea in the parlour. Her harebell tea set was admired, as was Dot's pink-rose china. The sponge cake was cut and passed round on the matching tea plates while everyone chatted.

'Tell me some good news,' said Mrs Cooper. 'I want summat to smile at. It doesn't have to be brand-new good news. It just has to be cheerful, the kind of thing my Lizzie would have come home and told me.'

'I don't have anything brand new,' said Joan, 'but I'm happy going out with Bob.'

Mrs Cooper nodded. 'Lizzie said you'd found yourself a good 'un, though his foxtrot could do with improving.'

Joan laughed. 'He's got a lovely family. They've taken to me ever so well.'

'I'm pleased for you, love,' said Mrs Cooper. 'Who's next?'

'Me,' said Mabel, 'and this probably does count as brand new.'

'That's what we want,' said Dot, 'a spot of gossip.'

Mabel drew in a breath and seemed to hold it for a moment before she plunged in. 'I've got a new chap. His name's Harry Knatchbull.' Encouraged by the others, she made an amusing tale out of what a cheeky blighter this Harry Knatchbull was.

'To think he was there when I visited you in hospital,' mused Dot. 'I'd have paid more attention if I'd known.'

Mabel laughed. 'You'd have had to be a fortune-teller, Dot, because I didn't know myself at that point.'

'Is it serious?' asked Alison.

Mabel shrugged and blushed. 'Let's wait and see.'

'Well, don't wait too long,' said Mrs Cooper. 'You never know what's round the corner.'

'That's true.' Cordelia looked at Dot. 'Do you think now is the moment . . . ?'

Dot reached over the side of her chair for her shopping bag. 'We've got a special present for you, Mrs Cooper.'

'You shouldn't have . . .' Mrs Cooper began.

'Yes, we should,' said Persephone. 'It's in honour of Lizzie's birthday.'

Dot brought it out of her bag and handed it across. Mrs Cooper didn't move, so Mabel took it and placed it in her lap. Dot hadn't wrapped it. After a moment, Mrs Cooper, without lifting it up, opened the notebook.

'It's the book we kept under the counter in the buffet,' Cordelia explained. 'It's how we made our arrangements to meet up.'

'Yes, Lizzie told me.'

'It isn't just a stream of old messages,' Mabel said quietly. 'We've all written our memories of Lizzie.'

Mrs Cooper uttered a short, breathy cry and wiped a knuckle across her face.

'We wanted you to know how much she means to us,' said Colette.

Cordelia leaned across and closed the book beneath Mrs Cooper's trembling hands. 'Save it for later.'

With a sniff, Mrs Cooper nodded vigorously. 'Oh, my poor Lizzie. I miss her so much.' She sat up straight, pushing back her shoulders. 'But that's war for you, and I'm not the only one.'

The names of some of the dead and injured from recent weeks – the Andrews family of 47 Peel Street, the Prices of 30 Yew Tree Avenue, and various folk from Whalley Avenue, not far from Mrs Cooper's house – flashed through Dot's mind.

'All we can do is carry on,' she said. 'Me, I work full-time and then I go home and fettle for my family. It might not sound much, but with all of us doing the same, it'll add up to a worthwhile amount. That's what it's all about. That's why we do it – for King and country, for home and family.'

'And for Lizzie,' said Joan.

'Aye, lass,' said Dot. 'And for our Lizzie.'

Welcome to

Penny Street

where your favourite authors and stories live.

Meet casts of characters you'll never forget,
create memories you'll treasure forever,
and discover places that will stay with
you long after the last page.

Turn the page to step into the home of

MAISIE THOMAS

and discover more about

The Railway Girls

Dear Readers,

Welcome to the first book in The Railway Girls series. How exciting for me to be able to write those words! I hope you have enjoyed reading it and that you have come to love the characters as dearly as I do.

I have had Joan's story kicking around in my head for several years and Mabel's story for even longer, around fifteen years, so it was a great pleasure to find the right home for these two girls in this book. But Dot's story was a different matter. Since Mabel and Joan were both quite young, it seemed obvious that the third character ought to be older – and that was as much as I knew about Dot. I don't mind telling you I was worried about her at the time. I knew so much about Joan and Mabel – their family backgrounds, their personalities and what was going to happen to them throughout the series, while I knew nothing about Dot.

I needn't have been concerned. The moment I put pen to paper, Dot blossomed into the lovely lady you have met in these pages – warm-hearted, hard-working, adoring her sons and grandchildren and frustrated with Ratty Reg. Dot has captured my heart. She represents so many working wives and mothers of the time, who worked punishingly long hours and then went home and started work all over again; cooking, cleaning and taking care of their families. These women were the backbone of the country. It was taken for granted – in so far as anyone thought of it at all – that they would keep up their duties as mothers and housewives at the same time as doing their bit for the war effort.

Although this book is a work of fiction, certain events are real – for example, every air raid in the story took place in real life and when, towards the end of the book, Dot thinks about the names of people who lost their lives, these are a small handful of Manchester's air raid victims. The only liberty I have taken regarding the air raids is the destruction of the park-keeper's house.

Other events are also based on real happenings. There really was a young woman who arrived at Hunts Bank expecting to be interviewed for a bank teller's job and I also borrowed the story of the runaway goat escaping down the platform – although, in real life, it was actually a dog. And I'm sorry to tell you that, yes, the bottom-smacking incident was also based on a real event.

Was there a real Sister Medical Bellchambers? Yes, there was; but she wasn't a wartime Sister and her name wasn't Bellchambers. The former patient who told me about her was on her ward during the 1960s and witnessed the incident when the wife of a black gentleman had her bed pushed over to the other side of the ward.

On a happier note, the way in which Joan and Bob meet in the Ritz Ballroom is based on the way my parents met one another. My mum adored ballroom dancing and she was busy tripping the light fantastic one night at the Ritz when she caught sight of an old boyfriend. She didn't want him to see her, so she hid behind one of the pillars surrounding the dance floor . . . and my dad went over and asked her what she was doing.

When my original editor, Cassandra Di Bello, who is the person who asked me to write this series, finished reading *The Railway Girls*, she wrote to me, 'I finished this novel desperately wanting Dot to draw me into a hug and tell me I was one of the railway girls.' Now that you have read the book, I hope you feel that way too.

Much love

Maisie xx

Bibliography

In writing *The Railway Girls*, I have consulted various books. Some, such as John Peacock's excellent costume books, are among my regular research resources, but others I read for the first time. Top of the list, I must mention *Female Railway Workers in World War 2* by Susan Major (Pen & Sword, 2018), which provided me with masses of fascinating information and from which I chose the jobs for Mabel, Dot, Joan, Cordelia and Lizzie. Other railway history books I delved into include *Steaming to Victory* by Michael Williams (Arrow, 2014) and *Railwaywomen* by Helena Wojtczak (The Hastings Press, 2005).

I read various books about life on the Home Front; in particular *Put That Light Out! Britain's Civil Defence Services at War 1939-1945*, by Mike Brown (Sutton Publishing, 1999); Anne de Courcy's *Debs at War* (Phoenix, 2005); *Bombers and Mash; the Domestic Home Front 1939-45* by Raynes Minns (Virago Press, 1999); and *Millions Like Us: Women's Lives During the Second World War* by Virginia Nicholson (Penguin, 2011). Norman Longmate's *How We Lived Then: a History of Everyday Life During the Second World War* (Hutchinson, 1971), is quite simply the most comprehensive, informative and downright readable account of life on the Home Front that I have come across. I also found *Luftwaffe Over Manchester: The Blitz Years 1940-1944*, by Peter J C Smith (Neil Richardson, 2003) a very helpful book. I am indebted to all these authors. Any mistakes are, of course, my own.

Turn the page for an exclusive
extract from my new novel

Secrets *of the* Railway Girls

Coming September 2020
Available to pre-order now

Chapter One

Well! Wonders would never cease. Dot stared across the kitchen at Reg. Gawped would be a better word. She snapped her mouth shut. There stood Reg, her not-so-loving husband, in his Sunday suit, holding his homburg in his hands, his slicked-down hair thinner than it used to be and his once-firm neck looking stringy above his collar and tie, just come home from being interviewed to be an ARP warden. Reg – working for Air Raid Precautions.

Reg looked from Dot to Sheila and Pammy, their two daughters-in-law, who were sitting with Dot at her kitchen table, here to enjoy a secret meeting about Christmas while the children played tiddlywinks in the front parlour. Other folks kept their front parlour for best, meaning it was hardly ever used, and Dot, who was nothing if not house-proud, had been the same for years; but once her family had expanded and a new generation had come along, she had adopted a more flexible approach.

'Really, Mother,' Pammy had once remarked, 'it would be far more appropriate for us to sit in the parlour and the children to play at the kitchen table.'

But that wouldn't have suited Dot. She liked her kitchen. It felt like her natural place. She had grown up in a kitchen, enveloped in the aroma of onion stew, with a bottomless basket of darning in the corner, and more sharp elbows and scabby knees than you could shake a stick at. Meat was scarce for the likes of her family and what meat they had went on Dad's plate and, later, in smaller portions on the plates of each son as he started work, though working daughters were expected to get by on bread and carrot-and-swede mash, same as always. Folk today didn't know they had been born.

Anyroad, she loved her kitchen, did Dot, and she loved nowt better than having her family crammed round her table, tucking into a tasty meal into which she had poured all her love. When she dreamed of the end of the war, that was what she imagined. Not bunting and street parties; not deliriously happy crowds whooping and singing as they surged through the middle of town; but her beloved family squeezed around her kitchen table.

'What do you think?' asked Reg. 'Of me being an ARP man – what do you think?'

Dot blinked. Was he really seeking her opinion? Ever since the boys were small, he had derived pleasure from doing her down in front of them. Did he even care what she thought? And what *did* she think? She could hardly say, 'You spent the first year of the war at my kitchen table, waiting for me to put your dinner in front of you, and I thought you'd be there for the duration.'

'I think it's grand,' Pammy declared. She rose, her wool skirt flowing round her slender legs, and gave Reg a dainty kiss on the cheek.

'Aye, Reg,' said Dot. 'Good for you. We all have to pull our weight.'

'I reckoned it was time for me to sign up,' said Reg, 'after all the air raids we've had.'

God, yes. They had lived with air raids since late summer. The whole of Manchester had been affected one way or another as bombers had flown over time and again, dropping their deadly cargo of oil bombs and high explosives, the intimidation increasing after the Battle of Britain ended. In recent weeks, the abattoir had been hit, as had the Brooke Bond Tea Warehouse. The damage to Salford Town Hall had resulted in the burial of many records, though not in the burial of any people, thank God; and, mercifully, there had been no casualties when Manchester Royal Infirmary's nurses' home was hit.

It seemed there hadn't been so many casualties in November following the number of dead and injured after the bombings throughout October, and that was a blessing. Mind you, friends and relatives of the Winter family of 74 Button Lane in Wythenshawe probably wouldn't appreciate Dot's verdict. She had heard about the Winters from someone at work. That was one of the features of working on the railways. You were surrounded by folk from all over and so you got to hear the details from all over an' all; but, as shocking and heart-rending as it all was, you had to be grateful that Manchester hadn't been Coventrated.

Coventrated. A cold shudder passed through Dot in spite of the fire crackling in the grate and the heat from the oven in which she was cooking steak and kidney pie and baked potatoes. Poor Coventry had had seven bells bombed out of it two weeks ago.

Pray to God they never had cause to coin the word Manchestered.

Dot's heart swelled with love and concern for her young colleagues, Joan, Mabel and Alison, who were members of first aid parties, heading out each night they were on duty, not knowing whether they would spend a restless night where they were stationed, or whether they might be called upon to brave the streets during an air raid. Alison lived to the north of Manchester and did her first aiding over that way; but Joan and Mabel's depot was St Cuthbert's School, which wasn't much more than a hop and a skip from Dot's house. It hadn't always been Joan and Mabel. It used to be

Joan, Mabel and Lizzie; but all too soon and far too young, Lizzie had lost her life in an air raid. Poor Lizzie – and poor Lizzie's mum. Sometimes it felt like a hundred years ago; other times it might have happened yesterday.

'I'm proud of you, Reg,' said Dot.

She waited a moment. Would it happen again, that surge of love that had come over her during the Dunkirk evacuation? Along with hundreds of thousands all over the country, Reg had mucked in during that national emergency, helping local soldiers get home. He had even carried his shaving tackle in his pocket, just in case any of the filthy, battered, exhausted lads wanted a shave. Soppy old bugger. But he had done his bit and old remembered love had ballooned inside Dot's chest.

Would it happen again now? Did she want it to?

The door burst open and the kids threw themselves in.

'Mummy!' Jenny launched herself at Pammy. 'Jimmy's cheating.'

'It's only tiddlywinks,' Dot began.

'Jimmy would cheat at solitaire,' said Sheila, unperturbed.

'Never mind that now,' said Dot. 'Grandpa's going to be an ARP warden.'

'Isn't he brave?' said Pammy.

'Will they give you the money back on your gas mask?' Jimmy demanded, his blue eyes, just like Harry's, sparkling in his freckled face.

'What on earth is he talking about?' Pammy looked at Sheila.

Jimmy burst into song. He had a surprisingly good voice. It was a shame that when he was invited to sing in the choir, he had taken some indoor fireworks with him. He hadn't been invited back. *'Under the spreading chestnut tree, Neville Chamberlain said to me, "If you want to get your gas mask free, join the blinkin' ARP.'*

Jenny gasped. 'Jimmy said "blinking". Did you hear?'

'It's the words of the song,' Jimmy protested.

'It's swearing,' Jenny retorted. 'It's a pretend-polite way of saying the B word.'

'That's enough,' said Dot.

'Anyway,' said Jenny, 'it shouldn't be Mr Chamberlain any more. It should be Mr Churchill. You can't even get your facts right.'

'It's the song,' said Jimmy. 'Anyroad, are you going to get your money back, Grandpa?'

'The song's wrong, son,' said Reg. 'No one has to pay for gas masks.'

'Can we play air raids?' asked Jimmy.

'That's irresponsible,' said Jenny.

Oh, heavens. There were far too many times when Jenny opened her mouth and Pammy's words came out. Dot wanted her granddaughter to have fun and enjoy her childhood, in so far as that was possible these days, but Pammy seemed more concerned with having a child who was perfect and clean and good. Back when Jenny was a toddler, Dot and Reg had taken a day trip to Southport, where Archie had taken his little family for a week's holiday. Dot and Reg had offered to take Jenny off her parents' hands for the afternoon and had secretly taken her to the beach and made sand-pies and taken her paddling in the shallows and generally let her get covered in sand and ice-cream, before cleaning her up and returning her to her unsuspecting mother. Dot felt the same impulse now.

'Irresponsible?' she exclaimed. 'To play a game? Nonsense! Reg, take the kids in the parlour and you can all practise shouting "Turn that light out!" Me and the girls have business to discuss.'

'That means they want to talk about Christmas,' said Jimmy.

'Christmas? It's far too soon to talk about Christmas.'

Dot made shooing motions with her hands. 'Get gone, the lot of you.'

She shut the door on them and returned to her seat at the table, consciously shutting the recent air raids out of her mind. It was time for the good things. That was how you coped in wartime. You didn't ignore the bad things – that would be stupid – but you held them at bay and didn't let them overwhelm you. It was a piece of advice her dear late Mam had given her years ago and it was as true today as it had been during the Great War. Thanks, Mam.

'It's going to be a good Christmas this year,' she told her daughters-in-law.

'I hope so.' Pammy's voice was more refined than necessary. She had been fetched up by a mother whose status as the wife of a master butcher had given her ideas. 'Last Christmas was too awful for words.'

'Now then,' Dot said briskly, 'we'll have none of that, thank you. We want to make this Christmas—' Just in time she stopped herself saying *perfect*. '. . . as good as it can be, for the children's sakes.'

Aye, for the kiddies, her beloved Jimmy and Jenny. Their similar names might make them sound like brother and sister, but they were cousins. Jenny's real name was Genevieve, but that was Posh Pammy for you.

Posh Pammy and Sheila the Slattern. Dot dropped her gaze to the tablecloth, making a play out of straightening her cup in its saucer. Mrs Donoghue up the road's daughters-in-law were sensible, house-proud girls, who knew their place. Why couldn't Archie and Harry have brought home girls like that, girls Dot could have taken to her heart as real daughters? Instead she had been lumbered with Pammy with her flawless make-up, perfect vowels and fancy ideas, and Sheila, whose idea of housework was to wait for the spiders to choke on the dust before she ran round with a cloth.

Hear more from

MAISIE THOMAS